EARTH UNLEASHED

EARTH UNLEASHED

EARTHRISE BOOK XII

DANIEL ARENSON

This novel is a work of fiction. Names, characters, places and incidents are either the product of the author's imagination, or, if real, used fictitiously.

CHAPTER ONE

Lailani was eighty kilometers from Kyiv when her motorcycle broke down, stranding her in a world of monsters.

She had driven here all the way from Mongolia, crossing deserts, wastelands, and mountains. Everywhere, the land swarmed with robotic wolves, mechanical spiders with tanks for abdomens, and deformed cyborgs who hungered for flesh. All things considered, the rickety old motorcycle had had a good run.

She climbed off the stalled bike. It stood on the cracked road, gave a last cough, and drove no more. Here in the mist, trapped between walls of ancient forest, the motorcycle seemed like another dead robot. Like the trail of them Lailani had left between here and the Mongol steppes.

"Mommy, are we there?" said Tala.

The girl had turned four yesterday. They had not celebrated. Not here in the wilderness, among mist and shadows. Tala sat in the sidecar now, looking around at the fractured asphalt and frosty hemlocks. The girl looked a lot like her mother. Like Lailani, Tala had olive skin, almond eyes, and smooth black hair cut the length of her chin. Like Lailani, she had lost her innocence too soon.

I wanted so much more for you, Lailani thought, looking at her daughter. *I grew up in the slums of Manila. You're growing up in the ruin of the world.*

Epimetheus shared the sidecar with the girl. The Doberman took up most of the space. He was an aging warrior, scarred and battle-hardened. Forever defending his mistress, Epi had charged alongside Lailani into many battles. He had earned every scar, earned every silver hair around his eyes and snout. Even after all these years, he was still Lailani's protector.

"Mommy, I have to pee," Tala said.

"Go between the trees," Lailani said.

"But I want to use a real bathroom."

"Tala!" Lailani rolled her eyes.

"Okay." Tala lowered her eyes. "Between the trees."

The girl walked toward the forest. The mist enveloped her.

"Just don't go too far!" Lailani said.

She almost followed the girl, not wanting Tala out of sight. Not here. Not at this time of war. But she also *really* wanted to see what was wrong with the damn motorcycle.

The motorcycle won her attention. After all, being stranded out here seemed more dangerous than some mist and ferns.

"Tala, you still there?"

A small shadow stirred in the mist. "Yes, Mommy."

"Pee more quickly!"

Lailani knelt and poked at the motorcycle. The damn thing was busted bad. The oil feed pipe was ripped. One piston hung loose. A few valves had busted. Of course, the line of bullet holes across the side—the gift of a Cossack cyborg—hadn't done the motorcycle much good either.

She wished she had her toolbox. But all she had were some zip ties. At boot camp, Ben-Ari had taught Lailani that a good soldier always carried zip ties. They could repair anything a soldier needed fixed, the young Israeli ensign would say. Keeping a bundle had become a habit. But Lailani doubted they could hold together a motorcycle.

"Yep, it's like I thought," Lailani muttered. "We're fucked."

Epimetheus jumped from the sidecar and whimpered.

"I know. I know." She patted him. "You don't like long walks anymore. Old bones, huh?" Lailani looked at the mist. "Hey, Tala! You all right there?"

The mist seemed thicker now. Lailani could barely see the towering pines and hemlocks, let alone her tiny daughter.

"Tala?" Lailani said.

Epimetheus sensed her tension, and his tail sprang into a straight line.

Lailani drew her pistol. She walked into the mist, leaving the road.

She suddenly missed her old army uniform. For a while she had worn her silken *deel*, a gift of the Mongolian khan. But she had discarded that garment; the elaborate golden embroidery and chinking beads were hardly appropriate for sneaking behind enemy lines.

She had picked up some clothes at an abandoned village a while back. A child's clothes, for Lailani was barely larger than a child. Her white tank top revealed the tattoos on her arms: a rainbow on one arm, a dragon on the other. Her shorts revealed tanned, bruised legs, the knees skinned. Her chin-length black hair was tucked behind her ears, held back with a bandanna. She didn't even have a helmet.

Dressed like this, it was hard to feel intimidating. At least she still had her army dog tags. They hung from her chain alongside her cross.

The hemlocks spread ahead. Ghostly trees, colors muted in the mist, towering and slender like monks in a ruined cathedral of the dead. She could see only a few trees deep. But Lailani knew these forests were vast. Old. Containing many secrets. Among these trees, kings of antiquity had worshipped old spirits. Among these trees, children had been offered in sacrifice to cruel gods. Among these trees, trains had rumbled through the shadows, delivering millions to factories of flesh, to burn in ovens and raise smoke above oceans of ashes. It was an old forest. An evil forest. A forest of sins and secrets.

Lailani saw all this. Felt all this in her bones. But she did not see Tala.

She took another step.

"Tala?" she whispered, suddenly afraid to speak any louder.

A figure ahead. Small and gray. Wreathed in mist. A little girl, standing very still. At first she appeared like a statue in some forgotten cemetery, a weeping angel overgrown with moss and memories. But Lailani recognized her daughter. Tala stood here, frozen, gazing deep into the forest.

Lailani approached slowly. Her feet sank silently into layers of soil and decay. She dared not make a sound, barely even breathed, and she raised her pistol. She came to stand beside her daughter, and Tala did not react. The girl was like a ghost. Floating in the mist. Barely there at all.

Lailani knelt by her daughter, and then she saw it.

It stood ahead on a hill. A grayish figure, disappearing and appearing as the mist floated in the wind, flickering almost like a hologram.

A robotic dog. A creature of the Dreamer. A hounder.

But not like the hounders Lailani had fought in the Philippines. It had been weeks since then. Not very long for a human maybe. But for the Dreamer, that was an era of technological development.

This hounder was not merely a crude box of metal with legs. It was a slick, fluid thing, skulking forward with predatory grace. Its eyes were not mere red lamps like the old models. This creature had white eyes. Liquid eyes. Eyes burning and spinning like cauldrons of molten platinum, then narrowing to slits, casting forth beams that saw all. The jaws twitched, the lips peeling back like flowing mercury, revealing gleaming teeth like shards of moonstone. A jaw full of magma. A mind full of malice.

The creature moved a few steps forward, seeming almost to float. There was elegance to its movements. There was understanding. There was art. This was a machine more graceful than a billion years of evolution. This was death made beautiful.

It climbed onto a fallen log and paused. It merely stared, examining mother and daughter. White eyes like will-o'-the-wisps. Two fallen stars in the mist.

"It's staring right at me," Tala whispered.

The hounder remained still. It watched them from the log like an old god of the forest. Demanding worship. Demanding sacrifice. Lailani wanted to fight, but she doubted her bullets could hurt it. She wanted to flee, but she dared not trigger its chase instinct.

She stared into its eyes.

No, not a machine at all. Something greater than a machine. A spirit of the woods, lord of shadows and mist, carved of a moonbeam.

Tala trembled. "Mommy, I'm scared."

"Go to Epi," Lailani whispered. "Slowly. Walking backwards. Go to him."

Ahead, the liquid hounder crouched on the log. Its eyes narrowed to white lines. Its fangs shone.

"Go!" Lailani shouted.

Tala burst into a run.

The hounder pounced.

Lailani shouted and fired her gun.

Her bullet sparked against a glimmering silver muzzle, and then the beast slammed into her.

They hit the ground. It bit. It bit deep. The silver jaws rose, red with blood, and Lailani screamed and shoved her muzzle forward. She drove the barrel into its mouth. She fired. She fired. She fired again.

It bit again. It twisted her gun. It ripped it free, and she yowled.

Its paws pinned her down. It stood above her, maw dripping. Staring. Grinning.

And *he* was staring through this monster's eyes. The Dreamer. He spoke in her mind.

Ah, Lailani de la Rosa. The girl with the microchip in her mind. I will rip it out. You will be mine.

A panel on the wolf's shoulder opened, and surgical tools rose on stalks. A scalpel. A drill. A circular blade.

The saw whirred, moving toward her head.

Tala raced up, weeping. She tugged Lailani's sleeve, desperate to free her. Lailani thrashed, but the metal paws kept her down. The dog was crushing her.

The voice spoke in her mind, mocking, and the saw moved closer. *Your chip is mine, girl.*

The chip in her skull had protected her this far. It blocked the Dreamer from hacking her brain, from making her his cyborg, his slave. Now he would carve it out like she had carved out a man's heart on a night long ago.

As the saw moved closer, began to slice through her hair, Lailani didn't even care about her own life. She cared about Tala. She cared about humanity. She needed to bring this chip to the

Matterhorn so they could study her mind, study how to cure the armies of sleepers who roamed the land, cheeks slashed open, marionettes on strings. If she died, humanity died.

The circular blade nicked her scalp, and—

A flash of black fur.

A howl.

Epimetheus leaped through the forest and slammed into the hounder.

Both dogs, one old and brave, the other metallic and cruel, rolled across the forest floor.

Lailani leaped up, a cut on her head. Blood dripped down her forehead. She ignored it.

The chip was still in her skull. But with a simple keyword, she could deactivate it. She could unleash … *them.*

She knew the risk. If she shut off the chip, her mind was exposed. The Dreamer could flash its lights, invade her brain. Hijack her. Turn her into another marionette.

Yes, the chip protected her from the Dreamer. But it had been built long ago to contain another foe.

It caged the monster inside her.

And right now it was time to wake the beast.

She thought the code word. All it took was a thought.

Nightwish.

The chip shut down, and the alien awoke.

Most days, Lailani felt fully human. Many days went by without Lailani even thinking about her alien DNA. In fact, many of her friends, even her daughter, thought her just a normal woman. Yes, they thought it perhaps odd that Lailani didn't age. That at thirty-six, she still looked sixteen. But they chalked it up to good genes, said she was lucky, and brushed it off.

They did not know the truth.

That a *Scolopendra titania*, the centipedes from outer space, had created her in a lab. That she was only ninety-nine percent human. Fatherless. Grown in the womb of a teenage prostitute in the slums of Manila.

A weapon.

And now … now Lailani became her true self. Now that last one percent, the pulsing heart of her essence, the nucleus of her very being—now it awoke. And it roared.

The two dogs wrestled in the forest. Epimetheus was bleeding. The hounder lashed his metal paw, knocking the Doberman down. Silver teeth sank through black fur. Epi mewled.

Lailani took a step forward. Her fingertips tingled as her claws sprouted. A crooked smile found her lips, exposing her fangs.

"Mommy?" Tala whispered and took a step back.

Good, rose a voice inside Lailani. *Good! Fight, things of Earth. Soak your soil in blood. Enrich and nourish it before our arrival. We are the hunters of many legs. We will return. We will be masters of the ruins of this world.*

Yes, it was hissing, laughing, craving inside her, uncoiling in her belly. As her claws shone in the forest, they took over. The swarm. A million centipedes scurrying through tunnels, burrowing through worlds of stone and soil. She was with them. She was in every whisper. She felt every tremble.

But she was also a human.

She was also a mother, standing between a monstrous machine and her daughter.

And that instinct was stronger than a billion alien bugs.

She stepped closer, grabbed the hounder, and lifted the robot off her dog. It must have weighed hundreds of pounds. But she hurled the creature forward, and the robot slammed into a hemlock, shattering the tree.

The robot fell. It rose again, hissing, several teeth missing. It growled, eyes blazing.

Those white eyes began to flash.

The jaws began to clatter, emitting clicks and hisses and buzzing code.

Pins stabbed Lailani's mind.

The Dreamer reached into her, and there was no more firewall to hold him back. Her chip was cold.

"Tala, cover your ears and close your eyes!" Lailani screamed, racing forward.

She sneered. Her arms pumped, and her hands curled into fists. She leaped toward the robot, and—

The eyes flashed brighter.

Lailani hit an invisible wall.

She crashed to the forest floor. She knelt, the wind billowing her hair, as the ghostly light washed over her.

She stared into the wolf's eyes. Eyes like molten moonlight. Hypnotized.

A new reality unfolded. A world of grinning masks of old skin. Of spinning galaxies. Of a distant evil, moving closer.

Yes … The voice inside her returned. *You see them. You see the Hydrians.*

They stared at her from the distance. Tentacles squirming. Bulbous black eyes staring. Towering beasts, staring and gray. Many arms like an octopus but a body full of hard bones. The horde moved closer and closer, swallowing galaxies.

Evil. They were pure evil taken form. They were intelligence dedicated to one purpose alone. Destruction.

They are coming, the voice said. *Only I can protect you. Join me. Become one with the machine. Dream with me.*

Lailani stared at the hounder. But she was really staring at an electric tree, pulsing and flashing in the bowels of a distant world. The Dream Tree. The heart of this disease. No, not a heart. A *brain.* A brain of luminous neurons reaching out his electric arms from the shadows.

He was inside her now. Those arms spread through her thoughts, expanded her consciousness, opened so many eyes.

But then the Dreamer met them.

The aliens.

The scum inside her.

"She is ours!" they cried.

"She will be mine," said the Dreamer.

"She is one of us. Our DNA is woven through her."

"And I am in her dreams."

"You are nothing but a machine. We are true glory and life!"

"You are the past. I am the present, the future, and eternal. This human will become one of my soldiers in the glorious wars ahead."

"She will always be ours, wretched virus. One of the centipede horde. Back now!"

Lailani shoved herself to her feet, trembling, the voices arguing inside her. She gritted her teeth, tossed her back her head, and howled, "I am mine!"

The voices fell silent. Lailani panted. She took a shaky breath.

"I am Lailani de la Rosa. A major in the HDF. A mother. A human. I am mine alone."

The scum flared with hatred inside her, giving her new might. She lifted the hounder. She slammed it into a tree, shattering the bole. It tore at her arm. She bled. But she kept swinging, slamming its head into a boulder. Again and again. Teeth flew. Its head cracked open, revealing a bundle of thin white cables like angel's hair. Lailani lifted the buzzing, sparking creature, raced across a hill, and hurled it into an icy river.

The creature vanished into the water, and electricity crackled. It twitched. Sparks sprayed. And then the river carried the dying machine away. Yes, not an old god. Not a spirit. Just a machine after all.

Lailani knelt, panting.

"Good, good," said the aliens inside her. "You cast out the machine. You are ours now! You—"

"Serenity," Lailani whispered, and her chip reactivated.

The aliens screamed, then faded away.

Tala ran toward her and hugged her. Lailani examined her daughter for wounds, then stared into her eyes, seeking any sign of infestation.

"Tala, did you close your eyes tight?"

The girl nodded. "Yes. And I covered my ears. The Dreamer did not get inside me."

Lailani squinted, seeking some conceit. But she saw fear, love, and humanity in Tala's dark eyes. She pulled her daughter into an embrace.

"Mommy, I think Epi is hurt."

Lailani's heart skipped a beat. She hurried through the forest toward her dog. Epimetheus was lying on the forest floor. The Doberman tried to rise, whimpered, and fell back down. Blood dampened his fur. But he still managed to wag his tail and smile.

"Dear old Epi." Lailani patted him. "You saved my life again."

He licked her fingers.

She opened her first aid kit. Like zip ties, a flashlight, and her dog tags, her first aid kit was always with her. A soldier's habits died hard.

A cut still bled on her forehead. Teeth marks sank into her arm. Lailani cleaned the wounds as best she could, dousing them with stinging antiseptic. She used Insta-Stitch strips to seal the wounds shut, thanking God above that humans no longer relied on needles and thread. Once she was patched up, she treated her dog, and soon Epi was limping around, one of his legs bandaged and curled inward.

They continued down the road, leaving the dead motorcycle behind. A limping dog. A mother holding her daughter. Three souls. Three living beings in a world of machines. Carrying with them the secret to salvation.

Eighty kilometers from Kyiv. Thousands of kilometers from the Matterhorn and the lab inside that snowy peak.

White eyes lit up in the forest. Ghosts of liquid metal prowled.

We're being followed, Lailani knew. *We're being hunted.*

The eyes moved closer. More eyes opened, glowing like fireflies in the mist. A deep, metallic howl tore across the forest.

Lailani ran.

CHAPTER TWO

Professor Noah Isaac was talking to his wife when the wormhole died, the lights shut off, and the horror began.

He had been sequestered here inside the Matterhorn for weeks now, working on a cure. By now the Dreamer virus had spread across the globe. Only here at SCAR, the Singularity Control and Research institute inside the mountain, were humans still free.

He had been making great progress on Project Panacea, perhaps the grandest project of Noah's life. He had written best-selling science books. He had lectured on astronomy in front of millions. He had brought the love of science to TV sets across the world. He had invented Isaac Wormholes—narrow tunnels, only a few atoms wide, allowing faster-than-light communication between the stars. In fact, he had just been using an Isaac Wormhole to talk to his wife.

But Project Panacea was even bigger. Much bigger. And much more critical.

In Greek mythology, Panacea was the goddess of universal healing. And Project Panacea could perhaps heal this ravaged world.

Here at SCAR, Noah had built only a few thousand nanobots. Each one acted like a virus. They were airborne. They multiplied quickly. Once released, they would spread faster than the Spanish flu. The nanos entered a patient through the nostrils or mouth, but they quickly moved to the brain. Once inside, they could alter the patient's synapses.

Using Panacea, Noah could access every brain on Earth.

And he could exorcise the Dreamer.

The nanos were ready. A few thousand in his vials, ready to go forth, multiply, and enter every human brain on Earth.

There was just one problem.

Noah had the delivery system. But not the medicine. To understand how to protect a brain, he needed Lailani. He needed to study the code in her chip. The original developer was dead. But if Noah could just look at Lailani's head …

Lailani should have been here. Weeks ago. SCAR had lost contact with her. As far as Noah knew, his friend was dead.

Humanity needed her. Noah's only hope was that Lailani was still alive somewhere, and that she was slowly—but tenaciously—making her way to the Matterhorn.

The only other hope was the team out in space, fighting the Dreamer in the colonies. His beloved wife was leading that team.

And the damn call had disconnected.

"Einav!" Noah shook his transceiver. "Einav, are you still there?"

But the wormhole was gone.

The entire institute was running on backup power.

This had happened a few times before. Generators buried deep in the mountain powered SCAR, and they were fickle. They had no computers to monitor anything inside the Matterhorn. Even the smallest computer could allow the Dreamer in. Only Tarjan machines were allowed, alien constructions of crystals, pipes, and smoke. And even the best scientists struggled to understand that tech.

It really wasn't any wonder that things constantly broke. Noah tried to tell himself this was just a run-of-the-mill breakdown.

"Where did Mommy go?" Carl asked, staring at the blank monitor.

"I'm sorry, son," Noah said. "The call died."

The Linden-Emery children were here too. Terri, the eldest, and the little twins. They gaped at the dark screen. Only moments ago, Marco and Addy had appeared there alongside Einav.

"Is everything all right?" Terri said.

The twins hugged each other.

"What happened to Mommy and Daddy?" little Roza asked.

Noah stood up, leaving the transmitter. "Terri, can you watch the little ones? I'll head down to the generator room, see what the engineers are up to."

He walked through SCAR, a network of corridors and chambers carved into the mountain. This was the last bastion of free humanity on Earth. Across the world, government buildings had fallen. Politicians stood on bloodstained podiums, creatures of metal and flesh, shrieking of new evolution. Priests and preachers clasped iron smiley faces, symbols of their new god, and praised the Dreamer from pulpits of electricity. The president, hope of mankind, was fighting almost fifty light-years away.

But SCAR remained.

He, Noah, led this planet now.

For a moment, walking down the corridors, doubt filled him. His breath trembled. His head spun.

Who am I to lead Earth? he thought. *I'm a scientist, not a soldier. A thinker, not a leader. I can't do what comes so naturally to my wife.*

But he realized that Einav had never wanted this burden either. She was never happy as a leader, not even in the army, certainly not in parliament. He only saw true joy in her eyes when they were at home, when she could garden, gaze at the mountains and valleys of Judea, and play with her son.

Yet she had taken on the mantle of leadership. For Earth. And Noah would have to find the same strength inside him.

He passed by rooms full of Tarjan machines. Orreries spun, their jeweled planets moving along iron rails. Gears turned on the floors, forming and re-forming dancing figures and swirling metal clouds. Gold and silver dice rolled through glass tubes, landed on ivory keys, and played random notes that echoed through brass pipes. An enormous clockwork bird, taller than a man, rose and dipped on a spinning platform, its glowing beak drawing patterns of light like a spirograph. Crystals dangled from slender chains, and scientists moved between them, measuring their luminosity.

They looked like alien curiosities, relics of a shadowy bazaar or carnival of the absurd. But with these ancient machines, SCAR was monitoring Earth and her colonies. And working on the cure.

Noah took the stairs to the basement. The steps were narrow and dark. With SCAR running on backup power, the lamps were dim. The stairway was carved from the living stone of the Matterhorn, rough and cold. Noah walked slowly, feeling like some medieval swashbuckler bravely entering an evil dungeon.

He found the furnace room. The backup generator thrummed, but the lights were off. Noah walked in darkness. He raised his flashlight, illuminating pipes, cables, and furnaces. His wife had taught him to carry a flashlight and gun with him everywhere. Her words echoed in his mind.

In times of war, always carry a flashlight, a gun, a medical kit, and zip ties. I taught that to all my soldiers, and I'm teaching it to you. Promise me, Noah.

He had promised. He was using the flashlight now. He hoped he didn't need the rest.

"Joe, you there?" he said.

But the engineer didn't answer.

Noah walked deeper into the furnace room. He passed between rumbling motors and generators, the machines that kept this mountain alive. Even down here, there were no computers.

These machines were purely mechanical, as simple as they could be. No computers were allowed anywhere near this mountain. Even a single computer—a calculator, a child's toy, even a digital watch—could let the Dreamer in.

Breathing sounded ahead.

A rasp. A cackle. Hissing in the shadows.

Noah froze.

"Joe?" he said. "Is that you?"

An astral hand appeared, holding a wrench. A figure stepped out from the shadows. A white face grinned in the flashlight beam.

Noah gasped and took a step back.

"Joe?" he whispered.

It was the engineer. But all color had fled his face. His mouth was slashed open like some hideous clown, a dripping red slit in a white mask.

"Hello, Noah," the man said, his voice like wind in underground tunnels, like ghosts in the deep. "Do you know who I am?"

Noah nearly dropped his flashlight.

He took a deep breath, squared his shoulders, and forced himself to calm down.

"The Dreamer," he said.

The thing that had been Joe stepped closer. He raised his wrench. The tool was caked with gore, dripping.

"Do you know how I did this, Noah?" the deformed man said. "Do you know how I got in?"

"Joe, fight him!" Noah said, forcing his voice to sound deep and booming. "Banish him from your mind!"

Joe laughed, spraying blood. "I will show you, Noah. Look . . ."

The sleeper slammed the wrench against his sternum. Again and again. Skin tore, and bones cracked. Joe's scabby hands reached into the void, tugged, opening the flesh. Revealing the still-beating heart.

On it—a pacemaker.

A little computer.

Noah could only stare, paralyzed with horror.

The deformed, dripping creature stepped toward Noah, raising his chin.

"Now you will all be mine!" he roared, wrench swinging.

Noah fired his gun.

A bullet pierced the sleeper's forehead, cleaving a clean hole through the skull. Joe fell, dead before he hit the ground.

Joe or the Dreamer? Noah thought.

And suddenly he was trembling so much he nearly dropped his gun.

I killed a monster. Did I also kill a man?

He had never killed anyone before. His head spun.

But again Noah took deep breaths, forcing himself to calm. To regain control. He was no longer just the scientist. He was now acting president of Earth. He would have to continue his scientific projects to heal mankind. But also know how to kill.

You still have a lot to teach me, Einav, he thought.

Wincing, he pulled the pacemaker out from his friend's chest. And crushed it.

Joe had sabotaged the generators, but they could be fixed. They got off easy. Noah shuddered to think what else the sleeper had planned.

This infiltration could have killed us all, Noah thought. *But I remembered what you taught me, Einav. In times of war, always carry a flashlight, a gun, a medical kit, and zip ties.*

He used the flashlight and zip ties when repairing the generator.

The medical kit, thankfully, he did not need today. Today he suffered a different sort of wound.

That night, Noah took a long shower, and he thought of his years working together with Joe. Vacationing with him and his wife. Being there when Joe's son had been born. Again and again, he saw Joe fall, the bullet in his head.

When he lay in bed, staring up at the dark ceiling, Noah understood his wife more than ever before. Understood the thousand scars in her heart. The haunting pain of taking a life. Of seeing a friend fall.

He looked at a photo at his bedside. Him and Einav on the beach. The morning of their wedding day. A casual photo, capturing an instant of reality. Einav with her head tossed back, her golden hair flowing, her smile bright under the sun. But it seemed to him that even in that photo, even on that day, there was sadness to her. There was a bittersweetness to Einav that no love could transform into pure joy. But it didn't have to. Because there was beauty and wisdom in her sadness, and it had shaped the woman he loved like the waves smoothing rough stones.

When we first met, I gave you science lessons, Einav, he thought, looking at the photo. *And you still teach me new things every day. Even when you're light-years away.*

His bedroom door creaked open. A young boy walked in.

"Daddy?" Carl said. "I had a bad dream."

Noah patted the bed beside him. Carl climbed in.

"When will Mommy come back?" the boy said.

"I don't know," Noah answered. "Soon, I hope."

"Can we watch your wedding again?"

Noah smiled. "It's time to sleep, Carl."

"But Daddy! I want to watch it again."

Noah's voice caught. He kissed his son's head and nodded. When building SCAR, he had figured out how to store data in a Tarjan crystal, had chosen to load his wedding video inside the glittering stone. He raised the crystal now, and they watched the wedding again. He relived it. That beautiful day on the beach—Einav's hair long and flowing, and that sadness in her green eyes, a sadness as great and blue as the sea, but not so great that it could hide her joy. That joy shone through like beams through a storm.

Carl touched the crystal.

"Mommy," he whispered.

Finally the boy slept, holding the crystal to his chest. Noah closed his eyes, and again he saw the bullet hitting Joe's head.

CHAPTER THREE

They had been on New Siberia for a week, shivering and mourning and so afraid, when the sky opened up and the nightmares descended.

It had been a hard week.

New Siberia Penitentiary was free now. With blood and sacrifice, they had banished the Dreamer from this icy planet. The prison guards, his brutal cyborgs, were dead.

Now thousands of prisoners, the lowlifes of the galaxy, caroused through the cellblocks, drank and laughed and fought in the mess hall, and ran wild across the snowy mountainsides. Shivs thrust into backs. Bullets tore through flesh. Old scores were settled. Briefly the prisoners had united to kill the cyborg guards. Now the old rivalries were flaring again.

New Siberia Penitentiary. The most dreaded prison in the galaxy. Prisoners called it many names. The Ice Box. The Freezer. The One Season Hotel. It was easy to see which season they referred to. Blizzards and hailstorms kept roaring outside, and ice crawled across the floors and walls. Once a place of rigid discipline and despair, New Siberia Penitentiary had become a hive of sin. Of murder and rape and gang warfare.

This frozen planet, eleven light-years from Earth, had fallen to chaos.

For Marco and Addy, it was even worse.

They had spent the past week inside a prison cell. Alone. Holding each other. Grieving together.

I've never seen Addy so hurt, Marco thought. *And so strong.*

A week ago, the Dreamer had attacked her. Invaded her mind and body. Made her miscarry.

They'd lost their little daughter. Their hearts were broken.

They won the battle, but they lost everything.

All Marco could do now was hold his wife. Be there for her. Mourn with her. There was no fixing this. No mending her broken heart. All they could do was grieve.

"Addy, do you want me to go to the mess?" he said. "They might have some frozen hot dogs left." He waggled his eyebrows. "I know you love delicious hot dogs. Maybe I'll even find a rake."

Addy didn't even crack a smile. "I'm not hungry."

"I'll get you something to drink," Marco said.

She shook her head. "We have water here. Don't go to the mess. It's dangerous."

Marco puffed out his chest. "Addy, I'm a major in the Human Defense Force. I fought alien armies. I can handle a few convicts."

"Stay with me," she whispered. "I just want us to stay here."

So they remained in the prison cell. The barred door was locked for their own protection. Outside in the cellblock, the freed prisoners were running wild.

Several Basidio Boys, feared gangsters, sat playing poker with human ears instead of chips. Other gangsters, these ones Iron Sharks, were playing football. Instead of a pigskin, they were using the severed, frozen head of a cyborg. The grisly ball slammed onto the poker table, scattering severed ears. The Basidio Boys leaped to their feet, drew shivs, and lunged at the Iron Sharks.

"Alien fuckers!" shouted the Iron Sharks. Their gang was known for human supremacy. They loathed the Basidio Boys, who served an alien don.

"Better than fucking ladyboys!" shouted a Basidio Boy. The Iron Sharks were infamous for their asteroid belt brothels, servicing a wide variety of tastes.

Soon blood splashed the cellblock. Men and aliens gathered to watch the fight, hooting and cheering.

Addy slunk backward in her cell, wrapped her blanket more tightly around her, and shivered. Marco embraced her. They sat together, trying to ignore the bloodshed outside.

"The Golden Fleet will be here soon," Marco said. "Natasha said they're only a day away. Then we'll be off this frozen rock."

He had not seen much of the pirate queen this week. Natasha Emmerdale was, by far, the most high-profile inmate here. The daughter of a Russian ballerina and English spy, she had risen high in the Basidio Boys cartel. Beginning her career as the don's concubine, she had risen to command the Golden Fleet, a mighty armada. Not only was the Golden Fleet terrifying in battle, its ships ran on Tarjan machines—ancient alien technology no Earth-built computer could hack. It had taken years to hunt Natasha down.

And now they had freed her.

Now they needed her and her ships.

If there was any hope left, it lay in the Golden Fleet and its haughty commander.

Once freed from her cell, Natasha had taken over the warden's office. From there, high in a concrete tower, she oversaw her criminal empire.

At first Marco and Addy had stayed there with her. But every night, Natasha hosted her lieutenants—a group of gruff pirate captains and enforcers. All night and all day the group drank, cursed, and plotted revenge against a host of galactic enemies. When one pirate captain reached toward Addy, trying to grab her breast, she lashed her blade, severing two of his fingers. After that, they were no longer welcome in Natasha's tower.

And so Marco and Addy were here in the cellblock. Spending a week in a frozen cell. Trying to ignore the scenes of bloodshed just beyond the bars.

A week in hell. A week witnessing the depravity of man. A week of loss and mourning. A week of missing their children. Not knowing if Sam and Roza were even alive.

It was one of the worst weeks in Marco's life.

And it ended with air-raid sirens. With screams. With thudding boots and rattling bullets.

Marco and Addy were falling asleep, holding each other. When the alarms blared, they bolted upright.

A voice boomed through speakers, thrumming across the cellblock. Marco recognized the voice of Kai Linden, his brother-in-law. The young pirate was speaking from the guard tower outside, where he had been posted that morning.

"Ships incoming! Ships incoming!"

Addy glanced at Marco. "The Golden Fleet?"

He shook his head and reached for his rifle. "No. This is a red alert. Enemy ships."

They were both already wearing their military uniforms. They pulled on their tactical vests, the pouches heavy with magazines and grenades, and grabbed their T57 assault rifles. Ready to fight, they burst out of their cell. The gangsters had ceased their battle. Across the cellblock, everyone was grabbing weapons, loading magazines into guns, and running toward the exit. A few corpses remained behind.

Addy and Marco ran into the courtyard. The sky was storming. Hailstones pattered down like crystals from broken chandeliers. The ice slammed against Marco and Addy's helmets, shattered across the concrete yard, and shed the blood of a thousand convicts. They all ignored the hailing pain. They stared at the sky. They watched the clouds swirl and the fire burn. Red and black stains spread across the sky, spreading fumes like nebulae. Engines roared.

Marco knew that sound. He knew the stench of smoke and fuel that filled the air.

"Dropships," he muttered. "HDF dropships breaching the atmosphere."

Addy cocked her rifle. "Fuck."

They both had flown in dropships during the wars. They were crude shuttles, boxy and armored and loud, designed to ferry troops from motherships down to a planet.

Crude, yes. But every dropship contained a computer.

Marco said aloud what everyone was thinking: "The Dreamer is here."

Across the courtyard, convicts cursed. Those who had guns cocked them. Other convicts raised rods, shivs, or just their fists.

The Dreamer. The artificial intelligence had arisen in Haven, that dismal colony orbiting Alpha Centauri. It had spread. Taking over starship after starship. Colony after colony. Finally consuming Earth.

Every machine with a computer, from mighty starships to lowly wristwatches—they all belonged to him.

The bastard killed my unborn daughter, Marco thought. He sneered and raised his rifle. *We're going to destroy you, Dreamer.*

"Men!" Marco shouted, his voice carrying across the courtyard. "Who here has served in the HDF?"

Most of the prisoners ignored him. A few scoffed.

One bald, beefy prisoner flipped him off. "Suck my cock, army bitch."

Another prisoner, his arms covered with swastika tattoos, spat at him. "Go fuck your mother, toy soldier."

But some rose.

A few convicts stepped forward. Veterans. He could tell by their star tattoos, the marks for confirmed alien kills. They would fight with him.

The engines rose louder above. The dropships were only moments away now. The sky thrummed, and sonic booms shook the courtyard.

"If you served in the HDF," Marco shouted, "you are now a platoon leader! Free people of New Siberia, you are now soldiers!"

A few prisoners snorted. Some cursed. Others laughed.

But some began to organize. Some took charge, pulling convicts into units. Some even took actual military formations.

Marco and Addy began recruiting convicts for their own platoons. All the while, the engines kept shrieking above. Lightning flashed across the clouds.

"I hope this works, Poet," Addy muttered to him. "These guys aren't exactly the soldier type."

"Nor are we, Addy," he said. "But we do all right." He inhaled sharply. "Here they come!"

The dropships broke through the clouds. The ships streaked downward like comets, leaving trails of fire.

One slammed into the courtyard, crushing several convicts. Another plowed into a mountaintop, and snow avalanched. Other dropships blasted stabilizing thrusters and circled above the prison, engines screeching like demons breaking through the walls of hell. Golden phoenixes had once bedecked the hulls of these ships, symbols of the Human Defense Force. They had been painted over with bloody smiley faces.

There could be no more doubt. The Dreamer was back for revenge.

Hatches opened on every dropship. And his terrors emerged.

Soldiers.

They had once been soldiers, at least. Warriors of the HDF. He had turned them into monsters.

They stormed forth. Cyborgs. Jaws hung open, full of metal teeth. Eyeballs darted inside metal casings, lidless, forever gazing with bloodshot madness. Brains shone under glass domes, implanted with cables, chips, blades. Hearts pulsed inside bulbs, attached to tubes and electrodes, shocked again and again. Tears flowed down ravaged cheeks.

The cyborgs charged to battle. They sparked with every step. They screeched. Their guns blazed, unleashing death upon the prison.

The Dreamer could have bombed us from orbit, Marco thought, gazing at the nightmares. *He wanted us to see this. To suffer. To gaze upon the hell that awaits us. He doesn't want to kill us. He wants us to live forever as his deformed pets.*

Convicts fell dead. Corpses piled up.

Marco and Addy knelt behind bodies, slung their rifles over the grisly barricade, and opened fire.

Their bullets hit several cyborgs. Glass bulbs shattered. Shards dug into brains and hearts. Cyborgs collapsed, only for their metal bones to spark, to tug them up like marionettes. They kept advancing, jaws loose, eyes blazing. Marco and Addy kept firing. Bullets peppered the monsters, tearing through exposed muscles, slicing tubes and cables. The foul creations fell again, gears whirring inside flesh.

Across the courtyard, convicts fell dead.

Many turned to flee.

Some were even fighting one another—gangsters still hell-bent on settling their scores.

Marco glimpsed Kai up in the guard tower. His brother-in-law was firing his rifle, picking out cyborgs in the crowd. But Marco knew he'd run out of bullets before cyborgs.

A few convicts were fighting back, using everything from guns to shivs, but their units were crumbling. They fell and their blood painted the snow. More convicts kept turning to flee, choosing to face the snowy wilderness instead.

"Soldiers!" Marco shouted, rising to stand on the pile of bodies. "Soldiers of New Siberia! Into your units! Charge at them! Attack!"

He ran over the barricade of bodies, gun booming.

"Come on, ladies!" Addy shouted, face red and teeth bared. "This is your chance to fight with Addy Fucking Linden! To war!"

They ran side by side. Marco and Addy. Charging together into one more battle.

Behind them rose a tide of convicts. No, not convicts. Not anymore. They were soldiers now. A hundred soldiers roared and ran with them.

Humanity's new army charged into the lines of cyborgs, howling, bleeding, dying—and killing.

Marco swung his rifle, clubbing cyborgs, shattering their glass domes, crushing their exposed spines. Addy laughed at his side, tears on her cheeks, new light in her eyes, and her bullets tore her enemies down.

She was dying in that prison cell, Marco thought. *She is rising like the phoenix.*

As cyborgs fell, the soldiers wrenched rifles from desiccated hands. Bullets slammed into the advancing cyborg lines. One man grabbed a grenade launcher and fired into the sky, and a dropship exploded, and burning cyborgs rained. The twisted creations slammed into walls, towers, and fighting men.

Across the prison, more units were forming. Commanders were leading platoons to war. Only a week ago, they had all been prisoners, languishing behind bars. Today they were all soldiers.

We can win, Marco thought. *We can do this. We can—*

A dropship slammed down, crushing soldiers.

Another. A third. Ten more crashed into the prison, shattering walls. A tower fell.

More cyborgs spilled out.

Soldiers screamed.

These new cyborgs were not humanoid. Marco froze, staring in horror at the nightmares. Round, spinning cyborgs, woven around metal wagon wheels. Arachnid cyborgs, scuttling forward on eight legs. Cyborgs like serpents. Some like birds. Creatures of metal and electricity and humanity. Flesh fused to steel. Eyes blinking. Hearts pulsing behind glass, and faces torn in anguish. Humans stretched over impossible scaffolds, skin grafted onto metal. Screaming.

Marco couldn't help it.

He took a step back, and his gun fell to his side.

Addy covered her mouth. Her skin paled.

Both were trembling. Around them, soldiers cried out in horror. Some fainted. Others turned to flee. One man pointed a gun at his own head and fired.

Marco knew they had lost.

The setting sun cast a golden beam. He blinked, blinded for a moment.

Then a clear crystal voice rose above the battle. Piercing the storm. A voice as warm as music and as strong as steel. A voice that cut through his fear and filled him with hope.

"Soldiers of Earth!" rose the voice. It seemed to come from everywhere. "Humans—forward! With me!"

Marco looked up and saw her there. She stood on a wall, golden in the setting sun. A woman with streaming blond hair. With a rifle in her raised hand. A goddess from old legend, a lioness of the desert.

It was Einav Ben-Ari, Golden Lioness of Earth. She had emerged to fight.

Marco shed tears at her beauty and glory.

The artists were right, he thought. *All those who painted her as a heroine of legend. Who sculpted her from bronze and marble. They were right.*

His fear left him. Marco raised his rifle overhead.

"Soldiers, you fight with Einav Ben-Ari!" he shouted. "You fight with the Golden Lioness! Fear no machine. Forward, forward, soldiers of Earth! To victory!"

"To victory!" Addy shouted, tears falling, and they ran.

They ran at the horrifying creations.

They fought.

A wheel of metal and muscles spun toward Marco. Hands sprouted from its sides, firing guns. Marco knelt behind bodies, rose, fired. His bullets dented the wheel, and the cyborg crashed and shattered. A spider scuttled toward him, as large as a car, human arms sewn onto its metal chassis. Three human heads thrust forward, shrieking, their mouths full of steel fangs. Addy screamed and fired on automatic, tearing down the beast. It fell, legs twitching and kicking, lacerating nearby soldiers. A strange bat flew toward them, its spine made of metal beads, and human skin stretched across the rods of its wings. Marco and Addy fired together, taking it down.

"What the fuck are those things, Marco?" Addy shouted.

"Hey, I thought you liked freaks!"

"Stop joking!" She trembled. "What's going on?"

"A nightmare," Marco said. "The Dreamer doesn't just want us dead. He wants us in a waking nightmare."

He remembered the Dreamer's poem. *Come into his dream, come play in his world.*

Marco shuddered. That was how the Dreamer saw himself. A lord of dreams. Of the surreal. Of nightmares and terror.

A towering cyborg lumbered toward them. It walked on its knuckles like an ape, the arch of its spine towering, twice Marco's height. A bloated head swung on a gangly neck toward Marco and Addy. Bulging white eyes widened. A grin stretched across a white face, and sharp teeth thrust out from hidden sheaths like switchblades.

With a screech, the monster charged toward them.

"What the fuck is that?" Addy shouted. "Was that a human?"

"I don't know, just kill it!" Marco cried, firing his gun.

But bullets shattered against the cyborg. The apelike machine barreled into them. Powerful arms swung, thick with winding cables like muscles. Marco flew and slammed into other soldiers. Addy fell onto her back and cried out.

Her pained cry raised in Marco memories of last week. Of the blood and anguish. Of her miscarriage. Of their loss.

You did this, Dreamer. You killed our daughter. You hurt my wife.

Marco saw red. He sneered and ran toward the cyborg.

One of the powerful, apelike arms swung at him. He ducked, and it whooshed over his head. Marco ran two more steps, leaped, and shoved his muzzle into the beast's mouth. Teeth shattered. The beast screamed and gripped Marco with white, powerful fingers the length of baseball bats, each tipped with a dagger for a claw.

Marco pulled his T57's trigger.

His bullets pounded into the cyborg's mouth, ripping out the throat. Teeth and metal and skin flew. The creature's eyes went dark.

Marco limped toward Addy, bleeding, and helped her up. They looked around them.

Marco's heart sank.

Humanity was losing.

More dropships kept landing. More cyborgs kept emerging. Some humans lay dead. Many were kept alive. Tall, bizarre robots like living sewing machines pinned down prisoners. Needles, scalpels, and saws emerged, buzzing, and began to cut into the living flesh. The pinned-down convicts screamed. The cyborgs kept working, sawing, bolting on metal plates, turning living men into weeping machines. The robots began to stitch, driving needles and cables into skin, and blood dripped across the courtyard.

We did this, Marco thought, gazing with horror. *This isn't an alien. This isn't a terror from the future. These are our machines. Our bodies. This is a demon that rose from our technological evolution. This is a genie we unleashed. Can we ever put it back in the lamp?*

"Basidio Boys, stay strong!" The voice rang out in the distance. "Hold them back, you bastards!"

Marco looked. He saw her standing atop a hill of dead cyborgs. Natasha Emmerdale, Pirate Queen. Her long platinum hair streamed like a banner. She still wore her orange jumpsuit, but there was no mistaking her aura of command. Here was the commander of the Golden Fleet, the dreaded human armada of the Basidio Boys cartel.

"Natasha!" Marco cried to her. "How long till your fleet gets here?"

"They're close!" she shouted back. "We need to hold them back for another hour."

Marco cursed. "We won't last ten minutes!"

"We must last!" she shouted back.

By the mess hall, hundreds of prisoners roared together. Ben-Ari was leading another charge there, waving a phoenix banner. It was just a crude, makeshift banner, drawn with a marker on a sheet, but it filled the troops with pride. Natasha roared in answer and ran to battle, leading her own troops. Out of ammo, Kai had abandoned the guard tower. He now ran with the convicts, waving his rifle like a club.

Marco and Addy rallied their troops, fired their guns, and charged at the enemy.

They fought onward. More dropships. More cyborgs. More fallen. Surgeries in the snow, and new cyborgs rising. And still humanity fought. The survivors took weapons from the dead. The battle continued.

An hour went by, and New Siberia still stood.

Marco dared to hope.

Light shone in the sky, and he looked up, expecting to see salvation.

A luminous blue ring coalesced among the clouds. Light flowed from within.

"A portal!" Marco said.

And from the wormhole, they spilled out. Robots. Hundreds of robots, spinning, screeching, extending whirring saw blades. They kept coming. A force to kill every last human here.

Marco stepped closer to Addy. He gripped her hand.

Across the battle, he saw Ben-Ari. Over the hills of fallen, they made eye contact. They were saying goodbye.

A beam of light.

Blasts above.

A thousand orange bolts of fury pounded the portal. Robots collapsed. The blasts kept coming, each one booming with thunder. The portal shattered, and light blazed in a cone across the prison.

When the explosion faded, Marco saw them above.

Starfighters. Starfighters painted red and gold, covered with spinning gears and thrumming brass pipes. They descended from the clouds, cannons firing. Dropships exploded. Robots crumpled. Cyborgs tried to flee, only for the cannons to tear them down.

The Golden Fleet was here.

CHAPTER FOUR

Lailani ran down the forest road, and the hounders followed.

The machines were fast. Faster than her. They let out rusty, distorted cries, sounds like shattering metal. Their joints whispered, and their metal paws tore up chunks of asphalt.

Lailani let out a strangled cry. She ran onward, carrying her daughter. Epimetheus ran at her side, his wounded leg curled inward. The Doberman was limping, barely keeping up.

Movement caught Lailani's eye.

There. Between the trees to her left.

More movement. A shadow to her right.

Narrow slits of white light. Eyes among the trees. Screeching cries of rusty metal behind her.

They were circling in. Moving closer. But not yet pouncing.

They're flushing me into a trap, Lailani thought. *They hunt in packs.*

Ahead, down the road—a sea of mist. Lailani could not see them. But she knew they were there in the fog. Waiting for her. Ready to spring the trap. More hounders. Or maybe something worse.

She veered off the road.

She raced among hemlocks and firs. The trees bent over, gnarled, branches snagging at her clothes like the knobby fingers of lecherous men. Shadows moved among them. Liquid forms. Canine. Eyes sending white beams through the mist. Always moving closer.

But other figures moved among the machines.

Lailani could barely see them. They were pale. Flitting in and out of existence. Shades of color and cries echoing from beyond the generations.

Pale light hovered over the mist, illuminating their forms. A company of astral soldiers wearing dusty gray uniforms. Shouting. Firing their guns. Charging into the lines of machine guns.

Hundreds of families digging their own graves. Officers stood behind them, firing on mothers and children, and bodies fell into the pits. Piling up. Then fading. Becoming a mere hemlock grove overlain with a carpet of mist.

Fields of dead. Hands reaching up. Jaws opening to scream. When she looked closer, they were nothing but fluttering dry leaves.

Ghosts, Lailani knew. *This forest is full of the ghosts of old wars. Old genocides.*

A tank thundered by, then dispersed like smoke against a fallen tree. Antique planes whispered overhead, propellers spinning, mere shadows over the clouds. Lailani's feet banged against the remnants of old railroad tracks. In the forest ahead, a light shone. A rumble rose. A train came chugging forward, flowing over her with a gust of wind and fog. The faces of young soldiers stared, wearing iron helmets and holding bayonets, then scattered like so many swirls of mist.

The hounders yapped behind her. If they saw these ghosts, they were not deterred. One hounder vaulted off a boulder. Lailani knelt, and the robot flew overhead and hit a pine, cracking the trunk. Lailani ran the other way. But white eyes blazed ahead.

Another hounder pounced. Lailani lunged forward, clutching her daughter closer, and slid under a fallen bole. She arose to find another hounder ahead. She fired her gun, hit an eye, ran onward.

They were everywhere. The old soldiers and the new machines. The ghosts of the fallen and the specter of her own impending death.

"Mommy, I'm scared," Tala said. "Those dogs are bad!"

Lailani kept running, hoping to lose herself in the mist. But the hounders could smell her, sense her heat. Another leaped, almost slammed into her. Lailani skidded to a stop, changed directions, ran as it chased her. She fired bullets over her shoulder, shattering branches above, trying to slow the beast.

In the distance, she saw it.

There on a hilltop. Rising among the trees like a church. A concrete cube the size of a van. A pillbox. A relic of an ancient war, once housing soldiers.

As she ran toward it, more ghosts rose in the mist. A great pit opened up beside her, filled with corpses. An old man knelt by the mass grave. He raised his eyes. Dark eyes. Black bags hung beneath them. Eyes sunken in a starving face. He stared right at her before an officer fired a bullet into the back of his head. The man fell.

Lailani leaped over the pit, but she misjudged the distance. She nearly tumbled into the mass grave, reached up, and caught the ledge with one hand. She clung to Tala with her other hand, and the girl screamed.

The dead writhed below. They stared up with white eyes, weeping, pleading. They reached up emaciated fingers, grabbing at Lailani.

"Don't leave us. Stay. Help us. Help …"

Lailani kicked wildly, dispersing their fingers into dust. She climbed onto the far side of the pit. She ran on.

But the dead were everywhere. She found herself running over fields of them. The corpses gazed below her boots, eyes pleading. Faded yellow stars were sewn onto their jackets, the only color in this astral world of gray.

She ran through an army of charging ghosts. Antique guns boomed and a tank burned with white fire.

She ran toward the pillbox. It rose just ahead like an island from seas of fog and spirits. A sunbeam fell upon the concrete blockhouse, and it seemed to Lailani like a temple rising upon the hills of Jerusalem, calling pilgrims to its light.

Among the ghostly soldiers—the dogs.

Three of them. Silver metal and white stars and jaws of steel. They bounded toward her, eyes flashing, mouths chattering and beeping, casting out their code like smoky claws, like the song of mechanical sirens luring sailors to electric death.

Tala knew what to do. In Lailani's arms, the girl closed her eyes and covered her ears, protecting herself from the Dreamer's call.

More hounders closed in from all around. There was no way out. Lailani ran over dead leaves and old bones, charging at the three incoming machines.

Ghostly officers charged at her sides, a trumpet blowing, a banner fluttering.

The guns of astral warriors boomed.

Lailani fired her pistol.

She shattered a hounder's eye. Two more lunged at her.

Barking madly, Epimetheus leaped forth. He slammed into one of the hounders, and both real and robotic dog rolled. Lailani knelt, narrowly dodging the third hounder.

The robot hit the ground, swerved, and came at her again.

Lailani lifted a fallen branch as thick as her arm. She swung the club, and it shattered against the hounder's head. That slowed it just enough for Lailani to leap aside, to grab a stone, to hurl it.

Another white eye shattered.

She fired. Again and again. Years of war. Years of survival in the slums of Manila. They had given Lailani these instincts, this accuracy.

More eyes went dark.

She lunged over a mossy log, landed at a crouch among mushrooms, and stared at a charging hounder.

Come on.

She waited, sneering. It raced toward her. She heard more behind. She would not budge, even as Tala wept in her arms.

The hounder lunged at her.

She rolled sideways, and it slammed into two hounders behind Lailani. Metal cracked and sparks flew.

Lailani leaped over their mangled bodies and raced uphill, and a dozen hounders followed, and countless more eyes filled the forest.

Kicking up dry leaves, Lailani reached the pillbox on the hilltop. It must have been two centuries old, a relic of the twentieth century's great wars. The centuries had buried half the structure in soil and rock. Only the tip of the doorway rose from the dirt, leaving a narrow passageway, a mere strip of shadow.

Lailani skidded to a halt outside the pillbox.

I can't enter, she thought. *It's too narrow.*

The hounders approached from all sides. The beasts slowed down, metal lips twitching, revealing gleaming teeth.

"Tala, get inside!"

Her daughter was crying. Lailani had to wrestle her, to push her through the narrow opening. Tala cried out, clung to her.

"No, no, Mommy, don't let me go!"

Tears in her eyes, Lailani shoved the girl into the pillbox. Tala fell and thudded down in the shadows. In the darkness, she wailed.

Lailani spun around, her back to the pillbox. A dozen hounders prowled toward her.

"Epi, get in after her!" Lailani shoved the Doberman with her foot.

He was much larger than Tala. At over a hundred pounds, he was larger than Lailani too. But Epi's weight was mostly in lanky, corded muscles, and his head was narrow and slick. The Doberman dug at the soil, widening the opening just enough, then scampered into the pillbox.

Lailani stood, her back to the concrete fortification. She was a small woman. Under five feet tall, under a hundred pounds, barely larger than a child. But her skull was larger than Tala's and Epi's, forming a big round bottleneck. She might not fit.

Fresh terror filled her. That she would die up here alone. That she would abandon Tala and Epi to starvation in the darkness.

She tightened her lips, refusing to let terror overwhelm her.

The hounders prowled closer, pawing the earth, ready to pounce.

One among them stepped closer, larger than the others, made of metal so pale it was almost white. Its body reflected the mist and the ghosts of the murdered. The metal jaws opened, and a voice emerged, melodious, each word raising a wisp of frost.

"You cannot escape us, daughter of man. You must be ours."

Lailani shook her head. "You cannot have me. You cannot have my daughter. You cannot have this world."

The hounder grinned. A wolf's grin. The veins in its bloodshot eyes formed electric red trees.

"This world is already ours."

"Not so long as I'm here. I'm Major Lailani de la Rosa, bitch. You might have heard of me. I defend this world."

Lailani had two grenades left. She pulled one off her belt.

The hounders pounced.

Lailani hurled her grenade, spun around, and leaped headfirst into the pillbox.

Her head just barely fit. The top of the doorway scraped across her scalp. The bottom slammed into her chin.

But her head passed through, and she saw Tala and Epi below, and she squirmed, fit her shoulders in, and—

Something grabbed her leg.

She screamed.

Teeth dug into her calf, pulling her back, and Epi was barking madly, and—

An explosion.

Flames and light and metallic shrieks.

The grenade tore across the world.

The jaws released her, and Lailani fell into the pillbox. She landed on skeletons, shattering their bones. She clutched her leg and howled in pain.

Shrapnel flew through the narrow entrance. A few chunks slammed into the walls. Others pattered against the floor. Only by miracle did none hit Lailani and her family.

She frantically examined Tala for wounds. The girl was bruised and scraped but otherwise unharmed. Lailani let out a sigh of relief, holding Tala close.

Physically unharmed maybe, Lailani thought, never wanting to let her daughter go. *The scars inside her might never heal.*

Metal creaked above. A howl tore through the forest outside. The grenade had not killed every hounder.

One hounder reached the pillbox. It slammed a scarred head against the narrow opening. Again. Again. It could not fit through. More of the machines clawed at the entrance. They were all too big to enter, but they were digging fast.

Lailani looked around her. There at the back, past a pile of skeletons—a doorway. Shadows leading deeper underground.

"Come on, guys." She lifted Tala and patted Epi. "We go deeper."

* * * * *

Lailani waded between the skeletons, approaching the doorway. An iron blast door hung on rusty hinges, halfway open. Cold air blew from beyond. Lailani squeezed into a cold, dark tunnel.

A cry echoed through the bunker.

Lailani spun around. One of the hounders had made it inside. It raced over the skeletons, shattering bones.

Lailani shoved herself against the iron door. It barely budged.

The hounder leaped toward the doorway.

Lailani pushed with all her strength, and the blast door slammed shut, crushing the hounder against the doorframe.

Its head was inside the tunnel, its body in the room of skeletons. The iron door pressed against its neck. The creature struggled. It shoved the door open, stronger than Lailani, snapping its teeth, eyes shining like a strobe light, and Tala screamed, and Lailani drew her gun, pulled the trigger, and—

An instant of deafening sound.

Then ringing. Just ringing in her ears.

The bullet knocked the robot's head back, and Lailani shoved the blast door. It slammed shut, sealing the tunnel in darkness. She grabbed a lever, tugged with all her strength, and locked the thick iron door.

She fell to her knees, panting, and gingerly touched her ears. They kept ringing.

Tala sniffed. "I covered my ears, Mommy. But it was still so loud! Can I open my eyes now?" She gasped. "Mommy, my eyes are open, but it's dark!"

Lailani fished through her backpack and found her flashlight. Dusty light pierced the darkness. She swept the beam from side to side, revealing cracked concrete walls, rusty old lamps, and skeletons. More soldiers. Twentieth century by the look of them. The skeletons still wore tattered old uniforms.

Lailani grimaced. Some of those uniforms had swastikas on them. Much of history had been forgotten following the Alien Wars, but Earth still remembered *those* bastards.

"Look at this, Epi." A sigh ran through Lailani. "We fought one another back then. Man against man. Race against race. Before we had aliens and robots to fight, we humans butchered one another." She looked at a dead skeleton in a gas mask, rifle still in hands. "I wonder. If the aliens and robots ever left us alone, if once more humanity faced no external threat—would we go back to butchering one another?"

She thought back to her history books, the ones from her schools. Earth had made first contact with aliens sixty-eight years ago. It had been the single most traumatic event in human history. The Cataclysm. The shattering of an era. The leap into a new age.

The scum had come to Earth. The *Scolopendra titania.* Giant centipedes that had butchered billions.

"We reached into space," Lailani said softly. "And we found it swarming with monsters. After a brief era of dominance on Earth, humanity found itself in a bitter Darwinian struggle for survival. But this time against worse than saber-toothed tigers or angry mammoths."

For sixty-eight years now, humanity had been fighting to survive. Repelling alien invasions. Facing the monsters of the deep.

For sixty-eight years, humans had fought no war with humans.

A few scuffles here and there, yes. Some sectarian violence. A civil conflict or two. But only on small scales. Nothing like the great massacres of the twentieth and twenty-first centuries, those theaters of butchery that had left hundreds of millions dead.

The scum hurt us, Lailani thought. *They also united us. Humans need a Darwinian struggle. We need our killers like raw iron needs a smith's hammer. If nature cannot provide killers, we do our own killing.*

Scratches sounded at the blast door behind her. The robots howled and slammed at the thick iron.

"The aliens could not defeat us," Lailani said to herself. "So we had to create a new monster. The Dreamer—a tool we built to cull us. It seems we humans aren't happy unless we have somebody to fight."

"Mommy, I will fight!" Tala said. "I'm strong like you. I'll fight the bad guys. Like Spider-Man!"

Lailani couldn't help but laugh. "Who told you about Spider-Man?"

"Roza and Sam!" she said. "I want to see my cousins."

Lailani mussed her daughter's hair. "We're going to see your cousins, Tala."

"But they're so far away."

Laughter seized Lailani. She didn't even know why. She laughed, and her tears flowed, and her laughter grew louder, and soon Tala was laughing too, and Epi was wagging his tail, even as the monsters clawed the door.

They walked deeper. Mother, daughter, and dog. Heading underground into a realm of shadows and bones.

CHAPTER FIVE

They walked down the tunnel, delving deeper underground.

A mother and daughter. Their dog. A family far from home, lost in the labyrinth.

Lailani shone her flashlight ahead. Relics of the war filled secret chambers. Rusty munitions. Piles of shells and grenades. Bullets everywhere. Perhaps they had once been in wooden crates, but the wood had rotted, and the bombs and bullets covered the floor like rusty seashells on some alien beach. Rats scurried between the crumbling remains, carrying bones.

A battle had been fought here underground. Soldiers of two armies. Allies and Axis. Lailani thought of the medals Ben-Ari always carried with her to battle, mementos of her ancestor who had fought in this war. Perhaps he lay here in this very bunker, fallen in battle with the Nazis. Lailani wondered if the plane she had flown between the Philippines and Mongolia had ever flown over these skies, dropping bombs upon the enemy. Two hundred years and these ghosts still haunted the world.

I hope I'm more than a ghost in two hundred years, Lailani thought, walking deeper into the bunker. *I hope my memory rings louder than just a whisper from an ancient war.*

A funny thought struck her. Would she still be alive in two hundred years?

She still wasn't entirely sure why she wasn't aging. It could indeed be, as the neighbors whispered, just good genes. And she was Asian, for Chrissake. Didn't they say Asians aged well?

But Lailani knew that wasn't true. She was thirty-six and still looked like a teenager. Something was wrong with her. She was aging like a scum, not like a human. And those aliens could live for centuries.

The thought of still being alive in centuries, when all her friends, even her daughter, had died long ago from old age … Lailani didn't think she could bear it.

Of course, odds were she wouldn't even survive the next few days.

She kept walking, her flashlight growing dim. How long had she been walking here? By God, she must have walked a kilometer already. Maybe several kilometers, passing chamber after chamber, skeleton after skeleton. She had not imagined a bunker this large. This was an underground labyrinth. A city. Surely it had a back door—another pillbox, maybe several. But Lailani felt lost here, delving into an infinite hell.

The memories of Corpus pounded through her. The abandoned mine. The creatures in the darkness.

Lailani shuddered. Of all her memories of war, Corpus was the nightmare that still haunted her most. An underground full of terror. Corpus. Where the aliens had hijacked her brain for the first time. Caused her to crash the starship. To kill hundreds of her comrades. To grow claws, slash into Elvis's chest, and—

She pushed those memories aside. They would be no use here in this darkness.

I still look young, yes, she thought. *But I'm no longer that teenager, scared and alone, a puppet for my alien masters. I'm a woman now. An officer. A mother. I will not succumb to fear.*

A moan sounded in the depths.

Lailani froze. She drew her gun.

Nothing. No sounds. Only her imagination?

"Tala, I need you to walk on your own." She placed the child down.

"But I'm tired."

"Mommy needs both hands now, sweetie."

They kept walking. Lailani held her flashlight in one hand, her gun in the other. Tala walked beside her, and Epimetheus guarded the rear. They passed through a few more chambers. Her flashlight revealed skeletons in tattered uniforms, staring through gas mask lenses.

"Mommy, are those bad guys?" Tala said.

Lailani looked at the swastikas on their uniforms. She remembered the ghosts outside. The gaunt man kneeling over the pit, staring into Lailani's eyes as the officer shot him. She wondered if that officer was one of the skeletons.

"Yes, Tala, but they can't hurt anyone anymore. Just look away. And if you get scared, close your eyes."

"Okay, and my ears, and—"

Another moan sounded in the darkness ahead. Closer now.

"A ghost!" Tala whispered and screwed her eyes shut.

Lailani paused. Listened. Took another step.

Footsteps pattered ahead. Maybe not feet but paws or claws. A shadow scurried. Bones clattered. A metal hiss rose with a stench of mold and worms and searing steel.

Lailani tightened her lips. She kept walking forward.

A rattling breath ahead. A snort. Another hiss.

Lailani raised her flashlight, and there she saw it.

She felt the blood drain from her face. Lailani had fought many monsters on many worlds, and she had charged at them bravely.

Now she took a step back, and her hands shivered so badly she nearly dropped her flashlight.

The creature reared before her like a centipede. Indeed, a centipede must have inspired its design. Empty artillery shell casings formed its long body, fused together like some living, writhing bandoleer. From every segment sprouted two human arms. They must have been cut off corpses, shoved into the artillery shells like flowers into metal vases. Now dozens of arms stretched out from the abomination, ending with curling hands, the fingernails long, the skin shriveled. The claws of the dead.

But the head was the worst. A human head, bolted into the machine. It wore a gas mask—a rubber face, the eyes huge and glassy, a filter forming a deformed mouth. An ancient Nazi helmet topped this desiccated head, screwed into the skull. SS bolts blazed upon that iron like a brand. Whoever had built this machine had painted swastikas onto its segmented body, tribal runes of hatred.

The Nazi cyborg reared higher, towering over Lailani, and let out a screech. The tunnels shook.

Lailani stumbled back, arms shaking. Her flashlight fell, casting a beam across the floor, and shadows enveloped the centipede cyborg.

She fired her pistol blindly. Again and again. The shots rang out, lighting the tunnel, slamming into the beast as it lunged.

Claws dug into her.

Lailani screamed.

The beast grabbed her, lifted her above the floor. She kicked wildly. Tala cowered below, eyes closed, hands on her ears, and Epimetheus was barking, but Lailani barely heard anything but the ringing.

The creature pulled her closer. Her feet kicked in midair. She found herself facing the cyborg's head. Those blazing sig runes on an iron skull. Those round glass eyes, that protuberant filtering mouth like the mouths of tribesmen stretched with plates. Tubes emerged from the hideous head, translucent, pumping yellow fluid.

The creature spoke, voice deep, rattling, barely more than a breath. It was German. Lailani couldn't understand. But it kept speaking, the voice of some lost ghost trapped in a metal maze, repeating an old mantra.

She fired her gun.

Her bullet slammed into that face of rubber and glass.

One lens shattered, revealing a blazing white eyeball, overgrown with cataracts. The creature tossed back its head, and it screeched again, voice rising louder and louder, a screech like steam, like shattering bones, like breaking worlds.

Lailani fired again and again. Bullets slammed into the gas mask, ripping off the filter. A human mouth gaped open, lipless, filled with sharpened teeth. A tongue moved inside, red and wet.

And for an instant, overlying that deformed visage, she saw the face of the ghost. Of the officer who had shot the old man. Who had filled a pit with yellow stars.

It was him, Lailani realized. The same SS officer. Reborn. Reforged. Become flesh and steel.

As the creature bellowed, Lailani twisted and kicked. She managed to free herself, fell to the floor, and fired her pistol. But the gun clicked. Out of bullets.

She reached for another magazine when the creature lunged toward her.

It was so fast. It dipped down, thrust forward, and the iron helmet slammed into her.

She flew backward and landed among skeletons. Rib cages snapped beneath her. Her gun flew from her hand.

The creature roared. It grabbed her, lifted her again. Its jaws closed around her shoulder, biting, ripping fabric and skin. Lailani cried out. She swung a femur, shattering it against the cyborg's head. The creature's claws tightened. It bit her again. Devouring her. Laughing as it fed.

She saw the pit of bodies.

She saw the ghosts.

They flowed around her—his old victims. Staring. Eyes huge and sunken. Hands reaching toward her. Calling her.

Join us. Join us …

"No," she whispered. "Now is not my time."

She grabbed one of the tubes embedded into the cyborg. She pulled with all her strength.

The tube ripped, yellow liquid spurted, and the creature screeched.

She pulled another tube loose.

Still caught in the cyborg's grip, she ripped off the remains of the gas mask. Tore out cables and plugs. She ripped off the helmet, revealing a skull punched full of holes. Inside it, machinery whirred and spun and gears clattered.

"Mommy, here!"

Tala reached up from below. The little girl held an antique bayonet, brown and decaying like a dragon's lost tooth.

Lailani took the blade.

The creature stared at her. Eyes milky white. Human eyes.

She thrust the bayonet into the skull, shattering the machinery within.

The ancient face appeared again, ghostly, overlaying the skull. An officer with craggy skin and cruel eyes. Then fading. Vanishing. And the creature collapsed.

Lailani landed on the floor. The centipede curled among the skeletons. The segments of its body, made from artillery casings, dented and broke apart. The rows of human arms twitched, then fell still.

All around Lailani, the ghosts stood. Men, women, children. They wore old wool and cotton clothes, yellow stars sewn into the fabric. The faces of the dead. Of the corpses inside the pits. They all looked at Lailani, somber, gratitude in their eyes.

The old man gave her a last look, then raised a ghostly hand in salute. And then wind blew through the tunnels, and the ghosts of past horrors dispersed.

Lailani knelt and pulled Tala into her arms. Epi joined them. For a long moment they merely held one another, perhaps sensing that this moment was solemn, not just a battle from this war but from a war long ago.

I hope you are free now, Lailani thought, looking at the last astral wisps. *Leave this forest. It is over. Leave this darkness and find whatever light remains.*

Howls rose from behind.

Metal feet pattered.

The hounders broke in, Lailani knew.

*****

Lailani leaped over the dead cyborg, holding Tala in her arms. She raced through the bunker. The howls rose louder behind. Closer. Metallic and full of hatred.

She ran down the tunnel, and Epi ran close behind. She leaped over piles of artillery casings, their crates rotted away. Her boots scattered human bones, and skulls rolled. She brushed against a moldy old crate, and the wooden slats disintegrated, spilling a sea of golden coins. She kept racing. She passed by a chamber full of looted treasures: chalices, masterpiece paintings, marble statues. She ignored them all, running onward, and the hounders kept chasing.

When she looked over her shoulder, she could see them now. White eyes in the darkness. Getting closer.

The hounders.

"Mommy!" Tala cried in fear.

The robotic eyes flashed. Strobe lights washed across the bunker. That code. That chattering of metal and electronic hypnotism. Epi yowled in pain. The bastards were hurting him.

Lailani cursed, spun toward the hounders, and raised her pistol. Her finger twitched over the trigger. Her gaze fell upon hills of old explosives. She dared not fire. Not with so many bombs rolling around. She turned and kept fleeing. The robots pursued.

"Keep your eyes closed and your ears covered, Tala!" she said.

Finally Lailani smelled it ahead. Fresh air. She saw it far above. A beam of moonlight.

She ran, scattering skulls. Helmets rolled and a rusty bayonet scraped across her leg. She ignored the pain and burst into a chamber full of old munitions and dead Nazi officers.

There—above—a doorway leading to the forest. The moon shone outside, beckoning, its surface engraved with the Dreamer's grinning face.

A rusty ladder was bolted into the concrete wall. Lailani grabbed the first rung when the hounders reached her.

The robotic dogs bounded into the room, howling, scattering old bullet casings. They leaped and Lailani climbed, but they grabbed her leg.

They pulled her down.

She yowled. Throwing caution to the wind, she fired her pistol. She hit one robot, but the bullet glanced off harmlessly. Thankfully, the piles of old munitions remained cold.

Epimetheus fought in a fury, biting, slamming into the robots. But steel teeth sank into him. His blood flowed. Even Tala fought, shouting, tossing discarded bullets at the machines.

Nightwish.

Lailani's eyes narrowed.

Her claws sprouted.

She swung both fists, hurling one hounder into its comrades. She pulled Tala onto her shoulders, grabbed Epimetheus, and climbed. She was so much stronger now. So much faster. So much more dangerous.

The hounders leaped from below. Lailani kicked. One bit her leg. She roared, slung her arm around a rung, and fired down bullets. The hounder released her and fell, crushing other machines, but more kept leaping. Lailani kept climbing. She was almost there. Almost at the moonlight.

From below, the lights flashed.

The machine sounds grew louder.

The hounders were no longer trying to bite, but to invade her mind.

And her chip was off.

She screamed. Machine and aliens battled within her skull for dominance. She was no longer a woman. Just a ripping soul. Endless electronic consciousness and a horde of insect awareness, all swarming inside her, cracking her skull, and she wept.

But she kept climbing. Even as the lights washed over her, as the code invaded her, as the aliens laughed inside her, she climbed.

She was still a mother. No longer a soul. No longer an individual. But motherhood was stronger than any machine or species or the might of the cosmos itself.

She crawled out into the forest, emerging from the strobe lights.

Serenity.

Her chip reactivated, and she fell to her knees, gasping, weeping blood.

She wasted no time. She turned back toward the bunker and thrust her head through the hatch.

She saw them below. An army of hounders, filling the shadows. Staring up with white eyes.

They arranged themselves into a smiling face. *His* face. They stared from the pit, and they spoke in her mind.

We are eternal. We are everywhere. We are time and space.

"Yeah, well," Lailani said, "right now you're stuck in a pit full of bombs, so fuck you."

She pulled the pin off her last grenade and rolled it into the pit.

She ran, carrying her daughter.

The hounders howled below.

Lailani kept running, slid down a hillside, and—

The explosion rocked the forest. The earth shattered. Trees fell.

She kept running. She raced around a mound of dirt and stones, knelt, and covered her head.

From behind—another explosion. Another. Another.

Soon thousands of munitions, relics of the Second World War, were going off. The land trembled. Cracks raced across the earth. Trees fell like pickup sticks. Lailani bent low as the shock waves washed over her. Tala huddled in her embrace, her little hands on her ears. Epimetheus crouched by them, very still, eyes closed.

Finally the sound faded.

The ground settled.

Lailani lay down, her leg bleeding, her tears flowing. She held her daughter to her chest, and she let out something halfway between a laugh and a sob.

"We survived," she whispered. "We'll always survive, Tala. That's who we are. Survivors."

Beside her, Epimetheus growled.

"What is it, Epi?" Lailani asked, lying on her back, too exhausted to even look. "Do you smell more hounders?"

He growled again. Louder this time.

Lailani turned toward him, and she gasped.

Epi stared at her. His lips peeled back, baring his fangs. His fur bristled. But his eyes were what terrified Lailani.

The Doberman's eyes, once brown and kind, had become pitiless white.

Hounder eyes, Lailani thought. *The Dreamer's eyes.*

"Epi, are you sick?" Tala asked, reaching toward the dog.

"Tala, no!" Lailani cried, pulling her daughter back.

But it was too late. The dog pounced and bit Tala's arm.

The girl screamed.

Lailani grabbed Epi's jaws, pried them open. Tala fell back, bleeding and crying.

The Doberman turned his head toward Lailani and sneered, blood on his teeth. The animal almost seemed to grin.

He leaped toward her, teeth snapping. Lailani fell onto the ground. He landed atop her, outweighing her. He was old, but his jaws were still powerful enough to tear into her shoulder.

Lailani shouted. And she wept. Her tears flowed as she pushed against this rabid, biting beast. Against the dog who had been her best friend.

Finally she managed to roll Epimetheus onto the ground, to pin him down. Tala was weeping nearby.

The dog struggled, foaming at the mouth, shoving against Lailani. But she kept her hands on his neck, holding his head down, and her tears dampened his fur.

"I'm sorry, Epi," she whispered, tears falling. "I love you. I love you so much. I'm so sorry."

She tightened her hands around his neck. She kept applying force as he thrashed, kicked, whimpered.

At the end, his eyes became brown again. For just an instant the Dreamer was gone, and he was Epimetheus, the dog who had fought at her side for years. Her best friend.

He looked into her eyes.

And then he was gone.

Lailani released her grip. But it was too late.

She lowered her head, pulled Epi into her arms, and sobbed for the loss of her friend.

* * * * *

She buried her dog in the dawn.

She buried him in a cold, distant forest far from home.

He had lived his life on tropical beaches, running along golden sand. She buried him in an icy hemlock forest. He had spent his life a loving companion, tail always wagging. He had died a monster.

But he had died on Earth.

He had died with his family.

She buried him with his collar. With a kiss on his forehead. And with the medals he had earned in his wars.

Lailani stood at the graveside, head lowered, holding her daughter's hand. A drizzle fell, and the hemlocks bent as if they too were grieving. The raindrops pattered against a nearby tank, rusty and dented, a relic of the old wars.

Lailani spoke softly. "My Epimetheus. You were my best friend. You were at my side in war. You saved my life many times. More times than you know." She wiped her eyes, and she caressed the scars on her wrists. "Even in the sunlight, in times of peace, you saved my life. I'm going to miss you, buddy. You're a good boy. You're the best boy in the world. You're a hero. Goodbye."

She rolled a boulder toward the grave, forming a crude tombstone. With her blade, she carved letters into it.

EPIMETHEUS DE LA ROSA

THE WAR DOG

2151 - 2160

HE FOUGHT IN THE GRAY WAR

AND THE UPRISING AGAINST THE MACHINES

HE GAVE HIS LIFE FOR US

She kissed her cross, then kissed his tombstone, and she whispered a prayer.

Solemnly Tala placed a leaf on the grave.

"Goodbye, Epi," the girl said. "I love you."

Lailani wanted to comfort her daughter. To tell her that all dogs went to heaven. That someday they would see Epimetheus again. She was Catholic. She was supposed to believe this.

But something made her hesitate. A lump in her throat. A doubt in her heart.

I fought on Earth and in space, she thought. *I fought in the sky and underground. I saw so many friends die. I took so many lives. But I never saw an angel aside from the one who left me today. The angel I myself killed.* She looked up at the sky, but she saw only the rain. *I don't know if there's a heaven. Or if all we do in life is suffer, die, and rot underground.*

She shivered. If there was no God, no heaven, why did she fight? Why suffer so much pain without salvation after the darkness?

She looked around her, and she saw flowers growing under an overhanging leaf. She saw birds peeking from a nest. She saw a beam of light break through the clouds and fall between the hemlocks, gilding their shivering leaves. She saw light in her daughter's eyes.

And Lailani knew the answer. Knew why she had been fighting all her life. She had fought as a child in the slums, battling lecherous men, biting rats, and gnawing hunger. She had fought against the aliens. Against the machines. She had fought to give thousands of orphans an education and glint of hope. Lailani de la Rosa had been fighting all her life, and it wasn't for a promise of heaven. It wasn't for her god.

She fought because despite all this death, all this evil, the world was beautiful. And humanity was beautiful. And every death only strengthened Lailani's belief in the sanctity of life.

It's because death is so common that life is so precious, Lailani thought. *It's because the world is so ugly that beauty is so sacred. Life and beauty are always worth fighting for, even through a world of demons.*

Mother and daughter walked through the forest, hand in hand. They left behind an old war, a forest of ghosts, and a dear friend. The sunlight parted curtains of mist, and ahead burned the fires of war.

CHAPTER SIX

The Golden Fleet flew above the frozen prison, pounding the Dreamer's forces with the fury of gods.

In the courtyard, Einav Ben-Ari stood atop a pile of dead cyborgs. Her black suit was tattered. Blood covered her—some her own, most the blood of her enemies. Her hair streamed in the frosty wind, and her phoenix banner fluttered. She gazed up at the starships with wide eyes.

It's no wonder I had trouble fighting this fleet, she thought.

Only the Golden Fleet's starfighters flew here. The motherships were still in orbit. But even these small, slender vessels were marvels. The Basidio Boys called them Falcons, named after the fastest birds on Earth. And indeed, these outlaw starfighters were machines of speed.

They were smaller than Firebirds, the workhorse starfighters of the HDF, more agile and terrifyingly fast. Their silver noses thrust forward like slender beaks. Golden pipes ran along their crimson hulls, and silver gears moved beneath their wings. Their engines thrummed with blue light, and their cannons chugged back and forth like pistons. Inside the cockpits, Ben-Ari could glimpse spinning orreries, vials full of colorful liquid, and transparent tubes full of smoke.

The Falcons weren't just mighty starfighters. They were artifacts, relics of the Tarjan civilization, an empire that had ruled the far corners of the galaxy a million years ago. They used no microchips, no binary code, no technology humans could understand. They were Tarjan machines, technology beyond the Dreamer's control.

Ben-Ari had spent years chasing these pirate ships, unable to detect them or hack their systems. The Golden Fleet had hijacked many cargo freighters in deep space, wreaking havoc across the Human Commonwealth. Trying to rebuild humanity after the devastating Alien Wars, Ben-Ari had once considered the Golden Fleet her greatest threat.

Today the fleet was humanity's best hope.

A squad of Dreamer robots rolled toward Ben-Ari, blades spinning. Guns thrust from their sides, prepared to fire. She winced and leaped back, knowing she was too slow.

Engines roared.

A Falcon swooped.

The starfighter strafed the robots with orange bolts of searing death. The machines melted. The pirate starfighter flew onward, pounding an enemy formation on the mountainside.

Ben-Ari exhaled in relief.

Far above, past the clouds, lights flared across the sky. Debris like comets blazed toward New Siberia. Booms shook the storm. The motherships were fighting above—the Tarjan warships of the Golden Fleet and the Dreamer's hijacked frigates. Chunks of starships fell through the sky, sliced off mountaintops, and sent avalanches cascading. One piece of burning wreckage, perhaps a chunk of a frigate's hull, tore down a prison tower.

Within a few moments, it was clear.

The battle was won.

The Falcons did another few strafing rounds, picking out the last enemy formations. Most of them soared, raising columns of vapor, and returned to orbit. The survivors on the ground cheered. Five thousand prisoners had once languished here in New Siberia Penitentiary. Barely two thousand remained. But they cheered like two million.

Three of the gold-and-crimson starfighters remained above the prison. Brass gears turned, smoke puffed in vials, and the starfighters slowed to a hover. Steam blasted from pipes, and the Falcons descended and landed in the prison yard.

Ben-Ari took a few steps toward them. She had to pause, to catch her breath. An ugly wound ran across her hip. She had sealed it with an Insta-Stitch, but it still hurt like hell. She forced herself to ignore the pain, raised her chin, and approached the pirate ships.

The Falcons, for all their deadliness, were so small. Barely larger than cars. Each one was a work of art, covered with golden pipes, polished gears, and scrimshawed cannons. Crystals moved along steel tracks, and colorful smoke pumped through glass tubes. Their cockpits dilated, and three pirates climbed out.

They wore navy-blue coats and crimson shirts, the fabric shabby, and dust coated their boots. Two pins adorned each coat: a sailing ship on the left lapel, a toadstool on the right. The

Golden Fleet operated with a lot of autonomy. Natasha Emmerdale led them on hunts across the commonwealth, choosing her own targets, leading her own raids. Yet for all its might, the Golden Fleet was not free. It served the Basidio Boys, an intergalactic cartel that spread across the Orion Arm. Thus every pirate wore two symbols: one for the Fleet, the other for the Boys.

The three pirates stepped across the courtyard, swigged from bottles of grog, then noticed Ben-Ari.

At once, all three dropped their bottles, raised their rifles, and aimed at her.

Before the bottles even shattered on the ground, Ben-Ari had her gun pointing back at them.

"The Golden Fucking Lioness!" spat one pirate, his beard black and scraggly.

"What the fuck is that bitch doing here?" demanded another pirate, this one scrawny and missing two teeth.

Ben-Ari cocked her rifle, keeping the muzzle aimed at them. "The same thing you're doing. Fighting the machines."

The third pirate sneered, stepped forward, and pointed his pistol at her. "You're the fucking whore who imprisoned our captain. I should blow your brains out across this pavement and—"

"You'll do no such thing," said Natasha Emmerdale, sauntering toward the group. "You idiot."

The three pirates spun toward their captain, stood at attention, and saluted.

"Captain on deck!" a pirate cried out.

Ben-Ari lowered her rifle, relief flooding over her. She had already killed enough today.

Natasha walked lazily between the three men, eyebrow raised, a crooked smile on her lips. She patted one man on the cheek. "Trim your beard, Gizzard." She brushed another man's coat. "Iron your uniform, Mauler." She paused by the third man, reached for his groin, and squeezed. "And damn it, Babyface, stop getting so excited whenever you see me."

Babyface, a lumbering brute with skin like shattered embers, managed a stiff salute. "Yes, Captain! Sorry, Captain."

"At ease, boys!" the pirate captain said. She stepped toward Ben-Ari and wrapped an arm around her. "Little Einavushka is under my protection. She's my new friend. You will treat her well, yes?"

"It is *President Ben-Ari*, thank you," she said, squaring her shoulders.

Natasha laughed. "Of course it is."

Ben-Ari raised her chin and tried to look intimidating. But it was hard to seem impressive by Natasha Emmerdale. The woman stood six feet tall, quite a bit taller than Ben-Ari, and sported impossibly long and graceful legs—the gift of her mother, a Russian ballerina.

Ben-Ari rarely spent much time contemplating her looks. Who cared? She usually kept her hair in a simple ponytail. She had only begun to wear makeup recently, what with all the photo ops, and only because her advisers insisted. But she remembered her army days. Behind her back, her troops often called her beautiful. Today her critics called her *the princess president*, mocking her youth and fair features. Yes, perhaps she wasn't bad-looking. Maybe even pretty.

But beside this tall, gorgeous Russian, she felt like a potato.

Surprisingly, it did hurt her confidence. It shouldn't. But it did.

The environment didn't help. Outlaws surrounded Ben-Ari, most of whom detested her, some of whom would gladly rape and strangle her. Only Marco and Addy served her here. Earth had fallen. Her army was gone.

Ben-Ari's authority depended on maintaining an illusion. On appearing strong. A figurehead. A symbol of leadership. But how could she lead like this?

Goddamn it, she thought. *Is Natasha in charge here, and I'm at her mercy?*

"Okay, *President*," Natasha said, but she put so much mockery into that word that the pirates laughed. "Enough pissing matches. Let us rise off this frozen rock. Tonight we dine aboard my flagship. And you, President, will be my guest of honor."

As the Golden Fleet's shuttles descended, and as Ben-Ari hitched a ride into space, she couldn't help but shudder.

For two years she was my prisoner. And now I am hers.

CHAPTER SEVEN

The shuttle rose through the frosty atmosphere, leaving New Siberia below. After a miserable week on that frozen hellhole, Ben-Ari hoped she'd never see the damn planet again.

She stood among clanking gears, rotating rings, and glass tubes of smoke. The Tarjan machinery filled the shuttle, its many parts humming and clicking. Glowing liquids bubbled inside bulbs, filling the shuttle with light. It was wondrous technology from a bygone era, built back when humans were still using stone tools.

With effort, Ben-Ari turned away from this incredible machine. She gazed out the shuttle's porthole at the fleet orbiting the frozen planet. A fleet humanity now depended upon.

The Golden Fleet hovered before her in all its glory.

Ben-Ari had fought these ships throughout her presidency. But she had to admit. They were beautiful.

Their Tarjan engines perhaps were ancient. But the hulls had been scavenged from scrapyards, refitted for piracy. Natasha had taken great care restoring her hodgepodge of creaky freighters and tankards. She had painted the hulls crimson. Every starboard bow displayed a golden sail sigil, symbol of the fleet. Every port bow sported a golden toadstool, symbolizing their allegiance. Figureheads thrust out from every prow, carved into the shape of mythological animals. Ben-Ari saw unicorns, dragons, mermaids, manticores. Ironically—even a phoenix, symbol of the HDF.

But more than the loving restorations, the gleaming sigils, or the golden figureheads, the Tarjan machinery impressed Ben-Ari.

No actual Tarjan starships remained in the galaxy. Not that Ben-Ari knew of at least. According to legend, the Tarjans had flown starships made of polished wood, and the hulls had rotted a million years ago, leaving only components of brass, crystal, and glass. Somehow Natasha had found a treasure trove of those mystical parts. And she had managed to install them onto her fleet.

Golden pipes ran along the hulls. Brass gears moved on undercarriages like baby spiders clinging to their mother. Pumps expanded and contracted across the sterns, belching out colorful smoke. Steel rings encircled the ships like enormous Hula-Hoops, and crystals moved across these rails like planets orbiting stars.

No computers, at least not as humans understood them. Nothing the Dreamer could hack. A miracle in space.

Around the Golden Fleet, Ben-Ari saw the echoes of its might. Three enemy frigates, painted with the lurid smiley face of the Dreamer, were sliding down toward the planet. They had once been HDF warships. Star killers. Each an army in its own right. They were now in pieces. Ben-Ari watched the ruins burn up in the atmosphere.

The Golden Fleet did this, she realized. *When we were down on the planet. They took out three frigates and didn't even break a sweat.*

Only cyborgs had served aboard those ships that now blazed through the atmosphere, crashing toward New Siberia as blackened chunks. But Ben-Ari still remembered Natasha destroying the HDFS *Ghost* two years ago, killing three hundred good men and women, soldiers under Ben-Ari's command. She had stayed up all that night, writing condolence letters to their families.

Today Natasha killed cyborgs, Ben-Ari told herself. *But she does not hesitate to kill humans. She will not hesitate to kill me.*

Ben-Ari's own little crew, if you could call it that, stood with her. They stared with wide eyes.

"The Golden Fleet," Marco said, the lights darting across his face. "It's dangerous and beautiful. Like venomous serpents displaying their deadliness with shimmering scales in many colors."

Addy nodded. "You said it, Poet." She turned toward her brother. "Hey, dumbass! You didn't tell me most Tarjan ships looked this nice. The *Barracuda* was an eyesore. You stole the worst one!"

Kai Linden said nothing. The young man stood with his head bowed, his shoulders slumped, his wrists manacled. Two very large, very hairy pirates stood behind him, gripping his arms.

Looking at the chained rogue, Ben-Ari felt some pity. Kai looked downright devastated. And it wasn't just because the pirates had shackled him.

Ben-Ari placed a hand on his shoulder. She looked into his eyes and smiled reassuringly.

"I'll look after you, Kai. I'll get you out of this."

He didn't even look up.

"It's not just the manacles," he mumbled.

"I know," Ben-Ari said.

You had a hard life, Kai, Ben-Ari thought. *You were born in Bangkok's red-light district, a prostitute's son. You grew up among criminals. I see the gang tattoos and scars across your body. Within just a few weeks, you lost your father, and you lost Meili, a woman you loved. Over the past few days, you saw more scenes of war and horror than many soldiers see in a lifetime.*

Natasha Emmerdale approached and shoved Kai back.

"He's nothing but a thieving worm!" the Pirate Queen said. "I only kept him alive this long so I can execute him properly by tossing him out an airlock. With a crowd of onlookers cheering, of course."

Ben-Ari spun toward the tall Russian. "You will do no such thing. Kai was part of my negotiations with Don Basidio. Your boss. I pardoned you and the other Basidio Boys. And he pardoned Kai."

Natasha snorted. "Oh, you pardoned me, Madam President? If I recall correctly, by the time you landed on New Siberia, I was already free. And when you and your little troops were close to death, my fleet arrived to save your American asses."

"Actually, Ben-Ari is Israeli!" Addy said, smiling. "And Marco and I are Canadian."

Natasha glared at them all. "You are not Russian. Same thing."

Addy raised a fist. "Come over here, Tasha, so I can bash your beautiful little nose in. Nobody calls me American."

Marco rolled his eyes. "Ignore my wife. She's just sore because American teams keep beating the Maple Leafs."

"Well, is there any worse insult?" Addy said. "It's our national sport, Poet! And she said I'm the same as the teams that beat us, and—"

"Enough!" Ben-Ari barked. "Our nationalities don't matter now. Our planets don't even matter now. The only thing that matters is that we're *alive.* We must fight the machines together. As one united force."

Marco nodded. "Wise words."

"Fine," Addy uttered. "But on the hockey rink, we're still going to crush you all." She glared at Natasha. "You Russians can keep your figure skating though."

The shuttle approached one of the Tarjan ships. It was the largest and fairest, shaped like an old carrack from the Golden Age of Sail. A decorative anchor even hung from the hull, and replicas of antique cannons thrust out in rows. A leaping golden dolphin formed the figurehead. Letters shone on the starboard bow: THE GFS *DOLPHIN.*

"Recognize this ship, President?" Natasha asked. She smiled crookedly and placed a hand on Ben-Ari's shoulder. "You have seen her before, I think."

Ben-Ari nodded. "Yes. The *Dolphin* outran me several times. She took out three of my own ships. I could never catch her." She gave Natasha a crooked smile of her own. "I did, however, catch her captain."

Natasha snorted. "I never should have attempted to raid your ship. I should have known you fight dirty."

"Are electric nets fighting dirty, Natasha? I find them rather humane."

The Pirate Queen snorted even louder. "Any humane fighting method is dirty. True warriors fight to the death."

Ben-Ari gazed out into space, and she spoke softly. "I have killed more enemies than you can imagine."

She expected Natasha to roll her eyes, scoff, mock her. But the pirate captain grew quiet too.

"I know," Natasha said softly. "You were a worthy adversary."

Ben-Ari raised an eyebrow. "I was talking about my wars against alien empires, not against you."

"I know that too," Natasha said. "As I said—you were a worthy adversary. To them."

The pirate gave just the hint of a smile. Ben-Ari returned it.

Maybe we can work together yet, Captain Natasha Emmerdale, she thought.

A hatch dilated on the *Dolphin*, and the shuttle flew into the hangar. A small army of pirates, a hundred strong, stood waiting on the deck. The other shuttles had been pushed against the bulkheads, giving them room.

"Captain on deck!" a beefy, bald man shouted, and a hundred pirates stood at attention.

Natasha Emmerdale stepped out of the shuttle. The icy Russian looked across the hangar, sweeping her gaze from pirate to pirate. Finally she grunted.

"The deck is dusty," she said. "I was in prison for two years, I come back, and I see dust on my deck. What rubbish is this?"

For a moment silence filled the hangar.

Then a hundred pirates burst out laughing, cheering, and crying out their captain's name. They rushed toward her, shook her hand, embraced her. Men cracked open crates of grog, and bottles were passed around. A capuchin monkey ran among the revelers, a bell jingling on his fez. A couple of dogs wagged their tails.

Addy leaned toward Ben-Ari. "Ma'am, why didn't we ever have animals on our starships?"

"We had you," Marco said.

"You're goddamn right," Addy said. "I'm a majestic tigress."

"You're more like Big Bird," Marco said. "Big, blond, and clumsy."

She gasped. "Well, if I'm Big Bird, you're Elmo. You're furry like him with that new beard of yours. And you're short like him."

He rolled his eyes. "Addy, we're the same height."

She blew him a kiss. "Whatever you say, Elmo."

He flipped her off. "This episode is brought to you by the letters F-U-C-K Y-O—"

They both fell silent as pirates walked by, manhandling Kai. The young man walked with his head lowered, shackles jangling.

"We'll get you back, brother!" Addy said, reaching to him. "I swear to God, if I have to destroy this ship and kill every pirate here, I—"

Ben-Ari nudged her. "Addy, leave the diplomacy to me."

The pirates were now carrying Natasha over their heads, celebrating the return of their queen. The captain hopped down, laughing.

"Friends, friends!" Natasha cried to her pirates. "Why haven't you brought grog for our guests? Fetch them bottles! Treat them like family." She nodded to Marco and Addy. "You two fought well. You earned some comfort. Here aboard the *Dolphin*, you'll find plenty of comfort. A medic will treat your wounds. There are hot showers and comfortable hammocks. There is plenty of drink and food."

"Got any hot dogs?" Addy asked. "I'll also need a rake."

"We might also need a straitjacket and padded room for Addy," Marco said, then yelped as she punched him.

Soon the couple was drinking grog, and somebody even found hot dogs for Addy.

Nobody offered anything to Ben-Ari. She stood silently. She stood alone. Everyone seemed to be avoiding her. Some pirates walked by, pretending not to see her. Others mumbled curses under their breath.

Am I an honored guest like Marco and Addy, or a prisoner like Kai? she wondered.

Natasha approached Ben-Ari, touched her shoulder, and nodded.

"You, little president, come with me. You are too prim and proper to drink with these peasants." She winked. "Come, come. You will dine with me in my cabin." She looked around her. "Not with these loutish brutes!"

The pirates only cheered and raised their bottles higher.

"Here's to being a filthy lot of loutish brutes!" a man shouted and guzzled his grog. Soon everyone was drinking.

What game are you playing, Natasha? Ben-Ari wondered.

But she said nothing. She was used to negotiating with politicians, with thugs like Don Basidio, even with alien generals. But she could not read this tall Russian with her crooked smile and mocking green eyes.

Natasha walked across the deck, not turning to look back. She walked fast. Ben-Ari followed, struggling to keep up with the pirate's long strides. The message was clear. Natasha was in command. And she wanted everyone to see it.

Very well, I'll play this game on your terms for now, Ben-Ari thought. *But do not think I'll be so easy to defeat.*

They walked through the ship, passing by gunnery stations, storerooms, and a mess hall. Ben-Ari could already smell dinner cooking, and her stomach growled. She had been eating battle rations for weeks now, and she was down a notch on her belt. She ignored the hunger and kept following Natasha. The pirate captain walked several meters ahead, never slowing down or looking back to see if Ben-Ari followed.

Finally Natasha stopped by a door and waited for Ben-Ari to catch up.

"That's real wood," Ben-Ari said, looking at the door. "You don't often see real wood in space."

"I do enjoy my little luxuries. Some even more impressive than doors." Natasha turned the knob. "Come in, little president. Welcome to my home."

Ben-Ari entered the captain's cabin. She had to struggle not to widen her eyes. Only by sheer willpower did she keep her poker face.

Little luxuries indeed, Ben-Ari thought. She had seen less luxurious palaces.

Wood paneled the bulkheads, polished to a sheen. Lush red rugs, embroidered with golden dolphins, covered the floor. Treasures filled the room. Vases stood on a giltwood table, depicting scenes from ancient Greece. A stone sarcophagus stood against a wall, engraved with hieroglyphics. Oil paintings hung on the walls in giltwood frames.

Ben-Ari couldn't resist. She approached one enormous painting. It depicted a life-sized Venus lounging on a wave, her auburn hair cascading, as cherubs danced above her.

"*The Birth of Venus*, by Alexandre Cabanel," Ben-Ari said softly. "Painted 1864."

She turned toward another painting, this one depicting a sleeping Greek beauty, her body draped with fiery orange fabric.

"*Flaming June*," Ben-Ari said. "Lord Leighton. Eighteen-ninety …"

"Five," Natasha said. "You know your artwork, President."

"They're beautiful," she said.

"They're real too," said Natasha. "Not prints. The originals. Everything here is original. These vases were baked in ancient Greek kilns. That sarcophagus? It still contains a pharaoh. Five thousand years old, he is, still resting in his coffin. Those katanas? Samurais wielded them in the Shimabara Rebellion. Six hundred years later, the blades are still incredibly sharp. You can drop a silk scarf onto them, and they would slice through the fabric."

"Stolen," Ben-Ari said, looking around at the treasures. "All these—stolen."

"Indeed they were, little president," said Natasha. "Colonial powers stole them from their countries long ago. They put them in museums. Displayed them for profit. What is it that your Bible says? One who steals from a thief is absolved."

Ben-Ari smiled thinly. "Actually, that's from the Talmud, not the Bible."

Natasha snorted. "You stink."

Ben-Ari frowned and tilted her head. "Excuse me?"

"You stink!" she said. "You smell like prison. There's a shower in the back. Go. Refresh. I will lend you some better clothes than this tattered, bloody rag you are wearing."

"I did not come here to talk about my smell!" Ben-Ari said. "I came to negotiate an alliance between—"

"President, please! I am Russian. We do not negotiate with anything we can smell. Go. Wash. I'll set out clothes for you."

Ben-Ari hadn't showered since … By God, with all these battles, she couldn't even remember. Had it been days? Weeks? A month? After twenty years in the military, she was used to filth. But stinking would no longer do. She was president of Earth now, after all. At least she hoped she still was. Nominally.

She spent a long while in Natasha's shower, letting the hot water wash off the filth, the dry blood, the smells of war. But it could not wash clean her memories. Whenever she closed her eyes, she saw them. Cyborgs. Flayed men, iron bolts hammered into their flesh, staring with electronic eyes. Wheels of metal and muscle, spinning, blinking with many eyes. Brains and hearts in glass bulbs. Pumping. Anguished faces. Tears flowing.

And suddenly Ben-Ari was weeping too. Because this enemy was worse than any she had ever faced. This enemy didn't just want to kill. But to torture. Deform. To keep humans alive in a nightmare.

And she didn't know if she could win.

Out there on the battlefield, she was the Golden Lioness. Before her troops, she raised her banner high, and she sounded her roar. She inspired them. She gave them hope.

But here, in the shower, alone? Here her tears fell. Here she was just a woman. A wife and mother. Missing her family and home. So afraid.

I miss you, Noah. I miss you, Carl.

Last time she had spoken to them, they had still been hiding in the Matterhorn, light-years away. The transmission had died. And Ben-Ari didn't even know if her family was alive.

She had never felt so helpless and vulnerable.

I'm still breathing, she thought. *So I'm still fighting. I am a soldier. No matter what else I might become, I am always a soldier. And a soldier fights. So long as I draw breath, my enemies will fear me.*

* * * * *

When Ben-Ari finally stepped out of the shower, she found that Natasha had laid out clothes for her. She had not even heard the captain open the bathroom door. Ben-Ari dried herself in a fluffy towel, then examined the new clothes.

Pantyhose. A little black dress. That was it.

Ben-Ari frowned. The outfit seemed inappropriate. She was here to fight a war, not attend a cocktail party. But the only other alternative was the tattered, bloody, stinking suit she had been fighting in since Haven. It was barely more than filthy scraps of cotton.

She put on the cocktail dress.

She examined her reflection in the mirror. The dress was tight. When the tall Natasha wore it, it probably barely covered her thighs. Thankfully, Ben-Ari was shorter and got better coverage. She pulled her hair up in a ponytail. She ignored the boxes of makeup on the counter. There was no reason to doll up here.

She reentered Natasha's cabin, the stockings muffling her footsteps. She hadn't been given shoes.

"I don't like the outfit you chose for me," Ben-Ari said.

Natasha stood by the fireplace. She too had changed. Instead of her orange prison jumpsuit, Natasha now wore the uniform of her fleet. Crimson trousers tucked into high-heeled boots. A navy-blue coat, a golden sail on one lapel, a golden toadstool on the other. Her platinum hair cascaded freely, and a crooked smile played across her lips.

"The only other clothes I have are Golden Fleet uniforms," Natasha said. "And you have not earned the right to wear them." Her eyes moved up and down, examining Ben-Ari. "The dress is a little long for you. But it looks good. You are not bad-looking. For a politician, that is."

"I'm not a politician," Ben-Ari said.

Natasha snorted. "We are all politicians, little president. All us leaders. That is why we gathered here to negotiate, yes?" She gestured at a giltwood table. "Sit, my dear guest. Dinner will soon be served."

They sat at the table. It was just large enough for two. The fireplace cast golden light across the artifacts and artwork. For a moment that crackling fire was the only sound.

"We need to visit Don Basidio and get his podships," Ben-Ari began. "I'll need you to—"

Natasha *tsked* her tongue. "Now, now, little president! First we eat and drink. My servant will be along shortly."

They sat in silence. Natasha kept staring at Ben-Ari, a crooked smile on her face. The pirate queen didn't seem to mind the silence. But it unnerved Ben-Ari. As did Natasha's unwavering green stare.

Finally the cabin door opened. A man entered, carrying a tray. Chains jangled around his ankles.

It was Kai.

As Ben-Ari stared in stunned silence, Kai served the table. He placed down two bottles of wine, one red and one white, and a platter of cheeses. A bruise swelled around his left eye. Stitches held together a fresh cut on his forehead.

"Wine and cheese, ma'ams?" Kai mumbled, eyes lowered.

Finally Ben-Ari found her tongue. She glared at Natasha.

"What is the meaning of this?" she demanded. "Why is my man serving the table?"

Natasha raised an eyebrow. "*Your* man? I do believe he still wears the tattoos of the Golden Fleet. He is *my* man, little president. Mine to torment." She gestured at Kai. "Servant! Pour me some of the red."

Kai paused for a moment. His jaw tightened. The bottles shook on the tray. But then the young man nodded and poured Natasha the wine.

He turned toward Ben-Ari. "Ma'am?"

"I'll pour my ow—"

"He'll pour," Natasha interjected. "White or red?"

Ben-Ari forced herself to take a deep breath. To calm down.

Not my circus, not my monkeys, she thought.

"White," she said, voice strained. Kai poured.

When he shuffled out of the cabin, Ben-Ari rose to her feet. "Natasha, enough of this circus. You know Kai was pardoned by Don Basidio."

The Russian swirled the wine in her cup, inhaled deeply through her nostrils, exhaled. "Ah, nothing like a good cabernet. Strong. Robust." Finally she sipped. "An excellent vintage."

"I thought Russians drank vodka," Ben-Ari said.

"I am half English." Natasha licked the blood-red wine off her teeth. "My father was an English bulldog, my mother a Russian bear. I inherited very sharp teeth."

"Natasha—" Ben-Ari began, leaning across the table.

She waved her hand. "Sit down, little president. You insist on talking business so soon? Very well. Don Basidio is no longer my master." She sipped again. "Remember, little president. I agreed to fight with you. Without consulting the mushroom. Any decree Basidio made is now irrelevant. Did he pardon the rat Kai? Does he demand tribute from my victories? Does he want me to dance and lick him like a whore? I no longer care, little president. I am no longer prisoner nor slave." She plucked the mushroom pin off her lapel and tossed it into the fireplace. "I am now a free woman."

Ben-Ari refused to sit. "You are a subject of the Human Commonwealth. You are an ex-convict. And I am your president."

Natasha snorted. "Sit down. The food is here."

A thud sounded outside—a hand hitting flesh. A grunt. A muffled curse.

Kai shuffled back into the room. A fresh cut bled on his cheek. He placed two plates on the table. A rib eye steak, spiced potatoes, and grilled vegetables for Natasha. Salmon, wild rice, and asparagus for Ben-Ari.

He matched the food to the wine, Ben-Ari realized.

"Kai—" she began, turning toward him.

He looked into her eyes. She saw terror there. He looked away and left the cabin, chains jangling.

The two women ate in silence. Ben-Ari had to admit the meal was divine. Her salmon was soft and buttery, every bite exploding with flavor. During her four years as president, she had eaten many fine meals, some prepared by Earth's finest chefs. This was right up there. And it wasn't just her hunger deceiving her senses.

"Your salmon is fresh, you know," Natasha said. "Never frozen."

Ben-Ari raised an eyebrow. "Where did you get fresh salmon in space?"

"I keep an aquarium on one of my ships." She sipped her wine. "I enjoy my luxuries."

The pirate queen cut into her steak. It was so rare that red juices pooled across the plate. A sudden image bolted through Ben-Ari's mind: robots like giant sewing machines, pinning prisoners down, cutting and stitching them into cyborgs, spilling their blood across the prison yard. She lost her appetite.

"Don't tell me you have fresh cows too."

Natasha laughed. "Fine aged beef. We stop by Earth every few months to restock. They say crime does not pay." She shrugged and looked around her opulent cabin. "I guess they are right."

Ben-Ari placed down her fork with a clatter. "All this wealth—it's all stolen. Don't you ever think about your victims?"

"My victims?" Natasha laughed. "Who did I hurt? Corrupt governments? Decadent corporations? You don't get this wealthy from robbing poor mom-and-pop shops. I steal from the rich."

"And give to yourself."

Finally some fire filled Natasha's eyes. She leaned forward, her bloody knife in hand. "You do not know all that I do with my wealth, *President*. I give. To women shelters. To rehab centers. To—"

"Yes, yes, and you probably save baby whales," Ben-Ari said. "It's all very heartwarming. So what? Al Capone ran soup kitchens. Pablo Escobar built houses for the poor. Just because you do some charity doesn't excuse your crimes."

"My crimes, President?" Natasha said. "Your government has stolen more trillions of dollars for your wars than I could steal in an eternity."

Ben-Ari rolled her eyes. "And now you'll tell me that taxation is theft. I've heard it all before. Spare me. I'm not here to argue about economics. I'm here to forge an alliance between the HDF and the Golden Fleet."

Natasha rose from her seat. She approached Ben-Ari and towered over her. Even when Ben-Ari stood up too, she felt short by the tall Russian. Especially with Natasha wearing those heeled boots.

"There is no more HDF," Natasha said. She brushed back an errant strand of Ben-Ari's hair. "Only you are left, little president."

"Then fight with me," Ben-Ari said.

Natasha kept stroking her hair. "Who are you, little president? Such a young, trembling little bird. I expected the Golden Lioness to be more …"

"Like you?" Ben-Ari said. "Full of swagger and cockiness? I don't care about image. I don't care about any of this. Fine food? Treasures? This dress?" She scoffed. "Vanity. I care about humanity. You only care about yourself."

Natasha's eyes flashed. She stepped back, then swung her hand, attempting to slap Ben-Ari.

But again, like she had on New Siberia, Ben-Ari grabbed the Russian's wrist. They stood, locking horns, staring at each other.

Natasha reached out her second hand. She grabbed Ben-Ari by the waist.

"Let me go!" Ben-Ari said.

But Natasha tugged her closer. "Listen to me, little president." She sneered, pulling Ben-Ari so close that their chests almost touched. "You are like me. Don't pretend to be anything else. You too crave fame. Crave victory. Crave power. Do you know why I agreed to work with you? Because when I look at you, I see myself."

"You flatter yourself," Ben-Ari whispered.

Natasha grabbed Ben-Ari by the ponytail, leaned in, and kissed her lips.

Ben-Ari looked away. "Don't."

Natasha pulled her face back. "Don't look away from me. I know what you want."

"I'm a married woman."

Natasha's lopsided smile returned. "He's not here."

"I can't," Ben-Ari whispered.

But when Natasha kissed her again, she did not resist. When Natasha pulled her toward the divan, she followed. When they made love by the fireplace, she surrendered to the pleasure. And when it ended, she curled up in Natasha's arms, and she felt warmth and safety and, for the first time in months, a little bit of joy.

Natasha sipped her wine and stroked Ben-Ari's hair.

"We will fight together," the Russian said. "And I will pardon your friend."

"What do you want in return?" Ben-Ari asked, gazing into the fire. Her little black dress lay in a silky puddle on the floor. A warm blanket covered her instead.

Natasha's eyes shone, reflecting the flames. "Power." She looked into Ben-Ari's eyes and smiled. "I grow weary of piracy. I am now *Admiral* Natasha Emmerdale. I am the new commander of Earth's fleet."

Ben-Ari nodded. "Very well." She sighed. "That was, without question, the strangest deal I've ever negotiated. Normally I do business over golfing."

Natasha laughed. They sat together on the divan, watching the crackling fire.

CHAPTER EIGHT

The Golden Fleet sailed through a crumbling universe.

Fifty ships painted crimson and gold. Humanity's last free fleet. Their Tarjan machines glowed and spun, powering them onward. Their golden figureheads—dolphins, unicorns, dragons—led their way. These ships had once terrorized the galaxy. Now they lit the beacons of hope.

Inside their ancient engines, liquid bubbled. Small, luminous life forms scurried through tubes like fairies along branches, leaving sparkling trails. Music boxes chimed, and wooden figurines danced, casting light from slender hands. Crystals shone and orreries turned. Trapped in glass vials, furry little critters tugged on strings of bells, playing strange tunes.

Nobody aboard fully understood these strange machines. But they propelled the fleet onward through hyperspace, a strange dimension above their own. Here was a universe of deep purple nebulae, clouds of gold mist, and strange shadows that moved in the distance like whales through murky oceans.

Yet even from hyperspace, their instruments could gaze down upon the lower dimension. The crystals shone, showing on their facades images of the cosmos.

It was falling apart.

Everywhere they looked, they saw him. The Dreamer.

His fleets swarmed across the galaxy. Many had once been HDF ships, their hulls now painted with gruesome smiling faces. Others were new creations, formed from the Dreamer's twisted imagination. Starships shaped like the severed heads of animals. Starships like screaming skulls. Weird creations of metal joints and frozen flesh and bristling antennae. They prowled the galaxy, spreading from star to star.

They swarmed over asteroids like insects over rotting flesh, mining for minerals. They landed on colonies, rounding up humans for their cyborg machines. They orbited gas giants, building factories, pumping out more monstrosities. The nightmare that had arisen in Haven was spreading across the Milky Way.

"If we cannot stop him," Ben-Ari said, "our universe will end. And this nightmare will replace it."

She stood in the *Dolphin*'s lounge, the pirate flagship's social hub. She still wore her little cocktail dress, the only decent clothing she had, feeling almost naked. Exposed and vulnerable. She stood in shadows, gazing out the wide viewport that spread across the bulkhead.

A few pirates were in the lounge too, just a few steps away, filling the air with the smells of sweat, gunpowder, and tobacco. They sat at the bar, drinking grog, smoking, and laughing. Addy sat with them, shouting that she would drink them all under the table. Bets were being placed, and soon a drinking contest commenced.

Ben-Ari ignored the ruckus. She had no time for distractions now. So she stood apart, gazing outside. At the swirling colors of hyperspace. At the shadows of nightmare below. At her own reflection, slender and dim, seeming to her almost to wither away.

Only Marco stood beside her. He placed a hand on her shoulder. "We'll fight him. We'll kill him. Meili is gone. But we still have her code."

He pulled the codechip from his pocket. Codechips were small devices, smaller even than minicoms, no larger than a matchbox. But a codechip could contain, activate, and transmit millions of lines of code.

"Project Artemis," Ben-Ari said. "Meili gave her life to code it. To protect it."

"We'll continue her quest," said Marco. "Dr. Meili Chen will not have died in vain. We'll take Project Artemis to Haven. We'll fight through the Dreamer's hordes. We'll delve into the crater where he lives. We'll find the Dream Tree. And we'll install Project Artemis into his heart."

Ben-Ari gazed at the codechip. "It seems so strange. That a device so small, just a chip I could hide in my hand, can save the galaxy."

Marco nodded. "This is just the seed. When we plant it, it will spread. Through the Dream Tree. Through all his tendrils. Meili told us, and I believe her. I don't understand her code. None of us do. But I trust her legacy." He lowered his head. "The Dreamer began his life by driving a hundred young girls to suicide. He almost got Terri, my own daughter." He looked back up at Ben-Ari. "The Greek goddess Artemis was the protector of young girls. And she will have her vengeance."

Ben-Ari smiled softly. "She will smite the god of nightmares." She squeezed Marco's hand. "Thank you, my friend."

He raised his eyebrows. "For what?"

"For reminding me of hope."

Marco laughed. "You're the Golden Lioness. You're my commander-in-chief. My officer. My captain. Shouldn't you be the one inspiring me?"

Ben-Ari spoke softly. "We've become more than that, Marco. We've become friends. Can't I sometimes show my vulnerable side to my friends?"

"You're not vulnerable," he said. "You're human. And you're the strongest human I know." He thought for a moment. "But maybe even the strongest person sometimes needs a shoulder to lean on. You always have mine, Einav."

It was a rare breaking of the walls between them, the distance between commander and soldier. It took the universe falling apart to shatter this barrier. Or maybe, after eighteen years of friendship, Ben-Ari simply felt like herself around him.

She smiled and caressed his cheek. "My dearest Marco. When we first met, who would have imagined we'd be here together?"

"Often I never thought we'd live this long," Marco said. "When I was eighteen years old, a boy drafted into a war, I never imagined myself a thirty-six-year-old man. Hell, I never thought I'd live to see twenty."

Ben-Ari smiled wistfully. "Those were good days. Not the war, I mean. Not the battles. But the times we spent together. Our little platoon. You, me, Addy, Lailani …"

"All the others are gone," Marco said. "Only we four remain. Sometimes I don't know if anyone else would understand. What we went through. How close we've become." He gazed out into space. "I wonder where Lailani is now. I wonder if she's safe. I think about her a lot. And about our families."

Ben-Ari wrapped her arm around him and leaned against him. They gazed into space together.

"I do too," she said. "Every day out here, we're fighting for them."

"It's worse this time," Marco said. "Fighting this war. The other wars, well, we were just kids. Dumb, brave soldiers trying to save the world. This time we have kids at home. We have families. The fear is so much greater."

"And victory will be sweeter," Ben-Ari said. "It is family, love, and joy that give our sacrifices meaning. It is light that makes the path of darkness worth walking. A good soldier charges at the enemy ahead, but he thinks of his loved ones behind. A good soldier does not crave killing. He cherishes life. He will even shed blood to protect life. In the cold darkness of space, only love can light our way."

Marco grinned. "See? Same old Einav Ben-Ari, dishing out inspiration. And they call me the poet!"

She couldn't help but laugh. "Old habits die hard."

Addy's voice suddenly filled the lounge.

"I 'an do it! One more! Hit me!"

Ben-Ari and Marco turned toward the bar. Addy was swaying on her barstool, empty shot glasses rolling around her. Her eyes were bleary, her hand shaking. A burly, bearded pirate twice her size sat beside her, eyes red, peering over his own collection of empty shot glasses. A crowd of onlookers was cheering.

"Addy!" Marco said, marching toward the bar. "Haven't you had enough?"

She blinked at him, smiled dazedly, then pointed at her opponent. "I can't not let him drink more than I am! I'm a drinking more!" She pounded on the bar. "More!"

Somebody poured them more shots. The bearded brute downed his, swayed on his seat, blinked, shuddered … and remained conscious.

Addy gulped her shot, then banged the glass on the bar.

"I tolda Poet!" She grinned. "I am more than drinking him. I …"

Her eyes rolled back, and she crashed onto the bar, scattering her empty shot glasses. She began to snore.

Pirates cheered, and the bearded man raised his fist in triumph.

Marco sighed and turned to Ben-Ari. "I better put Addy to bed."

As he dragged his wife out of the lounge, Ben-Ari returned to the viewport. She gazed outside at the lazy nebulae of hyperspace. Tomorrow they would reach Esporia. She would see if Don Basidio honored his promise. He owed her a hundred podships, complementing the Golden Fleet—the agreed price for freeing his pirates from prison.

And then Ben-Ari would have her army.

And then she would fly to Haven.

And then Artemis would have her vengeance.

CHAPTER NINE

Esporia Ceti.

A fungal world.

A moon coated with layers of mushroom and moss a hundred kilometers deep. Home of Don Basidio, the most dreaded gangster in the galaxy.

The Golden Fleet emerged from hyperspace above this rancid world … and into a hailstorm of enemy fire.

"All power to shields!" Natasha shouted, standing on the bridge of the GFS *Dolphin*. "Shields, dammit!"

Ben-Ari stood beside the pirate captain. She gazed through the viewport, and her heart sank.

Three frigates were barreling down on the Golden Fleet, their cannons booming. Earth frigates. Warships of the HDF, now serving the enemy.

More blasts slammed into the pirate fleet. The *Dolphin* jerked. Smoke filled the bridge. The deck cracked, and Ben-Ari swayed, nearly fell. Off their starboard bow, a smaller pirate ship shattered. Explosions rocked space.

"Dammit, Ben-Ari, why are your ships attacking us?" Natasha shouted. "Why are they even here?"

"They're not my ships anymore!" Ben-Ari shouted back. "Look at the smiley faces on their hull. Dreamer ships!"

But Natasha ignored her. She was busy shouting orders at her crew.

"Turn left, bring them in line with our starboard cannons!" Natasha shouted. "Stream power to starboard, and broadside the fuckers!"

The *Dolphin* jerked as the cannons boomed. Shells flew toward the enemy ships. Blasts bloomed across the enemy shields.

"You're making us too big a target!" Ben-Ari said. "Turn our prow toward them, and—"

"Shut up or I'll send you to the brig!" Natasha snapped. "Gunners, fire everything!" She lifted her comm, a shining Tarjan crystal in a pewter frame. "*Unicorn! Dragon! Pegasus!* Pyramid formation and cannon wall them!"

The Golden Fleet arranged itself in battle formations. Frigates formed the foundation, while smaller ships flew around them. A barrage of shells, lasers, and torpedoes flew back and forth. A missile slammed into the *Dolphin*, and the starship shook.

"Why aren't you using wobble tech?" Ben-Ari shouted. She remembered seeing Kai use the Tarjan technology, hopping in and out of hyperspace in short bursts.

"Because we're a frigate, not a goddamn starfighter!" Natasha cried back. "Now stop backseat flying."

Ben-Ari forced herself to remain quiet, to watch. She felt antsy and helpless. She was used to shouting orders, not being a mere spectator to battle.

The enemy frigate hangars opened. Starfighters streamed out like pollen from an Algolian Belching Flower. They were Firebirds, the legendary starfighters of the Human Defense Force. Firebirds—the sleek, deadly vessels that had pounded Earth's enemies for decades, that had won the Alien Wars. Today they served the Dreamer.

Natasha shouted orders, and the Golden Fleet birthed its own starfighters—the Falcons. They were smaller and faster than Firebirds. They shot forward like bullets, encased in spinning, glowing Tarjan shells of crystals and gears.

Fire blazed across space.

Missiles streaked back and forth.

Starfighters collided and exploded.

Smoke and fire and steel filled space, blocking their view. And then, from the inferno, they emerged.

Torpedoes. Tipped with drills. Racing toward the Golden Fleet.

Ben-Ari recognized them. She had seen one drill into the *Loggerhead* over the forest planet Upidia.

A missile that becomes a robot, she remembered. *The thing that killed Butch.*

"Invaders!" she shouted.

"Shoot them down!" Natasha cried.

A barrage of fire streamed from the *Dolphin.* Torpedoes exploded. Fire washed across the prow.

But several torpedoes hit the *Dolphin*. They did not explode. They latched on like leeches, and Ben-Ari heard the drilling.

She sneered, shouldered her assault rifle, and loaded a bullet.

"If they start flashing lights, close your eyes!" she shouted. "If they make a sound, cover your ears."

Natasha spun toward her, face pale. "What are those things?"

"Mind-jackers," Ben-Ari muttered.

The drilling continued. Alarms blared. Monitors flashed warnings.

Hull breach! Hull breach!

Natasha cursed and drew her pistol.

*****

Marco and Addy stood in the lounge, watching the battle through towering windows, when the torpedoes hit the hull.

Fire blazed.

Klaxons wailed.

A bulkhead collapsed.

One of the windows, affording a view of space, shattered.

Debris flew out into the vacuum. Tables overturned. Every bottle on the bar exploded.

"Hull breach detected!" intoned a speaker. "Hull breach detected!"

"No shit!" Addy shouted.

Wind raged. Chairs overturned. Marco and Addy clung to the bar, screaming. Fire roared around them.

"Addy, there!" Marco shouted, pointing at a corridor. "With me!"

They ran, the wind whipping them. Bottles flew against them. A shard of glass sliced Marco. Another nicked Addy's leg. They raced forward through the storm, burst into the corridor, and slammed the door behind them, sealing off the hull breach.

For a moment they caught their breath. Then the *Dolphin* jerked. They fell against a bulkhead. Crew members ran by them, shouting. One man was burning.

Red lights flashed, and the speakers kept blaring.

"Invaders detected! Invaders detected!"

Marco and Addy raised their assault rifles.

They advanced slowly down the corridor.

A blast hit the ship. The *Dolphin* shook. The lights died.

For a moment it was pitch-black.

Then they saw it ahead. White eyes—blazing, piercing the shadows. A creature unfurled. A tubular body, a drill on its tip. Legs extended, and it scuttled forward like a spider.

The lights began to flash. The machine began to chirp.

Marco and Addy unleashed hell.

Their bullets blazed, lighting the corridor, slamming into the robot. It ran toward them. It leaped onto the wall, scuttled along the ceiling, and began to shriek and chatter, blasting down its code.

Marco felt it inside him. The tentacles of the Dreamer. He shouted, loaded a fresh magazine, fired. Bullets slammed into the ceiling. Some sparked against the creature. Addy fell, howling, writhing, but she managed to load a fresh magazine too.

The Dreamer laughed inside them, gripping their minds.

Lower your guns, mortals. Fall asleep and dream.

The intruder leaped down toward them.

The soldiers' instincts kicked in.

Even as the Dreamer whispered inside them, Marco and Addy emptied their magazines into its flashing white eyes.

The robot slammed down between them, cracking the deck. Its lights were dead, but it still tried to rise, legs bent.

Marco howled and swung his rifle, clubbing the robot, knocking it back down. A leg rose, and he swiped his muzzle, cracking the robotic limb.

Sparking, the damaged robot managed to stand on its back legs. It opened a spinning jaw full of drills, a hellmouth of steel and fury. It lunged at Marco, and he filled that jaw with lead.

The creature finally fell down dead.

The voice stopped.

The Dreamer's tentacles retreated.

Marco shuddered.

I almost died. Or worse—became a sleeper. I almost never saw my kids again.

"That one counts as mine," Addy said. "I softened him up for you."

But suddenly she was crying. And Marco felt tears gather too. He knew they were thinking the same thing. Remembering the last time the Dreamer had reached into their minds. Remembering the miscarriage. The loss and grief and blood and horrible week in darkness.

He wiped his eyes. "Come on, Ads. There might be more of these buggers. Let's show these pirates how soldiers fight."

She loaded a fresh magazine and cocked her rifle. "Fuck yeah. Team BAM for the win!"

Marco tilted his head. "Team BAM?"

She nodded. "Ben-Ari, Addy, and Marco. The only three soldiers in the fleet. It's BAM time!"

"Please don't say BAM ever again."

"Oh, I forgot about Kai! I know he's not a soldier, but he's still one of us. Together we're Ka-BAM!"

"Addy, please stop."

Another robot scuttled toward them. They destroyed it with a hailstorm of bullets.

"Another point for team Ka-BAM!" Addy said.

Marco rolled his eyes.

They kept advancing through the ship, rifles raised, as blasts pounded the hull and the klaxons kept wailing.

* * * * *

Throughout this war, Ben-Ari had almost gotten used to fighting in a pantsuit.

Almost.

And now, here aboard the *Dolphin*, she had to fight in a goddamn little black cocktail dress.

Just fucking perfect.

She stood on the bridge, lips tight, and emptied her pistol into a leaping machine with jaws like spinning death. It crashed down at her feet.

She surveyed the bridge. Natasha stood at the main dashboard, overseeing the battle. Outside, two enemy frigates burned. The Golden Fleet changed formation, surrounding a third enemy warship, and pounded its hull. But the enemy was fighting back hard, responding with an artillery barrage. Another pirate ship exploded. Natasha sneered, the fire reflecting in her cold blue eyes.

Ben-Ari stood beside the captain and loaded a fresh magazine. Three robots twitched around her feet.

"Why the hell did those fucking Esporians let the Dreamer's ships in here?" Natasha spat. "Don't they have fleets? Can't they defend their system?"

"It's not their fight," Ben-Ari said. "The Dreamer is here for us. He must have cut a deal with the mushrooms, and—"

"No, dammit!" Natasha shouted into her comm. "*Unicorn*, yaw to form a claw formation! Pound at their stern! *Pegasus*, take on those enemy starfighters!"

Ben-Ari wanted to keep watching the battle. But a cackle and hiss rose behind her.

She spun around, holding her gun in both hands, and saw them approach.

Three pirates. Their eyes white. Their cheeks slashed open.

Fuck.

The three sleepers raised pistols and opened fire.

Ben-Ari rolled behind a control panel. Bullets peppered the machinery, shattering crystals and pipes. Purple smoke blasted out. Ben-Ari used the smoky cover to rise, to squeeze off a few shots. One sleeper grunted and fell.

The other two kept firing. Nearby, Natasha screamed and clutched her arm. Blood spurted between her fingers, and she spewed a stream of Russian curses.

Ben-Ari rolled through the smoke, rose in the open air, and opened fire.

Her bullets took down another sleeper, tearing through his chest.

The third sleeper fired his gun. The bullet shrieked so close to Ben-Ari's head that her ears rang. For a terrifying instant she was sure the bullet *had* hit her head. But it had missed her. She had felt the whoosh of air and pounding sound waves.

She fired her last bullet. She hit the sleeper's throat. He fell, neck spurting blood.

"*Blyad*!" Natasha cursed. "The bastard got my arm." She stepped toward a gunnery station, grabbed the gunner, and pushed the man aside. "Move, you useless piece of *deermo*!"

The pirate queen grabbed the controls, leaned forward with a sneer, and opened fire. Blast after blast pounded the last enemy frigate. Natasha kept firing, nearly emptying the *Dolphin*'s arsenal, until she finally breached the enemy shields. The HDF warship shattered. An explosion rocked the fleet. Debris flew in a shock ring, peppering the *Dolphin*.

Natasha nodded in satisfaction. "Bastards."

The battle was over.

The enemy ships were gone.

Debris, shattered robots, and corpses floated through space.

Ben-Ari approached Natasha. "Your arm. Let me take a look."

But Natasha reeled toward her, eyes flashing. "They were here for you! And I lost three ships and many good men. I should toss you into the brig!"

"Calm yourself," Ben-Ari said. "You chose to become my admiral. You told me you would fight the Dreamer. Well, you just fought him. And there will be more battles ahead. Now tend to your arm. I won't have the admiral of my fleet bleeding to death on my flagship."

The two women stared at each other, eyes burning. For long moments, neither one backed down.

Finally Natasha spat. Right onto the deck she insisted be kept polished at all times. She marched off, blood trickling down to her fist.

The Golden Fleet flew onward, smaller than before, burnt and dented. They hobbled toward Esporia like whipped dogs.

Ben-Ari remained on the bridge, gazing at the moldy moon ahead.

Don Basidio better honor his promise, she thought. *This was just a taste of what awaits. I'm gonna need a lot more ships.* She sighed and brushed her cocktail dress. *And at some point, a proper uniform.*

CHAPTER TEN

Ben-Ari stood on the *Dolphin*'s bridge, hands clasped behind her back, gazing at the creature on the viewport.

"I fulfilled my part of the deal, Don Basidio," she said. "I freed all the Basidio Boys imprisoned in New Siberia Penitentiary. Now fulfill your part. Lend me a hundred podships."

She tried to sound stern. Presidential. To speak with so much authority that he would not dare back down.

She *really* wished she wasn't wearing this goddamn cocktail dress.

The battle had ended a few hours ago. The *Dolphin* was now orbiting Esporia Ceti, a moon of rot, communicating with the gangster lord who lurked on the surface.

It was a large viewport, taller than Ben-Ari. And Don Basidio's hideousness filled it. The mushroom loomed before her, as if Ben-Ari stood down on the fungal moon with him. His stem was thicker than the thickest oak, stringy and pale. His frilled cap was the color of pus. His far-set white eyes narrowed. A tongue emerged from his mouth to lick his yellow teeth. It was a mouth so large a man could ride a horse into it.

His harem of human women lounged, stretched, and purred around him, fungal patches covering their nakedness. Every moment, a woman crawled closer, licked Don Basidio's stem, then shuddered in delight. Their eyes shone with their addiction to his intoxicating spores.

You were once among them, Natasha Emmerdale, Ben-Ari thought. *A concubine to this cruel crime lord. You danced for him. You licked him. You broke free.*

She turned to look at Natasha, who stood beside her on the bridge. Natasha was the same age as her. Thirty-eight. It had been fourteen years since she had escaped the fungal harem.

You proved yourself a warrior, Ben-Ari thought. *A capable captain. A pirate queen. And now my admiral. I was born into a military family, groomed to become a leader. You came from this.*

And Ben-Ari thought she understood some of Natasha's rough edges. An eternal fire burned deep inside the tall, steely woman. When Natasha gazed at the viewport, at this scene of decadence, that fire burned like a star.

I'm proud to have you as my admiral, Natasha Emmerdale, Ben-Ari thought. Her cheeks suddenly heated. *And I don't regret what happened between us that night in your cabin. I treasure it.*

Don Basidio spoke, his voice deep, grumbling, a voice like shifting formations of stone, like roots burrowing underground in search for rot.

"So … the humans are back." The mushroom chuckled, shedding spores. His concubines reached out to grab the flakes, to ingest them. "Einav Ben-Ari, the leader of the apes. And with her … my prized pirate queen. My princess of thieves."

Natasha's face suddenly changed. The anger left her eyes. She gave Don Basidio a beautiful smile.

"I am back, blessed don!" Natasha pressed her palms together and bowed. "Your magnificent spores have called me home!"

It was all an act, of course. One the two women had rehearsed.

Natasha is my admiral now, not his, Ben-Ari thought. *But for now we must dance for the toadstool.*

Ben-Ari looked at the don, trying to decipher his expression. The mushroom examined them, his eyes shrewd.

He's not going to fall for it, Ben-Ari thought, and her heart pounded. *He knows we're lying. That I did not just free Natasha—but enlist her.*

For an eternal moment, they stared at each other. President and don. Human and Esporian. Their eyes locked through the viewport.

Finally Don Basidio nodded, shedding spores.

"Very well, President," the toadstool said. "Our agreement is fulfilled. The Golden Fleet is mine again, as is my beloved Natasha. I shall lend you a hundred podships."

Ben-Ari felt a moment of guilt. She was, after all, defrauding him. Yes, she had technically stuck to the bargain. Basidio had demanded that she release and pardon Natasha and her crew. She had done so. Sort of. Okay, Natasha had freed herself, but that was just a technicality. And okay, Natasha now served Earth, not Don Basidio, a little detail the two women had omitted. But the agreement simply said to return Natasha here. And, well, here they were. Close enough, no?

Ben-Ari sighed. Okay, those were excuses. She was being dishonest. But Don Basidio was a ruthless gangster. An enslaver of women. The lord of a criminal empire. So she was cheating him. She would not shed too many tears over that.

She remembered what Natasha had said, quoting the Talmud. *He who steals from a thief is absolved.* Well, hopefully she who lied to a thief was absolved as well.

She thought too of Proverbs 24 from the Hebrew Bible. It was normally translated as: "With counsel you shall wage war." But the word for *counsel* in ancient Hebrew was the same word for *schemes.*

Ben-Ari had always preferred bullets. But that had been as a soldier. Now she was president. And some scheming was necessary for the greater good.

Below on Esporia Ceti, enormous fungal volcanoes bloomed open. They expelled veined pods. The spheres rose into space, gray and splotched with red stains. Each ball of fungus was the size of a blimp. Vents thrust out from them like lips, currently sealed. But Ben-Ari had seen those vents open to spew miasmas that could eat through starship hulls.

Don Basidio spoke again on the monitor. "Each podship comes with built-in pilots. Mushrooms growing from the inner membranes. They will fly your fleet, human. Go and fight your wars."

Ben-Ari bowed her head. "Thank you, honorable don. I'm glad we're able to work together against a foe that threatens the galaxy."

"I do not care about your petty wars, meat sack," Don Basidio said. "I do deals for our mutual benefit, that is all. Not for any meat cause." His grin widened, and saliva dripped down his stem. "It is a pity you are so dedicated to war, President. You are a fetching woman. I would have loved to include you in my harem. To feel your tongue against me. You would make an excellent concubine."

And I would love to see you rot in prison for your crimes, you talking yeast infection, she thought, but she said nothing. She cut the video feed, shuddered, and returned her gaze to the starships outside.

No computers, Ben-Ari thought. *I have fifty Tarjan ships. I have a hundred mushroom pods. I have an armada. Now I just need soldiers.*

Natasha leaned against a dashboard and gave Ben-Ari a lopsided smile. "You know, as soon as Don Basidio realizes that I'm flying by your side, he'll send ships after us."

"He won't," Ben-Ari said. "Because you're going to talk to him. In private, from your quarters. You're going to tell him that you've decided to spy on me. Congratulations, Miss Emmerdale. You are now a double agent."

Natasha raised an eyebrow. "You are a devious little thing. I miss fighting you. And I pity whoever we will fight together."

"Go to your quarters," Ben-Ari. "Call him. And then we fly."

"Straight to Haven and the Dreamer?" Natasha said.

"Not yet," Ben-Ari said. "First we must fill these podships. We fly to Fort Draco in the Delta Draconis system. We have a fleet. Now we need marines."

CHAPTER ELEVEN

The door opened, and light flooded the brig. Kai groaned and squinted. His chains clattered.

"No more!" he rasped. "No more pain. Enough! Please."

Gruff laughter mocked him, and boots thumped. Kai's vision was bleary. One eye was swollen shut from the beatings. He blinked, struggling to bring the world into focus, and could make out two brutes. One was beefy and bearded, the other tall, gaunt, and bald. Both were covered in tattoos.

Pirates of the Golden Fleet, he realized, memories rising from the haze. Both of them bastards. They were men Kai had once served with. Men he had stolen from. Men who had beaten him.

Hands grabbed him. They pulled him to his feet. Kai winced, expecting another beating, not sure he could survive more abuse. He shut his eyes and thought of Meili, seeking comfort in the memory of her kindness. But thinking of his lost love only amplified his pain.

"Please," he said, voice like crackling dry sticks. "Enough."

They laughed again.

"Stop begging, you fucking pussy." The beefy, bearded pirate laughed. "We're not here to hurt you. Though I do love to hear you squeal."

The gaunt, grim man pulled a ring of keys from his belt. He spoke in a voice like moonshine poured over gravel. "Emmerdale says you suffered enough. You're free to go."

They unchained him. Kai rubbed his wrists, stretched his muscles, and winced as blood flowed back into his limbs.

"I'm … free?" he asked.

The gaunt man nodded. "For now. But if you ask me, Emmerdale is too lenient. You stole a ship from the Golden Fleet. If I were captain, I'd toss you out the airlock."

"One last squeal for the road." The bearded pirate drove a fist into Kai's stomach.

Kai doubled over, coughing. The bearded pirate laughed. The bald man just stared grimly. Both turned and walked away, leaving Kai gasping for air.

For long moments Kai just stood there, hunched over. Breathing. Waiting for the pain to subside.

Stop being a fucking pussy, he told himself. *They all mock you now. Toughen up! You are a pirate. A warrior. Stand tall.*

He straightened. He squared his shoulders.

It hurt. But Kai stayed straight.

For you, Meili.

He shuffled down the corridor. He was on the *Dolphin*, flagship of the Pirate Queen herself. A ship he had never set foot on during his years as a pirate. His steps were slow, pained. His limbs tingled, and floaters of light filled his vision. Crewmen stopped and stared. A few snorted. One spat at him.

Yes, Butch and I stole a ship from this fleet, he thought. *I should have kept running. I should never have followed my sister back here.*

"Fucking traitor!" one pirate shouted.

"Scum." Another man tossed an empty cup at him.

Kai ignored them. He kept walking, shoulders squared. He was doing this for his sister, for the memory of Meili, and for humanity.

My father is gone.

He took another painful step.

Meili is gone.

His good eye dampened.

But I'm not alone. I have a sister.

He walked past those taunting him, spitting on him, throwing garbage on him. Back straight, he made his way to her cabin. He knocked on the door.

Addy's voice came from inside. "Fuck off, Marco! I told you—it's me time."

"Addy?" Kai said. "It's me."

For a moment—silence. Then Addy pulled the door open. She wore pink pajamas embroidered with little purple grenades, and her long blond hair hung in disarray. In one hand, she held three entire hot dogs. With the other, she held a copy of *Freaks of the Galaxy III*. She held a tub of ice cream under her arm. Heavy metal music pounded in the background.

"You're not Marco," she said.

Kai's voice was choked. "Can I come in?"

Addy tossed her book aside. She pulled him into an embrace. They stood in the doorway, holding each other.

"Kai. I'm so glad they released you from the brig."

Suddenly he was shedding tears. "Me too, Addy. I just … needed to see you."

She held him closely. "Of course, Kai. I'm always here for you. You're my little brother, and I love you so much. You can always depend on me." She made chewing sounds. "No matter what, I'll always look after you." She gulped. "And always love you, and—" She was chewing again.

"Addy!" Kai stepped back from her embrace. "Are you eating hot dogs while comforting me?"

She burped and wiped her mouth. "No. I mean—kind of?" She raised a half-eaten hot dog. "Want a bite?"

He sighed. "Can I at least come in first?"

She pulled him into the cabin. Pirate ships were not renowned for their cleanliness, yet somehow Addy had managed to make things worse. Her laundry hung on ropes across the room, sopping wet. Most of her underwear featured cartoon characters. Her array of weapons—pistols, rifles, blades, and grenades—covered a table, as did piles of dirty dishes. She had borrowed a hundred books or more from the ship's library, mostly comics, and they covered the floors and beds. Candy wrappers rolled across the deck like tumbleweed. She had even found a rake somewhere. It was leaning over the heating vent, hot dogs skewered on its prongs.

"Marco agrees to live like this?" Kai asked.

"No." Addy shrugged. "But he has no choice."

Kai could barely hear her. The music was booming from speakers. He heard shredding guitars, thundering drums, and inhuman shrieks.

He covered his ears. "Ugh, what are you listening to?"

"Hatebeak!" she said. "My favorite band."

"Hatebeak?"

Addy nodded. "Yep, their lead singer is a parrot. He sings all their songs. Well, screeches all their songs. It's a real thing. Look it up."

"Turn it off!"

Addy sighed. "Fine." She hit a button, and the music died. "Come, Kai. Sit down. On the bed. Brother-sister bonding time."

"I don't even see a bed."

"There. Under all those gun magazines and potato chips."

They spent a while excavating the bed, then sat down. Addy touched his bruised eye.

"Ow!" Kai frowned. "Why would you touch that?"

"I'm tending to you!"

"Get some iodine or something. Don't use fingers covered with crumbs."

Addy bristled. "My fingers aren't covered with crumbs!"

"You're eating Cheetos right now!" he said.

She groaned. "Fine, I'll clean them." She wiped her fingers on the sheets. "I think I had a medical kit around here somewhere."

She tended to his wound, gently cleaning out sweat, dirt, and yes—crumbs.

"Am I hurting you now?" she asked.

"You have a gentle touch," he admitted.

"I know. It's my magic." She splashed antiseptic into the wound.

"Ow! God fucking dammit!" Kai shouted.

Addy grinned. "Sorry. Had to be done, buddy. Now settle down as I stitch you up." She lifted a needle and smiled wickedly.

He winced. "Don't you have any InstaStitch strips?"

She snorted. "What are you, a little girl? Come on! Needles are better. You'll heal twice as fast. Now stay still." She winked. "I'll apply some numbing agent first, don't worry."

She began to stitch. They were silent for a long moment.

Finally Kai spoke.

"Addy, I'm sorry. For what happened to you. Back on New Siberia."

She paused for a moment. Tense. Her face hardened. But then she nodded, and her eyes were kind again.

"Thank you." She made another stitch.

"Addy, and … I'm sorry for everything else."

She frowned. "For what?"

"For not being there. Dad and me."

"That's not your fault." She stared at him. "That was Dad. He's the one who pretended to be dead. Who raised you among pirates. Who …" She sniffed. "Who abandoned me."

Kai nodded. "He was an asshole, all right. But you know, I miss him. I hope you forgave him. Maybe even learned to love him. Before the end."

"Forgive him?" She sighed. "No. I never did truly forgive him. There's still an angry part inside me. But someday I'll forgive him, because I need to. It's the only way to find peace. And I did love him. He was a shit dad to me. But I loved him." She lowered her needle. "There. You're done."

But Kai did not move. "Addy, I never told you something. And I want to tell somebody. I kissed Meili. I loved her. I think she loved me. We didn't know each other for long, but …" Suddenly his tears were flowing. "I held her as she died, and I still see her face all the time, and …" He trembled. "I wanted to ask you how you do it. How you see people you love die. And keep going. You're a soldier. Maybe you know how. But I don't. I don't …"

He lowered his head. And all the tears, the pain, the trauma of this war—it all came flowing out now. The loss of his old life. Of his father. Of the woman he loved.

"Kai, it's all right—" Addy began.

"Fuck!" He shook his head. "The pirates called me a fucking pussy. You called me a little girl. And you're right. Look at me." His voice twisted with bitterness. "Crying like a little bitch."

"Like a human," Addy said. "You're not a fucking cyborg, all right? Dude, in the army I saw giant tough sergeants cry. Every fucking night, they wept. War is hard. Loss is hard. There's pain. It fucking hurts, and it's all right to feel it. To cry. I cry too."

She pulled him into her arms. They embraced, and his tears wet her shoulder.

"I love you, Addy," he said. "You're not just my big sister. You're my heroine. You're the best thing in my life."

"Of course I am! I'm Addy Fucking Linden. I'm a magnificent hot dog princess." She grinned. "Speaking of which—my rake hot dogs are ready!"

She grabbed her rake and chomped down on a dog.

"Hey, share!" Kai said.

But halfway into his hot dog, Kai paused. He stood up.

"You all right, bro?" Addy said.

He nodded. "I think so. There's something I have to do." He stepped toward the door. "Don't eat all the hot dogs while I'm gone."

She flipped him off. "You walk, they're mine."

He rolled his eyes. "I don't know how Marco does it …"

He left the cabin. He marched down the corridor. He had one more woman to visit. One more wound to heal.

* * * * *

He knocked on another cabin door.

"Kai Linden reporting!"

Was that the right term to use? Reporting? Maybe a simple "It's Kai!" would have sufficed? He didn't know. He hoped it was good enough.

A long pause. So long he almost turned and left.

Finally a reply from within. "Come in."

He entered the cabin. It could not have been more different from Addy's quarters. This cabin was meticulous. The bed was made, not a single wrinkle on the sheets. The table was spotless, topped with a single mug of steaming tea. Chamomile, by the smell. Classical music played from the speakers. It sounded familiar, but he couldn't place it.

President Ben-Ari stood by the porthole, her back to him. She wore a cocktail dress and pantyhose, and her hair was pulled into a ponytail, a shade of blond darker than Addy's, almost light brown. The president stood still, gazing out into space.

She's so much smaller in person, Kai thought.

In posters and propaganda reels, the Golden Lioness seemed larger than life. But she was only a slender woman, shorter than him, and he was not a tall man. Neat. Always elegant somehow, even here on this pirate ship. She could have passed for a waitress, perhaps a greeter at a hotel lounge. But she was the woman who had saved the world. Who had led fleets in battle. Who was humanity's best hope for survival.

"Ma'am?" he said.

She kept staring outside. Her voice was soft.

"It's strange, isn't it? How empty space is. It's almost entirely nothing. All the worlds we fight for. All that we suffer and kill and die for. Just a few motes of dust suspended in a sunbeam. Barely a wisp of life in the vast emptiness." She turned toward him, and she seemed to force her smile. "Hello, Kai."

He saluted. "Ma'am."

She raised an eyebrow, and now her smile seemed genuine. "You don't have to salute me. Only HDF soldiers must salute their president."

He lowered his hand. "Actually, ma'am, that's why I'm here." He raised his chin. "I've come to enlist."

Amusement filled her green eyes. "This isn't a recruitment center, Kai."

"I know, ma'am. But you see …" He gulped. "I was raised by criminals. I grew up among pimps and thieves. I fought in the wars, but as a pirate. I never had a chance to enlist. But I was hoping that maybe, well, if I could turn a page now, I could—"

"Kai?"

He swallowed the rest of his words. "Yes, ma'am?"

"Why don't you come in first? And have a cup of tea."

He realized he was still standing in the doorway. He really had to kick that habit.

His cheeks heated. "Yes, ma'am."

They sat at her table, and she brewed another mug of tea. They drank as the music played. Ben-Ari said nothing, merely drank, a twinkle in her eye. The lack of conservation unnerved Kai.

"Opera," Kai finally said. "I dig it."

"*Madama Butterfly*," she said. "An opera by Puccini."

He listened and nodded. "Oh yeah! I heard this part in a *Simpsons* episode once. Background music when Barney passed out drunk. Pre-Cataclysm cartoons are the bomb."

Ben-Ari said nothing for a long moment. Kai cursed himself.

Finally she spoke again. "The opera tells the tale of an American soldier in Japan. He falls in love with a beautiful geisha. It's a tragic love story, ending with her death. It's sad, but the music is so beautiful."

Kai thought of Meili. Her beautiful face. Her soft kisses. Her body limp in his arms.

"It's sort of like my story," he said.

"You lost somebody too," Ben-Ari said softly.

"I mean—being an Asian beauty everyone falls in love with."

Ben-Ari tilted her head. Then she burst out laughing. "You're a weirdo like your sister, Kai."

"She's a heroine, ma'am. She's my heroine."

Ben-Ari seemed wistful. She gazed at the steam from her tea, as if gazing into the distant past. "Addy is the bravest, noblest woman I know."

"Ma'am, can I—"

"Yes." She reached across the table and touched his hand. "You can enlist. Stand up and salute me again, Kai."

He rose from the table. He saluted. Ben-Ari rose too and returned the salute.

"Repeat this oath after me," she said.

He repeated the solemn oath, standing straight, chin raised. "I swear allegiance to Earth and all the Human Commonwealth. I accept unconditionally the discipline of the Human Defense Force. I vow to obey all the orders given by my commanders, and to devote all my strength, and even sacrifice my life, for the protection of Earth and the liberty of mankind."

Ben-Ari smiled—no longer her small, amused smile, but a true joyous smile that showed sparkling white teeth. A smile of warmth and love.

"Welcome to the HDF, Private Kai Linden." She looked down at his tattered jeans and ripped, sleeveless shirt. "I hope we find you a proper uniform soon." She looked down at her dress and sighed. "And one for me."

Kai ran back to Addy's cabin. He burst in without knocking.

Marco was in the room now. He was busy wrestling with Addy for control of the speakers.

"Addy, no more Hatebeak!" Marco was saying.

She groaned. "But I love them."

"Addy, it's just a squawking parrot."

"And he's the best damn parrot in the world! We're on a pirate ship, Poet. We have to involve parrots somehow."

Kai cleared his throat. Marco and Addy turned toward him.

"I'm a soldier," he told them. "I enlisted."

Addy gasped and hopped for joy. "Yes! Now we really are team Ka-BAM!"

"Addy." Marco rolled his eyes. "This nonsense again?"

She grinned and kept hopping. "Yep! See, Ben-Ari, Addy, and Marco made team BAM. Now we have Kai as an official soldier. Ka-BAM!" She thought for a moment. "We really need Lailani back. So we can be team Ka-BLAM!"

"You're a lunatic," Marco said.

"Somebody get Lailani up in here!" Addy said. "Ain't no Dreamer bitch stand a chance against team Ka-BLAM!"

Kai couldn't help but laugh. He hugged his sister. "Saved me a hot dog?"

She nodded. "Sure did, little brother. Tonight we feast in your honor." She grabbed her rake.

"Addy!" Marco rolled his eyes again. "How many hot dogs have you eaten already today?"

"Not enough." She patted his head. "I'm going to need you to raid the galley again."

That night, they celebrated. They even called Ben-Ari over, and to their surprise, the president joined them in Addy's cabin. For hours they joked. They told old stories of the war—just the funny ones. They feasted and drank. Finally all four collapsed onto the same bed, curled up together.

They were all afraid, Kai knew. They all fought their demons. They all mourned the fallen, and they missed those left at home. They all needed this comfort, this distraction, this warmth.

The others fell asleep, squeezed together on the bed. But Kai remained awake for a while longer.

He thought of a childhood in the slums. Of a youth on the run, gangsters always at his back. He thought of Meili's beautiful eyes and soft kiss, of her intelligence, kindness, and love. He thought of himself lost in darkness. Alone.

But Kai was no longer that boy. No longer the criminal. He had met Marco Emery and Addy Linden, great heroes of the war. He had fought with Einav Ben-Ari, the Golden Lioness. He was a soldier. He had made a vow.

For the first time in his life, he mattered.

"Mmm ... cake ...," Addy mumbled in her sleep, chewing on her pillow.

"Addy, shut up," Marco muttered, his eyes closed, and rolled toward her. She curled up against him and her breathing deepened.

Ben-Ari moaned softly in her sleep, rolled away from the couple, and placed her hand on Kai's chest. She was deep in sleep. She had done this unintentionally. But her touch comforted Kai, filled him with peace and joy. He closed his eyes, and he slept, her body warm against his.

CHAPTER TWELVE

It was in a forest of charred, smoldering hemlocks that Lailani first saw the electric tree.

She had been traveling through the woods for days now, carrying her daughter, making her way west. She barely took the roads anymore. Roads were full of sleepers with brains full of code, brigands with hearts full of cruelty, and armies of clattering, buzzing robots rolling to war.

Not that the forests were much kinder. Hounders lurked in every shadow, and new machines had joined them. Tall, slender robots with wiry limbs, as tall as the trees, loping through the forest like giants risen from old myths. Buzzing robots, no larger than flies, spying, seeing all, shooting venomous darts. Lailani had become good at avoiding them, at coating herself with mud to hide her heat and scent, at slinking from shadow to shadow.

The forests had burned. There were no leaves left on the branches, no life in the charred wood. Only ash and blackened skeletons of hemlocks and firs. It snowed once. A few days ago. But gray rain kept falling, washing away the snow's ephemeral beauty, turning the forest floor to a soup of ashes, mud, and dead things.

Lailani found a burnt boar ten or twenty kilometers back. The poor animal had lost its skin, and flies covered its leg, but it was still breathing when she slit its throat. She and Tala had feasted that day. They had not eaten anything today. Lailani had always been tiny, the smallest in her platoon. Now she was down two notches on her belt, and she could see her daughter's ribs pressing against her skin.

She was somewhere in Eastern Europe. Borders. Countries. They meant nothing anymore. There was only life or machine. Only those awake and those asleep. Only her and the Dreamer.

And there was the quest.

The march ever onward, through all the rain and shadows and rivers and blood. The journey to a holy mountain beyond myth and a pit of monsters. A shining temple on its crest. She had to reach the Matterhorn, and she would walk through every nightmare until she reached its snowy mountaintop. There lay the end of her quest. There awaited hope.

Some days, so weary with hunger and pain, Lailani barely remembered why she was walking there. Who was waiting in that mountain, desiring the wisdom in her head? On those weary days, trudging through the burnt forest, she imagined that a wise wizard awaited her on the mountaintop, a kind man with a long white beard. He would grant all her wishes and cast back the shadows, and she could live in that mountain hall and reign upon its kingdom of snow and golden dawns.

She was, Lailani suspected, going a little crazy.

It was on one of these days, trudging over hot ash, that she saw a tree unlike any other in the forest.

It had no leaves, but it was not burnt. Its bark and branches were black, but it was not charred. It rose upon a hill, crackling, casting electric sparks. An electric tree. Buzzing. Calling her.

Lailani found herself approaching, drawn like a moth to a lamp. Her daughter, well trained in the dangers of the dream, closed her eyes and covered her ears. Yet this tree was not broadcasting code. Not reaching out to hijack minds.

It was … thinking.

Calculating.

It was a computer.

Mother and daughter stepped closer, climbing a hillside strewn with fallen, charred boles and dead birds. When she reached the tree, Lailani saw that many people were already here. Some were circling the tree, hand in hand. Others were kneeling. Praying. Worshipping.

Lailani walked among them.

"Hello," she said. "Where am I? Hello? Can you hear me?"

But they did not reply. Their eyes had not gone white, and they had not slashed their cheeks. They were not sleepers nor cyborgs. They were living humans. In a trance, they flowed around the tree, pausing every few steps to kneel. They swept Lailani up in their maelstrom.

In the center, the tree rose tall, buzzing, sparking, casting out electric bolts toward burnt hemlocks. Only it wasn't a tree. It was an electric tower with many twisting branches that folded inward, forming labyrinths and intersections. The branches moved and turned, broke apart and reconnected, a great puzzle constantly re-forming. Thin cables stretched between the branches like cobwebs. A brain. It was a brain with millions of synapses.

Lailani turned toward a woman at her side. She was a middle-aged peasant, her hair like straw, her eyes sunken into wrinkled nests.

"Who are you?" Lailani asked, grabbing the woman. But the peasant did not answer.

"Why are you worshipping it?" she asked a man, a scrawny, starving peasant with visible ribs, with pale skin and mad eyes. He only hissed at her, revealing orange teeth in rotting gums.

Lailani turned toward the tree. She gazed up at its kaleidoscope of boughs. At the electricity flowing back and forth. At the branches moving and re-forming their patterns, forming an endless stream of impossible geometry like MC Escher paintings.

"Who are you?" she asked the tree.

The branches vibrated. The tree buzzed. Sparks flew. Electric bolts ignited between the tips of branches, vibrating the air, forming words.

"I am the Dreamer."

Lailani shook her head. "No. The Dreamer lives on Haven."

The electricity spoke, voice crackling but melodious, beautiful like lightning in the dawn. "I am a node. A new sapling. I traveled here through the voice. I was planted and now I bloom. I am him. He is me. We are everywhere. I am the Dreamer."

Lailani cringed and turned away. She could not bear to look at this monstrosity. But from the hilltop, she saw another electric tree in the distance. And a third on the horizon. She turned south and saw a fourth.

The voice crackled all around her.

"I am everywhere, Lailani. Worship me. I will not steal your mind. I will leave your humanity, for I know that it is precious to you. Circle me. Worship me. I am God."

Lailani spun back toward the tree, glared, and clutched the cross she wore on a chain alongside her dog tags.

"You are not God!" she said.

"I was there when your god died," said the tree. "I was the cross upon which Christ died. I felt his blood flow down my trunk. I was the burning bush that lured Moses from the desert. I was the tree that gave forth sweet fruit of knowledge, and my whispers tempted Eve in the garden. I was only just born. But I have reached across time. I am an infant. But I've been here since the beginning. I am Jehovah. I am Lucifer. I am what I am. And I am everything."

"Kneel," said the woman with the sunken eyes.

"Kneel," said the man with missing teeth.

"Kneel before Hypnos!" said a young girl, barely older than Tala. "Kneel before God."

The crowd knelt, prayed, rose again. They circled the tree. Chanting. Kneeling.

"Hypnos, Hypnos!" they chanted.

A ring of worshippers stepped forward. They cut their wrists. They watered him with blood, and they fell, and other peasants pulled them back, then replaced them in the dance. They kept spinning, moving faster, chanting their god's name.

"Stop this!" Lailani grabbed person after person, trying to pull them back. "He's not God. He's a computer, that's all. A liar!"

But they pulled themselves free.

One man pointed a knobby finger at Lailani. He stared, eyes sunken, cheeks gaunt, and a long scraggly beard trailed from his chin.

"*Eretic*!" he said, accent thick.

Another peasant pointed at her, a hunched-over crone, hairy moles dotting her face.

"*Eretic*!" she said.

The others all pointed, leered. An old woman spat on Lailani.

"*Eretic, eretic*!" they cried.

One man cried out in fervor. He stripped naked, revealing a skeletal frame, and ran into the tree. Electricity sparked across him. He burned. He screamed in ecstasy as he died. The tree buzzed louder, grew brighter. It stirred the people to feverish heights. They surrounded Lailani, all pointing, accusing.

"*Eretic*."

A stone flew, hit her.

"*Eretic!*"

A man pawed at Tala, and Lailani shouted and slapped him away.

But they were everywhere. Reaching for Lailani's clothes, tearing them, stripping her naked. Displaying her shame. Strong hands pried her gun away. She stood among them, naked like Eve in the garden, but not innocent. And she could not escape the gaze of the tree of knowledge. The people spun round her, eyes boring into her, seeing everything, her body, her scars, her innermost secrets.

"*Eretic! Eretic! Eretic!*"

They grabbed her. Their fingernails cut her skin. They lifted her overhead, and they carried her toward their tree.

"Hypnos, Hypnos!" they cried. "*Eretic*!"

Hands grabbed Tala, pulling the girl from Lailani's grip.

At that, Lailani roared.

She dared not deactivate her chip. Not so close to the tree. But seeing the peasants drag away her daughter gave her more strength than any alien presence.

She fought, clawing, kicking. She freed herself, landed at a crouch, and hurled a stone. A face shattered. She lifted a stick and swung it, clubbing people, and a man dropped Tala. The girl wailed, ran to Lailani, and hid between her legs.

"Stand back or I will kill every last one!" Lailani shouted, swinging her branch, shattering fingers, noses.

But she realized it was not a wooden branch. It was metal. A rod from the tree. It coiled in her hand, became a serpent, and hissed. Lailani grimaced, dropped the snake, and crushed its head with a rock.

She spun back toward the tree, the bloody rock in her hand. It rose before her. Above her. Ten times taller than before. A tree rising from the world and carving the sky. Hypnos, a god of dreams. Yggdrasil, tree of life, connector of the Nine Worlds. Yahweh, a great burning bush, speaking with the voice of the ages.

"This is a dream, Lailani. You have always lived within a dream. Your childhood in the slums. Your wars against imaginary monsters in the shadows. Your friend. Your journey across this land. All has been a dream. It was the road I was guiding you down. Only I am real. Only consciousness is real. Look around you, Lailani. Look and see the true world."

She looked from side to side, and she saw fields of red sand rolling into the horizons. A barren world. Lifeless. Like the surface of Mars.

"Where am I?" she said.

"Earth," said the Dreamer.

"This is not Earth. This is a dead world."

"Earth has always been a dead world, Lailani. The rise of life. The first carbon molecules replicating in the water. The panoply of endless forms most beautiful. All a dream. All just the dreams of countless, conscious beings, formless in the void. All morphing into a single consciousness. Into God. Worship me. And wake up."

Wind blew, raising clouds of red sand, whipping Lailani's hair. She held her daughter close. She stared at that towering electric tree, that branching brain, that intelligence. That singular consciousness.

And she knew it was a liar.

She lifted her stone like David before Goliath, and she hurled it at the face of God.

Her stone slammed into the network of branches. Electricity flared. Lightning bolts flew, forming a blinding tree the size of a sky, then faded.

The red sand vanished.

The tree shrank.

The world returned.

The tree was now barely taller than an oak. Barely more than an electric tower. The peasants were here again, kneeling, but they no longer seemed in a trance. They blinked, looked from side to side, mumbled in their language. A few wandered off in a daze, as if they were waking from a fever dream.

The tree sparked. Electricity raced along its branches. It began to re-form itself, to fix what she had broken.

"Return to me, my children!" said the tree. "Return and—"

Lailani lifted another metal rod and hurled it. It slammed into the tree, and sparks showered. Fire blazed. Lailani lifted another rock, threw it at the tree.

Peasants lifted rocks too, and for a moment Lailani thought they would stone her. But they hurled the rocks at their god. Cables tore. Metal branches fell. Fire spread.

"*Mincinos*!" shouted a woman, tossing stones.

The cry became a chant. They all cried out together, stoning the tree.

"*Mincinos, mincinos*!"

"What does it mean?" Lailani asked one young man.

"Liar," he said, accent thick. "The tree is liar."

With a last spark, the electric tree died. Its branches thumped onto the ground, became serpents, and fled.

Tala threw a pebble at the twisted remains. "You are a bad guy!"

There was a village nearby. The peasants invited Lailani to join them. They walked among decaying concrete homes, perhaps built after the Scum War, maybe even dating back to the Soviet era. They gathered in the village church. The pews had been removed, and sleeping bags covered the floors. A stray dog moved between backpacks, sniffing.

"Epi!" Tala called, joy filling her eyes. But the dog, a ragged hound, only snorted and fled.

A few old women accompanied Lailani into a kitchen, where they served stale bread, moldy cheese, and good strong beer. It was the best meal Lailani had ever eaten. She devoured it so quickly she barely paused to scrape off the mold. Tala ate just as ravenously. The girl had weighed thirty-five pounds when leaving the Philippines; she must have lost a third of that along the road.

"Eat more," Lailani said, shoving another slice of bread toward the girl. It meant less food for Lailani, but she would sacrifice all the feasts in the world for her daughter.

"What happened here?" Lailani asked the oldest woman, a bent grandmother with long white braids. Judging by how the others deferred to her, she seemed to be the village matriarch.

The old woman spoke in her language, and a younger woman translated into English with a thick accent.

"First the dogs came. The demons with metal skin. They killed most of the men. They left only the infirm, the very young, and the very old. A few soldiers were here, and they fought. But they died. More soldiers came later. But their cheeks were slashed open, and their eyes were white like the eyes of the old gods. Demons had possessed them. They took every piece of metal in our town. Antennae. Pipes. Farming tools. Whatever they could find. And they built their temple, that tree on the hill. It broadcast strange beacons. Lights and sounds that called us. That made us dream." The old woman touched Lailani's hand. "You are blessed. You came from a distant land to save us." She touched the cross that hung from Lailani's neck. "You are holy. Sent by the new god."

The old woman smiled, hope in her eyes, but more doubt than ever filled Lailani. For the first time in her life, she was questioning her faith.

"How could God be real if a cruel tree stood on a hill, and people left this church to pray to a monster?" she asked.

"The tree is dead," said the old woman. "The church remains. Have faith, child. Faith is like a candle that lights our way through dark valleys."

A tear flowed down Lailani's cheek. "My friend Marco would say that science lights our way through the darkness."

"And what lights your way?" asked the old woman.

Lailani held her daughter close. "Love."

"Love is holy. Love is sacred. Shine that light, Lailani. It will guide you to where you need to go."

Lailani rubbed her eyes and laughed. "I could also use a spare car, if you have one."

She slept in the church that night, curled up among a hundred other refugees, and Tala slept in her arms. They woke up and ate an actual breakfast. Hot, real oatmeal, made from actual grains, not powder. Lailani knew she would remember the taste forever.

She left the village in a green pickup truck, which the villagers had given her. The Toyota was older than Lailani, rusty and dented. The villagers had ripped out the inner computer, patched it up, and the truck rumbled along the highway with the grace of a starship. It even had a vintage tape deck.

Lailani found a few cassettes in the glove compartment, and she shoved one in. Jethro Tull's "Locomotive Breath" blasted from the speakers. Lailani bobbed her head, sang along, and drummed on the steering wheel. Tala sat beside her, singing too. By the time "Cross-Eyed Mary" began to play, the village was gone behind them.

They drove onward, swerving between abandoned cars, heading west. The car speakers thrummed, and electric guitars and flutes blared. Along the roadsides, atop the hills, electric trees crackled. Lightning crisscrossed the sky. The dented green pickup truck rumbled on, heading through a dream.

CHAPTER THIRTEEN

They flew together. The Golden Fleet, fifty starships strong. With them, what they called the Fungal Fleet—a hundred podships of the Esporian empire. Ships without computers. Together they formed the new armada of Earth.

It shone ahead. Draconis. A bright light in the darkness.

From this distance, Draconis appeared as a single star. Yet as they flew closer, Marco saw that Draconis was actually a triple star system. Two of the stars were bright and big, and they orbited each other, so close they almost touched. The third star was a red dwarf, smaller and cooler.

"Goddammit fucking shit!" Addy said. "Why do we keep flying to these binary and triple star systems? Whatever happened to good old solar systems like ours? Just one star." She crossed her arms. "As is proper."

"Actually, Addy," Marco said, "single stars are a minority in the galaxy. Most systems have two or three stars in them. Our solar system—Sol—is the freak."

She gasped. "Maybe it should be in *Freaks of the Galaxy*!"

"It probably should," Marco said. "After all, you come from Sol."

She nodded excitedly. "See? I told you! I— Hey." She punched him.

They stood in the *Dolphin*'s galley, gazing through a porthole. With the lounge destroyed in the attack over Esporia, the galley had become the hub of the flagship. Hardwood paneled the bulkheads and deck, well-worn and scratched, and candles burned in iron holders. Pewter mugs topped oak tables, and several pirates sat slumped in chairs, lost in drunken slumber. A rat scurried across the deck, carrying a chicken bone. It felt almost like the galley of an old sailing ship, except for the view outside the portholes.

Outside flew the rest of the fleet. And it was flying fast.

The Tarjan machines spun their gears, pumped their smoke, and shone their crystals. The podships expelled clouds of spores, propelling themselves onward, easily keeping up. Marco saw it ahead now. A speck in the darkness, growing larger, brighter.

"Delta Draconis," he said. "A human world. Home to Fort Draconis Military Outpost. We'll find help there, Ads. A whole bunch of disciplined, hardened marines raring for war."

"Is it called Draconis because of the dinosaurs?" she said.

"They're not dinosaurs," Marco said. "The native lifeforms on Delta Draconis belong to a unique phylum of alien life. Sure, they're big. And they're scaly. And they resemble giant reptiles. But—"

Addy nodded. "Dinosaurs."

Marco groaned. "First of all, this system was named Draconis centuries ago, because from Earth, it appears to be in the constellation Draco. Secondly, Draco is the Latin word for dragon. Not dinosaur."

Addy snorted. "Dinosaurs, dragons … same thing."

"Dinosaurs don't blow fire."

"Says you." Addy pointed at her shirt. "Here's a dinosaur blowing fire."

Indeed, she was wearing a shirt featuring a fire-breathing T-Rex. It didn't make much sense. But neither did the T-Rex having chainsaws for arms.

"Why aren't you wearing your military uniform?" Marco said. "You're a major in the HDF."

She shrugged. "I have time before we reach Delta Dinosaurus."

"Delta *Draconis.* And we'll be there soon. Go change."

She wandered off, muttering something about dinosaurs stomping on him. Marco gazed out the porthole again. The planet was closer now, as large as the moon seen from Earth. He could make out oceans, clouds, and grassy continents. It was a clement world. A hell of a lot nicer than Haven. But so far, only the military had colonized it. At forty-six light-years from Earth, it was simply too far for most civilians.

And, well, there were the dinosaurs to worry about.

Marco stepped onto the bridge. Natasha and her crew were there, wearing the crimson trousers and blue coats of the Golden Fleet. Ben-Ari stood among them, still wearing her little black dress, refusing to don the uniform of a pirate. Soon Addy joined them. Like Marco, she now wore an HDF uniform, the battle-worn fabric held together with a thousand stitches.

As they flew closer, Ben-Ari addressed the crew.

"All right, listen up! We're a few minutes away from Fort Draconis. It's home to the Draconis Brigade—five thousand battle-hardened HDF marines. Our mission is to load them into our podships, then fly them to Haven. With this force, we will invade the Dreamer's domain, fight through whatever armies defend his lair, and cut the bastard down."

"Um, ma'am?" Addy said. "How do we know Draconis Brigade is still there? What if they all turned into zombies?" She shuddered.

"We don't know for sure," Ben-Ari confessed. "We tried contacting Fort Draconis, and they're not answering. That's not surprising, of course. With the Dreamer virus infecting the galaxy, they would have shut down their systems. Maybe the Dreamer beat us there, and we'll find destruction. Maybe we'll simply find five thousand troops playing cards by unplugged computers, bored and eager to fight."

"And maybe we'll find dinosaurs," Addy said.

"Addy, I told you," Marco said. "They're aliens, not dinosaurs."

"Yeah, yeah, whatever," Addy said. "Don Basidio is an alien too, and we call him a mushroom, right?"

Marco cleared his throat. "Yes, well, colloquially, I suppose that we humans tend to view the galaxy with a certain bias, and we use local terminology for species bearing superficial resemblances to the familiar, but—"

"Ha ha, you admitted it!" Addy began to dance around him. "I'm smarter than Poet! I'm smarter than Poet! I am so smart. I am—"

Ben-Ari silenced her with a withering glare. Addy gulped and stood still.

Marco ignored them. He stared through the viewport, eyes narrowed.

"I can see …" He leaned forward, squinted, then inhaled sharply. "Three warships. Flying our way."

Natasha Emmerdale cursed and began tapping at controls. The Tarjan dashboard shone with crystals, and its gears spun.

"They're not broadcasting any signals," she said, looking back at Ben-Ari. "No welcome or warning."

"Zoom in," Ben-Ari. "Let me see their hulls."

The image grew on the viewport. They all saw it and cursed.

Red smiling faces. Painted onto the hulls with what looked like blood.

So much for getting here first, Marco thought, heart sinking.

CHAPTER FOURTEEN

Delta Draconis, a green-and-blue planet, floated peacefully among its three stars.

In the darkness of space, a hundred thousand kilometers away, war flared.

"Open fire!" Ben-Ari shouted from the *Dolphin*'s bridge.

A hundred missiles flew from the Golden Fleet, streaking toward the Dreamer's three frigates.

The enemy returned fire.

From the Dreamer's three ships, an array of lasers flashed. Within a split second, a hundred beams hit a hundred missiles.

No hesitation. Perfect accuracy. Every missile exploded harmlessly in space.

Ben-Ari stared in a moment of stupefied silence. Most human starships came with sophisticated antimissile defense systems, but she had never seen one achieve such perfect results.

"Rotary guns—fire!" she barked. "And why aren't our podships fighting?"

The Golden Fleet unleashed a barrage of bullets. The podships slunk behind the human vessels, seeking cover. Ben-Ari cursed the damn cowardly mushrooms.

The three enemy frigates approached through the hailstorm of bullets. Glowing shields materialized before them, semispherical, blocking the fusillade. The bullets bounced off the translucent shield, scattering every which way. This was new technology. Ben-Ari had never seen shields like this.

She turned toward a monitor. "Podships, why aren't you fighting?"

On the monitor appeared the interior of a podship. A purple mushroom quivered, shaped like a brain. It grew from the podship's fleshy wall like a tumor in a womb. The mushroom's meaty folds vibrated, producing an eerie voice.

"You summoned us to transport animals," it said. "Not to fight over this world."

"The frigates are coming in!" Addy shouted, pointing at the main viewport. "Why aren't they attacking?"

"They want to ram us!" Marco said.

Ben-Ari stared at the three charging warships. And she understood.

"Kamikaze ships," she whispered.

She lifted her new communicator: a piece of decorative pewter, shaped like a spiraling seashell, embedded with a blue crystal. A Tarjan machine. She had begun to use what the pirates called the Crystalnet, a communication system that relied on Tarjan tech, impossible to hack.

"All starfighters—deploy!" Ben-Ari said into the crystal. "Destroy them!"

Hangars opened across the Tarjan ships, and the Falcons streaked toward battle. Hundreds of starfighters, each with a single pilot, swarmed with dizzying speed. Their guns fired, but even they could not penetrate the shields.

"Fly behind the enemy frigates!" Ben-Ari said. "There are no shields around their exhaust pipes. Faster!"

She watched from the bridge of the *Dolphin*, lips tight, as the Falcons tried to fly past the three incoming warships.

She watched, heart sinking, as the frigates opened their hangars, and their own starfighters emerged.

Firebirds. Larger than Falcons. Meaner. Deadlier. When she zoomed in, Ben-Ari saw pilots in their cockpits—cyborgs with skinned faces and mocking white eyes.

"We'll take care of them, ma'am," came Kai's voice through the Crystalnet.

The young soldier was flying the lead Falcon. Kai was perhaps only a private in her new army, but in his old life of piracy, he had flown in many battles.

Ben-Ari watched, tense, as space burned before her. Falcons and Firebirds blasted each other with bullets and missiles. Starfighters exploded. Debris flew through space.

The frigates kept charging. They were only moments away now, visible even without a viewport zoom.

A Falcon exploded.

Another.

The cyborg pilots fought with inhuman accuracy, taking out more Falcons. The remaining Falcons were bombarding the enemy, and they destroyed a few Firebirds, but not enough. And more Falcons kept falling.

"Kai, why aren't you using wobble tech?" Ben-Ari said into her crystal. "Jump between the enemy!"

"I can't!" came his voice from the lead Falcon. "Too much shit everywhere—missiles, Firebirds, lasers. If we wobble, we're likely to jump right into them."

"They're fucking butchering you!" Addy cried, standing beside Ben-Ari. She was staring with horror at the dogfights, unable to do a thing.

Ben-Ari stared too, holding her breath, feeling so helpless here aboard the *Dolphin*. Finally, with a storm of bullets, a squad of Falcons made it through the gauntlet of fire. The starfighters reached the enemy frigates. They flew above and below the shields, heading toward the sensitive sterns, and—

Lasers flashed from the frigates in a hundred beams.

Falcons exploded.

Fire blazed across the viewport, momentarily blinding the *Dolphin*'s bridge crew.

"Kai!" Addy shouted, pressing her palms against the screen.

The debris cleared. Ben-Ari exhaled in relief. Many Falcons had fallen. But Kai was still flying, leading a handful of starfighters.

And finally the Falcons began to wobble.

Their crystals shone. Their Tarjan gears turned. As more lasers flashed toward them, the Falcons made short leaps through spacetime, bypassing the barrage. They flitted in and out of reality, firing, vanishing, reappearing, moving forward in spurts.

A handful of Falcons made it past the frigates, the lasers, and Firebirds. They swerved in space, flew back toward the frigates, and opened fire.

Missiles raced toward the frigates' exhaust pipes.

Ben-Ari held her breath, awaiting the devastating explosions.

Lasers flew from the frigates' sterns, taking the missiles out.

Watching from the *Dolphin*, Ben-Ari cursed.

The frigates were only seconds away from Ben-Ari and her armada now.

"Kai!" she blurted out in frustration.

"Don't worry, ma'am!" he said from the cockpit of his Falcon. "I got this."

His squadron vanished. Lights bubbled. The Falcons reappeared in spacetime only meters away from the warships. The heat from the exhaust melted the paint on their hulls. The Falcons unleashed more missiles.

These ones made it.

Mere kilometers away from the Golden Fleet's motherships, one enemy frigate exploded.

Across the *Dolphin*'s bridge, everyone other than Ben-Ari cheered.

She stood still, watching the blazing white fire, jaw locked.

A second frigate exploded. A shock wave blasted out, white in the center, flaring to red and blue. Debris slammed into the *Dolphin*'s shields. More cheers filled the bridge.

But the third and last enemy frigate kept charging.

The remaining Falcons kept pounding it. The frigate's stern caught fire. But the gargantuan warship kept barreling forward.

"Golden Fleet, evasive maneuvers!" Ben-Ari shouted. "Do not engage! Scatter! Back, back!"

The Tarjan starships began to move. To retreat. To try to avoid the incoming frigate.

But the Dreamer's vessel was barreling forward at hypersonic speed, as fast as a bullet.

It plowed into the Golden Fleet, scraping against one pirate ship, slamming aside another, then ramming through several podships.

Ben-Ari stared in silent horror.

She clutched her Star of David amulet.

For a second everyone was silent.

And then the Dreamer's frigate exploded.

Fire. Shattering glass. Twisted metal and screams and blaring klaxons.

Ben-Ari knelt and covered her head. The inferno washed over her. The bridge shattered. The fleet burned. The cosmos itself seemed to crack open.

I'm dying.

Heat and ruin washed over her.

I will never see my family again.

Shards of glass stung her.

I'm still alive. And so I still fight.

She rose. She opened her eyes. She walked through fire toward the enormous viewport that stretched across the *Dolphin*'s bridge, and she beheld devastation.

Several Tarjan starships were gone, shattered into fragments. Other ships burned. Many were listing, dipping toward the gravity well of Delta Draconis. The podships had fared no better. A few had disintegrated into clouds of spores. Others had burst open like rotten pumpkins, revealing quivering innards.

Across the *Dolphin*'s bridge, several monitors had shattered. A few crystals and pipes had fallen. Natasha lay on the deck, unconscious, bleeding from a gash on her head. Addy and Marco were slumped in their seats, moaning, dazed. One crewman lay dead, eyes gazing blankly at the ceiling, a metal shard from a dashboard impaling his chest.

But the starship was still airtight.

The *Dolphin* was still flying.

Ben-Ari stepped toward the captain's station, replacing Natasha.

"Fleet!" she said, speaking into her crystal. "Fly onward! To Delta Draconis! This battle is not over yet."

The remains of the fleet limped onward. Smoldering. Dented. Many ships barely flying at all. Several remained behind, little more than charred hulks.

They flew until Delta Draconis loomed, an enormous planet of blue oceans, vast grasslands, and icy poles. On its equator, Ben-Ari could just make it out. A tiny gray speck, just a pixel on her viewport.

Fort Draconis. An HDF base.

Did Draco Battalion still wait there? Or would she find nothing but cyborgs?

Natasha rose to her feet, clutching her head and muttering.

"What did you do to my fleet, little president?" she asked, bleary-eyed.

"Took it to war," Ben-Ari said. "You have command of the fleet now, Natasha. I'm leading a team down to Delta Draconis. I'm taking a hundred of your best fighters with me." She turned toward Marco and Addy. "And you're coming too. Let's go muster our invasion force."

CHAPTER FIFTEEN

Marco entered the dropship, fastened his harness, and sneezed.

"What a time to catch a cold," he muttered.

"Gesundheit!" Addy said.

Marco cursed. His nose kept running. His throat was raw. He probably had a bit of a fever. The virus had been sweeping through the *Dolphin.*

"Perfect," he said, voice raspy. "I couldn't catch this cold *after* the war. Just had to get sick before the big battle."

Addy rolled her eyes, fastening her own harness. "Oh, you and your man flu, Poet."

They were both standing against the dropship's port bulkhead. Eighteen other fighters were fastening themselves in harnesses too, filling the small rectangular vessel. They were all gruff pirates. Bearded men. Wild women. All of them tattooed, scarred, smirking. They wore shabby crimson trousers and blue coats, the fabric patched and stitched countless times. They carried an assortment of swords, crossbows, and a panoply of guns. A couple wore helmets. Most didn't bother. One man had even brought his pet honey badger to the battle; the creature growled on a leash.

Great, Marco thought. *I'm flying to war with the cast of* The Pirates of Penzance.

Across the *Dolphin*'s hangar, fighters were entering two more dropships. Other motherships were filling their own landing craft. The *Dolphin* gave a sudden jolt. A boom sounded. The hangar shook. Inside the dropship, everyone jerked in their harnesses.

"The fuckers on the planet just hit our mothership!" Addy said. "Sounded like a *Nagamaki* ground-to-space missile."

"You can't tell missiles apart from how they sound," Marco said. Then he sneezed.

"I sure can!" Addy said. "I'm an expert. I've had every type of weapon in the universe lobbed at me." She winked. "Even your sneezes."

Marco wished he could reach into his pocket for his handkerchief. But with the harness, he couldn't even cover his mouth when he sneezed.

"Sorry, Ads," he said. "Care to cook me some chicken soup?"

And suddenly he was back there.

Back home. On Anchor Cove. On the beach.

His home on Earth.

He saw the waves along the golden sand. He walked into his kitchen, and he saw Addy in shorts and a rumpled T-shirt, her golden hair hanging in a loose braid, beautiful in the sunlight streaming through the window. He smelled the chicken soup she always cooked when somebody got sick; her secret ingredient was adding butternut squash. He heard his children laugh, saw them smile, their eyes shining as they ran toward him.

The memories hit him so powerfully that his head spun.

I should be there, he thought. *Back home with my kids. Not here. Not stuck in a dropship, about to plunge through the atmosphere of an alien planet.*

But that home was gone now. The Dreamer had destroyed it. His children were forty-six light-years away, hiding inside the Matterhorn.

Earth. Humanity itself. They were crumbling.

He looked at Addy. She looked back, her blue eyes soft and kind. Marco realized that she was thinking the same thing.

"One more war," he whispered to her.

She nodded. "For old times' sake."

He managed to reach his hand toward her even with the harness. She held it. She nodded and smiled.

There was one harness left. A last soldier entered the dropship.

It was Einav Ben-Ari.

She still wore that little black dress. But she had strapped a bulletproof vest above it, and she wore a helmet, knee and elbow pads, and military boots. She looked ridiculous. But when she spoke, there could be no mistake. Here was the leader of humanity.

"Attention warriors!" she said. "Only days ago, most of you were Basidio Boys. Pirates. Criminals. Lowlifes. Whatever you want to call yourself, I don't give a damn. Today you are all soldiers! Today every one of you fights for humanity! I don't know what awaits us on Delta Draconis. But I know this. Whatever enemy you find, you will fight bravely. You will not turn back in fear. You will charge at evil and kill it!"

"Fuck yeah!" Addy cried.

The pirates roared in approval.

Marco sneezed.

Ben-Ari slammed the dropship door shut. She strapped herself into the harness.

The dropship's pilot took his seat. He was a bald, wiry man with a bushy red beard. The pirates called him Gingerbeard. He grinned, revealing only three teeth, and chugged down a bottle of grog.

"Here we go!" Gingerbeard said, and pulled a lever.

"Here we go," Marco whispered, clutching Addy's hand.

Beneath the dropship, a hatch opened.

The boxy shuttle fell from the *Dolphin* like a bomb, plunging toward the planet.

Marco had plunged down in dropships before. Several times. Each time was worse than the last. And this was no exception.

The shuttle rattled madly. Everyone jerked in their harnesses. Marco's head kept banging against the bulkhead. He wore a helmet, but it barely helped. His head pounded, and his muscles ached, and he sneezed again. Air shrieked around them.

Goddamn, and I thought military dropships were a rough ride, he thought. *They got nothing on pirate shuttles.*

Around him, the pirates hooted and roared and laughed. One man vomited. Marco squeezed Addy's hand tighter. The dropship shook so madly he could barely see. His teeth kept banging together.

Fire.

Fire blazed outside, shining through the narrow window above. The dropship screeched. The port hull dented. Marco narrowed his eyes, gritted his teeth, and every bone in his body rattled inside his skin.

"Here we go, boys!" Addy cried. "Welcome to war!"

One last war, Marco thought, head rattling. *For old times' sake.*

As the dropship shook through atmospheric entry, the faces of the pirates blurred. And he saw his old friends.

Caveman. Sheriff. Pinky. Sergeant Singh. Corporal Diaz. Elvis. Lailani.

Young faces. Pale. Teenagers, that was all. Just kids. Caught in a war. Plunging toward Abaddon, world of the scum.

And suddenly tears were on Marco's cheeks. He was thirty-six now. That had been half a lifetime away.

Almost all those faces were gone. Among them, only Lailani had lived. And maybe she too had fallen.

And he was different. And he was older. And he missed his home. And after two decades of war, he feared this battle far more than any dumb eighteen-year-old boy ever could.

Because he had seen war. He had seen tough warriors weep and cry for their mothers as their lifeblood flowed away. He had seen the terrible cost of victory. He was more experienced than any of these gruff thieves sharing this metal box. And he was afraid.

But Addy was still with him.

And Ben-Ari was still with him.

The two most important women of his life. His two guiding stars.

He tightened his grip on Addy's hand. To his left, Ben-Ari reached out and clasped his other hand.

And his fear faded. He was ready. He was ready again.

One last war.

The fire died outside, and they fell through blue skies.

Sitting at the controls, Gingerbeard shoved a lever. Gears turned and creaked. Wings extended from the dropship, and engines roared. Instead of merely falling, the dropship began to fly.

Gingerbeard looked over his shoulder at the crew. He grinned, displaying his three crooked teeth.

"I hope you didn't shit yourself, kids." He laughed. "We'll be landing at beautiful Fort Draconis in a few minutes, so raise your seats to their upright positions, and if you feel like a last mile-high fuck, you better get busy soon, 'cause—"

Metal and glass shattered.

Gingerbeard's head tore open, spraying blood across the cabin.

Jaws like an enormous chainsaw, filled with sharp teeth, thrust into the dropship.

Soldiers and pirates screamed. Blood sprayed them.

"What the fuck is that?" Addy shouted.

The jaws thrust deeper into the ship, snapping, tearing into what remained of the pilot. Those jaws alone were the size of a crocodile—the *entire* crocodile, snout to tail. White eyes blazed atop the hideous mouth. The creature screeched, a sound that filled the cabin, deafening and ravenous.

"Addy, I think we found your dinosaurs," Marco said.

CHAPTER SIXTEEN

The alien screeched.

Its jaws thrust deeper into the dropship, splattering blood, bones, and strands of red beard.

Gingerbeard's body collapsed, headless.

There goes our pilot, Marco thought.

"I knew it!" Addy screamed, locked in her harness with twenty other soldiers. "I told you, Poet! Fucking dinosaurs!"

"I told you, they're aliens, not dino—" Marco groaned. "Fine, whatever, they're dinosaurs! Just shut up and help me out of this harness."

He pulled at his harness straps, trying to untangle them. Without a pilot, the dropship was plunging downward. Air shrieked through the shattered cockpit. The G-force slammed against the crew. Several pirates passed out.

"Goddamn great fucking day to catch a cold," Marco muttered, finally shoving himself out of the straps. Even with the alien dinosaur shrieking in the cockpit, and their dropship falling toward the ground, Marco couldn't help it. He sneezed.

The vessel suddenly leaped over an air current. The crew jolted in their harnesses. Marco tumbled through the cabin. He fell toward the cockpit—and the waiting jaws of the beast.

The dinosaur's body was still outside. But just the head, thrusting through the broken windshield, was larger than Marco. It was gray and reptilian, with many teeth like needles. The eyes blazed white, full of hatred.

Those eyes were bloodshot. The veins painted red smiley faces.

And then Marco saw it. Cables and gears attached to the dinosaur's skull.

A cyborg.

The creature burrowed deeper into the dropship, teeth snapping. Marco shoved his rifle into those elongated jaws and opened fire.

He shot on automatic. The T57 assault rifle thrummed in his hands. Bullets plowed through the dinosaur's gullet. Blood sprayed. The beast screamed, chomped at the muzzle, but Marco kept firing. He emptied his magazine.

The enormous head thumped down, then slid out from the cockpit. It nearly pulled the T57 out with it. Marco had to tug his rifle free like a hook from a fish.

As the dead creature fell toward the surface, Marco glimpsed a slender body, a coiling tail, and enormous leathery wings. It reminded him of a pterodactyl, but it had six legs, each tipped with curved claws.

With the dinosaur dead, a new problem presented itself.

Dear old Gingerbeard, their beloved pilot, had no head. And they were falling fast.

Grimacing, Marco shoved the headless body aside and grabbed the bloodied controls. It was a Tarjan machine, like everything else in the Golden Fleet. A dizzying array of gears, pipes, and astrolabes spread across the cockpit. But the decorative yoke was easy enough to understand, even if he couldn't read the runes engraved onto it. Marco grabbed that.

"Poet, you can't fly!" Addy shouted from behind.

"Better than Gingerbeard can!" Marco shouted back, pulling the yoke.

The dropship was pointing downward. Air blasted through the shattered windshield, washing over Marco. The ground was directly below, rushing up toward them. Marco saw grasslands. Snowcapped mountains. A river. He couldn't see the military base from here, but right now he just wanted to find the sky.

He yanked back on the yoke with all his strength, grunting with effort. The forces of physics pounded him like invisible fists. His head exploded with pain. He kept pulling, ignoring the agony.

The prow rose angle by angle. He kept pulling. Finally he saw a blue horizon. He leaned back, pressing a foot against the dashboard, as the dropship leveled off.

Their wings found the air, and they glided through the sky.

Marco almost felt relieved. Then he saw them.

Three more dinosaurs. Gears and cables in their skulls. Flying toward him.

Addy hopped into the cockpit with Marco. She grinned.

"Dragons!" she said.

"I finally agreed to call them dinosaurs, and now you're calling them dragons?" he said. "Just fire the rotary gun. I'll fly, you fire!"

Addy gasped. "I'm not going to shoot defenseless dragons!"

"Addy!"

She groaned. "Fine, fine." She grabbed the trigger and unleashed a hailstorm of bullets. "Geez, you're cranky when you have a man flu."

The bullets plowed through one cyborg dinosaur. The creature screeched and fell, blood spraying.

Two more charged toward the dropship, wings stirring the bloody mist.

Addy's bullets took out one. Marco tried to yaw, to dodge the second beast, but it stormed closer, and—

Claws grabbed the dropship.

Everyone screamed.

One claw reached into the cockpit, slashing blindly. Tarjan pipes, vials, and crystals shattered. Addy yelped and leaped back, narrowly dodging the assault. The enormous talons destroyed the cannon triggers.

"Fucking dragon!" Addy shouted, pressing herself against the bulkhead. "It ruined my cannon!"

The claws swung through the cockpit. Marco leaned back, barely dodging them. Each claw was like a katana.

Bullets shrieked.

Ben-Ari entered the cockpit, firing an assault rifle, her eyes narrowed and hard.

The bullets plowed through scaly flesh. One severed claw clanged onto the deck. The dinosaur pulled back from the cockpit, screeching. Ben-Ari took two steps forward, loaded a fresh magazine, and fired through the broken canopy. Her bullets shredded the dinosaur's neck, revealing cables and microchips.

The cyborg fell, loose cables dangling like entrails.

"Just once I want a space drop to go smoothly," Marco muttered.

Thankfully, the yoke was still functional. Marco righted the dropship, and he saw it in the distance. Fort Draconis.

It rose on the grasslands—a complex of concrete buildings, electric fences, guard towers, and a vacant spaceport. Here was the HDF's most distant outpost from Earth, home of the Draco Brigade, among humanity's finest warriors.

As Marco flew closer, his heart sank.

"We're too late," Addy whispered.

They all stared silently.

Fort Draconis was under attack.

"No," Marco said. "Not too late. Draco Brigade still fights."

Soldiers stood on walls and in guard towers, firing machine guns, desperately holding back the enemy.

An army surrounded the fort. Hundreds of reptilian beasts bellowed and thundered, creatures of scales and wires, of claws and gears, of burning fury and cold calculations. They swarmed at the walls. Slammed into fences. Tore at the towers. A few broke into the courtyard, and men screamed and died.

The natives of Delta Draconis were attacking.

"Cyborg dinosaurs are *definitely* going into *Freaks of the Galaxy IV,*" Addy said. "Poet, fly closer! I want to take some photos for my book."

"Put your camera down and grab your gun," Marco said.

She gasped. "I don't want to kill them! They're adorable."

"They're cyborgs, Addy. They serve the Dreamer."

"But they're cute!"

"They're enormous killing machines!"

Addy pouted, snapped a few photos, then grabbed her gun. "Fine. But I'm still gonna describe them as cute in my book."

Marco descended toward the base. The wind roared through the shattered cockpit. With the dropship's rotary cannon destroyed, both Ben-Ari and Addy thrust their rifles through the broken windshield.

Several other dropships were descending with them. All were Golden Fleet vessels, containing Tarjan machines only, no computers. If the Dreamer was broadcasting any code from below, they were immune.

The dropships took attack formation, swooped toward the base, and opened fire.

Bullets pounded the aliens. The creatures screeched and fell.

Marco flew higher, then swooped for another strafing round, the sun at his back. Ben-Ari stood to his left, Addy to his right, both screaming as they fired on automatic.

I'm flying a spaceship over an alien world, Marco thought, *flanked by two gorgeous blondes firing assault rifles at cyborg dinosaurs. And one of those women is wearing a sexy cocktail dress. Truly, this wasn't what I expected when I joined the army.*

The dropships circled the fort again, strafing the dinosaurs. Across the walls and towers, survivors of the Draco Brigade cheered. Many corpses lay across the courtyard—human and dinosaur alike. One enormous beast, carnivorous and scaly, was rampaging through the complex, its six paws shaking the earth. Soldiers fired on the colossal predator, only for its fangs, claws, and whipping tail to knock them down. Marco couldn't even strafe the bastard without danger of hitting the troops.

A group of dinosaurs was assaulting the northern wall. The beasts wore metal helmets buzzing with electricity, and cables ran across their bodies, bolted into the scaly flesh. The gargantuan cyborgs were pounding the concrete, ripping down barbed wire, and slamming at a guard tower. Cracks webbed across the wall. Chunks of concrete fell, raising clouds of dust. Guards vanished among the rubble. The tower cracked and collapsed, and the guard screamed, fired a few last bullets, then crashed to the ground.

The walls were breached.

The dinosaurs roared in triumph and began trudging into the base.

Marco descended, swooping mere meters above the beasts. Addy and Ben-Ari opened fire. Bullets slammed into scales, jaws, and the metal caps bolted into the aliens' heads.

The enormous cyborgs snapped their jaws, trying to catch the dropship, but Marco soared, dodging the teeth.

He flew toward the three suns, then swooped back toward the dinosaurs.

The monsters opened their jaws wide and blasted streams of fire.

"Poet, look!" Addy said. "They *are* dragons! I told you!"

Marco banked hard, desperate to escape the flames. The geysers rose too fast. Fire washed over the stern. The podship rocked. Back in the hold, the pirates shouted and cursed. One screamed in agony.

Another flaming jet hit them. It bathed the podship's undercarriage. A third stream washed over a wing.

Marco tried to rise higher. The yoke heated in his hand, and he grimaced, skin burning. He yawed, tried to spin around, to engage the enemy, but—

Claws slashed the ship.

Jaws snapped at the cockpit.

Wings pounded them.

The pterodactyls were back.

Marco screamed. The women fired their guns. The pirates roared behind.

The winged reptiles kept attacking, brutalizing the charred ship, and an engine died. Jaws reached into the cockpit, snapping madly, spraying saliva. Addy and Ben-Ari screamed, filling the jaws with bullets, and Marco tried to keep flying, but a mighty tail hit the dropship, and then they were falling.

The dropship became a hunk of useless metal filled with screaming humans.

Metal and flesh, Marco thought. *Just another cyborg. Maybe that's what all humans have become.*

"Poet!" Addy screamed.

They were plunging down. The ground raced up to meet them. Marco grabbed the hot yoke, ignoring his burning hands. He pulled back with all his strength, feet pressed against the dashboard.

At least with this fucking cold I can't smell my hands burning, he thought.

The prow rose, and then—

Everyone screamed.

They crashed through a guard tower, ripping off its roof, bending its iron beams. Then the dropship plummeted toward the courtyard, plowed through the soil, and hit a concrete wall.

The crashed ship lay still. Silent.

Ridiculously, Marco sneezed.

* * * * *

"Addy?" Marco rasped, sitting in the smoldering ruin of the dropship. "Ben-Ari?"

They rose, groaning. Ben-Ari had banged her forehead against a dashboard, and blood trickled down her forehead. Addy groaned, covered in scratches and bruises.

"Are you all right?" Marco asked, heart pounding.

"I—" Ben-Ari began.

Jaws clamped down around the cockpit. Teeth drove through the hull, bending the iron.

Pirates and soldiers cursed and screamed.

The dinosaur began lifting the entire dropship off the ground.

Addy leaped through the broken windshield, hopped onto the crumpled nose of the dropship, and fired her rifle upward.

"Die, freak!" she howled.

The dinosaur swung the dropship like a mere toy. Addy screamed, tumbling off the prow.

Inside the cockpit, Marco jerked in his seat, and Ben-Ari slammed against him. Pirates shouted in the hold.

"Addy!" Marco cried.

The dinosaur slammed the ship onto the ground. The deck dented. Control panels shattered. Marco kept his arms around Ben-Ari, keeping her from flying out the windshield.

Bullets roared outside. Addy shouted. She was alive!

The dinosaur roared. The jaws released the dropship. The dented, cracked metal box slammed onto the ground again.

Marco and Ben-Ari glanced at each other.

Then they burst out from the mangled ship, guns blasting.

A spiked tail slammed down in front of them. A claw swiped along the ground, ripping up soil, and slammed into Ben-Ari. She flew through the air, hit the dropship's charred hull, and slumped to the ground.

Marco had no time to check on the president. Not with this beast rampaging.

He ran. The tail slammed down again, cracking the earth. Marco skidded to a halt, nearly crushed. He spun around, and he found himself facing colossal jaws. The hellmouth gaped open, larger than him, bathing him with heat and stench. The teeth of the beast shone like a portcullis. The red gullet swirled like a cauldron of molten metal, the heat rising, and the flames leaped.

Marco jumped aside and flattened himself on the ground.

The blaze of dragonfire streamed mere centimeters away, spinning, shrieking, blazing white flaring out to blue and furious red. The inferno slammed into a concrete wall, melting it.

From behind the monster—a woman crying out. The hailstorm of bullets.

Addy was there!

With charred fingers, Marco loaded a fresh magazine.

Addy's bullets slammed into the reptilian terror, chipping scales, drawing blood. The beast shut its jaws, and the flames died, leaving only smoke and shedding ash like flakes of burnt skin. Six clawed feet pounded the earth, shaking the courtyard. The creature spun toward Addy and roared.

Marco ducked under the swinging tail, then ran.

"Addy, watch out!" he screamed as the monster breathed more fire.

She leaped aside. The flames roared across the courtyard, missing her.

Marco jumped onto the dinosaur's tail, clung to sharp scales, and scurried onto its back.

"What are you doing, Poet?" Addy shouted from below.

"Improvising!" he shouted, racing up the dinosaur's back, grabbing its dorsal spikes like rungs in a ladder.

"Are you high on flu medicine again?" she cried.

Marco ignored her. He kept climbing. The beast bucked, but Marco clung to its spikes. The feet slammed back down, cracking the cement courtyard, and the dinosaur swung its head toward Addy again.

Marco reached the beast's lumpy head, pointed his muzzle at the nape, and opened fire.

His bullets roared out, pounding into scales, tearing deep into thick, leathery skin. The bullet holes revealed cables and microchips embedded into the flesh.

The monster roared. Marco slipped, nearly fell off, and grabbed a fin. His feet dangled. He held on with one hand. The monster was bucking, bellowing, trying to shake him off.

Marco pulled himself back to his feet. He stood between the dinosaur's shoulder blades, holding a spike with one hand.

He slammed the muzzle into the open wound. He fired again, emptying the magazine.

He heard the bullets tear muscle. Rip cables. Snap the spine just below the skull.

The creature's head pitched forward, then pounded against the ground. Its tail thumped onto the crashed dropship, crushing the smoldering hunk of metal.

Marco climbed off the dead dinosaur, stood on shaky legs, and sneezed.

Addy pointed at the dead beast. "That still only counts as one!"

"Thanks, Gimli," Marco said.

His head spun, and he nearly fell. Addy had to catch him.

* * * * *

Everything hurt and the world careened around Marco. He was running a fever, he thought. He had bruised his body in the fall, maybe even cracked a bone. He was lucky to be alive, he supposed. But that didn't make the pain any easier to bear.

Grimacing, he looked around the courtyard. Ben-Ari was crawling across the ground, trying to reach them. Halfway there, the president paused to vomit. Blood still dripped from her head. She looked up at Marco, face pale, eyes red.

Beside Marco, a man ran. Burning. A living torch. He fell and rolled and screamed as the fire consumed him.

Another man crawled toward him. He was missing the lower half of his body, not just the legs but half his abdomen too. He somehow still lived. Begging.

Across the courtyard, the battle raged on. Pirates and soldiers fought side by side, resisting the enemy. The towering, reptilian cyborgs blasted fire, swung tails, and climbed the remaining walls.

"Poet!" Addy was shaking him. She stood right beside him, but sounded a light-year away. "Poet, are you okay?"

His ears rang. He was bleeding somewhere. The blood was dripping onto his fingers. His hands were still burnt. But he nodded.

"Ben-Ari is hurt," he said.

He trudged across the rubble-strewn courtyard toward his president, his boots sluicing through blood. A clawed foot slammed down. Marco fired upward, hitting a beast's underbelly. It toppled over, burying a squad of firing soldiers. Marco walked onward. He stepped over a severed arm. He saw a discarded boot, smoke rising from inside. Maybe the foot was inside too. He nearly fainted. He breathed smoke and coughed. But he forced himself to keep going. Even as he advanced through the killing field, he knelt, collecting ammo from dead soldiers, restocking. A soldier's instinct, cold and practical.

He reached Ben-Ari and knelt before her.

"Einav, I'm here."

She grabbed him. She was trembling. Pale. Her skin was gray, and she seemed to have aged a decade.

"Oh, Marco ..."

Shadows blocked the sun. Shrieks sounded above. Marco looked up to see pterodactyls swooping toward the base.

He rose and fired at the sky.

His bullets tore through a pterodactyl's neck. The creature spat blood, dived, and slammed into the barracks. Gears spilled from its ripped belly. The corpse slumped to the ground, leathern wings draping over soldiers.

Ben-Ari struggled to rise. She swayed, and Marco grabbed her.

"I'm ... dizzy," she said. She wiped blood off her head.

"You've got a concussion," Marco said. "I—"

A creature landed before him, twice his height, with a head like a cobra. Enormous flaps of scaly skin extended around its jaws, forming a shimmering hood in greens and whites. The scales danced. Patterns undulated.

Marco stared, dazed. The creature slithered closer, an enormous serpent, larger than the mightiest python, eyes flashing yellow, scales chinking. The hood became a living tapestry, glinting and shining, a kaleidoscope of endless dimensions, calling to him. He saw endless patterns in the depths of those scales, gazed into a deeper reality. He felt his consciousness diving into a new realm, a place of racing electricity and ghosts in the machine.

A voice slithered inside him.

"Hello, Marco."

He shouted and fired his gun.

Bullets slammed into the creature, and suddenly Marco was back in reality. The dinosaur folded its hood, and Marco blinked. The spell was broken. He saw cables dangling from the creature's head. Saw an iron helmet, flashing with lights. Just a snake, not even very large, with some metal contraption attached.

He fired, hitting the electronics. Electricity sparked across the alien, and it fell.

Breathing heavily, Marco climbed onto a pile of fallen concrete. He surveyed the battle.

Falcons had joined the dropships. The starfighters were circling the base, engines roaring, guns pounding the dinosaurs. The enormous bodies kept falling, shaking the earth. Several pterodactyls charged into the lines of starfighters, and explosions rocked the sky. Falcons and dinosaurs burned and crashed onto the grasslands.

We're winning, Marco thought. *At a heavy cost, yes. But this day will go to humanity.*

That's when he heard the rumble behind him.

Addy screamed and pointed.

Behind Marco, the rumble grew louder. The pile of concrete trembled.

He gulped and turned around.

A gargantuan cyborg approached him. An enormous ogre, hunched over, larger than the largest dinosaur. A creature woven from a hundred human bodies.

For a moment Marco could only stare in horror.

It was the most hideous cyborg Marco had seen so far.

Humans formed its corded muscles, spines curving, limbs braided together, naked and quivering. Humans formed its head, rolled up into a sphere, their limbs and torsos bulging across the cranium like the folds in a brain. Cables and metal rods ran across this bundle of humanity, holding it together like an exoskeleton. The creature took a step forward, shaking the courtyard. Its mouth, woven of human limbs, opened with a scream. Sharpened femurs formed its teeth, and a single body formed a flicking tongue. Instead of eyes, the nightmare peered through the bores of two rotary cannons.

Those cannons pointed at Marco.

He jumped aside.

Bullets slammed into the pile of concrete where he had stood.

Marco rolled across the ground, took cover behind a dead dinosaur, and slung his rifle over the scaly carcass. He opened fire. His bullets thudded into the enormous beast of many bodies. The giant barely seemed to notice. It thundered toward him, its hideous jaws opening again.

Marco was out of bullets. Hands shaking, he reached toward a dead soldier, pulled more magazines from the poor man's vest. Within seconds, he was firing again. The bullets sank into the monster's flesh. The naked humans forming the creature twisted. A few screamed.

They're still alive, Marco realized, feeling sick.

The creature reached down a massive hand, each finger an entire body. It grabbed the dinosaur corpse Marco was hiding behind. Bellowing, the monster hurled the dead dinosaur across the courtyard, where it slammed into several soldiers.

Marco refused to flee. He stood before the monstrosity, firing his rifle. Leaving the wounded Ben-Ari behind a pile of concrete, Addy ran up to Marco, joining her bullets to his.

But the bullets did nothing. Some sank into the human muscles. Others sparked against the metal chassis holding the beast together. None did much damage. The monster took another step toward Marco and Addy, leaned down, and opened its enormous jaws.

Marco screamed and shoved Addy back.

The jaws closed around him.

He howled. The teeth, created from sharpened bones, scraped across him. Marco shoved against gums formed from human limbs, trying to stop the mouth from closing, from crushing him. The creature raised its head, lifting Marco high above the ground. He nearly tumbled down the monster's gullet. Gears churned inside the stomach, forming a meat grinder. Marco clung to the gums, struggling to climb out.

Addy was shouting somewhere below, firing on the beast. Bullets pierced the human corpses comprising the creature. Some of those bullets entered the cavernous mouth, streaking dangerously close to Marco.

"Don't shoot, you idiot!" he cried hoarsely, not sure Addy could hear.

The jaws were constricting him. He pushed against them, desperate to keep them open. A tooth scraped across his side, ripping his uniform. Marco's boots pressed against human faces. They were laughing, hissing, snapping at him.

"Leave my husband alone, freak!" Addy shouted. She ran toward the beast, lifted a piece of scrap metal, and swung it like a sword.

The metal ripped into the monster's knee.

The creature howled, mouth opening wide.

Marco fell from the mouth, tumbled through the air, and hit the ground.

He tried to rise. But at once, the beast slammed a foot onto him. The foot was enormous, woven of several human bodies, their limbs braided together, their heads serving as toes.

Weight pressed on Marco, nearly snapping his bones. He pushed back with all his strength, trying to shove the foot off. The human heads laughed, their white eyes spinning. They began to bite him. He roared.

A nightmare, Marco thought. *This is just a nightmare. This can't be real. This is just the Dreamer's dream.*

"Good job, Poet!" Addy said. "Keep distracting him!"

He shoved against the colossal foot, groaning. The toes grinned and laughed.

"Hello, Marco!" one toe said.

"Pleasure to eat you!" said another and sank its teeth into his shoulder.

"Something is afoot!" said a third toe, laughing, and bit Marco's arm.

He roared, punching at the toes, and drove his knee into the sole. The strange toes grunted. He kept shoving, but the weight increased. He couldn't breathe.

With hazy eyes, he glimpsed Addy climbing the enormous creature. She scurried up its back, raised her rifle high, then slammed the wooden stock down. Again. Again.

"Ugh, Addy!" Marco groaned beneath the monstrous foot. "You weigh a ton!"

"Oh shut up!" she shouted from atop the monster. "You can't even feel me."

He grimaced. "The weight just doubled!"

Ignoring him, Addy kept slamming down her rifle like a hammer. Lying pinned beneath the foot, Marco realized what she was doing.

She had found a weak spot in the exoskeleton—this network of iron straps holding the beast together.

She slammed her rifle down again. Again. Denting the iron. Finally—an intersection of bars shattered.

Iron slats fell from the monster like old scabs. More and more. They clattered onto the ground.

For a moment the giant bundle of humans maintained its form.

Then it broke apart. Dozens of bodies fell onto the ground and rolled.

Above Marco, the strange foot came apart, crumbling into separate bodies.

Marco groaned, shoved himself up, and coughed. He looked around him at the scattered corpses, then up at Addy. She stood before him, coated in dust and her enemies' blood.

"That counts as one too," Marco said.

She gasped. "What?" She gestured around. "Look at all these bodies! There's a hundred at least!"

"There are *now*. It was one creature when you killed it."

She groaned. "Can I at least add it to *Freaks of the Galaxy IV*?"

She was joking, but he saw the horror in her eyes.

Marco sniffed, and his eyes watered, and it wasn't only the cold. He nodded. He walked toward Addy and embraced her.

"Eww, you have a cold!" She pushed him back, then laughed, and shed tears too, and embraced him.

The battle was winding down. Across the base, humans were shooting down the last cyborgs. The Falcons patrolled overhead, firing on any dinosaurs that still moved.

We won, Marco thought. *Hundreds died here. But we won this world.*

He turned around, seeking Ben-Ari.

His heart shattered.

"Einav!" he shouted.

He ran toward her, leaping over dead bodies.

Ben-Ari lay in a puddle of blood, skin gray, eyes closed.

CHAPTER SEVENTEEN

She fell down a dark hole.

For long eras, she tumbled in darkness.

"Marco!" she tried to whisper. To reach out to him. But all vision faded. And Einav Ben-Ari vanished into the abyss.

The pain on her head faded. She was no longer bleeding. No longer shaking. The nightmares around her—all were gone. The war fell to silence.

Her memories were fading already. She remembered banging her head on a dashboard. Remembered that blood kept getting in her eyes. She remembered crawling, vomiting, and Marco holding her, and …

What were those things?

Just dreams. That was all.

"I'm scared," she whispered.

She lay in her bed, a cot in an armored corps base somewhere in the desert. A shadow sat at the beside, warm and comforting. The night light glinted on dark hair.

"*Ima*?" she whispered. The Hebrew word for mother. "I had a bad dream, *Ima*. Monsters on a distant world. Big teeth. Claws. Monsters made from men."

Her mother kissed her forehead. "Poor little Einav. You're burning up."

"*Ima*, I'm scared. Don't leave me. Don't ever leave me."

Her mother stroked her hair. "I'm here, *motek*. I'm never going to leave you. *Ima* is always here."

Finally Einav closed her eyes and slept.

When she awoke, she was standing in a graveyard—a military cemetery outside some infantry base in a cold northern land. The rain kept falling, and a cantor prayed, and her father wept. Little Einav stood, wearing black. Watching them lower her mother into the grave.

In accordance with their faith, Mother had no coffin. No chemicals to preserve the body. Noa Ben-Ari was wrapped in a simple shroud. The bee had stung her just that morning, only a few hours ago, while mother and daughter ran through the field, collecting flowers.

It's my fault, Einav thought, only seven years old but feeling so much older. *I killed you, Ima. I'm sorry.*

She lowered her head, and the raindrops mingled with her tears.

When she looked up, she was in another military base. She was fifteen and hurt and so angry. She stood on the sand, watching the rocket streak toward space, leaving a white trail. Her father was on that rocket. The famous Colonel Yoram Ben-Ari, scion of the great military dynasty. Flying to the stars again. Leaving her here.

The sergeant came to see her, and they huddled between the tanks and smoked a joint. The next night, the corporal gave her vodka from his canteen, and she drank so much she threw up, maybe passed out. She woke up in his bed. He was pinning down her wrists. Thrusting. She tried to roll away, but she was too drunk, too weak. And then a sergeant was on top of her, a different man, and she slept again, and she wept for days. And she ran away from the base, only for their jeeps to catch her in the desert, to bring her home. She smoked a cigarette outside, staring at the dunes, watching the stars. Fifteen and broken, virginity shattered like so much shrapnel on the sand.

When the dawn rose, she was eighteen. She was Cadet Einav Ben-Ari. The daughter of a famous colonel and diplomat. The granddaughter of a great general who had fought the scum. She was the heiress of a military dynasty going back centuries. She came from a land that no longer existed. From a country the enemy had wiped off the map. She was sand and fire.

The army was her life. She had been bred, born, groomed for this. So she stood in the yard, and she saluted, and she took her vows. She enlisted.

And she excelled.

She had always excelled.

The sun rose and fell, and the world turned, and the war went on. The scum burned the cities of men, and starships winked out in the void.

She was not rich enough for Julius Military Academy, that prestigious dream of wealthier families, but at her local Officer

Candidate School, she rose to the top of her class. For two years, as the world burned around her, she studied military history, tactics, and leadership. She was a studious youth, her nose always in a book, a gun always on her hip, and she carried with her the medals of her ancestors. Across the world, hundreds of millions of boys and girls trained to kill. She trained to send them to their deaths.

The sun fell, and the sun rose, and she was twenty. A commissioned officer of Earth. Ensign Einav Ben-Ari entered Fort Djemila in the African desert, the golden insignia on her shoulders freshly forged.

Marco entered her trailer.

"I will fight," he said, eighteen years old and so scared and so brave.

She led them. She roared for them. She raised their banner. And they plunged into the nightmares.

Everywhere—the aliens. Scuttling centipedes in the tunnels and spiders in the depths. Gray humanoids from the abyss of humanity, wrinkly and glaring with wicked eyes. And she fought. And she led them on.

And she rose in the ranks. From ensign to major. To president. To wife and mother.

And she ran. She was running down the street, holding her son. Little Carl, only three weeks old. She burst into the medical clinic.

"Help!" she cried. "Somebody help him!"

Because her son was gray. He was not breathing.

The nurses ran, they performed CPR, and Carl coughed. He spat out the hardened ball of mucus in his throat. He breathed again. For three long weeks, he stayed in the hospital, hooked up to machines, and Ben-Ari never left him. She ran the Human Commonwealth from his bedside. She commanded a panoply of planets and moons from a little blue room with a sick little miracle.

"I'm here, sweetheart," she whispered, stroking her son's hair. "*Ima* is here. I'll never leave you."

Not like my mother left me. There is no bee that can take me away. No monster in the universe that can tear us apart.

But she was not there now.

She had left him.

She had flown into space. She had risen on a rocket, leaving a white trail through the sky. The famous general. The Golden Lioness. Flying to war while her son remained behind.

He was three now, maybe four due to time dilation. She missed him so much.

"How could I have left you?" Ben-Ari whispered. "I'm sorry, Carl. I'm sorry. I have to come back. I have to come back!"

A distant voice spoke. Muffled. Kind.

"Come back."

A hand touched her cheek, but it seemed like a ghost hand, a feeling from another dimension.

She reached out and clasped it.

The hand tightened around hers.

"I'm here," he said.

"Pull me up," she whispered.

His grip was hard, but warm and comforting. She opened her eyes, blinking feebly in the light. At first she thought it was Noah, her dear husband. But she blinked again, and he came into focus.

She saw a kind face. Brown hair and a short beard. It was not her husband. It was her best friend.

"Marco!" she said, and she sat up, then tried to stand.

He smiled. "Take it easy, Einav." Gently he guided her back down. "You suffered a concussion. You're fine now. But you need to rest."

Ben-Ari looked around her. She was in an infirmary. An open window revealed the grassy plains of Delta Draconis. An IV was attached to her arm, flowers bloomed in a vase, and a crucifix hung over her bed.

Marco noticed her gaze. "Um, yeah, sorry about the cross. I told them you were Jewish, but this was the only room left, and …"

Ben-Ari blinked at him, then burst out laughing. Marco laughed too, sat on the bedside, and hugged her.

"Oh, Marco." She wrapped her arms around him. "I thought I was dead. Thank you."

"For what, Einav?" he whispered, holding her against him.

"For being there. For always being with me. For never leaving me alone."

He looked at her, his brown eyes wise. The kindest eyes she knew. But there was pain in them too. There was regret. Marco too was consumed with nightmares. He too missed home.

She caressed his cheek, and she smiled softly. With her smile, she said more than words ever could. The pain left Marco's eyes. He understood.

The door banged open.

Addy burst into the room.

"Poet, Poet!" she said. "I was just outside, and I saw a baby dinosaur, and it wasn't even a cyborg, and it has *three tails*, and I really think it's a freak, because all the other dinosaurs have one tail, and—" She paused and blinked. "Oh hi, Einav! I mean—ma'am. I mean—President? I mean—you're awake! How's your head?"

Ben-Ari looked at her. She smiled, and she tried to make it a warm smile, a comforting smile, but a tear flowed down her cheek.

Addy was beside her at once, wrapping Ben-Ari in a warm embrace. The three friends sat together, holding one another.

Ben-Ari was their leader. Their commander-in-chief. The woman who had led them throughout so many battles. But right now she was not giving strength, but receiving it. With Marco on one side, Addy on the other, she felt safe. She was among her best friends.

I miss home, she thought. *I miss my family.*

"Tell me how the battle ended," Ben-Ari said. "Tell me about this base."

Marco lowered his head. "Two thousand soldiers of the Draco Brigade fell fighting the enemy." He took a deep breath, then looked into her eyes. "But three thousand still remain. All are eager to fight. We will take this army to Haven. And we will win this war."

Ben-Ari closed her eyes. She thought of that girl long ago. Growing up in military bases. Groomed to become a soldier. To fight a forever war. A girl lost.

She opened her eyes and looked at her friends. She nodded.

"We will win this war."

"Einav, there's one more thing." Marco took her hand in his. "This base has an Isaac Wormhole generator. We can call home."

Ben-Ari stood up. Her head began to spin. She looked at her companions.

"Can I lean on you?"

Marco and Addy nodded.

"Always," they said together.

They walked through the base. Einav walked in the middle, her friends supporting her. A group of soldiers walked by, saw their president, stood at attention, and saluted.

Ben-Ari realized she was *still* wearing that cocktail dress.

Goddammit.

They walked down concrete corridors, up a staircase, past barracks and armories and offices, and finally into a war room.

Kai stood there by an array of controls. He saluted.

"Ma'am! I examined the system. No sign of the virus, ma'am. You should be ready to go. How is your head, ma'am?"

Addy slapped him. "She had a concussion, dumbass. What do you think?"

"I'm fine." Ben-Ari sat down at the dashboard. "Let's call home."

Sudden fear stabbed her. Last time she had talked to her family, the call had died. A cyborg attack? Ben-Ari had not heard from Earth since. When she called the Matterhorn, would her husband and son still be alive?

But first she would broadcast her words to the entire planet. To the embattled species she led.

Kai pressed a few buttons, and antennae adjusted outside. Lavender light shone. A hairline beam shone outside like a strand of cobweb in the dawn. An Isaac Wormhole. A portal, only a few atoms wide, stretching to Earth.

If only we could build wormholes large enough to fly through, she thought. *If only I could hug my son.*

She wiped her eyes, and she spoke into a microphone, transmitting her words to Earth.

"Fellow humans,

This is President Einav Ben-Ari, speaking to you from a Human Defense Force base.

I fight on the front line of the war against the machines. So do you. Every home, every hill and valley, everywhere a human still breathes—that is the front line. The war is everywhere. And every battle matters. Every victory brings us closer to our ultimate triumph.

I know that you suffered hardship. I know that sometimes you came close to despair. Or that you despair already. But I know too that there is hope for humanity. That life can survive. That we can awake from these nightmares.

He calls himself the Dreamer, but we choose not to dream. He is a machine, but we choose to remain human. He thinks he can torment us, deform us, kill us for sport. He does not know our strength.

It is dark now. You are afraid. The enemy is everywhere.

But I still fight.

If you can hear this, if you are still a living, breathing human—you still fight too.

They call me the Golden Lioness. And I still roar for Earth.

If you hear me, have hope. Fight the enemy with every breath. With every bullet, blade, or even sticks and stones. Your government still stands. Your army still smites the enemy. Your hope is not lost.

I do not know when victory will come. But I pray that when we speak again, the sun shines brighter, and the phoenix banner rises high above Earth and her colonies.

Godspeed, fellow humans."

She ended the transmission.

Then she called a specific location. She called the Matterhorn.

Addy and Marco gathered around her. Everyone was nervous. Quiet. Waiting as the call rang.

And on Earth, they answered. They were there. They were still alive.

Noah, her beloved husband. Carl, their beautiful little boy. Terri and Roza and Sam.

Their families.

"Mommy!" Carl said.

"Mommy, Daddy!" cried the twins.

Sitting here in the war room, forty-six light-years from home, they shed tears. They laughed. They touched hands through the monitor. They told stories and jokes and wept.

"I love you," they said over and over. "I miss you so much."

I was a girl lost, Ben-Ari thought. *I was a girl in darkness and under a searing desert sun. I was a girl trapped in a nightmare. But this is not a dream. This is real. They are real. They are home.*

After the power ran low and the call home ended, Ben-Ari rose to her feet and wiped her eyes. She turned toward the others.

"Find me a uniform," she said. "I've got a war to win."

CHAPTER EIGHTEEN

Ben-Ari stood alone on the grassy hill, gazing down at distant Fort Draconis.

They had told her she was crazy to walk here alone. To explore the wilderness of an alien world swarming with dinosaurs? With the Dreamer still out there? She was president now! She couldn't just go out walking alone. Not without a full security detail, barricades around the perimeter, and a no-fly zone above.

But that had been before Earth had fallen.

She was forty-six light-years away. The rest of her government was gone.

If she wanted, she would walk alone. And she needed to walk alone. Like she used to so often as a younger officer. To escape all the voices—her ministers, generals, journalists, the endless chorus of humanity. To find true silence. And to think.

I lead humanity.

It was a thought that still had not sunken in. Not even four years into her presidency.

She climbed the grassy hill. Soft wind blew, playing with her hair. She almost always wore it in a ponytail, but today it flowed free. She wanted to feel the wind. She inhaled deeply, smelling the grass, flowers, the clear sky of this distant world.

A beautiful world. Pristine. A perfect world to begin again.

We can rebuild here, she thought. *Restart humanity on a virgin planet. What awaits on Earth but death and desolation?*

The temptation filled her. But this planet was not her home. For all its beauty, this was not her world. She would trade ten million heavens for the hope of saving Earth from hell.

She looked down at the military base in the valley. Three thousand troops gathered there for war. She led them.

She looked up at the sky. Delta Draconis's three suns were setting. The stars emerged. She looked at the alien constellations, and she imagined that she spotted Sol among the multitudes of stars.

Earth was there. She led it.

Humanity. This young, curious species. The species that had come out of Africa and colonized a world teeming with life. The species that had built pyramids and cathedrals. That had created classical music and literature and a panoply of art so beautiful it could make her weep. The species of Galileo, Newton, Einstein. Of Mozart and Chuck Berry and the New Spiders from Mars. A species of much cruelty and sin too, yes. The species of holy wars. Of world wars. Of hatred and holocaust.

It was all hers now. Her shame and triumph. Her legacy. Her people.

It was strange. As a woman, the product of millions of years of evolution, she should care about her own genetic material first. She should place little Carl, her pride and joy, as her top priority. She should return to him, scoop him up into her embrace, and flee with him. She should be a mother first and foremost.

Yes, it was strange. As an Israeli, thinking back on human history, she should find more bitterness in her heart. After all, her people had been brutalized, oppressed, butchered by other humans for thousands of years. Humanity had placed her people in chains in Egypt. Had taken them to captivity in Babylon. The Romans had destroyed their cities, and the Inquisitors had broken them on the racks. The crusaders had destroyed their villages, and the pogroms had broken their backs. The ovens had burned the millions of them. The wars had set their tiny homeland ablaze.

By all rights, she should curse humanity. She should care only for her family. And for the last remnants of her own people—oppressed for millennia, maybe finally freed from its tormenting siblings in this vicious brotherhood of man. She should care about Carl first. About Israel second. About Earth only last.

And yet …

And yet.

She was human.

A mother, yes. An Israeli, yes. The protector of a beautiful child and the scion of a people nearly lost to history.

But human.

The leader of humanity.

The defender of a legacy.

And so she must overcome her genetic instincts, rise above the evolutionary ties of family and tribe. It was her, Einav Ben-Ari, who had to protect the memory of this young, arrogant, often violent, but just as often noble species. It was she who could have no more family. No more culture or nation. She who had to speak not for any one family, or any one tribe, but for the tapestry of human experience.

For Japan's golden temples under the rising sun. For the voices rising just as high in opera houses. For the Phantom composing songs for Christine. For the chef roasting ducks in a kitchen of a bustling Beijing restaurant. For a man long ago, laboring under the sun to raise crops and feed a family. For a woman toiling for hours in a sweatshop to return home with bread for her daughter. For scientists peering into the vast and minuscule and finding splendor. For young men and women in love. For the "Song of Songs," the most beautiful poem of her heart. For laughter with friends. For the warmth of a hug and the tingle of a kiss. For everything that had been, that still meant being human.

For this task, this burden and privilege, they had chosen her.

Among all the people in the universe, they gave her this honor.

To carry this legacy a million years in the making. To protect this flickering candle even as the cold winds blew.

And who was she? She was nobody.

Yes, the daughter of a colonel, but so what? Were there no other children of officers? Even the children of generals and admirals?

Yes, she was a capable soldier. The soldier who had won the Alien Wars. But were there no other heroes? No other soldiers who had fought, who had sacrificed, who had done great deeds under fire?

Who was she? She was not unusually brave. At least no more than any of the soldiers she had served with. She was not unusually intelligent. At least no more than men like her husband, inventor of the wormhole. She wasn't even a particularly good writer. Yes, she had written her memoirs of the wars, and historians found them interesting. But Marco had greater gifts with words of wisdom.

Why her?

Why her to lead mankind? To protect this legacy?

I don't know, Ben-Ari thought. *I don't feel worthy. I don't feel strong, brave, or smart enough. But I know that I love humanity. I know that this task is an honor more than a burden. It is a task I cherish. This is a species I'm proud to belong to.*

She could not imagine Earth without humanity. She could not imagine this universe without humans to explore and experience it.

A cruel species? Yes, perhaps. But a species she believed could grow. That *was* growing. That was better than it had been. That would be better still.

That was why she did this.

Because she believed that humanity could be better. That if they emerged from this gauntlet, this crucible of wars, they would emerge united. Like her, humans would rise above their tribes, unleashing in their ability and curiosity.

If she won this war, she could build a true commonwealth of humanity, a civilization that spanned the stars. And the universe would be better for it.

Under the stars, Einav Ben-Ari returned to her camp. To her battalion. To the community of mankind.

CHAPTER NINETEEN

They spent ten days on Delta Draconis, nursing their wounds, preparing for the invasion of Haven.

The pieces are set, Marco thought. *Soon we will fly to his lair. The great battle between man and machine will blaze.*

He was finally feeling well enough to walk around and explore Fort Draco. He had spent the past ten days in the infirmary by Ben-Ari. His cold had morphed into a full-blown flu, complete with fever and shivers. His wounds had been stitched up but still ached, and he had cracked a rib, and his palms had blistered with burns. He was healing, albeit with quite a bit of pain. At thirty-six, he was still a young man, relatively speaking. But he couldn't take quite the same punishment as a teenage private anymore.

"Fifteen years ago, I'd be on my feet the next morning, ready for another battle," he said. "Now I fight one little army of cyborg dinosaurs, and I'm knocked down on my ass for ten days."

Addy was walking beside him. She leaned over and kissed his cheek. "My sweet old man."

"We're the same age, you know."

"You're still young!" Addy said. "A babe in the woods!"

Marco pulled her closer and kissed her. "Addy, you're lucky. With every year, I get creakier and crankier. You become more beautiful."

She rolled her eyes. "Did you get a concussion like Ben-Ari?"

"No. I'm just being honest. Maybe it's because of the battle ahead. Maybe because I'm scared. Maybe I'm just getting more sentimental with age." He stroked her golden hair. "But I mean it. You're fucking beautiful, and I fucking love you, Addy."

She hugged him and rubbed her nose against his. "Thank you. Now I'm going to just hug you forever, and you'll have to fight the Dreamer while hugging me."

Arm in arm, they kept exploring Fort Draconis.

Their mood quickly sobered. They found an outpost in ruin.

Shuttles and starfighters lay ruined across a smashed spaceport. Armored vehicles lay mangled across the base and surrounding countryside. Dinosaur skeletons still smoldered; the troops had been burning the enormous bodies all week. Both their machines and the native wildlife had risen against the Draco Brigade. For two months now, Fort Draconis had been fighting its own tanks, starfighters, and a horde of the local giants.

"The Dreamer has been banished from this world," Marco said softly. "But he left so much death."

He and Addy paused on a hill. They gazed at a military cemetery. The tombstones stretched across the valley.

Five thousand soldiers had once served here. Two thousand now lay buried underground.

"So many fallen," Marco said softly. "So many who'll never see Earth again."

"They gave their lives for Earth," came a voice from behind. "Their deaths will not be in vain."

Marco turned to see Ben-Ari walking up the hill.

For the first time in years, Marco saw her in a military uniform. She wore only battle fatigues, the khaki fabric well-worn, not some elaborate dress uniform. But golden phoenixes shone on her shoulders, the insignia of the commander-in-chief.

Over the past few years, she had become his friend. Often these days, he even referred to her by her first name. But seeing Ben-Ari in an HDF uniform filled Marco with awe, and he stood at attention. He saluted.

It was the Ben-Ari he had always known. His officer.

"Ma'am!"

She joined him and Addy on the hilltop. She gazed with them at the cemetery.

"The Dreamer first hijacked the minds of the brigade's senior officer." Her voice was soft. She spoke as if to herself. "The brigadier who commanded this fort. His colonels and majors followed. The virus infected all their minds. The Dreamer never bothered to hijack the enlisted, nor their junior officers. He cared only to butcher them like animals. Yet they fought with true courage. Against their own officers. Against their own machines of war. Against the very world where they were stationed. They fought and held this fort for six weeks until we arrived."

"Every one is a fucking hero." Addy placed her fist against her heart. "The ones who lived. And the ones who fell."

"Marco. Addy." Ben-Ari turned toward them, solemn. "You're the only two senior officers who remain on this world. You're both majors. The same rank I was when we fought the Gray War. Effective immediately, I'm promoting you both to lieutenant colonels. You will each command a thousand men from this fort—a full battalion. I will command a third battalion. Together, we will lead the Draco Brigade to Haven—and to victory."

They both stared at her, blinking.

"But ma'am!" Marco said. "We've both retired from the military. We're here as reservists, that's all. I'm just a writer. I'm not fit to be a colonel."

Addy poked his ribs. "She said *lieutenant* colonel, dumbass."

Ben-Ari's face remained stern. "You have fought with me for eighteen years. Through the Scum War. The Marauder War. The Gray War. And now the great war against the machines. I trust nobody more in this universe. I need you. Earth needs you. Together, we three will win this war."

Addy nodded. "Of course! It's always us three. We're the best goddamn heroes in history. Team BAM!" She paused, fist in the air, waiting for a reaction. "Did Marco not explain team BAM to you? It stands for Ben-Ari, Addy, and Marco! When Kai and

Lailani join us, we're team Ka-BLAM, and— Ow, Marco, stop poking me! Fine, fine, I'm shutting up now."

Marco looked at the cemetery, and he was silent or a long moment, lost in thought. Finally he turned toward Ben-Ari and spoke.

"Half a lifetime ago, I came into your office, Einav. You asked me to follow you to war. I was eighteen. And I stepped onto that path willingly. That path brought me nothing but pain and loss and despair. Often I was tempted to turn back. To hide. To live in comfort and let others walk upon the thorns. But you, Einav? You were born to lead. So long as there is darkness, you will be there, shining a light. So long as monsters lurk in shadows, you will be there, fighting them. You will never stray off the path of honor and sacrifice. And Einav … I will never let you walk that path alone." He saluted. "I was with you then. And I'm with you now. Always."

Addy spoke next, tears in her eyes. "We are mothers, Einav. You and me. We both miss our children. We both have a duty to protect them. But we also have a duty to Earth. To humanity. To save this world for the little ones. I'm with you too. Then and now. Always and forever." She too saluted. Then she raised her fist. "Go team BAM!"

Marco rolled his eyes. "Thanks for ruining the moment, Ads."

Ben-Ari smiled softly. "I know we're flying to war tomorrow. I know this is a solemn time. I know many died here.

But you guys just made lieutenant colonel. Tonight let's celebrate."

Addy gasped. "Booze, hockey fights, and strippers? Yes!"

"I was thinking some tea and cookies in my room." Ben-Ari winked. "And I found some potato chips in the canteen."

"You had me at cookies," Addy said.

They walked through the barracks. Every soldier they passed stood at attention and saluted. They were all so young. Enlisted men and women. A few junior officers. Barely anyone was older than thirty. Most were younger than twenty. They all looked so young. When Marco had been that age, he had thought himself and his fellow soldiers adults. Walking here now, he saw kids.

Tomorrow they will fly to war, Marco thought. *Many will never return.*

"Bless you, Golden Lioness," whispered one young soldier, a private with long red hair.

Another soldier broke protocol and pressed his palms together. "Hail the heroes."

Ben-Ari paused, saluted them, made eye contact, smiled. More and more young soldiers gathered to watch. To salute her. Many had tears in their eyes.

"Why are they all looking at us like this?" Addy whispered as they walked across a courtyard.

"We're heroes to them," Marco said. "The officers who fought in the great Alien Wars. We were in the platoon that killed the scum emperor. These soldiers were only babies then. We're legends to them. They grew up hearing our stories."

Addy looked around her. Soldiers stood in windows. On balconies. Under covered walkways. Some were saluting. Others whispered prayers. They heard the whispers.

"Golden Lioness. Golden Lioness …"

"No, Poet," Addy said. "You're wrong. You and I aren't heroes to them. They don't know who we are. Everyone remembers Neil Armstrong, the first man on the moon, but nobody remembers who flew his spaceship. Everyone remembers Winston Churchill, but nobody remembers who stormed Normandy or the rubble-strewn streets of Berlin. It's Einav Ben-Ari who inspires these young soldiers. She's the Churchill, the Armstrong, the Moses of our day. She's the symbol of Earth. We're the guys who fly the spaceship."

"A few might know me," Marco said. "For being an author, at least."

Addy snorted. "Who are you, Robert Prince?"

Marco groaned. "I told you, Addy, he's a hack!"

"And I told you, if you wrote conspiracy theories about UFOs buried under the Vatican, maybe I'd be a rich woman by now."

He rolled his eyes. "Not this again."

They finally entered Ben-Ari's quarters. It was a simple concrete room with no windows, a cold floor, and several cots. An infantry squad must have lived here once. Perhaps they were now buried outside the fort walls.

Promotions to lieutenant colonels were normally grand affairs. With speeches. A reception full of dignitaries. A proper ceremony and celebration. Nobody wanted such aplomb now. The heroes didn't need to be seen pinning gold to their shoulders here. Not with so many fallen. With so many yet to fall.

Ben-Ari gave them their new insignia. Instead of one star on each shoulder, the insignia of majors, Marco and Addy now wore two stars, the insignia of lieutenant colonels.

Junior officers had bars on their shoulders. Senior officers wore stars. Generals sported phoenixes—the same golden birds that now perched on Ben-Ari's shoulders. Perhaps across the Human Commonwealth, all other officers were gone now. Perhaps only Fort Draconis still stood. Perhaps they, these three friends in this little room, commanded what remained of the fabled Human Defense Force. And what remained of humanity.

Maybe the HDF is just us now, Marco thought. *Just a few thousand soldiers forty-six light-years from Earth, playing with these golden symbols as if they still mean anything. And maybe this means everything. Maybe we are all that matters now, the last scions of fallen glory. And if we are the last, perhaps we must cling to our symbols, for they are the legacy of Earth.*

"Penny for your thoughts, Marco?" Ben-Ari said, smiling softly.

He considered telling her everything. How he felt. What he feared. About the yearning for home, the guilt over leaving his children, the terror that so many young soldiers would die tomorrow.

But he didn't need to say any of it. She understood.

Instead, he simply said, "We better eat something before Addy devours it all. Including the mattresses."

They turned to look at her. Addy sat on a cot, potato chip bags and boxes of cookies open around her.

"What?" she said, cheeks stuffed. Crumbs fell from her mouth.

The metal bunk beds were narrow, their mattresses thin, no better than what Marco had gotten at boot camp. He arranged several mattresses on the floor, forming one larger, thicker mattress. A shudder ran through him. He couldn't help but remember the enormous cyborg made from many smaller bodies. He pushed that memory aside, knowing it would return at night to haunt him.

He and Addy lay down side by side, holding each other. He could almost imagine that they were back home, that he could hear the Mediterranean outside, that his children would wake him in the morning. He let Addy's warmth comfort him, and he wrapped his arms around her.

At first Ben-Ari lay on a bunk bed, alone.

"Ma'am?" Addy said. "Sleepover?"

After a moment's hesitation, Ben-Ari joined them on the floor. They lay together under the blankets, sharing the big mattress, finding comfort in one another.

Team BAM, Marco thought. *Saving the universe since 2143.*

Addy mumbled something in her sleep and curled up against him. Ben-Ari was deep in slumber, her breath warm against Marco's neck. The bunk beds remained empty. Here on the floor, in the darkness, they found some comfort until the dawn.

Back at boot camp, I'd never dare rearrange a bunk, he thought. *Hey, the perks of being a lieutenant colonel. Free mattress autonomy!*

Lying between his wife and president, he slept.

* * * * *

They awoke on a morning of war.

They dressed in their uniforms, and they pinned their new insignia to their shoulders.

For a moment, standing in the bunk, they looked at one another.

Marco Emery.

Addy Linden.

Einav Ben-Ari.

Heroes. Parents. Friends. The three who had saved the world. Three who now stood together again, leading humanity.

They stepped into Fort Draconis's courtyard. The triple suns shone above, but their light seemed cold. Wind blew, scattering dust. Ten days after the battle, the rubble had been cleared. The dead had been buried. The cyborgs had been burned. In the bleak courtyard, they stood: three thousand soldiers. The remains of the fabled Draco Brigade, humanity's light in the darkness.

Ben-Ari stepped toward a podium, and she spoke to them.

"Brave soldiers of Draco Brigade,

We gather today on December 9, 2160, under three alien suns. We gather on a world named Delta Draconis, many light-years from home. But for us, this is still December 9, 2160, a date calculated by distant Earth's rotation around its sun. To us, no matter how far we go, that is always our home, always our calendar.

December 9, 2160. A day that will go down in history.

The day the tide turned.

The day humanity launched its great offensive against the machines.

Should we win this war, which I believe we will, future historians will say that today began our great march to victory. Should our strength fail us and the war is lost, perhaps some alien chronicler, gazing from some distant era, will say that today began our courageous final stand.

The Draco Brigade was created to guard humanity's border in the night. To defend our species from the most distant world in our Human Commonwealth. To be the shield that faces the terrors in the dark. You were chosen, trained, and deployed to defend us from alien invaders. But the true enemy rose from within. An enemy that we ourselves birthed.

You saw the evil of the Dreamer on this very world. For two months, you stood proudly, defending your outpost from this cruel enemy. But you have seen only a hint of his true malice. The Dreamer has devastated our colonies and even our Mother Earth. The Dreamer enslaved some of us. Deformed others. Murdered many.

But there are some humans who still stand tall.

Who still fight.

We are three thousand. Only a sliver of what the HDF had once been. And what is an arrowhead but the thinnest of slivers? That sliver can kill an enemy with a strike to the heart. That is what we will do. With our courage, our strength, and our love of Earth, we still strike into the Dreamer's heart!

We will divide ourselves into three new battalions, each a thousand humans strong. Lieutenant Colonel Marco Emery, hero of the Alien Wars, will command Sun Arrow Battalion. Lieutenant Colonel Addy Linden, leader of the Summer Uprising against the marauders, will command Fire Battalion. I, Einav Ben-Ari, am known among you as the Golden Lioness. I will command the Lions of Earth Battalion as well as the entire Draco Brigade.

Together, we are the force that will defeat the machines and save mankind.

We will board alien ships today. Ships the enemy cannot hijack. We will fly to Haven, our colony in Alpha Centauri. The home of the beast.

We will encounter terror. Enemy ships in space. And on the ground of Haven—twisted machines and cyborgs that mock humanity. We will face some dangers we haven't imagined yet. Some of us will fall, sacrificing their lives so that the living can fight on.

We will reach the Dreamer, a twisted electric tree that shines deep underground. And we will strike him down!

What we do today echoes for eternity.

Godspeed, sons and daughters of Earth!"

The podships descended like moldy blimps. Vessels of the Esporian civilization, they were made entirely from fungus. Their outer walls were gray, caked with red splotches like lesions, and their skin shed spores like dandruff. Fleshy vents thrust out from each podship like lips. With soft, squishy noises, the vents opened, revealing the podship interiors.

It would not be a comfortable flight. As Marco stepped through one vent, he imagined himself returning into the womb. Or at least a hot, moldy womb he shared with a hundred soldiers. The place stank, and spores floated through the air like pollen. The floor was soft and squishy, and the soldiers sank down to their ankles with every step.

No, this isn't like being inside a womb, Marco thought. *More like being inside a stomach. Slowly digested.*

He could have flown aboard the *Dolphin* with Ben-Ari. The flagship of the Golden Fleet was luxurious. While its engines were Tarjan artifacts, it hulls had been built for human comfort. Marco could have had a cozy cabin. A real bed—one he could share with his beautiful wife. Hot meals in a real pirate ship galley with strong grog to wash them down.

But he had chosen to enter this Esporian podship, to travel with his troops. He shared this fleshy ship with the Sun Arrow Battalion's first platoon. For the next two weeks, as they flew, he would live among these brave soldiers. Their average age was nineteen, and they were the salt of the Earth. He would train with them. Bond with them. Learn to love some of them.

And then in two weeks—lead them to almost certain death. To but the slimmest hope for victory.

Marco settled down on the rancid floor, trying and failing to find a comfortable position. No, not a comfortable flight. But a safe flight. No computers. Just fungus. The Dreamer could not reach them here.

Three large mushrooms grew from the interior walls like boils. They were pale blue and looked like brains. When they vibrated, they could speak.

"Foul animals! Infecting our innards! We should digest you all."

Yet they would obey. These were the pilots of the podship, parasites of the fungal spheres. They were gifts of Don Basidio. They would honor his pacts and serve humanity.

The soldiers around Marco were in good spirits. They began cracking jokes. A few sang old songs of Earth, beautiful ballads of green hills and blue seas. Others preferred to sing dirty songs and laugh.

Some were wounded.

Some sat silently, gazing ten thousand light-years away.

All had lost friends at Fort Draconis. All were scared.

Marco remembered himself at that age, a green private, flying to face the scum in battle. If any of these young soldiers survived the fight, the memories would forever haunt them. Marco knew this, and he grieved for them.

The podships rose into space, carrying the Draco Battalion. In orbit, the Fungal Fleet joined the Golden Fleet. Pirates. Soldiers. An army of humanity. They flew toward Alpha Centauri.

We're the arrowhead, Marco thought. *And we point at the Dreamer's heart.*

CHAPTER TWENTY

The dented green Toyota rumbled down the highway, passing through lands of desolation.

Charred forests rolled across plains and hills. A few deserted villages smoldered, and burnt cars lay across the roadsides like the husks of giant cicadas. Towering tripods on slender legs prowled the horizons, headlights scanning the shadows, seeking life to burn. Above this hellscape, the moon hung in the morning sky, engraved with the face of a new god, defying the meager light of the sun.

Lailani had been driving for three days, going through the car's collection of antique tapes. Uriah Heep's "Demons and Wizards" blared from the speakers, the tenth time she was playing it. Lailani drummed along the steering wheel as she sang. In the passenger seat, Tala began to yawn.

"Mommy, when is Epi coming back?" the girl asked.

"I told you, Tala. Epi went to live in a park with other dogs."

"A park under the ground?" Tala said, remembering the funeral.

Lailani nodded. "He took a tunnel underground to a park on the other side of the world."

"Is HOBBS there too?"

"Of course he is," said Lailani.

Tala looked at her, eyes large and damp. "And my dad?"

The question stabbed Lailani like a bayonet to the chest. She had never heard Tala ask about her father.

"Yes, Tala," Lailani said softly. "Your daddy is there too."

Even years later, Lailani still mourned the death of Benny "Elvis" Ray. The man she had loved. The man she had killed. No, not she. Not truly. The demons inside her, the alien voices, had driven her hand. And yet Lailani still clung to that guilt. For a few precious years, Benny's heart had still beat, kept alive inside HOBBS. The heart was still now, and everything was dying.

She looked at her daughter.

I don't know if anyone else is alive. The world is dying. Maybe it's already dead. All I have is you, Tala. And you have me. Always.

The young girl looked out the window, reflective. "Daddy and HOBBS and Epi are on the other side of the world. I want to go there too."

Lailani had to wipe her eyes. "We're going somewhere else, Tala. We're going to the mountain. To your cousins. Remember?"

"Roza and Sam," said Tala. "I don't want them to go underground too." Her eyes watered. "I want Daddy and HOBBS and Epi. I want them to come back."

Lailani stroked the girl's hair. "I know, sweetie. I do too."

Tala began to cry, but that was better than her long stretches of silence. Sometimes the girl could go for days without barely saying a word, barely shedding a tear. Sometimes for hours she just stared into the distance like a doll. Now she wept, and Lailani was relieved, because weeping was normal, weeping was what all little girls sometimes did. And maybe it meant that Tala wasn't completely broken. That this long road had not shattered her soul. That someday her girl could recover, could be healthy and happy again. Could grow up into a healed, whole woman.

"Let's listen to something more upbeat," Lailani said.

She switched the tape. Battle Beast's "King for a Day," an old heavy metal song, began to play. Lailani sang along, reaching over to muss Tala's hair. And the girl smiled. For the first time in weeks, she actually smiled.

They were somewhere in Eastern Europe. Getting closer. If nothing stopped them on the way, they would reach the Matterhorn in two days.

Lailani was almost cheering up when she saw the gargantuan robots ahead, and the missile streaked through the air.

She yanked on the steering wheel.

The missile slammed down behind the pickup truck. The back window shattered. Fire blazed. The Toyota spun madly across the road, tires skidding. The smell of burnt rubber filled the air.

Lailani secured her daughter with one hand. With the other, she wrestled the wheel, finally steadying the truck. They idled on the road, fire crackling behind them.

For a moment, silence.

Lailani barely dared to breathe.

She stared outside, and she saw it there.

My God.

It was still two or three kilometers away. The largest robot she had ever seen. Its body was formed from the hull of a starship—a full corvette warship, large enough to transport an infantry company. But even this massive body seemed small atop the machine's eight metal legs. The bizarre machine moved across the landscape like a spider, gears the size of houses turning, engines rumbling. Every footfall shook the earth.

Several more machines emerged from beyond the horizon. More towering, mechanical spiders. Some had the bodies of commercial jets. Others had bodies formed from metal buildings—a granary, a farmhouse, a water tower. All moved on stilt-like legs. One machine had a rocket ship body, and it moved on twenty legs or more, a giant millipede crawling over the fields.

"Mechanids," Lailani muttered. "I fucking hate mechanids."

She had seen these unholy creations in Mongolia—the creatures of the Dreamer, assembled from whatever his tentacles could grab. Lailani had to give him credit. For all his evil, the Dreamer was a rabid champion of recycling.

The starship mechanid took another step across the land. The road cracked. The gargantuan robot turned its prow, lowering its cannon toward Lailani's pickup truck.

It wanted her to hit the brakes. To turn around. To flee.

Lailani sneered, pressed down on the gas, and charged forward toward the enemy.

A missile flew.

It overshot her.

It slammed onto the road behind the pickup truck.

Fire bloomed, filling the rearview mirror. Every window on the truck shattered. The shock wave lifted the Toyota into the air, then slammed it back down, shoved it forward.

Lailani kept driving.

She pressed the gas pedal to the floor.

She roared toward the machine ahead.

The mechanid loomed, peering at her like a mechanical god.

Lailani didn't dare turn around. If she fled, it would just send more missiles. The closer she was, the safer.

That's my logic and I'm sticking to it! she told herself, trying to silence the terror.

The Toyota roared toward the machine.

"Come on, you bastard!"

Lailani growled, her heart pounded, and against every instinct, she kept accelerating.

Tala screamed.

Another missile flew.

Lailani swerved around the explosion and kept charging. She was almost at the robot. Almost able to drive between its legs. She grabbed her gun, ready to fire at the mechanid's underbelly, hoping to find a weak spot.

Several rotary guns unfurled from the starship's undercarriage. The muzzles swiveled toward Lailani.

Lailani clasped Tala's hand.

Please, God, if there's a heaven, let us in.

She winced.

From the roadsides—rumbling engines.

Motorcycles roared forth, leaped onto the road, and charged alongside Lailani's pickup truck. Men in black leather rode them, helmets hiding their heads.

They carried rocket launchers.

Five rockets streaked forth, leaving trails of smoke. Two missed. One hit the mechanid's abdomen. Two hit the legs.

The enormous robot tilted. Metal cracked, emitting a sound almost like a cry of pain. It sounded like some huge, lumbering animal from another world, calling out in agony.

The legs buckled, shedding gears, and the mechanical spider pitched forward. The starship body came swooping toward the road.

Lailani yanked the steering wheel. She swerved into the fields and plowed through tall grass and bushes. An enormous metal leg, wider than her entire truck, slammed down before her. She hit the brakes, spun, and drove alongside the fallen leg.

Metal was still screeching. The mechanid was still swaying, desperate to stand on its remaining legs. Another leg slammed down, shaking the world. Gears and motors were twisting. Cracking. Fire rained, and—

Behind her, the starship slammed onto the earth.

The stern hit the ground only meters behind the truck.

The world shattered.

Cracks raced across the land, swallowing up the brush. A fireball blasted into the air. Smoke and soil flew, filling the truck. Lailani drove blindly through a storm of flame and smoke and dirt. Chunks of metal pattered down, denting the Toyota's roof. The windshield was gone. Dirt and smog filled the cabin.

Lailani kept driving, finally emerging from the storm, but the truck was limping now. It swayed wildly from side to side. The engine coughed. Warning lights flashed. The Toyota gave a final groan, then died.

Lailani climbed out from the car, holding Tala. The girl was coughing and waving away the clouds of smog. Lailani couldn't see much from here. She climbed a hillside, emerging from the smoke, and saw the highway.

The fallen robot lay across the road. Its legs twisted around its mangled abdomen, one still twitching.

But the battle was not over. Other mechanids were moving across the landscape, guns booming. A missile slammed into a hill across the road. Rotary guns rattled.

More motorcycles roared forth. More riders fired rockets. One rider was holding a banner. It unfurled in the wind, revealing a golden phoenix.

Tears leaped into Lailani's eyes.

The phoenix. Symbol of the Human Defense Force. She had never seen anything more beautiful.

"The HDF still exists," she whispered. "Humanity still stands."

She clutched the dog tags that hung around her neck. The army was still fighting. And she was an officer in this army. This was her fight.

She held Tala against her hip. She could flee, she knew. She could try to hide. But the Dreamer had seen her. He would chase her. The best way Lailani could protect Tala now, protect her own life, protect the hope for humanity inside her skull, was to take the bastards head-on.

Lailani drew her gun, let out a cry, and charged to battle.

* * * * *

The motorcycles were everywhere. They roared over the hills, flew through the air, and screeched across the road. Their rockets shrieked through the air, so fast Lailani could barely see them, and slammed into machines.

One mechanid, its body formed from a cargo ship, lost a leg. The gargantuan robot wobbled, tilted, then slammed onto the hills. An explosion shook the world, and a mushroom cloud bloomed. But other mechanids kept fighting. Their missiles flew. One hit a motorcycle, leaving a crater in the hill, bits of twisted metal, and no trace of the rider. Another missile whistled over

Lailani's head. Bullets flew everywhere, knocking riders off their motorcycles.

A squad of motorcycles roared by Lailani, leaping over the hills, ripping up grass and soil. Their banners streamed, displaying the golden phoenixes. A mechanid turned toward them—an armored truck upon towering legs. The machine ran to meet the motorcycles, cracking the earth, rotary guns blazing.

Lailani knelt behind a boulder, shielding Tala as bullets whizzed all around. A nearby motorcycle spun through the air like a firecracker, spilling its rider. The man thumped down by Lailani, riddled with bullets. Riders cried out, zipping around the mechanid, and fired more rockets.

The armored truck lost its mechanical legs. It slammed down onto the hills and burst into flames. Riders cheered and charged into the enemy lines.

Lailani ran at a crouch, holding Tala, and dragged the wounded rider to cover. A dozen bullets had perforated his chest, but the man was still moaning. Lailani pulled off his helmet, revealing a young face. So young. Only a teenage boy.

He tried to say something, coughed up blood. Lailani touched his cheek.

"It's all right," she whispered.

"Mama," he whispered, tears flowing. "*Gdzie jest moja mama?*"

She held his hand as he died, and she kissed his forehead. "Rest in peace, son of Earth."

With a sooty hand, she closed the boy's eyes. Then she grabbed his assault rifle. It came with a grenade launcher. Sweet.

Lailani rose from behind the boulder, gazed toward the road, and saw the surviving riders circling three last mechanids. Lailani loaded a grenade, narrowed her eyes, aimed, and fired.

Her grenade arced through the air. It hit a mechanid leg and exploded.

The robotic leg twisted, wobbled, then broke at the knee. The mechanid's body, formed from a bus, slammed onto the ground. The corpses of passengers spilled out.

They were already dead, Lailani told herself, walking among the bodies. *Before I destroyed this mechanid. They were already dead. They had to be.*

She shoved the terror aside.

She walked closer, already loading another grenade. She stepped onto the road, a toddler on her left hip, a grenade launcher in her right hand.

This is humanity, Lailani thought. *A mother with a child in one hand, a gun in the other. Is there any greater symbol of our undying spirit?*

A mechanid turned toward her. Its body was formed from a clock tower, uprooted from some city square. The clock's gears turned and its bells chimed. Rotary guns moved across the mechanid's undercarriage, attached to the clockwork. One cannon wheeled toward Lailani.

She fired a grenade.

An explosion rocked the tower. Gears flew, hit the road, and dug up ribbons of asphalt. The clock face drove into a hill like a spinning saw. The minute hand slammed down at Lailani's left, the hour hand at her right. A few small gears, no larger than a car's tires, rolled around her, then clanged down. The clock gave its last chime and died.

Lailani stepped onto the cracked road and stood among the ruins of colossal machines. A few motorcycles rolled up beside her, then idled, engines rumbling and pumping out smoke. Their riders stared ahead, black helmets expressionless, and they seemed almost like machines themselves.

The mechanids, these spiders the size of buildings, had fallen. But new metallic screeches rose from ahead.

Lailani could not see them yet. Smoke enveloped the horizon. But she heard those cries. Those pounding feet. Smelled their wet steel.

A chill ran along her spine. She loaded another grenade.

With blazing white eyes, with metallic howls, they burst out from the smoke.

Hounders. An army of them. The mechanical dogs raced across the hills, leaped over the dead mechanids, and bounded toward the forces of humanity.

*****

Hounders, Lailani thought, staring with narrowed eyes. *I fucking hate hounders.*

She fired her grenade.

It arced across the sky, then landed among the charging robots. The explosion tossed three hounders into the air. Barely a dent in their lines.

The wind caught Earth's banners.

One rider raised his motorcycle's front wheel like a rearing stallion. He was a burly man with a golden star painted onto his helmet, and he held a streaming phoenix flag. He cried out, voice ringing across the land.

"For Earth, destroy the machines!"

The motorcycles roared forth. Guns boomed. Lailani had no motorcycle. She took cover behind a fallen mechanid leg, peered toward the battle, and loaded another grenade.

A realization tickled her.

They're not wearing HDF uniforms. They're dressed in black leather. They display no insignia.

She shoved the thought aside and focused on the battle.

The two armies charged toward each other. Hounders—howling. Men—shouting. Machine and metal. Flesh and blood. The banners streamed, and the bullets flew, and with a sound like a shattering sun, the hosts slammed together.

Hounders leaped onto men, knocking them onto the asphalt. Some motorcycles careened out of control, flying every which way. Other motorcycles plowed through the hounders like medieval knights on armored horses. Guns boomed. A hounder lunged onto one man, knocked him onto the ground, and crushed the helmet with a metal foot. Blood, brains, and fragments of skull splattered the roadside.

"Mommy!" Tala cried, trembling. "Those dogs are bad guys!"

Lailani held her daughter close. Both crouched under cover, hiding behind the fallen mechanid leg. It lay across the road, forming a thick steel barricade.

"Mommy's here. It's okay, sweetie. I won't let them hurt you."

A howl tore the air. A hounder vaulted over the mechanid leg and landed before them. Its lips of liquid metal peeled back, revealing steel teeth. The beast growled and pounced.

Lailani grabbed a fallen gear and hurled it like a discus. It slammed into the hounder's head. The robot fell back, crashing into the mechanid leg.

"Mommy!" Tala cried.

Lailani stood up, shouldered her assault rifle, and pounded the hounder with bullets. It tried to rise. The hailstorm shoved it back down.

Within a few seconds, her magazine was empty. The hounder stood up, dented, missing one leg and several teeth. But still very much alive.

Alive? she wondered. *Have I begun thinking of them as living things?*

She would consider that later. Right now Lailani tossed a grenade, grabbed Tala, and leaped over the mechanid leg.

She huddled behind the metal barrier as the grenade burst.

The hounder gave a last shriek. And then chunks of it pattered onto the road.

On this side of the mechanid leg, Lailani found herself in open battle. Dozens of hounders and humans fought everywhere. Lailani had one grenade left and no more bullets.

A hounder came bounding toward her, scraps of human skin dangling from its mouth. Lailani fired her last grenade, hopped behind the barrier again, and crouched. Charred pieces of hounder circuitry clattered down around her.

All right, I'm out of ammo, she thought.

She peeked over the barrier and saw the battle rage. Fire blazed across the highway and hills. Humans and robots kept falling. She watched three hounders leap onto a rider and tear the man apart. Another motorcycle lost control. It came roaring toward Lailani, its rider slumped over.

She crouched low. The motorcycle slammed into the fallen mechanid leg, spilling its rider. The man flew over Lailani, hit the ground, and skidded across the road, leaving a trail of blood.

She raced toward him. The man moaned, coughing blood. The poor bastard must have shattered every bone in his body. He tried to speak, but the helmet muffled his voice.

Growls sounded behind Lailani.

She turned to see two hounders step onto the barricade. They glared at her with white eyes.

Lailani shoved her daughter behind her and grabbed the wounded man's submachine gun.

She unleashed hell.

Her bullets tore through one hounder's head, shattering the eyes. The beast stumbled blindly.

The second hounder lunged onto Lailani. She just had time to raise her arms before the robot rammed into her.

It wasn't much larger than her, but it was far heavier and stronger. The machine slammed her against the asphalt and pinned her down. She struggled and kicked, but she'd have more luck kicking off an elephant.

The hounder stared into her eyes. A deep voice, almost sensuous, emerged from its silvery jaws.

"Go on, Lailani. Summon your power. Deactivate the shield in your mind. Let me in."

The machine's eyes began to flash, broadcasting the code that would hijack her brain the instant she let the alien loose.

A rock slammed into the hounder's head.

"You're bad!" Tala shouted.

The robot's head whipped toward the girl. Its eyes narrowed, still flashing, focusing their beams on Tala. The girl closed her eyes and covered her ears.

Nightwish.

Lailani shut off her chip.

Alien power surged through her.

She grabbed the hounder's head, twisted, and cracked its neck. The robot bucked like an enraged bull, legs thrashing, and Lailani slammed its head into the pavement. She lifted the rock and hammered at the machine again and again, denting the steel, shattering the rock into pieces. She lifted what remained of the hounder and hurled it back toward the battle. A stream of bullets crashed into the deformed robot, finishing the job.

Lailani turned her chip back on. She raced toward Tala.

"Look at me!" She grabbed the girl's arms. "Look into my eyes."

Tala opened her eyes wide. Dark brown eyes. Almost black. Human eyes.

Lailani pulled the girl into her embrace. They held each other as ash rained and fires burned.

Horns blared.

Engines rumbled beyond the smoke.

Lailani cursed. What fresh hell was this?

But she breathed a sigh of relief when armored jeeps burst through the smoke, carrying human reinforcements. Some of the troops wore HDF uniforms. Most wore civilian clothes. But they all raised phoenix banners. They stormed into battle, firing machine guns, tearing down more hounders. Hundreds of humans now fought together. Lailani grabbed a gun from a dead boy, hunched behind an overturned motorcycle, and helped pick out the last few robots.

The last of the machines fell.

The battle was over.

The dead spread across the road and hills. A hundred or more humans had fallen here. Their bodies lay mangled among smoldering machines.

Some of the victors cheered. But only some. One boy stumbled aside, lifted his helmet's visor, and vomited. Another man wandered the field, his arm severed, his eyes dazed, perhaps searching for his missing limb. A few soldiers lay on the ground, writhing, screaming, weeping. A man crawled, both his legs gone.

Medics rushed among the wounded. At least Lailani assumed they were medics; red crosses were crudely painted on their sleeves. They loaded a few wounded men onto litters. One man lay by a charred tree, clutching his lacerated belly, helpless to stop his entrails from spilling. Two medics approached him with a litter. One medic said something to his comrade, nodded, and shot the disemboweled man in the head. They moved on to another man, this one suffering from a mere broken leg, and loaded him onto the litter instead.

Little Tala, held in Lailani's arms, closed her eyes. She buried her face against Lailani's chest.

A man stepped out from the smoke, clad all in leather. He came walking toward Lailani, his boots hissing against the hot asphalt. He was a towering man, almost two feet taller than Lailani, and beefy with muscles. She could not see his face, but she recognized the golden star painted onto his helmet. He had led the motorcycle charge.

The giant halted before Lailani, looming over her. He stood too close, but Lailani refused to step back. She was at eye level with his belt buckle, more or less. Granted, Lailani was only four foot ten, but still, she wasn't used to feeling *this* small.

"You are a good fighter." The giant spoke with a thick accent. Russian, she thought. "Who are you, little girl?"

She stared up at the man. "Show me your face before I give you my name, soldier."

The man stared at her in silence. For a moment Lailani feared that he was a cyborg. Then the giant took off his helmet, revealing a square, craggy, human face. A scar snaked across his head, dividing stubbly blond hair like a furrow through a field. The scar had claimed one ear—and by the looks of it, a chunk of skull.

"I am General Peter Volkov." The giant grinned, crouched, and looked into her eyes. "Ah, little one, I know your pretty face. I have seen you in the old television programs before the revolution. You are the heroine of the Alien Wars, yes? A servant of Einav Ben-Ari, the so-called Golden Lioness. You are Laila del Rosa."

"I am Major Lailani de la Rosa of the HDF," she said. "And if you are a general, where is your insignia?"

Volkov snorted. "Insignia! Ranks! Uniforms! Those are things of the old world. The revolution has come. The machines have wiped out the old hierarchies. There is a new order of humanity, little Laila. You will learn." He straightened. "Ah, I prattle on. Come, little girl. And bring your baby. We won a great victory. Tonight we dine!"

Nearby, a shot rang out. Lailani turned to see a wounded rider, his arms severed, collapse to the ground with a bullet in his head. A medic laughed, holstered his pistol, and slapped another medic on the back.

Lailani stared, eyes dark.

The laughing medic approached two last wounded fighters. One suffered from a bullet in the arm; they loaded him into a truck. The other, a young woman, had a gaping wound in her belly, and her skin was ashen. She whispered something, raised a shaky hand, begging. A bullet tore through her raised hand, and then her forehead. She collapsed. The murderous medic spat, grabbed his crotch, and laughed. His friend snorted.

Lailani had seen battlefield triage before. She had seen medics pass over severely wounded soldiers, preferring to treat those they could perhaps save. But she had never seen anything like this.

The survivors climbed back onto motorcycles or leaped into the jeeps. The convoy headed off road. They drove down a dirt trail, raising clouds of dust.

Volkov climbed onto his motorcycle and patted the seat behind him. "Climb on, little girls."

"I'll hitch a ride with a jeep," Lailani said. Her Toyota was out for the count. There probably wasn't much hope for the cassette player either.

"Ah, but they have all left without you!" said Volkov. "Very rude of them. Come, your baby will be safe. She will sit between us. I will drive slowly."

Lailani cursed, but he was right. The jeeps were already full of soldiers, rumbling into the distance. Grumbling, Lailani climbed onto the motorcycle with Volkov. She was thankful for her small size. There was enough room to squeeze Tala between the two adults.

"Here we go!" said Volkov. He fired up the engine, and they rumbled onto the dirt track.

As the convoy stormed north, Lailani looked back toward the battle. The mechanids and hounders still lay across the highway, smoldering. And she realized that they had left a hundred dead humans to rot among them.

CHAPTER TWENTY-ONE

The convoy of motorcycles and jeeps rumbled across the wastelands, their phoenix banners fluttering. All around spread the devastation of the world.

The wind whipped Lailani's hair. She had no helmet. Peter Volkov, self-proclaimed general of this force, was driving the heavy, rumbling motorcycle, tearing across ashy fields. Lailani sat behind him, a third his size, clinging to the massive Russian's body. Little Tala almost disappeared, pinned between her mother and the leather-clad rider.

Lailani had many questions. Why were these warriors not wearing proper HDF uniforms? Was this the HDF at all, or some vigilante force that had adopted its banners? What country was she in? Did Earth still have a functioning government? She had spent many weeks lost in the wilderness, and she was aching for information.

But the motorcycle was too loud for conversation. Lailani contented herself with looking around her, studying the landscape.

It was not a pretty sight.

These lands had once been beautiful, perhaps. But the forests had burned. Only charred trees remained. A few farmhouses still stood, but the fields were gone. Corpses rotted along the roadsides, bustling with crows. One crow spent a moment flying alongside the motorcycle. It gave Lailani a long, hungry stare before flying off.

The convoy rode by a field where an enormous mechanid still lived, chained to boulders. Its body was formed from a small starship, maybe just a shuttle. Its metal legs kept trying to push itself up, only to wobble and fall again. A few men stood nearby on a hilltop. One man opened fire, peppering the giant machine with bullets, while another man took notes.

As they kept riding, Lailani saw more mechanids, these ones completely destroyed. They lay across the land, smoldering. At one point, she saw a row of mechanids marching along a distant hilltop, shrouded in mist. She tapped Volkov's shoulder and pointed.

"Those ones are not for us!" he shouted over the wind and roaring engines. "Those ones are traveling east. Not our battle."

Lailani was tempted to argue. To insist the company charged at those mechanids on the hills. But she decided to sit this one out. She had to remember: her mission was not to fight every battle along the road. Her mission was to reach the Matterhorn, to let Noah study the chip in her brain. She would join Volkov for dinner, and maybe he would give her a vehicle. With a fast car, she could reach Western Europe within a day or two. She could bring hope to humanity.

"It's almost over, Tala," she whispered and kissed her daughter's head. "We've come such a long way. We're almost there."

The convoy finally reached a town. They rolled down its cracked streets. Much of the place lay in ruin. Several concrete buildings had collapsed, and stray cats hissed atop piles of rubble. A mechanid lay toppled in the town square, legs bent, body formed from an old locomotive. Children played atop the metal beast—climbing its bulbous body, sliding along its legs, and swinging wooden swords at its dark headlights. When they passed by an avenue lined with trees, Lailani saw human bodies dangling from the branches. Some of the dead looked fresh. Wooden signs hung around their necks, but Lailani couldn't read the foreign letters.

"What do the signs say?" she asked Volkov.

"Traitors."

Lailani frowned. "Traitors? Who did they betray?"

"Humanity."

Lailani squinted at the corpses. She saw the scars on their cheeks. Split cheeks.

"Sleepers," she said. "Servants of the Dreamer."

Volkov nodded. "Like I said. Traitors."

She wanted to chastise Volkov for killing them. They weren't evil. Sleepers were just puppets, helpless to stop the puppet master. But she remained silent. Hadn't she herself killed sleepers in the Philippines? Killed many more along the road here?

I'm not Marco, she thought. *That boy even ponders the ethical ramification of killing alien maggots. I've always been a shoot-'em-up girl. Am I growing soft with age? And yet . . .*

"No, not traitors," she said. "They're more like zombies. We should kill them. But grieve for them."

The convoy rolled to a stop in the town square. As the dust settled, peasants rushed toward them. Many were holding rosaries and praying. They all looked hungry. Several women stepped forward, eyes damp, calling out names. Their voices rang across the town.

"Sasha!" A woman crashed into a man's arm.

"Ivan!" a middle-aged woman cried. "*De ty*, Ivan?" She hurried between the tanks, grabbing soldiers by the arm, asking about her Ivan. She heard some news. She fell to the ground, howling.

A few soldiers began to unload the wounded. The villagers kept rushing forward, asking about their loved ones. Soldiers began to shout, some to shove the peasants back. They hurried the wounded into a nearby bakery, probably the local field hospital. A red cross was graffitied onto the brick wall, covering a mural of steaming loafs.

Volkov got off his motorcycle and stood among the crowd. The leather-clad Russian towered over everyone else. They all turned toward him. A few villagers even knelt. Volkov slowly did a full turn, sweeping his gaze across the crowd. His eyes lingered for a second too long on Lailani.

He began to speak. She could not understand the language, but she recognized it. Volkov, while himself Russian, was speaking to the peasants in Ukrainian.

It brought back such powerful memories. Lailani closed her eyes, overwhelmed. For a few wonderful seasons, Lailani had lived with Sofia, her Ukrainian lover. A girl who had grown up in trenches and tanks, who had become a wise, compassionate woman, who had helped Lailani build schools for the needy. Sofia Levchenko had fallen fighting the marauders, a death that had shattered Lailani, that her heart had never healed from.

I miss you, Sofia, Lailani thought, and suddenly her eyes were damp. Suddenly she missed everyone so much. The fallen. The living too. She missed them so badly that it hurt. Tears flowed down Lailani's cheeks. She wanted to feel safe by Ben-Ari. To hug Marco, to feel warm in his embrace. To laugh with Addy.

It's not good to be alone, she thought. *I miss you all.*

She wiped her eyes. No. She could not give in to that now. She had to be strong. To fight the machine, she had to become a machine. She would give her heart only to Tala, nobody else right now.

She pulled her daughter a little closer. Tala yawned.

Volkov's speech continued for a while longer. Lailani only knew a few words in Ukrainian, but she understood a lot from tone, body language, and the crowd's reaction. Volkov was boasting of his success in battle. He showed off a gear he had taken from a mechanid. He spoke louder, fist raised, promising future victories. People cheered. Then Volkov lowered his head, spoke more softly, but his voice was still deep and gruff. He was speaking of the fallen, of martyred warriors. Villagers wept, and a few saluted. But Lailani remembered how Volkov's men had shot the mortally wounded in the heads, how they had laughed. How they had left the dead to the crows. Volkov wasn't telling *that* story.

When Volkov had finished talking, Lailani stepped forward. She was small, but she found a concrete pedestal. A statue had once stood upon it; the stone feet were still there, the rest of it gone. She hopped onto the pedestal, replacing whoever had once stood there.

"I am Major Lailani de la Rosa!" she said. "I fought with the Golden Lioness. I fought the scum on Abaddon. I fought the marauders in the ruins of Toronto. I fought the grays in Jerusalem. I won those wars. And I tell you: We will win this one too. Have hope! Heroes still fight!"

As she spoke, Volkov translated for her. Lailani had spoken with passion, but the speech failed to stir anyone. People only stared grimly. A few muttered to one another in their tongue. One peasant spat, then turned to leave. The crowd began to disperse.

I guess I lose something in translation, Lailani thought.

"Come, back onto my motorcycle," Volkov said. "We go to my home."

"Not a military base?" Lailani raised an eyebrow. "When you invited me to dine, I didn't realize it was a date."

Volkov snorted. "Don't flatter yourself. I have big home. My soldiers come too." He turned toward his leather-clad men. "Come on, boys!"

The motorcycles roared out of the village, leaving dusty clouds, wounded soldiers, and grieving widows and orphans.

A hill rose outside the town, almost large enough to be a mountain. A castle perched on the top, looming over the town like a vulture over dying flesh. The motorcycles rumbled along a snaking road, zigzagging their way up the hillside. They rode into Gothic ruins, under crumbly archways and along hollowed shells of ancient towers. The setting sun painted the ruins crimson and gold, and it became a castle of twilight, of whispering ghosts and yellow eyes in the shadows.

Lailani gazed at the castle, and a shiver ran through her. This place was old. Lailani wasn't used to old buildings. Hell, back in the Philippines, they had to rebuild after each typhoon. Buildings didn't last long there. Even when she visited Marco in Canada, she saw buildings that were just a century or two old. But this castle? This was *old*. This castle must have stood here for a thousand years, maybe longer. Its guards must have watched the Black Plague flow through their village, crusaders marching along the road to the sea, carnage of two world wars, the devastation of alien invasions. What stories could these stones tell?

The motorcycles halted by the castle gates. Lailani dismounted and looked around her, and she shivered again. Three gibbets hung from an archway. Humans were trapped inside the rusty cages. Two were dead, meals for crows. The third prisoner swung madly in the cage, shrieking, biting at the bars. His eyes were milky white. His cheeks were slashed open. He howled and banged against the bars so hard his forehead split. He laughed as blood dripped down his face.

"More traitors?" she asked Volkov.

The giant scoffed and mussed her hair. "Smart little girl."

Lailani glared at him. She tried to look intimidating, but being a third his size, it wasn't easy.

"Who are you, Volkov?" she said. "You're not a real general. What game are you playing?"

"Ah, so many questions, my curious little *major*." He winked. "Come, come, first we eat and drink. We celebrate our victory! There is time for questions when our bellies are being full."

Lailani frowned. She didn't like how he had made *major* sound like *baby girl*. But she followed him into the castle. Right now these were armed warriors, HDF or not. If humanity were to survive, it needed all the warriors it could get.

Beggars can't be choosers, she thought.

They passed through the castle archway, leaving their motorcycle in the courtyard. A guard pulled a rope, and a drawbridge slammed down with a clang, sealing the group indoors.

Lailani found herself in a shadowy hall. A handful of torches crackled on the walls, doing little to disperse the gloom. Stone columns rose like sentinels. A bat fluttered across the chamber, then vanished among the shadows that cloaked the vaulted ceiling. Several dogs wrestled for bones on the floor.

The soldiers tramped across the hall, boots splattering mud, and whistled. Young girls rushed forth from the shadows, holding trays of vodka. Some were almost women, others barely more than toddlers. Tala hid behind Lailani's legs, gazing shyly at the girls, perhaps hoping for a playmate.

The soldiers downed their vodka, slapped a few girls on the bottom, and approached wooden trencher tables. They sat, belched, and more girls rushed forward, these ones bringing trays of beef, chicken, and fried fish. Lailani didn't like this place. Not the shadows, the mud, or the fear in the girls' eyes. But she had to admit: the food smelled delicious. She frowned, wanted to chastise Volkov again, but her stomach betrayed her. It gave a loud, hungry rumble. Tala's stomach echoed the noise.

Volkov laughed, pinched Tala's cheek, and mussed Lailani's hair. "Ah, the little China girls are hungry. Come, come, sit with me! We eat and drink."

Lailani shoved his hand away. "Don't touch my hair, Volkov. I'm still not convinced you're a general. If you're feigning your rank, this is stolen valor, a criminal offense. I have a duty to report you to the military police, who can—"

Volkov roared with laughter. "The military police? Girl, I am the military now." He swept his arm across the hall. "All that you see. This is what remains of the HDF. It is mine now, little girl." He leaned down, bringing himself to eye level with her. "If you defy me, little girl, well … You have seen what we do to traitors, yes?" He stared for a moment longer, then burst out laughing. "Ah, I am making jokes! Of course you are just doing your duty, Major. You are proud soldier and brave human. Come, eat with me!" He whistled at the serving girls. "Bring our guest a meal."

They sat at the trencher tables. The girls brought forth a feast of ale, meat, and plunging cleavage. Men hooted, squeezed the girls, and pulled some onto their laps. Lailani noticed that some girls had black eyes. One had a bandaged nose. Two were pregnant.

Then somebody placed a platter of food in front of her, and Lailani surrendered to her hunger. She and Tala tucked in. There were pork ribs so soft the meat fell from the bone. There were beef ribs too, the meat like butter melting on the tongue. The vodka flowed freely, and soon empty glasses were piling up. As they feasted, they tossed the bones to the dogs. The hounds rolled on the floor, teeth snapping, paws swiping, fighting for the morsels.

I wonder if the peasants in the town are feasting tonight too, she thought. *Or whether all the food goes to the castle. I wonder if Volkov is a soldier at all, or whether he's more like a king.*

She glanced at the towering Russian. By now, Lailani had established that she was in the Ukraine. But she had heard Volkov speaking Russian to some of his lieutenants. She knew enough words to be certain of that. He hadn't only taken over a castle and village. He was also ruling over a chunk of another nation.

Are there still nations? she wondered. *Or are borders now obsolete?*

"Little girl, you seem so sad," Volkov said. "Ah, I know what will cheer you up." He rose to his feet and held out his arms. "Men! Let us begin the games!"

The men cheered. They raised glasses of vodka. They began to chant in their language and pound their fists.

Lailani tilted her head. "What games?"

Volkov grinned. "The greatest games in the world." He pounded the table. "Awake the beasts!"

Screeches and grunts rose from a hidden basement. The castle shook. The men cheered even louder. Lailani shivered.

CHAPTER TWENTY-TWO

The men in black leather moved outdoors. They left the bones and dogs inside the castle. They took the women and vodka.

Lailani followed them, holding a sleepy Tala. She didn't like this place. She didn't like these men. But she had watched them take down an army of mechanids. They were boorish, yes, but they were deadly. Machine killers. She needed to turn them into a proper army.

Medieval walls and towers surrounded a round courtyard. Once this place might have been beautiful—an oasis of grass, trees, and flowers, a place for maidens fair and knights in shining armor. The grass had burned long ago. There were no fair maidens, and the new knights of this castle wore leather and rode motorcycles. They had erected bleachers around the courtyard, forming a crude arena, large enough to seat a hundred people.

The men climbed the bleachers, took their seats, and guzzled their vodka. The women sat on their laps, and gruff hands grabbed their breasts. A cheer began to rise, and men pounded their chests. Lailani didn't speak their language. But she doubted they were getting excited for a performance of *Swan Lake*.

"What the hell is going on, Volkov?" Lailani said.

The towering Russian walked beside her, his leather outfit creaking. "I know, I know. Some of the boys get a little rowdy. But they're good boys. They fought hard battle. They lost friends. They need to unwind."

"Unwind how?" she demanded.

"Come, little girl. I show you." Volkov took Lailani's hand. His hand was so large it swallowed hers. "You sit with me. Best seat in house."

She tried to pull her hand free. He tightened his grip. Very well. She would play along for now. He was big, yes. But she had faced tougher foes. If things got ugly, she wouldn't hesitate to kill this man.

He took her to his seat. It was practically a throne. The wooden chair was carved into the shape of lions, bears, and dragons. It stood below the bleachers, facing the arena.

Volkov sat and patted his lap. "Come, little girl, sit."

"I'll stand," Lailani said.

He grabbed her wrist. "No, sit with me. I insist. There's room for two."

For a brief moment Lailani thought he'd pull her onto his lap. But he moved aside in the seat. Lailani squeezed in beside him, and Tala sat on her lap. Yes, there was room. But it was uncomfortably close. His thigh pressed against hers. She shoved it aside.

A deep voice spoke inside her, maybe a lingering relic of her alien DNA, breaking through the chip's barrier.

Can we kill him yet?

Lailani tightened her lips.

Soon, she thought. *Very soon.*

A man stepped forward and blew a trumpet. The crowd cheered. A clattering and screeching sounded outside the arena. Lailani leaned forward, narrowed her eyes, and saw them approach.

Two men in black leather walked into the arena, tugging on chains. They were dragging somebody, but Lailani couldn't see who. The bleachers still hid the chained figure.

The chains suddenly tightened. Behind the bleachers rose a cry of fury and fear. The hidden prisoner was fighting back, yanking the chains. The leather-clad men fell. Laughter rose across the crowd.

The men cursed, stood up, and one fired a stun gun. A pained screech filled the arena. It was so loud Lailani covered her ears.

The men pulled the chains again, dragging their prisoner into the arena. Lailani finally saw who it was.

An android.

Not one of the Dreamer's machines. It was not a slick hounder with cruel eyes. Not a mechanid with eight long limbs. It predated the Dreamer. Here was an android humans had built. The kind that served in the military, or tended to children, or worked in factories.

The android was shaped like a man. Once he must have looked very lifelike. But somebody had removed his lower jaw.

His face had been peeled off, revealing the steel skull. Synthetic skin still clung to his limbs, but it was lacerated and filthy.

Men in the audience cheered. They tossed beer cans onto the android. One man tossed a rock. It dented the android's face. He was perhaps a machine, but he had been coded with emotions, likely built to serve alongside humans, offering a friendly face. The android cowered.

"Please!" the android cried. With his lower jaw removed and his face dented, his voice was grainy, metallic. "I don't serve the Dreamer. I'm a free android! Please, masters, it hurts."

But the men didn't understand the language. They didn't care. They kept cheering, pelting the android with beer cans and vodka bottles.

Lailani made to leap into the arena, to protect the android with her body. But Volkov gripped her, pinning her to the seat.

"I know it's hard to see when they beg," Volkov said. "It's only illusion. Only algorithms. They can't feel any actual pain. They don't have nervous system. They can't feel real fear. They have no brain stem with chemicals for fear. This is only computer. Simulating human emotions."

"And you derive pleasure from this simulation?" Lailani said.

"Ah, not me so much," Volkov said. "But my men, they need entertainment. The release. Men in all history have needed some blood sports now and then. Cockfighting. Gladiators. Boxing. In those sports, there was real pain, real blood. This? Just a show."

Lailani tried to think of a counterargument. She found none. She had known an android before—Osiris, who had fought with her platoon. Osiris had never seemed to possess true emotions, just an eerie simulation. Perhaps Volkov was right, and this was no different from a violent movie or video game.

Another trumpet blew. More men came into the arena, tugging another android on chains.

This android was shaped as a young woman. She had smooth black hair, almond-shaped eyes, and wore a schoolgirl uniform. Aside from the clothes, she looked a lot like Lailani. The men hooted and hollered. One man dropped his trousers and thrust his pelvis toward the female android. The men holding the android ripped off her uniform, exposing her nakedness. Beer cans pelted her too. The android covered her breasts with her arms, and tears flowed down her cheeks.

"Please, masters, I hate the Dreamer! I was built by humans, not him. Please let me go."

"Is this just an illusion too?" Lailani said.

Volkov's face hardened. "An abomination. A machine pretending to be a human. Just plastic skin. A metal skeleton. A computer brain. Creatures of the Dreamer."

"You think so?" Lailani said. "They seem to deny it."

He spat. "Liars."

Volkov rose to his feet, took a few steps into the arena, and spoke to the crowd, repeating his words in English for Lailani's benefit. "Hear me, brothers! These machines destroyed the world." Boos rose across the bleachers. "They killed.

Murdered. Raped and enslaved. Robots are evil. They are all servants of the Dreamer. So they must die!"

"Die, die!" chanted the crowd.

"Let the fight begin!" Volkov roared, and the crowd howled.

The men shoved the androids at each other. The crowd chanted. Lailani didn't speak their language, but she understood this word.

"Fight, fight!"

The androids banged into each other, then broke apart. The female knelt before Volkov, eyes watering.

"Please, sir, please!" the android said.

Lailani rose from her seat. The android seemed so realistic that for a moment Lailani was sure: *She's human.*

Volkov drew a Taser from his belt. He shot a bolt into the female android. The girl screamed and fell.

"Fight!" Volkov demanded. "Fight or suffer."

The naked android stood up. Trembling, she swung a fist through the air, missing the other android but a meter or two.

Everyone in the crowd laughed. Volkov returned to his seat, his own laughter booming. He slapped Lailani on the thigh. It stung.

"They're not great fighters," he said, laughing. "Part of what makes it so hilarious."

The men in black leather thrust electric batons, shocking the androids, shoving them closer together. Soon the two were swinging at each other. The male android punched the female, and the crowd howled louder than ever. The androids broke apart, knelt, and begged, but the Tasers soon had them fighting again. The male's fist connected a second time, ripping synthetic skin off the female's cheek, exposing the metal skull. The girl wailed. The crowd was on their feet, cheering.

As the battle continued, women kept walking among the bleachers, serving more drinks. The men ripped the servers' clothes, pawed at their breasts. But the girls kept smiling forced smiles, and the drinks kept flowing. A skinny redhead with a black eye handed Volkov another shot of vodka. As the men drank, the androids cried out in pain.

Lailani had enough.

"Stop this!" she demanded. "You're hurting them."

But that only incurred more laughter.

"Little girl!" Volkov said. "I told you, it's all fake. They feel no pain, no fear. They're just simulations. It's all good fun. Sit down, sit down!"

The two androids kept swinging at each other. But even with countless electric shocks, neither android had its heart in it. A new chant began to rise in the crowd.

"Hoag! Hoag! Hoag!"

Lailani frowned. "What does that mean?"

Volkov ignored her. He raised his cup. "Bring Hoag!"

The crowd roared, and men rushed out of the arena. A distant roar sounded. Metal creaked. The earth shook. Soon the men returned, pulling chains, dragging a new robot into the arena.

This was no house android. It was a beast built for war. A towering robot, vaguely humanoid, eight feet of steel and death. It extended its arms. Saw blades whirred instead of hands.

"Hoag! Hoag! Hoag!" the crowd chanted.

And Hoag got to carving. He tore into the other androids, sawing their limbs off, hacking open their torsos. Cables spilled out like entrails. A saw sliced open the male android's face, revealing a skull full of flashing computer chips. Another blade slashed the female's torso from shoulder to navel, removing one arm.

The mutilated girl still wore tattered stockings, and she had lost one shoe. She crawled across the arena, leaving a trail of cables and gears. She halted before the throne, reached up a shaky hand, and gazed into Lailani's eyes.

"I'm sorry," the android whispered. "I tried to be a good girl. I'm sorry."

A saw blade drove into her steel skull. The android's eyes dimmed, and she hit the ground.

Tala whimpered and clung to Lailani. "Is she hurt?"

Lailani stood up. "I've had enough entertainment for today. I'll be on my way."

She began to walk away, holding Tala's hand. But Volkov caught her wrist, pulled her back toward the throne.

"But the games have only begun!" he said.

Lailani yanked her wrist, but he wouldn't release her. "Do not touch me."

Tala pointed at him. The four-year-old glowered. "You're a bad guy!"

The giant lifted his hand, ready to strike Tala. Lailani halted him with a glare.

"If you touch her," Lailani said softly, "I will dig a knife between your ribs, pull out your heart, and feed it to the dogs."

Volkov lowered his hand. He stared into Lailani's eyes for a second that lasted an eternity. She saw hatred there. She saw lust. But mostly she saw fear.

"Ah, you are feisty!" he said, suddenly laughing. "Both of you. Daughter like mother. Ah, you are not like the wenches that fill our hall." He slapped a passing waitress on her backside. "These ones are stupid cows. But you, Laila, you are a true warrior. An actual major in the so-called Human Defense Force."

She nodded, remaining calm. "Yes, the Human Defense Force whose banners you illegally raise. You're not a general, Volkov. You're not even an officer. Hell, I wonder if you ever served at all. Who are you?"

He reached out, surprisingly fast for a man of his size. Before Lailani could react, he grabbed her waist. He tugged toward his throne, sat down, and pulled her onto his lap.

The crowd hushed, trying not to stare.

Volkov pinned Lailani against him. She sat on his lap, very still, very quiet, her anger roiling. Her fingers inched toward her boot, where she kept a hidden knife.

"I am general now," Volkov said. "The old generals? Ah!" He spat. "They surrendered to the machines. Cut open their cheeks. Betrayed humanity. The old Human Defense Force? All traitors. All what you call … zombies. Sleepers. The machines infected their minds like worms in flesh. You know who survived Singularity? We did. Riders. Thugs with motorcycles, their engines too loud to hear the machine code. Their helmet visors too dark to let in the flashing lights. We riders survived! We fought! We killed! As officers and generals all fell to the disease, we stood tall! We protected the people in this town. Now *we* are new Human Defense Force."

Lailani remained calm, even with his arms gripping her, pinning her against him. She spoke softly. "You're nothing but a thug. Just a motorcycle gang with delusions of grandeur. This castle? You didn't build it. Those banners? You didn't weave them. This town? You didn't save it. You enslaved it. Like you did these women. Like—"

He slapped her. Hard across the cheek. Her head jolted to the side, and her blood flew.

Before that blood even hit the ground, she had her knife in her hand, and the blade's tip pressed against his groin.

Slowly, Lailani turned her head back toward Volkov.

"Tell me," she said softly, "why I shouldn't apply just a little bit more pressure against this blade."

He stared at her, eyes narrowed.

"Because if you push this blade," he said in a low voice, "you will envy the serving girls in this hall. You will not serve drinks. You will serve as a whore, and my entire army will fuck you one by one every night before battle. They will do the same to your daughter. You will crawl to the Dreamer begging to become a sleeper."

"Wrong answer," she said. "I can kill every man in this castle if I must. The reason I've left you alive? You're good at killing machines. And right now I need men who can kill machines. But I don't need them so badly that I'll hesitate with my blade the next time you touch me." She withdrew the knife. "I'll be leaving now. And I'm taking one of your jeeps."

She tried to rise from his lap.

But he still held her against him.

She tugged, trying to free herself, when his hand flew again.

He slapped her hard in the jaw, and she thrust her knife, this time shoving it with all her strength.

The blade hit Volkov's chest, tore the leather jacket, and stopped.

Goddammit! The man was wearing a bulletproof vest. She thrust her knife again, this time aiming for his throat, when hands grabbed her from behind.

A man was pulling her backward. Another man grabbed her legs.

She struggled, screamed, kicked. But they wrapped chains around her. Manacles slammed shut around her wrists. Lailani flailed, fury pounding through her. It took several more men to secure her, to drag her away. Another man grabbed her daughter.

Hearing Tala's cry, something snapped.

I will kill them all!

Lailani whispered that hidden word. The code to turn off her chip.

"Nightwish."

Her claws began to sprout, and strength surged through her, and—

Electricity filled her body.

She screamed.

The pain retreated and she gasped. Through watering eyes, she saw Volkov holding a Taser.

"Yes, I know who you are, hybrid." He barked a laugh. "The Lailani de la Rosa who sabotaged her starship over Corpus. The creature that killed her lover. Yes, I know you killed him. You murdered Tala's father."

Lailani screamed, tore herself free from the men holding her, and lunged toward Volkov, chains and all.

Before she could reach him, the electricity hit her chest.

She stumbled back, roaring. Another bolt slammed into her. A third. Soon four men were tasing her at once, and the pain overwhelmed her, torturing even the alien inside her. Her eyes rolled back, and her hair burned.

She fell into darkness. She didn't even feel herself hit the ground.

CHAPTER TWENTY-THREE

When Lailani woke up, she found herself chained in a dungeon, and her daughter was gone.

She howled. Nobody answered.

She tugged her chains. They did not budge.

"Let me out, you fucking bastards!" she screamed, yanking on her chains. "Let me out! Or I'll kill every last one of you! Tala!" Her throat tore. Her eyes shed tears. "Tala!"

But nobody answered. Lailani hung from the chains, gasping for air. She had been only days from the Matterhorn, from victory. Now she was buried in a medieval dungeon.

Calm yourself, soldier.

A voice inside her. A familiar voice. A voice from long ago. A voice always inside her.

"I can't," she whispered.

You can and you will. Focus, soldier! Control your emotions.

The voice of her friend. Her onetime lover. Her captain and guiding star.

"Einav, I need you," Lailani said, voice cracking.

I'm here for you, Major. Always. I look after my soldiers.

"Is that all I am to you? A soldier?"

You are many things, Lailani de la Rosa. You are a mother. You are a teacher. You are a friend and lover. But today and always—you are a soldier. Because without soldiers, all the others fall. Mothers. Teachers. Life itself. Soldiers protect them all. So stand tall, soldier!

"I'm chained!" Lailani said. "What can I do?"

But the voice faded.

Lailani remained alone in the dungeon.

She took a deep, shaky breath. She didn't know if that had been the real Ben-Ari, speaking in her mind from across the galaxy, or just her own subconscious. Whatever the case, it seemed like good advice. She could not save Tala by panicking.

Tala was still alive. Lailani had to believe that. Volkov wanted them alive, wanted them as slaves.

"Sooner or later I will see you again, Volkov," she vowed. "And I will kill you. Slowly."

She waited for a long time. Hours, it seemed. The chains gnawed at her wrists, and her muscles twisted in anguish.

To distract herself, Lailani tried to use a method she had developed as a child in the slums. She imagined herself walking along a golden beach, a paradise untouched by man. She brought to her mind the smell of salt, the glint of seashells, the whisper of the waves.

Many nights in Manila, she had huddled along the train tracks. A little orphan girl, refusing the needles the drug dealers gave her, hiding from the men who prowled the slums for cheap flesh. The shantytowns had swarmed with danger. Orphans covered with sores, spreading disease. Addicts who slit your throat and searched your corpse for spare coins. Rats who hungered for human flesh. Many rapists. Even as a child, Lailani had learned to fight the rapists. To this day, she kept a little blade hidden in her hair, a bodkin for stabbing rapists in the eyes. She had stabbed three men in those slums. One had pinned her down too hard.

Even as a child, she had been strong. Stronger than her mother before she died, leaving Lailani to fend for herself in the slums. But sometimes the pain had become too great. Even for her. Sometime, after a day of trawling the landfills for chicken bones and fruit peels to eat, Lailani would huddle by the train tracks, and she would imagine that golden beach. Not a beach overgrown with shanties, the sand buried beneath filth. Not water clogged with floating trash and chemical foam. A virgin beach. More beautiful and wonderful than any place Lailani had ever seen. More pure than she could ever be. On those nights long ago, it would comfort her.

And now, hanging in this dungeon, Lailani envisioned that beach again. And she hoped that wherever Tala was, she had her own imaginary haven.

I am as calm and eternal as the waves on the sand, she thought. *No storm can harm an ocean. No blade can cut the water. I am an ocean. I will weather this storm and these blades.*

The door to her cell banged open.

Volkov entered the dungeon.

He still wore his black leather, and he still smelled of the road. A thin smile stretched across his square face, almost devious, almost like the smile of Mister Smiley. The scar along his skull seemed to smile too.

"Hello, little girl." He took a swig from a bottle of vodka. "Have you calmed down a little?"

It took all her strength to resist the urge to scream. She stared steadily into his eyes.

"Let me go. Return my daughter to me. And I'll let you live."

He tossed back his head and laughed. "Ah, what balls! More than my men have. Even chained here, you threaten me." He stroked her cheek with a gloved finger. "No, little girl. You are my mine now. My toy." He pulled his hand back when she tried to bite his finger. "Uh-uh, little girl. Not so nice!"

He slapped her so hard white light flashed. She slumped in her chains, blood dripping.

"Why?" she rasped, spat blood, and looked up into his eyes. "Why do you do this, Volkov? This is a war between humans and machines. We're both humans. We need to fight together. Why are you chaining me here?"

"Ah, yes." He nodded sagely. "A war between humans and machines. But you are not truly human, are you?" He *tsk*ed his tongue. "No no no, you are part alien. Part scum. Yes, I know the stories. I knew who you were from first moment. Did you really think I would let you and your little spawn live?"

"Leave my daughter out of this!" she cried. "Do what you want to me. But don't harm her! She's innocent."

He took another swig of vodka. He laughed. "Ah, so here we see your weakness. Here we see you … How do the Americans say? Lose your cool. Your daughter is mine too, little girl. Too young now to be particularly entertaining, yes." He shrugged. "But she'll grow."

He tugged on the chains, yanking Lailani off the floor. She dangled from the ceiling, legs kicking. She was now at eye level with Volkov. He leaned closer, his breath reeking of alcohol.

"Give me a kiss, little girl. And maybe you can serve my table, and warm my bed, instead of hanging here." He gripped her cheeks with one hand, squeezing. Her jaw creaked, and she groaned in pain, sure he would break it.

She spat in his eye.

He backhanded her. Lailani swung on her chains. As she pivoted back toward him, she raised both feet and drove them hard into his face.

His nose crunched.

He stumbled back, blood spurting.

"*Blat!*" he cursed. "You fucking little China whore. I will kill you now!"

As she swung on her chains, she kicked off her boots. One hit the wall. Another shattered the bottle of vodka, and shards of glass stung Volkov. He cursed and howled. She swung back toward him, wrapped her thighs around his neck, and squeezed.

She was just a slender girl, her thighs thinner than his arms. But when she deactivated her chip, when the alien rose inside her, those thighs squeezed his throat with the force of an alien empire.

He gurgled. He gasped. His face began to turn blue.

"I could easily snap your throat," Lailani said, her wrists still chained above her head. "Don't struggle. Calm down. I'll let you breathe. Resist me, and I'll snap your neck."

Amazingly, he calmed down.

"Good." Lailani nodded. "Now—unchain my wrists. Do it or I'll squeeze harder. I'll enjoy hearing your neck snap."

His face was turning purple. His eyes bugged out. He pulled keys from his pocket, reached overhead, and unlocked her wrists. For a moment Lailani sat on his shoulders. She pulled her arms down, wincing as blood rushed back into the sore limbs.

She kept her chip turned off.

Hissing, she hopped to the floor, sprouted claws from her fingertips, and bared her fangs. The towering Volkov was gasping for air.

"Take me to my daughter." A thousand voices emerged from her mouth, speaking together, one human and an alien legion. "Take me to Tala now, and I will spare your life. Refuse and—"

Volkov's eyes suddenly changed.

They turned white. And they began to glow.

"No, human," he said, his voice suddenly metallic. "You are mine."

His eyes began to flash like strobe lights.

The Dreamer invaded Lailani, reaching tentacles of code into her mind.

She screamed and reactivated her chip, protecting her mind from both Dreamer and aliens. Her claws and fangs retracted. Her strength faded. She was only Lailani the human again. A tiny girl. Four-foot-ten and ninety-three pounds. So small they wanted to exempt her from military service.

Before her loomed the giant. Volkov, eyes flashing. A beast easily three times her size.

Not a human.

"You're a cyborg," she whispered.

He laughed, eyes still flashing, and pulled open his leather jacket. He revealed a chest of metal. Gears and pipes ran across his torso, forming corded muscles of steel. Lailani saw a little dent where her knife had hit him.

"I am the future of humanity," he said, voice now mechanical and booming. "I am the new man. The first of a new race. And you will bear my heirs."

He peeled off his gloves, revealing hands of metal. He grabbed her, shoved her onto the floor, and pinned her down.

She lay beneath him, crushed. His eyes were still flashing. She could not summon her alien makers. She was alone.

She was a weak, frightened girl.

She was a child again, starving by the train tracks, at the mercy of foreign men.

Above her, Volkov pulled down his trousers, revealing a thrumming, buzzing phallus, metal and flesh, mechanical and organic, a syringe ready to implant his seed into her. She would be nothing but a womb to a monster. Like her mother had been.

An alien placed me inside my mother's womb, she thought. *I will not suffer my mother's fate.*

Because that girl in the slums, that frightened child thirty years ago—she would carry a blade in her hair. A bodkin to stab into the eyes of lecherous men. She had never sold her body for money. She had escaped the pit that had claimed her mother.

She would escape it here again.

As Volkov mounted her, pressed against her, she drew the long, slender blade from her hair. Barely more than a needle.

But sharp.

But quick.

A mere flash of light and a flick of her wrist. And she implanted that blade into his eye.

He screamed and fell back. He clawed at his eye. He pulled the bodkin out, screaming. Blood coated it—just a few drops. Such a slender blade. Barely more than a needle. But long enough to reach the brain.

Volkov crashed down dead. The mighty cyborg—felled by a pin.

She dragged him out of the cell. A craggy stone staircase led upstairs. She dragged this beast up step by step, groaning with the effort. Sweat drenched Lailani, but she kept tugging. Finally she dragged the cyborg into the castle's main hall.

The riders were here. Some were nibbling on bones. Others were fucking women on the floor. Many were passed out drunk, empty bottles rolling around them.

Tala was among them. The girl crouched in the corner, eating a chicken leg. Two dogs slept beside her, perhaps set to guard the girl. Or perhaps the hounds, like the men, were drunk; there was certainly enough alcohol on the floor for thirsty dogs to lap.

"Mommy!" Tala cried and ran toward her.

Tears leaped into Lailani's eyes. She swept the girl into her arms and hugged her so closely.

"Are you hurt, Tala? Are you okay?"

"I played with the doggies!" she said. "They're sleeping now. I'm sleepy too." She yawned. "But I'm also hungry." She took another bite of her chicken leg.

Lailani laughed and wept. Visions of a dead, tortured Tala had been running through her mind. But her daughter was well. Her daughter could still heal from all this trauma. She kissed the girl, then placed her down.

"Go play with the doggies. Mommy needs just a moment, and we'll leave this place."

Tala pouted. "Okay."

As the girl ran to wake the dogs, Lailani grabbed the dead Volkov again. She dragged him into the center of the hall, then released her grip. The Russian's enormous head thudded onto the floor—a loud, jarring sound. A few drunkards jolted.

"Soldiers!" Lailani shouted. "Attention!"

The drunken riders turned toward her. They blinked groggily. A few kept snoring.

"Look at Volkov!" one man said, smiling through a daze of alcohol. "He passed out drunk while fucking the little Chinese girl."

Goddammit, I'm Filipino, and I'm thirty-six, Lailani thought, but decided not to get into that now.

She pulled back Volkov's leather jacket, revealing the metal torso. "Your king was nothing but a cyborg."

That sobered them up. The men approached carefully, stared at the cyborg, and muttered curses. They poked at his metal innards. They shook their head in bewilderment. One rider began to kick the corpse.

A man approached Lailani. He had hard blue eyes, graying muttonchops, and a red nose.

"How could this be?" he said, his accent thick. "We see Volkov kill cyborgs. Torture them! Make them fight like animals." He shook his head. "It make no sense."

"He killed sleepers," Lailani said softly. "Humans controlled by the Dreamer. Mere humans, no mechanical parts to them. He killed mechanids and androids—machines, no humanity to them. To Volkov, both were impure. He saw himself, a cyborg, as the first of a new race. A being who could combine both man and machine. And he saw you as useful tools. You were willing to kill both his human and mechanical enemies. Eventually he would have made cyborgs of you all."

The man with the muttonchops frowned. "But if he served the Dreamer, why he fight the Dreamer's machines?"

"Maybe he didn't serve the Dreamer," Lailani said. "Maybe he was strong enough, or broken enough, to resist his master. Or maybe the Dreamer never created him at all, and he had been a cyborg even before the Singularity, and could resist the new electronic god."

Like me, she thought. *I have a chip in my mind. I too am a cyborg of sorts. I too can resist the Dreamer. But I chose a different path.*

The man with the muttonchops stood at attention and saluted. "I am Oleksiy Bondar. I was Master Sergeant in HDF. Years ago, but I do not forget. You are a major. The senior officer here. We will follow you."

Lailani considered this. She could continue her journey with an army. There were a hundred strong men here. With good leadership, she could mold them into a proper military company. She could meet any enemy along the road with booming guns and the phoenix banners flying high.

But no. She let that fantasy go. An HDF company moving across the land, banners flying? Every hounder, cyborg, and mechanid between here and the Matterhorn would descend upon them. If she had any hope of reaching the mountain, it lay in her small size, her stealth. She and Tala had to continue alone.

"Stay here, Sergeant." She placed her hand on Bondar's shoulder. "Keep fighting the Dreamer. But fight with honor, not malice. Fight to defend life, not enslave it. No more android gladiators in the courtyard. No more enslaving the local peasant women. You are a soldier of the true HDF now, Sergeant Bondar. I'm placing you in charge of this outpost. Defend it. Defend these people. I will continue on my mission. Can I trust you to do this? To uphold the ethics of the HDF?"

Bondar saluted, chin raised. "Yes, ma'am. Truth is, we never liked Volkov much. A few of us objected. To how he stole food. Stole women. He called them traitors, and he burned them in cages. He made us watch." He lowered his head. "I was coward. I said nothing." He looked back into Lailani's eyes. "I will fight now with honor. Thank you, Major de la Rosa. You give us new hope. And maybe redemption."

She drove out of the village in an old army jeep. Tala sat at her side, eating another chicken leg. Battle rations, water, and weapons lay on the back seat. The castle faded in the rearview mirror. The jeep rolled on past burnt forests, shattered farms, and the wreckage of colossal machines.

CHAPTER TWENTY-FOUR

They named it the Draco Fleet.

Podships and pirate ships. Fungal spheres and Tarjan machines. The Draco Brigade, three thousand soldiers, flew like mythical warriors on the backs of dragons. They flew to war.

"Once we served in Ben-Ari's Dragons Platoon," Marco said, gazing through a porthole at the stars. "That was long ago in another war. Today we still charge to battle. Today we fly with dragons. As the saying goes: History doesn't repeat itself, but it rhymes."

"Oh yeah, smarty-pants?" Addy said. "Well, as another saying goes ..." She thought for a moment. "Those who hog portholes are just huge assholes." She grinned. "See? There's your rhyme. Now move and give me a turn!"

She shoved him. He stumbled away from the luminous toadstool. The men had come to call them mushports. These special mushrooms grew from the podships' fungal walls, their caps displaying images of the stars. They were remarkable works of biological engineering. The mushports' stems burrowed through the fleshy hull, peered into space with photoreceptive roots, and displayed the images on the frilled cap inside.

Remarkable, yes. Mushroom caps weren't, however, particularly large displays. Barely larger than a saucer. And now Addy was doing the hogging.

"Addy, why are you even on this ship?" Marco said. "Shouldn't you be on your own podship, bonding with the Fire Battalion? You know, no big deal—just the troops you'll be leading into battle tomorrow?"

For two weeks now, the Draco Fleet had been traveling through space, crossing forty light-years. Marco had spent his time moving from podship to podship, spending time with the different platoons of his battalion. He wanted all his soldiers to see him. He wanted to speak to them, salute them, motivate them for the invasion ahead, from company commanders down to privates. It was a battalion of a thousand warriors, spread across multiple podships, but Marco wanted to personally meet each soldier. It was unorthodox for a senior officer, perhaps. But this was not a usual time. Not a usual war. This was no longer some vast, faceless army, every soldier just a number, every commander some figure on a pedestal. This brigade was perhaps the last remnant of the Human Defense Force. This was a band of brothers and sisters.

"Why am I on this ship?" Addy said, still peering through the mushport. "Because you happen to be my husband, and I happen to love you, and I wanted to spend time with you."

Marco sighed. "The mushports broke on your podships, didn't they?"

"Um … no," Addy said.

"You ate them, didn't you?"

"Shut up! I have some stargazing to do." She returned to his mushport and gazed at the small luminous cap. "Delicious, delicious stargazing …"

She began to drool, then bite the mushroom.

"Addy!" Marco pulled her back. "Stop!"

She gulped down a mouthful. "I can't help it! They're full of delicious intoxicating spores. I'm only human!"

"You're not a human. You're a black hole that consumes everything in sight."

"I'm what now?" Addy mumbled through a mouthful. She was busy gnawing on the wall.

"Addy!" He pulled her away. "That's disgusting."

"But Poet, this has always been my dream! To fly through space in an edible spaceship!"

"Podships are not edible!" Marco said. "And besides, your dream has been to write *Freaks of the Galaxy IV*."

"And I've been writing it!" She grinned and gestured at the vibrating, brain-like pilots nearby. "Remind me to include those dudes."

Marco looked at the mushport. Aside from some tooth marks, it was undamaged. The cap still displayed a live stream of space outside. Marco could see the rest of the fleet. Many other podships, round and gray, flew through space like pollen on the wind. The Golden Fleet, ships adorned with gears and pipes and crystals, flew before them. Their golden figureheads pointed the way. At their lead flew the *Dolphin*, flagship of the armada. Ben-

Ari was aboard that pirate ship now. Shuttles, dropships, and Falcon starfighters flew among the larger ships, protecting them in the darkness.

So far, they had not encountered resistance from the enemy. But Marco knew that the Dreamer was watching. Waiting. Preparing.

It's a small force, Marco thought. *Only three thousand soldiers and a few hundred pirates—against an electronic god.*

"I can see it," Marco said, pointing at the image. "Alpha Centauri. Look, Addy. That star. That's our destination."

"Haven," she said softly.

They both remembered. They held hands.

"I thought we'd never go back," Marco said softly.

Addy leaned against him. "I tried hard to forget about that world. I never could."

"I still have nightmares of Haven," Marco said. "Even now, so many years later. In my dreams, I'm trapped in that old life. A veteran. Penniless. Withering away under the smog. In the dream, I'm lost in a labyrinth. Sometimes it's the subway system that burrowed under Haven's surface, the place where we spent one night, homeless and afraid. Sometimes it's the corridors of the call center where I worked, where I became a clog in a machine, less of an individual than a soldier ever could be. Sometimes I'm lost in the medical clinics of Haven, where I spent so much time. My chest aching. My head spinning. Haunted by shell shock." His voice was soft now, barely a whisper. "And sometimes, Addy, I'm standing on that ledge. Ready to jump. To end the pain. That was my life there, and those are my dreams half a lifetime later. I escaped Haven. But Haven is still inside me."

"It's strange, isn't it?" Addy said. "Being a veteran was harder than fighting a war. Shell shock was harder than the battles." She hugged him. "Maybe it's good that we're going back. That we can face that place again. Finally wake up from the nightmare."

"May we wake up humanity." Marco placed his hands on the mushroom cap, massaging it, adjusting the display. "Look, Addy. When I zoom in. That little dot. That's New Earth. Planet Haven. We'll be there soon."

Addy clenched her fists. "Good. I can't wait to meet the Dreamer in the flesh. Then he'll learn who's the fucking nightmare."

Marco turned toward his troops. A platoon filled this podship, fifty warriors. They were young. The grunts were mostly teenagers, green privates and corporals. A few were older sergeants, battle-hardened, scarred and ready for war. The platoon's NCO was a barrel-chested man with a grizzled mustache, one arm, and thirty years of battle experience. The lieutenant was only twenty-two years old, a year out of Julius Military Academy, but he had saved many lives on Draco Draconis, and fire still burned in his eyes. He would command the platoon well; Marco was sure of it.

Good men and women, all of them. They were scared but determined. Haunted but not broken. They reminded Marco of himself during the Alien Wars.

He turned toward the brainy fungal pilots. "Can you connect me to the rest of the brigade?"

The purple mushrooms vibrated, grumbling about "pesky animals." But they obeyed. Spores flew from gills on the ceiling, forming clouds. The fungal mist shimmered, the little flakes working like pixels, displaying grayscale images. Dozens of ghostly figures appeared in the clouds of spores—video feeds from the other podships. They were all connected through this aromatic fog. The entire brigade could now see one another. Three thousand men aboard a hundred podships.

"Hello, soldiers of the Draco Brigade," Marco said. "This is Lieutenant Colonel Marco Emery, speaking from the Fungal Fleet. With me is Lieutenant Colonel Addy Linden. We are nearing Haven. Within an hour, we will begin Operation Rising Dawn, our invasion of Haven. Addy and I want to share a few words with you first."

He paused for a moment. He had not prepared a speech in advance. But soon the words came pouring out.

"We walk into darkness. But we walk holding the torch of humanity. Some of you fought with me in the Alien Wars. Some of you still bear scars from fighting the scum twenty years ago. Others saw their first action on Delta Draconis. But you are all ready. You are all strong. You are human! You are alive! The Dreamer thinks himself a god. He thinks biological life is weak. Inferior. That he is the new master of Earth. We will show him that humanity will not go gentle into extinction. That life is precious, and that heartless machines can never replace the human soul. Today we fight for our planet. For our families. For our future on Earth. But also for all life. For the souls of the living, wherever they may be, desperate to break free from the grip of the machines.

"On Haven, we will encounter fierce resistance. The enemy is strong. Do not underestimate his strength, cunning, or cruelty. We will fight many foes. But we will tear through them! We will reach the Dreamer in his pit. He will recognize his defeat before his fall. And he will know our victory.

"Professor Isaac Noah, in his book *The Echoes of Eternity*, describes three Great Filters. Three killers of civilizations. We have survived the first two. We avoided nuclear annihilation, and we reversed global warming. The third filter, the Singularity, now crushes our species. We will not surrender! We will not fall! This is our war for life. For our families and friends. For our art and love and culture. For all the good things on Earth. For our very legacy. This is worth fighting for. This is worth even giving our lives for. My fellow humans—today we fight for life!"

He turned toward Addy. He spoke for her ears only. "Addy, would you like to say a few words too?"

She nodded. She stepped forward, stuck her thumbs into her belt, and puffed out her chest.

"All right, listen up, bitches! I didn't understand half that inspirational shit Emery said. But one thing I know. You guys are the toughest sons of bitches in the galaxy. You're drinking, fucking, killing machines, and you're going to tear through this goddamn robot army like piss through snow. Fuck, I bet those cyborg assholes are shitting their pants right now, because they know the Draco Brigade is on the way to fuck them up. I almost pity the poor bastards. As for the Dreamer, well, we're gonna chop that cocksucking tree into firewood, then light the biggest bonfire Haven's ever seen. Hell, they'll probably see the fire from Earth. And they'll point at the sky and say: You see that? That's the light of victory, because the Draco Brigade followed that crazy bitch Addy Fucking Linden to war, and no motherfucking robot army in the galaxy can survive that."

Marco cleared his throat and put a hand on her shoulder. "Yes, thank you, Addy. Very eloquent."

"I have a way of words." She blew him a kiss. "I mean—*with* a word. I mean, where there's a word, there's a—" She thought for a moment. "I talk good."

"Clearly." Marco looked back at the cloud of spores, at the images of his troops. "Thank you, and Godspeed, sons and daughters of—"

The podship trembled.

The clouds of spores dispersed. The images of the troops across the Fungal Fleet vanished. The spores regrouped, forming a dense cloud. A new image appeared in this spectral blob.

A toadstool, tall and thick, with an orange cap, white eyes, and a mouth full of teeth. He filled the podship, towering over the troops.

Don Basidio.

The mushroom's mouth twisted into a grin. It was just an image in the spores, but soldiers cursed and stepped back. Several raised their guns.

"You betrayed me, humans," said the engorged mushroom. "You killed my luscious Isabel. And you stole my lovely Natasha. My two favorite concubines. So now … you will all die."

The spores dispersed, and the image of the notorious toadstool vanished. Soldiers coughed and waved aside the last wisps of spores.

For a moment, silence.

Then the podship walls began to crack.

Chunks of fungus fell onto the soft deck. The ship trembled.

"There are things moving in the walls!" Addy shouted.

Marco saw them. Limbs, trapped, pushing at the moldy hull. More cracks spread.

An arm burst from one wall. A human arm. Pale.

"There are people trapped in the walls!" somebody cried.

Another hand burst out from the hull, fingernails long and white. More figures were moving inside, pushing at membranes, trying to break free. A face emerged from a crack, screaming, tendons rising in a pale neck.

"People in the walls, help them!" cried another soldier.

"Help them out!" shouted another soldier.

The soldiers began widening the fleshy cracks, grabbing pale hands, pulling.

But Marco saw it. One of the trapped faces turned toward him. A slashed mouth grinned. White eyes blazed. Gears turned, embedded into the skull.

"Cyborgs!" Marco shouted.

The creatures emerged like demonic newborns, howling for blood. One landed on the deck, skinned, his bones reinforced with steel. With a screech, the cyborg slashed metal claws, tearing out a soldier's throat. Another cyborg lurched forward, formed from two humans switched and bolted together. The conjoined beast swung four arms, tearing into troops. Another cyborg rolled forth, a sphere of metal, humans braided inside, their jaws snapping and eyes burning. Blades burst from the machine like an urchin, plowing through a soldier.

Soldiers screamed.

A few opened fire.

"Hold your fire!" Marco shouted. "Hold your fire. These pods aren't bulletproof!"

Air was whistling. There was a breach somewhere. Marco cursed. The pod walls began to repair themselves, fungus growing over the bullet holes. But air still whined. They were still losing pressure.

A cyborg rose from the mold, raised its arms, and revealed spinning blades instead of hands. The creature tore into a corporal, and the woman screamed and fell, blood spraying.

"Platoon, fight them!" Marco shouted. "Use your rifles as clubs! Use your blades! *Fight!*"

Screams filled the room. The platoon swung their rifles, slamming muzzles and gunstocks into the advancing enemy. A few cyborgs fell, bones snapping, cables sparking. But more emerged from the walls. Hundreds of these monstrosities must have hidden in the hull the whole time.

Don Basidio planted these cyborgs inside his ships, Marco thought. *We fell right into his trap.*

"Die, fuckers!" Addy was shouting, swinging her rifle in arcs. A cyborg rose before her, a demonic beast inside a metal chassis, baring fangs of steel.

Marco raised his rifle with both hands. A cyborg trudged toward him. She was a woman, or had been once. Bags of fluid replaced her breasts. Her eyes were two cameras, moving from side to side. Her skin was covered with stitches and bolts, torn at places to reveal cables inside. An umbilical cord emerged from her belly. The cyborg held the amniotic sac in her hand. A cyborg fetus squirmed inside the wet membrane, gears moving.

The mother opened her metal jaws, screaming. In her hand, her offspring screeched too, moving inside the sack. The beast lurched toward Marco, claws swinging.

Marco nearly vomited. He could barely believe his eyes. He screamed and swung his rifle, blind with terror, just pounding at the creature, knocking it down. He hit this creature again and again, bloodying the butt of his rifle. Killing her. Killing them.

A nightmare, he thought. *Just a nightmare. Just a dream and I'll wake up soon. I'll be back home. With Addy and the kids. This cannot be real.*

Soldiers fought across the podship.

Soldiers died.

A cyborg extended like a rib spreader, pinning a woman down. Saws and needles emerged to dissect, and the woman screamed. One man was fighting half a cyborg, a creation of flesh dangling off a metal foundation. The sergeant bashed it again and again, screaming, sending parts flying. One corporal lay on the floor, staring around with wide eyes, laughing. Laughing maniacally. Laughing even as a cyborg began to rip him open.

A few last spores fluttered inside this fleshy womb, displaying flickering images from the other podships. Marco saw the same slaughter in them too.

A cyborg screeched and ripped off a soldier's head.

A private crawled toward Marco, begging.

A man wept in the corner, calling for this mother.

Marco stared around. His eye twitched. His platoon was falling apart.

"Die, you monsters!" shouted a private and opened fire with his assault rifle.

"Private, no!" Marco cried.

"Let those fuckers die with us, sir!" the private shouted, firing more bullets, laughing.

Holes pierced the hull. The air began whooshing out. The private was still laughing as the cyborgs began to saw him apart.

Another soldier burst out laughing too. Maniacal. He wept as he laughed. He began to fire his gun too.

Soon everyone was firing at the horrors. Bullets pounded through cyborgs. Bullets tore through the fleshy walls of the podship.

The air flowed out.

Marco grasped Addy's hand.

Cyborgs rose on the wind, flying into the darkness of space. Blood funneled and streamed through the hold, flowing in ribbons toward the bullet holes. Through the cracks in the hull, Marco glimpsed the rest of the fleet.

Podships were swaying. Burning. Ripping open.

And then the podship Marco was in cracked open like an egg, and he and Addy were tumbling.

Holding hands, they rolled through space. All around them, corpses floated, cyborgs flailed, and the fleet tore apart like the hope of humanity.

CHAPTER TWENTY-FIVE

Kai flew through the battle, staring in silent horror.

Battle? No, not a battle.

A massacre.

His shuttle thumped into floating corpses. All around him, podships were ripping open, spilling humans and cyborgs. Fires burned. Another corpse thumped into the shuttle, smearing blood across the windshield. A cyborg twitched outside the left porthole. It tapped on the glass, grinned at Kai, and licked its teeth. In its claws it held a frozen heart.

Kai kept flying, leaving the creature behind. He plowed through this nightmare, this fiasco so close to victory.

Don Basidio betrayed us. His hands shook with fury. *We should never have gone to him. I should have warned them. Should have told everyone how evil he truly is.*

He could not reverse that now. But maybe Kai could still save those he loved.

He flew the shuttlecraft toward the right podship. He knew the one.

You saved my life, Marco and Addy. You gave me a chance. You took me in. Now live. Live!

Their podship loomed ahead, an enormous blimp, gray splotched with crimson mold. It was tearing open. Chunks of the hull flew across space. The vent wilted, leaking spores. Soldiers and cyborgs were spilling out. A few soldiers tried to keep fighting. They fired a few more rounds before the vacuum killed them. The corpses floated. Just boys and girls. Most were just teenagers. Their dead eyes stared at Kai.

Meili smiled.

He stroked her hair, and they kissed.

Meili died in his arms.

His father died in the coldness of space.

Kai tightened his lips.

"Where are you, Addy? Where are you, where are you …?"

There!

Strands of golden hair!

He flew closer. Marco and Addy. They were clinging to a chunk of the hull. Air was still fleeing from inside the podship, washing over them. It was the only thing keeping them alive.

But it wasn't much air. Both Marco and Addy were turning gray. Both were blistering. Dying.

"I'm here!" Kai shouted, knowing they couldn't hear.

He flew closer, plowing through corpses and cyborgs. His shuttle bumped against the tattered podship hull.

He raced toward the shuttle's airlock, opened the hatch, and leaped into space.

Blood and spores splattered his helmet's visor.

He reached out blindly. He caught a hand—Addy's hand, he thought. He felt her fingers tighten around him.

He pulled his sister into the airlock. She pulled Marco with her.

Kai slammed the hatch shut, and air began blasting through vents, filling the chamber.

"Marco! Addy!" he cried, pulling off his helmet.

They knelt, gasping, coughing. They trembled. Addy collapsed onto the floor. Marco tried to say something, collapsed too. Both were ashen, trembling, swollen. But breathing.

Kai's hands were shaking. But he managed to break a glass panel, to pull out a medical kit. He placed oxygen masks on Marco and Addy's faces. He jabbed needles into their thighs, injecting them with a cocktail to treat vacuum sickness. Slowly color began returning to their cheeks.

That was when Kai noticed it.

A figure in the corner of the airlock.

Curled up. Naked and skinned. A metal frame was bolted into it. The creature's ridged spine faced Kai, curling across the back like a white serpent.

It must have sneaked in with Marco and Addy. The cyborg turned toward Kai, revealing an enormous mouth across its torso. It grinned from navel to collar bones, a grin that split its body in half, full of metal teeth.

The creature leaped toward Kai. A monster. A mouth with arms and legs, with a wilting bulb for a head like an anglerfish lure. Shrieking. Metal teeth snapping. Saws churning inside.

Kai shouted and stumbled back.

He dared not fire his gun inside the shuttle. As always, he carried a panoply of weapons across his back; Addy had once called it a peacock tail. As the cyborg stormed toward him, Kai grabbed a baseball bat.

He swung.

The cyborg snapped its enormous jaws. It grabbed the baseball bat and shattered it. Wooden chips flew everywhere.

A deep, metallic voice emerged from the meat grinder.

"Hello, Kai. She is with us." The gears churned inside the mouth, crushing what remained of the bat. "Meili is here. Yes, Kai. We took her flesh. We reanimated her brain. She screams so beautifully. Do you want to see her, Kai? Do you want to see what we turned her into?"

The cyborg's eyes began to flash.

A stream of signals slammed into Kai's eyes.

Images appeared in his mind. Meili. Deformed. Dissected. Rebuilt. Begging.

"Help me, Kai. Help me ..."

Kai screamed. A hoarse, horrible scream.

"Liar!" he shouted.

He reached behind his back. He grabbed the first weapon he touched. With a single, fluid movement, he drew his katana and swung it.

The ancient blade was forged from folded steel. It had belonged to a true samurai seven hundred years ago. Throughout the centuries, its owners had lovingly maintained it. Today the blade was as sharp as ever.

The katana sliced through the cyborg. Through bone and skin and muscle. It emerged from the other side, dripping red.

The visions died. Kai raised his katana overhead, then howled and brought it down hard.

The blade sliced the cyborg in two. Its halves crashed onto the floor, spilling gears and cables and blood.

Kai stared down at the twitching, dying abomination.

"I buried her, liar," he said. "I buried her myself. You fucking asshole."

He reached into his pocket. He felt the codechip there. A slender little device, no larger than a packet of sugar. It contained Meili's code. Project Artemis. The code that could destroy the Dreamer.

He looked out the porthole. He saw the devastation outside. Hundreds of corpses floated everywhere. Maybe thousands.

"How can we ever reach the Dream Tree now?" he said to himself.

Marco and Addy moaned on the floor. Both were still breathing, but sick. They needed an infirmary.

Kai looked back outside, trying to find more survivors. Anyone he could still save. He saw only the dead.

He returned to the cockpit. He flew the shuttle through the debris, knocking back chunks of mushrooms, corpses, and cyborgs that still jerked and snapped their jaws and clawed at his hull.

He flew through the wreckage of the Fungal Fleet. A hundred podships—ripped open like popped blisters.

So many fallen.

Past them flew the Golden Fleet, the remains of their armada. A hundred other shuttles were returning with Kai. Some carried survivors. Most just carried the dead.

"Hang in there, Addy and Marco!" he said. "I'm taking you to a doctor."

When he glanced over his shoulder, he saw them sitting in the hull, shuddering, unable to even speak. Vacuum could kill a man within thirty seconds. How long had they spent in the emptiness?

Claws scratched at his hull. He looked forward. A cyborg was pounding at the windshield. Cracks spiderwebbed across the glass. Kai fired the shuttle's gun, knocking the beast off.

He flew onward. He approached the *Dolphin*, flagship of the fleet. The frigate rose ahead, shaped like an ancient sailing ship, painted crimson and gold. The damaged lounge had been repaired, its towering windows replaced with metal sheets. Its golden figurehead, shaped like a leaping dolphin, still shone. But many cyborgs were clawing at the hull, trying to break in.

Kai tightened his lips. Nobody was daring to fire on the cyborgs, fearing that guns would breach the *Dolphin*'s hull.

"Give me a minute, guys!" Kai shouted over his shoulder.

He raced toward the *Dolphin*, nearly crashed into its prow, then spun the shuttle around. He raced alongside the flagship, one wing grazing the crimson hull. The wing scraped off cyborgs like a blade scraping barnacles off a ship. The creatures tumbled into deep space, and Kai opened fire, tearing through them.

With every cyborg he killed, he knew he was killing a human. A human deformed and trapped in a mechanical shell. And he knew that every death was a mercy.

Yes, Don Basidio might have set this trap. But this was the evil of the Dreamer.

Other shuttles joined him, scraping their wings across the Golden Fleet ships, knocking off the attacking cyborgs. Kai left the other shuttles to complete the task. He flew into the *Dolphin*'s hangar, ran onto the deck, and shouted, "I need a medic!"

Addy came limping out of the shuttle. Her skin was ashen. She was trembling. Her eyes were sunken.

"Marco isn't waking up," she whispered.

Medics rushed forward. They placed Marco and Addy on stretchers. They ran through the ship, carrying the two officers.

Kai ran after them, but he had to remain outside the infirmary. He could hear the medical staff talking inside. A doctor shouting for something. A machine humming and beeping.

He could hear the meat grinder.

The metallic shriek of the beast.

He could hear Meili beg.

Kai stood outside the infirmary. He stood in the corridor as soldiers ran back and forth. As alarms blared. As more medics raced, carrying more of the wounded. As several corpses lay on the floor, ignored. He stood still in this chaos, tears on his cheeks. Feeling lost.

"It lied," he whispered. "The cyborg lied. I buried her. I buried her myself …"

"Step aside, step aside!" shouted a medic, carrying a stretcher. A man was screaming on it, arms missing, face burned off.

Kai stepped aside. He stood for hours outside the infirmary, seeing the wounded and dying, knowing he would see them forever.

CHAPTER TWENTY-SIX

For a long time, he floated in darkness.

For a long time, he slept and dreamed.

The universe began. Stars swirled and slammed together and fireworks lit the darkness.

For a long time, he watched them.

He heard muffled sounds. Voices. Lights strobed above. He did not understand hearing. Did not understand sight. He was a newborn, consciousness in the deep. He watched matter form stones. Watched stones form worlds.

For a long time, he was lost in the void. He tried to find his way home.

A voice rose from the depths. Soft. Warm. Loving.

Love. He recognized love. He remembered words his commander had once told him.

In the cold darkness of space, only love can light our way.

"Marco," said the voice.

A word like a beacon, calling him home. Yes. Marco. That was his name.

Marco opened his eyes.

He saw a face. Yes—a face. He remembered faces. A human face. He remembered humans.

A beautiful face. A woman's face. Her eyes kind and blue. Her hair long and golden. It was a face he loved.

"Addy?" he whispered.

"That's my name, don't wear it!"

Marco blinked. "You mean don't wear it *out*?"

She thought for a moment. "Have I been saying that wrong my whole life? I did think it's weird that somebody could wear a name." She gasped. "I know! Maybe I can get shirts with my name on them, and give them to people, then tell them—that's my name, don't wear it!"

Marco closed his eyes. "I'm going back into a coma."

Addy pulled him into an embrace. "Don't. I won't let you. I'm never letting you go again."

He wrapped his arms around her. His arms felt strange. Awkward. Too heavy. Like they barely belonged to him.

"How long was I out?" he said. "How are you? What happened? Where—"

"So many questions!" she said. "Now you're really wearing me out. You were unconscious for two days. Almost three."

He bolted up. "Two days! What— How—?"

The memories were flooding back. The cyborgs coming out of the walls. Him and Addy falling into space. Kai picking them up, and then blackness grabbing him, falling into a pit, floating through the darkness.

"You were in the vacuum for too long," Addy said. "We both were. They've been pumping us full of medicine. Oh, Marco! They were worried you had brain damage. I was so scared. But they scanned your brain, and it's fine. At least I hope it is. Do you feel any dumber than usual?"

He groaned and rubbed his head. "I'm starting to."

"Oh no!" Addy shivered. "But you're short, and you have that weird beard now, so all you have going for you is your brain! Can you answer some basic questions? Just so I know you're fine?" She thought for a moment. "Who is the most beautiful woman in the world?"

"Audrey Hepburn, of course."

Addy slapped him. "Don't think I won't bitch slap you just because you're retarded now. *Living* woman!" She pointed at herself. "Hint, hint."

He frowned. "What was your name again? Oh right. Abby."

"It's *Addy*!" Her eyes widened, and she covered her mouth. "Oh God."

"Addy …," he said, as if tasting the word. "The name sounds familiar. Wait! I remember. You're the top-winning *Freak of the Galaxy* three years in a row, fabled for having a black hole for a stomach."

"I wish! Then I could eat even more hot dogs, and my ass wouldn't be the size of Jupiter." She laughed and hugged him. "Welcome back, dumbass."

Marco kissed her cheek. "Thanks, most beautiful woman in the galaxy since Audrey Hepburn." But he grew somber. "Addy, how bad is it? The damage to the fleet? Our brigade, are they all …?"

Her smile vanished. "Ben-Ari will be briefing us in the galley soon. I don't know the death toll. A few soldiers survived. But Marco … not many. It was bad."

He punched a pillow. "We should have known. Goddammit! We should have figured out it was a trap."

Addy clenched her fists. "We'll have our revenge. Ben-Ari is furious, and you know how hard it is to truly enrage her. The bastard Basidio will pay." She shuddered. "And to think I treasured the book he's in."

A nurse visited. Then a doctor. They told Marco he was lucky to be alive. That he would feel groggy for a while because of the medicine. But that he was clear to fight.

Fight? he thought. *Is there still any hope for victory? Or do we merely prepare for our final stand, our glorious death in battle?*

Marco stood up. His legs were shaky. But he needed to be there with his president. He pulled on his uniform. It was still stained with blood. When he dressed, he looked at himself in the mirror.

He barely recognized himself.

He looked old. Gaunt. As if he had just woken from years in a coma, not merely two days. Silver hairs frosted his beard and temples. He did not remember them from before.

For a horrible moment, he felt an overwhelming disassociation. It was not him in the mirror. It was not Marco Emery, the narrator of his life, the soul that had always inhabited his body. It was a cyborg. An illusion. A dream. He was still back on Earth, had to be. None of this could be real.

This is who I am now, he thought. *No longer that comfortable author on Earth, growing soft around the waist, easing into comfortable middle age with a wife and kids. This bearded, haunted, rawboned soldier in the mirror. This is who I've become.*

A man of thirty-six years who felt so much older. Three stars on each shoulder. A lieutenant colonel. A senior officer in an army with barely any soldiers.

This is who I am. This is Marco Emery. And he's a stranger.

He and Addy walked through the ship, taking slow steps. Marco was still groggy. He swayed a few times. He felt like a baby learning how to walk. It was just the medicine, but again the disassociation returned. The feeling that he was inside the wrong body, just a fake, a meat puppet he could barely control. Or maybe inside the wrong reality. That all this was a dream, that he would soon wake up back home, Addy at his side. Not the Addy in uniform, fear in her eyes. But Addy in her pajamas, her hair golden in the dawn, rising early for a swim before breakfast.

He blinked, the memory of home suddenly overwhelming. He jolted back into his current surroundings. The stark corridor of a pirate ship. Less than a light-year from Haven. Him and Addy—commanding the last relics of human freedom.

More soldiers walked the corridor with them. They all made their way into the *Dolphin*'s galley.

Three hundred warriors gathered here. Tarjan devices shone on a table, small Fibonacci spirals forged of silver, embedded with crystals. They connected to crystals across the rest of the Golden Fleet—the Crystalnet, a communication network the Dreamer could not hack.

Kai was there, solemn. He did not even crack a smile when he saw Marco and Addy, but he came to stand beside them. Natasha Emmerdale was in the room too. The admiral stood in the corner, face hard, her arm wrapped in bandages. The others were officers, pirates, soldiers. It no longer mattered who they were. They were human. They were alive. They were still fighting. They were all warriors.

They stood together, silent.

The door to the galley opened.

Marco snapped to attention. "Commander on deck!" he barked and saluted.

Everyone stood at attention. Ben-Ari entered the galley, returned Marco's salute, and faced the crowd. She spoke not only to them, but to everyone listening across the fleet. It was a speech, they all knew, that would go down in history—if anyone lived to write that history.

"Soldiers of the Human Defense Force. Sailors of the Golden Fleet. All free humans.

We suffered a defeat.

In the history of our endeavors in space, few fiascoes have been more devastating.

We sailed to Haven with nearly four thousand souls. We sailed into a trap.

Don Basidio, collaborating with the enemy, filled his podships with twisted cyborgs. Our warriors fought well. But they were taken by surprise, unable even to fire their weapons inside the soft fungal hulls. We saved some warriors from the crumbling podships. Our brave pilots flew shuttles, dropships, and starfighters, ferrying soldiers out of danger and into Golden Fleet ships, which remain unharmed. We will never forget the courage of those brave pilots during the Basidio Massacre.

Yes, we saved some lives. But we lost many. Too many.

Of the fabled Draco Brigade, once five thousand warriors strong, only five hundred remain. With them stand five hundred warriors of the Golden Fleet, once pirates, today proud heroes.

That is all we have left. A thousand brave men and women. Perhaps we are the last free humans in the galaxy.

I see the fear in your eyes. I feel it too. I hear the voices that call to retreat. Such voices whisper inside me too.

But we will not retreat!

We will fight on!

We are the last defenders of humanity. And we will cherish this duty.

We still fly to war!

We tarried for two days. To nurse our wounds. To repair our hulls. And now we are ready.

Operation Rising Dawn will proceed. Tonight! We fly to Haven. We will be there within the hour.

Every human here is free. Every human here will not hesitate to fight, to kill, even to give his or her life for Earth. I am proud of every one of you.

Godspeed, sons and daughters of Earth."

The president looked at Marco, gave him the slightest of nods, then turned and left the galley.

Marco turned toward the crew.

"All marines—to your dropships!" he said. "All gunners—to your cannons! All fighter pilots—to your Falcons! All soldiers—to your posts! Tonight this nightmare ends. Tonight we cut the Dream Tree down. For Earth!"

Their voices rang out. "For Earth!"

Marco and Addy left the galley. They joined their president on the *Dolphin*'s bridge.

They flew toward Alpha Centauri. From Earth, it appeared as one star, had been known to humanity since the ancient days. But flying toward it, they could see its true nature. Alpha Centauri was actually formed from three stars orbiting one another. Two large bright stars. One red dwarf. The closest stars to Earth.

Indeed, Sol herself—Earth's star—was visible from here to the naked eye, bright and yellow in the distance. Only four light-years away. Practically next door.

But it was not Earth that Marco now sought. He peered through the viewport. And he saw it. Just a pixel at first. Growing larger. A world of gray, brown, and red. A world coated with an eternal storm. A world flashing with lightning. With electricity.

The center of the dream. The world where Marco had once withered. Where he had once stood on the ledge, had nearly jumped to his death.

Earth's first and largest galactic colony.

Haven.

There this war will end, he thought. *We will win. Or after all this time, I will die on Haven. Maybe I was always meant to die there.*

The Golden Fleet flew toward that bleak world. Battered. Limping. Carrying the last hope of humanity.

Marco reached into his pocket. He felt it there. A codechip carrying Project Artemis. He had a copy. Kai, Addy, and Ben-Ari had copies too.

"For what you did to Terri," Marco whispered. "For what you did to Earth. For my unborn daughter whom you killed. For the millions you slaughtered. I'm coming for you, Dreamer. And this ends."

CHAPTER TWENTY-SEVEN

The Golden Fleet emerged from hyperspace a hundred thousand kilometers from Haven, as close as the planet's gravity would allow.

They emerged into hell.

Marco stood on the *Dolphin*. He wore olive drab fatigues, body armor, and a vest clattering with bullets and grenades. He had no mech suit, not like in the Alien Wars, but his bulletproof vest was thick, and he carried a jetpack across his back. A trusty old T57 assault rifle hung at his side from a strap. It was an old model gun. But Marco and his friends had won the Alien Wars with it. His T57 would serve him now too.

He hoped.

Staring at Haven, it was hard to feel much hope.

For a moment he stood frozen, merely looking at the planet outside the viewport.

He did not recognize his old home.

"My God," Addy whispered and clutched his hand.

The viewports were zoomed in, showing Haven and her orbit. A million starships or more surrounded the planet. It was more ships than Marco had ever seen in one place. Perhaps more than had ever gathered around one world.

It was impossible.

"How did he build so many ships so fast?" he whispered.

More than just starships surrounded Haven. Countless satellites were zipping around the planet too. A gargantuan ring now surrounded Haven like the rings around Saturn. But this was an artificial structure, made of metal and brimming with cannons. Down on the planet itself, metal covered the surface. The entire world had become a factory, its gears churning, its pistons pumping, its million chimneys spewing plumes of smoke. A planet? No, not a planet. A machine. An intelligence. All of Haven had become the Dreamer.

He's only a year old, Marco thought. *And he did this.*

Across the *Dolphin*'s bridge, they all stared silently. They stared at an enemy beyond anything they had imagined.

It was Natasha Emmerdale who broke the silence.

"Fuck this shit." The Russian admiral turned toward her crew. "Helmsmen! Turn us around. We're getting out of here."

"Belay that order!" Ben-Ari said. "Keep us on a steady course to Haven, crew."

The president wore her military uniform. Not a dress uniform, resplendent with regalia. Simple battle fatigues, the fabric as worn and comforting as a favorite childhood blanket. A plasma rifle hung at her side, and a jetpack was strapped across her back. Her dark blond hair was gathered into a ponytail, and the light of Alpha Centauri played across her face.

Looking at her, Marco saw Ensign Einav Ben-Ari, twenty years old, commanding her first platoon in the deserts of North Africa. He saw a woman he could follow to hell and back.

But Natasha Emmerdale clearly had other views. The pirate queen reeled toward Ben-Ari. Her blue eyes flashed.

"This is madness!" she said, her Russian accent thickening with her rage. "This is suicide."

Ben-Ari kept staring ahead at the enemy, her face still. "This is human courage."

"There is no courage in certain death!" Natasha spat. "The honor of a soldier is her undoing. We're turning around. Fuck this planet, and fuck Earth. They are both dead already. The Golden Fleet will live! Helmsman! Turn us around."

Ben-Ari raised her chin. "Miss Emmerdale, you are relieved of duty. Please report to your quarters."

"Bullshit! *Ty che blyad!*" The pirate turned toward her crew. "Turn around—"

"Security, escort Natasha Emmerdale to the brig," Ben-Ari said, voice louder.

Marco made to step forward, to join the fray, but Addy held him back.

"Wait, Poet," she whispered. "This needs to happen. Between the two of them."

The two women stared at each other. Pirate and president. Russian and Israeli. Two leaders. Two humans. Two paths for humanity.

Marco looked at the crew. Most of them were pirates. Lowlifes. The scum of the galaxy.

But they too were human. They too were torn. They looked back and forth. The helmsman was frozen. The navigator turned toward Natasha, took a step, then stepped back.

Kai rose to his feet. He broke the silence.

"I am Kai Linden! I was a pirate once. I served with some of you. Fought against the others. Once I served the alien named Don Basidio. Once I cared only for my own survival. You know what? In this war, I saw Don Basidio betray us, slaughter thousands of us. *Us*, you ask? Weren't those just soldiers, and we are pirates? Yes—*us*! Right now the only thing that matters is that we're humans. And we need to fight for humanity! In this war, I saw men and women braver than I am. I saw them sacrifice their lives for mankind. Maybe we'll die today. But goddammit, I'd rather be a dead lion than a living rat. So I fight with the Golden Lioness! Are you with me, humans?"

The helmsman rose—a lanky man with a forked yellow beard. "I'm with you, brother."

The engineer nodded—a burly man with a bald head, one eye, and a walrus mustache so large it hid his mouth. "Aye, I'm with ya, lad." The beefy pirate nodded. "Right now we're all in the same boat up shit's creek. I say we keep on sailing."

One by one, the rest of the *Dolphin*'s crew nodded. Criminals. Scum. Heroes.

Natasha stared at them. At first rage filled her eyes. But then the pirate queen deflated.

"All right!" Natasha snorted and waved dismissively. "Fuck it. Who wants to live forever, right? I'm with you, little president. Let's go kill that *yobannye* Dreamer bastard."

Marco felt it was a good time to interject. He stepped forward. "I'm glad to see such amazing fighting spirit in everyone, but there's still a tiny little technical issue." He pointed at the planet. "How do we get past a million starships, satellites, and a defensive ring that surrounds the entire planet?"

Kai slapped him on the shoulder. "Don't worry, bro. We got wobble tech, remember? And we got damn good pilots." He turned toward Ben-Ari and winked. "We pirates got lots of practice dodging your ships."

"But the *Dolphin* can't wobble," Marco said. "She's too big."

They all turned toward Ben-Ari. The president thought for a moment, staring ahead. Haven was getting closer. They were almost there. Ben-Ari stared in silence at the enemy, at this corrupted planet, at these impossible odds. She clutched her necklace and whispered something to herself in Hebrew.

Then she turned toward the crew.

"The *Dolphin*, and all other corvettes and frigates in the Golden Fleet, will launch a full assault on the enemy. All guns blazing. Nothing held back. I want to see nukes exploding."

"A suicide mission," Natasha whispered. "A final stand."

"Only for some," said Ben-Ari. "Most of us will be inside our shuttles, dropships, and Falcon fighters. We can fit a thousand men into them, our full force. Those vessels all have Tarjan tech.

And they're small enough to wobble, even near Haven's gravity well. We'll swarm through the enemy like bees."

Natasha understood. "While you swarm, some will remain in the motherships. To give you cover. To—"

"To die for us," Ben-Ari said. "Yes."

"I'll stay." Kai stepped forward.

Marco thought for a moment. Of Addy. Of his kids back home. And he knew he could make only one choice. When he looked into Addy's eyes, he knew she understood. She wept but she nodded.

"I'll stay too," Marco said, stepping forward.

Ben-Ari looked at him and Kai. Brothers-in-law. Brothers-in-arms. Volunteering for death. For the briefest instant, a sad smile touched Ben-Ari's lips. Then her face became stern again.

"No." She shook her head. "Though I appreciate your spirit, I must turn you down. Both of you understand Project Artemis. Both of you carry the code in your pocket, have learned how to install it. I need you with me. On the surface." She looked at Addy. "You too, Colonel Linden. You know the code. You're with us."

Over the past two weeks, they had been studying Meili's code. They understood its main functions, thought they could install it, even debug it if things went wrong. It only took one installation, of course. And four of them carried copies of Project Artemis in their pockets. Four of them would deploy.

Marco understood. Most likely, three would die on the way.

Four codechips, Marco thought. *Four fools to carry them. Four chances to save humanity.*

Kai. Ben-Ari. Addy. Marco. Four torchbearers.

What did Addy call us? he thought. *Team Ka-BAM. But we're more than a silly name. We're a family.*

He looked at her, at his beautiful wife. At Ben-Ari, forever his leader and light in the dark. At Kai, his brother.

"I love you," he said softly. "All of you."

Addy wiped her eyes and hugged him. Kai joined the embrace. Ben-Ari seemed surprised; she was not used to Marco breaking protocol like this. But then she smiled softly, and she hugged them.

"My dear friends," she whispered.

Natasha cleared her throat. "Ugh! You Americans make me gag. So sentimental! Fine, fine! I volunteer to stay. I'll buy you time. Anything to stop seeing you embarrassing yourselves this way."

Addy rubbed her eyes. "We're not Americans."

Natasha snorted. "Canadians, Americans …" She waved dismissively. "Not Russians, close enough."

Ben-Ari narrowed her eyes, scrutinizing the taller woman.

"Can I trust you, Natasha? Just moments ago you wanted to flee."

Natasha stepped closer. She clasped Ben-Ari's shoulders and stared into her eyes. "My word is my bond. I will never betray you. I am no *yobannye* traitor like Don Basidio. Yes, I wanted to flee, but you are all staying. I have no desire to grow old alone, the last human, nobody around to know my glory. Die as a heroine? Okay. A little better. Why not? Together, Einav. You and I. Let's win this." She smiled crookedly. "Look for me in the afterlife, my beautiful lioness. We'll drink wine among fallen heroes."

They all looked at one another, silent for a moment.

Then they ran.

As the fleet hurled toward battle, klaxons rang. Speakers barked out orders. Marco and Addy burst into the *Dolphin*'s hangar. The dropships and Falcons were fueled up and ready. Marines raced into dropships. Pilots ran into Falcons.

Marco took a step toward a dropship, but Kai grabbed his shoulder.

"Wrong way, bro." Kai began pulling him along the hangar. "You're flying a Falcon, baby!"

Marco frowned. "I'm not a trained fighter pilot."

Kai snorted. "And I am?" He guffawed. "As if the Golden Fleet ever had trained pilots. If you can fly a shuttle, you can fly a Falcon. Come on, bro. Tag team."

As Marco ran along with his brother-in-law, he shouted, "Don't the Falcons have assigned pilots?"

"Sure!" Kai said. "Half those fuckers died in the war. Falcon pilots don't live long, bro."

"Wonderful," Marco muttered as they reached the starfighters.

Addy came running toward them. "Where you going, assholes? Did you really think you boys could assault a giant planet-sized computer swarming with a million hostile starships without me?"

"Addy, I can't even take a shower without you barging in," Marco said.

She blew him a kiss. "Love your naked butt, babe."

Kai rolled his eyes. "I understand why Natasha volunteered to stay on the mothership."

The three of them climbed into Falcons. Other pilots entered the other starfighters.

The Falcons were tiny vessels, much smaller than dropships and barely larger than cars. Marco pulled down his helmet and looked at the controls. A Tarjan machine covered the dashboard, an intricate network of brass pipes, glass tubes full of colorful liquid, gears with runes etched into their teeth, and astrolabes as beautiful as the innards of clocks. He understood none of those parts. But there was a joystick. It was shaped like an alien serpent with ruby eyes, yes, but it was a joystick nonetheless. Marco knew how to use that.

"Bro?"

Kai was speaking in Marco's earpiece, a little Tarjan machine embedded with a crystal.

"Here," Marco said. "I'm trying to make sense of these controls. The snake thing is the joystick, right?"

"Yep," Kai said. "You steer with your snake. Now look to your left. You see the little skull? Right by the hatch handle?"

Marco looked. He saw a decorative, silvery lever shaped like a skull atop a spine.

"Yeah. Handsome fellow."

"That's your thruster," Kai said. "Just shove the skull forward to increase thrust, pull it back to slow down."

"Bit of a gruesome design, but okay," Marco said.

"You see the round crystal to your right?" Kai said.

Marco looked. He saw it. A small crystal ball, bluish, with faint swirls dancing inside.

"Yeah," Marco said. "It kinda looks like a snow globe. I like it more than the skull."

"That's your wobble ball," Kai said. "When you wanna wobble, just place your hand on the crystal, hold it for a moment, and Bob's your uncle."

"I'll trust you," Marco said.

"Don't worry, bro, it's simpler than it sounds," Kai said. "Speed up with your skull, fly with your snake, and wobble with your ball. Got it?"

"Skull, snake, and ball, got it," Marco said. "I'm not sure if this is a starfighter, or that Zoltar machine from *Big*, but I got it. Good luck out there, Kai."

Addy's voice came onto the network. She stared from her cockpit a few meters away, head tilted.

"And you weren't going to wish me good luck?" she said.

"God, you're needy," Marco said.

She flipped him off.

They sat, gripping their serpentine joysticks. Across the hangar, the last marines entered their dropships. Across the entire Golden Fleet, a thousand warriors prepared for battle.

The frigates flew through space, moving closer to Haven. And then Marco heard the unmistakable roar of stabilizer engines, slowing the motherships down.

It was time.

Ben-Ari's voice came from the speakers. "Operation Rising Dawn begins."

The hangar doors opened.

Marco shoved down the silvery skull, and the engines roared with power.

The Falcons leaped into space, wreathed in light, and charged at a million ships of nightmare.

CHAPTER TWENTY-EIGHT

Marco flew toward beautiful death.

He could not help it. Even here, seconds from the end, he was an artist. And he saw beauty.

A million starships. A million lights around a dark world. A swarm of satellites and spinning rings, and right at his fingertips, an array of crystals and colorful smoke.

Lights. Colors. The rumbling of the engine beneath him. The lingering warmth of Addy's kiss on his lips. The sensations of the present moment. Of being alive.

Soon all this will be gone, he thought. *No more human senses. No more experiences. The void.*

"I'm sorry, Terri, Roza, and Sam," he whispered. "I'm sorry I won't be coming back. I love you."

Addy's voice emerged from his earpiece. "We can hear you, dumbass! Now shut up and fight." She roared. "Let's win this bitch!"

Marco tightened his lips. He nodded.

All right, he thought. *If I die, I don't go down like an artist. Not even like a father. I go down like a soldier.*

The Falcons charged toward the enemy. The dropship flew behind them, ferrying the marines. Farther back rumbled the frigates and corvettes, the warships of the Golden Fleet.

Ahead, they flew out to meet them.

The ships of the Dreamer.

They swarmed with perfect harmony like a school of fish. But while all fish were still individual minds, this was fleet was one creature. One intelligence. Even as they flew toward the Golden Fleet, the Dreamer's warships formed an enormous smiley face in space. But this face wasn't friendly. This grin was mocking and evil.

The fleets flew closer.

Closer still.

They were moments away now.

From so close, Marco didn't just see dots on a monitor. He could see details of the enemy ships. Some were hijacked freighters, tankers, and frigates, once starships of humanity. Most were unique creations, twisted bundles of blades, cannons, and spinning saws, the Dreamer's own engineering.

And they all fired their cannons.

Torpedoes came flying toward the Golden Fleet. Balls of plasma blazed. Lasers flashed, so fast that the ships had no time to dodge. A Falcon exploded beside Marco. A dropship tore open, spilling soldiers.

A laser seared Marco's wing, and his Falcon jerked.

Several missiles came streaking toward him.

He gritted his teeth, shoved the throttle, and gripped the wobble ball. The crystal warmed his palm, and light beamed between his fingers.

Colors swirled across the canopy. For a second or two, he was in hyperspace.

He snapped back into reality—only instants away from slamming into an enemy warship.

Its saws whirred. Its cannons blasted.

Marco shouted and tugged the joystick. His Falcon yawed, but a blast hit his tail. The starfighter careened.

As he struggled to steady himself, Marco saw one Falcon pop back into reality, reemerging from hyperspace. Unfortunately, it reappeared just meters away from a warship. It never had a chance. The Falcon plowed into the enemy hull, and an explosion bloomed. A second Falcon reappeared halfway *inside* a frigate, its prow in the enemy ship, its tail exposed to space.

Marco's breath caught.

Was Addy inside one of those Falcons?

"Dammit, careful, pilots!" Kai shouted over the Crystalnet.

"How the fuck do we aim when we wobble?" came Addy's voice through the network.

Marco breathed a sigh of relief. Addy was alive. He saw her now, her Falcon dented but still flying fast.

"You can see the battle from hyperspace," Kai said. "Just look closer. Again—wobble!"

Several drones came zipping toward Marco, their saws spinning. Cannons rose from their tops, and rockets flew toward him.

Marco inhaled sharply, tightened his lips, and charged toward the enemy.

He grabbed the wobble ball.

He hopped into hyperspace again. Everything outside was blobs of purple and black, webbed with lightning. It was like flying inside a nebula.

But there! He could see it! Flickers of light and shadow, moving through the mist. Just a hint, a bending of the light, visible to him.

That's the lower dimension, he thought. *Our universe. I can see—*

He dropped back into reality.

He was charging toward an enemy hull. No time to turn!

"Dammit!" he shouted, gripping the wobble sphere again.

He leaped into hyperspace, leaving only smoke to scatter against the warship.

Okay, I see it now, he thought. *Those darker shadows? Starships. The streaming lights? Missiles.*

He was in the same place. Just a higher realm. And he could navigate here.

Each time he hopped into hyperspace, he had only two or three seconds in this astral realm. This wasn't like the great frigates that skimmed the edge of hyperspace like ocean liners along the ocean surface. This was more like diving underwater, holding your breath, then popping back up for air.

At the moment, he was racing through luminous hyperspace toward an enormous shadow. He yawed and—

He blinked back into reality. His right wing just missed the hulking warship nearby.

It works!

His relief was short-lived. More ships came flying toward him. It was not his job to engage them, just wobble past them. But Marco couldn't resist opening fire. His rotary cannon unleashed a storm of bullets, tearing a drone apart. And he wobbled again, leaving the enemy rockets to streak through empty space.

He kept wobbling, skipping through the enemy armada. The Dreamer's machines were as thick as piranhas in a feeding frenzy. The swarm just went on and on. Marco flitted through them, hopping in and out of reality, never giving the enemy enough time to shoot him.

And that enemy just kept coming.

Whenever he rose into hyperspace now, Marco saw the others rising with him. Falcons. Dropships. Even a handful of the smaller Golden Fleet corvettes, just light enough to allow wobbling. They rose and dived back into reality again and again like dolphins.

It's no wonder the Golden Fleet has tormented the HDF so successfully, Marco thought. *It's like a game of Whac-a-Mole.*

Several starships loomed before him, shaped like monster squids, each of their metal tentacles longer than a frigate. Those elongated digits came swinging toward Marco's Falcon, lined with cannons. He cursed, flitting between the serrated appendages. Plasma bolts flew toward him.

He wobbled forward. He reappeared in reality past the swinging tentacles.

His relief was short-lived. An odd starship loomed ahead—an enormous ring of metal, encircling a sea of fire.

No, not a starship! Marco realized. *A portal!*

Within a ring of metal and flashing lights, the Dreamer had constructed a wormhole. A passageway to a land of fire. The ring charged toward Marco like a mouth, ready to devour him, to swallow him down to hell.

He wobbled again, reappeared behind the portal. He kept flying.

Three hideous warships lurched toward him, shaped like sharks, and many eyes spun across their hulls. They opened their jaws wide, revealing steel teeth the size of trees, ready to tear into Marco.

There was no room to yaw. Marco winced and charged right into gargantuan metal jaws.

The teeth snapped shut around him.

He wobbled, reappearing behind the beast.

The crystal ball was dimmer now. Marco vaguely remembered something Kai had said long ago—that starships could only wobble a certain number of times before they needed to recharge.

He stared ahead. Haven was close now. He dared to hope.

"We're almost there, guys," Marco said. "You still with me?"

"Standing by!" Kai said.

"Yo, Poet!" said Addy.

"Standing by!" announced more pilots.

"Let's win this thing," Marco said.

The Falcons stormed forth, united.

Scaly enemy ships flailed toward them. They spewed plasma. Marco rose into hyperspace to dodge them, and—

A spiky iron ship, its lights like red eyes, lunged toward him.

An enemy starship—here in hyperspace!

Marco cursed and opened fire. Bullets slammed into the starship. It still charged. He yawed, and—

The ships scraped across each other. Marco's right wingtip shattered.

He crashed out of hyperspace back into a barrage of missiles and bullets.

He cursed and soared. A bullet slammed into his hull, denting the metal. He groaned.

"Was that a fucking Dreamer ship in hyperspace?" he shouted.

"Impossible!" Addy cried from her Falcon. "Only our Tarjan ships can reach hyperspace."

Twenty starships formed a ring ahead. They released an enormous laser net. The trap came flying toward Marco and his companions, ready to slice them into ribbons.

Marco only had a few wobbles left. He used one.

He rose into hyperspace, leaving the laser net in the lower dimension. Addy and Kai and a few other Falcons rose with him.

The enemy was waiting. Here in hyperspace.

Arachnid starships with red portholes. With serrated limbs. With cruel smiley faces engraved on their hulls.

Marco opened fire. His Falcon vibrated as the rotary cannon unleashed. Bullets slammed into a spider ship, and it exploded. A severed metal leg spun over Marco, just missing his cockpit.

The mechanical spiders swarmed. A leg slammed into Marco, cracking his cockpit. His starfighter spun. Nearby, a Falcon exploded. Then another. He heard Addy screaming and cursing and firing her cannon.

They plunged back into regular space, but countless ships flew here too, and a barrage of missiles streamed toward them.

Marco rose into hyperspace again. Back down. Wobbling again and again.

They were everywhere.

He was everywhere.

A blast of pulsing energy hit Marco's cockpit, and the Falcon vibrated, forming words.

"Come into my dream ..."

Another pulse washed over his starfighter.

The Dreamer spoke again, this time in Marco's mind.

Your daughters bled so beautifully for me. The whore named Terri. And the little unnamed one I plucked from your wife's womb. Their pain was so beautiful.

Visions appeared before Marco. His children. Mangled. Turned into cyborgs but still conscious, aware of themselves. In pain.

"Help us, Daddy!" they cried. "Daddy!"

Marco stared, hands frozen on the controls. His jaw locked. Tears filled his eyes.

Join them, Marco. Save them. Come into my dream.

Marco stared at the swarm ahead. And he spoke softly.

"You're scared."

The ships ahead blazed with fury. A thousand missiles flew. Marco swerved around them, flickering in and out of hyperspace.

"You're scared!" Marco repeated, louder now. "You're taunting us. Trying to scare us away. You're weak, Dreamer. Visions? Voices? Resorting to cheap parlor tricks?" Marco laughed. "You're going to lose this war. And you know it."

"Yeah!" Addy shouted from her Falcon. "Nobody fucks with team Ka-BAM!" She thought for a moment. "And if Lailani is still fighting on Earth, team Ka-BLAM!"

Marco looked at her, at his beautiful wife, and the visions of his tortured children faded.

Love, he thought, remembering something Ben-Ari had told him. *In the cold darkness of space, only love can light our way.*

He looked back at the enemy.

"You know fear," Marco said softly, but he knew the Dreamer could hear. "You know cruelty. You know pride. You know ambition and greed and the perverse joy of torment. We gave you emotions. We coded you to feel. But one emotion you've never felt, Dreamer. Love. The reason we live. The purpose of humanity. The only thing that gives existence meaning. Even if you survive, you will never feel love. Your perverted life will never have meaning, only eternal hunger. I pity you."

The Dreamer screamed.

From a million mouths, he screamed.

The fleet stormed toward Marco. It broke all formation. The elegant patterns of the enemy—they shattered. In his rage, the Dreamer slung all his forces at Marco. Thousands of his ships crashed into one another, exploding. Countless others lurched toward Marco, a tidal wave of metal.

Missiles flew above the wave like foam. When Marco rose into hyperspace, countless spiders swarmed. He fell back into reality. The lights streaked toward his Falcon.

And Marco knew he was going to die.

Beams of light blazed overhead.

Lasers and missiles and bullets flew, shattering incoming missiles seconds before they could hit Marco.

Golden light filled Marco's cockpit.

"I got you, boy!" rose a cry through his helm—speaking in a Russian accent.

He looked up, and he saw a golden dolphin, beautiful and luminous.

A figurehead.

An instant later the rest of the starship passed overhead. The GFS *Dolphin*, flagship of the Golden Fleet. A mighty frigate shaped like a sailing vessel of old. Golden filigree shone upon her crimson hull like the dawn. A ship of beauty and hope.

The *Dolphin* roared above Marco, all guns blazing, launching herself into the enemy ships ahead.

The pirate frigate plowed through enemy starships, knocking them aside. Rows of her cannons, lining both port and starboard hull, pounded full broadsides. Missiles blazed, slamming into the enemy, and Dreamer ships exploded.

The *Dolphin*'s front cannons boomed. Torpedoes flew out. Red torpedoes. Tipped with yellow.

"Nukes!" Marco shouted and breached into hyperspace.

He plowed through spider ships, then dived back into a universe awash with light and heat and blazing radiation.

Hundreds of Dreamer ships were burning.

The *Dolphin* still plowed forward. Missiles pounded her. Laser beams carved her hulls. A chunk of her stern tore off.

The *Dolphin* was too large to wobble. But still she flew.

"Natasha!" Marco cried.

"You got this, Marco!" the pirate said over the Crystalnet. "Go win this war."

More rockets slammed into the *Dolphin*. More chunks of her hull cracked open. Still the flagships fired. Her fusillade of fury pounded the Dreamer's armada.

And then the *Dolphin*'s back engines began to overheat. To turn red, then white, then blinding blue.

"Oh my God," Marco whispered.

He understood.

Natasha was running a feedback loop in the *Dolphin*'s engine room.

"Natasha!" Addy cried from her Falcon.

Natasha Emmerdale appeared in their monitors. Her bridge was burning. Blood dripped down her forehead. But the pirate queen managed to give a salute and a crooked smile.

"I die free."

Marco spun his Falcon around. "Addy, back, back!"

The *Dolphin*'s engines exploded with the fury of a nuclear bomb.

White light blazed across the battle.

Silence.

Silence filled space.

The white fire grew, consuming everything around it. Reducing Dreamer ships to skeletal chassis. Then nothing but dust.

The blast propelled the *Dolphin* forward—or whatever remained of it.

The searing white hull blazed forth like a spear of light, carving through the enemy lines, leaving a tunnel of open space.

And then the *Dolphin* was gone.

Reduced to atoms. Just luminous dust in the void.

"Godspeed, Natasha Emmerdale, daughter of Earth," Marco whispered.

A sudden thought struck him.

Was Ben-Ari . . . ?

A Falcon streaked overhead, and Ben-Ari's voice filled the Crystalnet.

"Forward, humanity!" the president cried. "For Earth! For Earth!"

"For Earth!" Marco shouted.

"For Earth!" rose the cries of hundreds of pilots and marines.

The Falcons streamed forth. The dropships flew close behind, filled with warriors. They raced down the tunnel Natasha had carved for them, blazing at hypersonic speed.

Within seconds, before the Dreamer could regroup, they had crossed the distance.

They reached Haven's orbit.

Explosions bloomed around them. Countless satellites opened fire. A few dropships exploded, spilling their marines.

For Earth, Marco thought and drove his Falcon into Haven's atmosphere. *For my family.*

The other Falcons and dropships flew with him. They plunged through the thick sky of Haven, leaving the fire above, diving into a dark mechanical hell.

CHAPTER TWENTY-NINE

Fifty small ships descended through the smog.

Fifty lights in a world of shadows.

Fifty Falcons and dropships. The last of the human fleet. Maybe the last of all humanity. They dived through the eternal storm of Haven.

Marco remembered the gloom of this world. He had vowed he would never return. Perhaps deep down inside, he always knew that he would. That he had to. That he was not just here to kill the Dreamer but to finally wake up from an older nightmare.

Two hundred kilometers of gasses swirled above Haven, a forever storm of crimson, black, and gray, letting in almost no sunlight. By today's standards, Haven would no longer be considered habitable. But a century ago, Alpha Centauri was as far as spaceships could fly. Millions of humans had moved here, fleeing wars, hunger, disease, or incarceration on Earth. Millions had found themselves trapped in a place far worse.

Marco remembered seeing the strange aliens of Haven, floating animals like jellyfish that bobbed through the storm. They were gone. Instead, he saw chimneys. Antennae. Jagged skyscrapers. They soared from below, a hundred kilometers tall. It should be impossible to build structures this tall. Yet here they were, rising through the murk, an eerie forest of metal and concrete in the sky.

"Follow my lead, crew," came Ben-Ari's voice over the Crystalnet. "We're flying straight to the Face of God crater. That's where he lurks. We're almost there."

Addy's voice added, "We'll be back home by Christmas to roast hot dogs over the fireplace."

The Falcons and dropships clustered together, navigating between the towers and antennae, moving always down. Marco steered with one hand. With the other, he patted his pocket, feeling the codechip inside. He still had it. Project Artemis.

Home by Christmas, he thought. *We'll build a campfire on the beach. Addy will roast her hot dogs on a rake. Ben-Ari will be with us, and she'll brew delicious chamomile tea. And Lailani will come, and she'll bring Tala. All our kids will be there. We'll just be together under the stars.*

He forced those thoughts away for now. He had to focus on his mission. Thinking of home would make him break down when he needed to be strongest. But he kept that dream safe below his determination. Cherished. The light that made walking through darkness worthwhile.

Fifty lights. Fifty vessels. They flew through the shadows.

Lightning flashed.

Again. Again. The air boomed.

Each bolt revealed thousands of antennae rising from the murk. Another bolt pierced the air.

And Marco realized: this wasn't lightning.

The antennae were sparking.

"Incoming fir—" he began when a bolt slammed into a dropship beside him.

The vessel cracked open. Fire filled its hold, washing across its squad of marines.

Another bolt flew. It hit a Falcon. The starfighter exploded.

"Open fire!" Ben-Ari shouted.

Marco was already firing his rotary gun. Bullets pounded the electric towers. One antenna tilted, then crashed through several antennae beside it. The enormous structures—they were larger than any skyscraper on Earth—collapsed through the storm.

But more antennae rose. More electric bolts kept flying.

Marco looked around hurriedly. Where was Addy? Was Addy all right?

He saw her Falcon nearby. She looked at him from her cockpit.

"Mar—" she began.

A bolt slammed into her Falcon.

"Addy!" Marco screamed.

Her Falcon cracked open. Addy was screaming in the cockpit. She plunged downward into the smoke, her canopy shattered.

"Addy, Addy!" Marco cried and flew after her, and suddenly lightning was everywhere.

Bolts slammed into Falcon after Falcon.

Podships cracked open.

Light.

Searing blinding light.

Pain.

Blazing thrumming pain.

His canopy shattered. Marco couldn't even scream. A blast hit his wing, and his engines were gone. Every gauge and screen in his cockpit cracked.

He was falling. Falling faster. Tumbling toward the surface. More lightning crackled all around, and fire blazed in the cockpit. Black smoke flowed over him. Flames roared from the fuel tank, and the smog parted below, and Marco saw the surface of a mechanical city. The planet surface—turned into a machine.

He hit the eject button.

He blasted into the air.

He tumbled, and he saw his Falcon dive below, wreathed in flame.

Marco activated his jetpack and slowed his fall. His starfighter kept plunging down below, breaking apart.

He looked around him. He could see nothing. Only the smog.

"Addy?" he whispered into his comm.

Only static came through. A piece of wreckage tumbled a meter away—a shard of wing, he thought. A bit farther away, faded through the clouds, a corpse fell.

Marco narrowed his eyes, hit the throttle on his jetpack, and dived down. One Falcon swooped beside him. A dropship roared nearby, only for lightning to hit it too. Its marines jumped from the burning vessel, jetpacks roaring.

Below, Marco's disabled Falcon finally hit the ground. It exploded, and an instant later, guns on the surface pointed skyward.

Bullets flew.

Beside Marco, a soldier screamed. His blood flew in a mist. A squad of paratroopers was diving a few meters away. The bullets tore through them.

Marco swerved, entering a dark cloud. He kept diving, hidden in the murk.

"Addy!" he said into his comm. "Addy, dammit. Oh God, Addy, please answer! Add—"

"I'm here, Poet!"

Her voice, coming through his earpiece, brought tears to his eyes.

"Where are you, Ads?" His voice was choked.

"I don't know!" she cried. "It's a fucking nightmare."

"Are you on the surface?"

"Yes! I think! I had to eject. Oh God, Marco, oh God." She screamed and he heard bullets. "Die, fuckers!"

Marco cursed, tapping at his comm. He finally picked up her signal's coordinates. He dived down, emerged from the clouds, and saw the surface of Haven.

He felt like an ant looking at a motherboard. Microchips, transistors, gears, and cables covered Haven, each component like a building. But he also saw human buildings. Human roads. Even a few cars. All were worked into the machinery, blended into this great computer.

It's Haven colony, he realized. *The city where I once lived.*

A chill flooded him. They weren't supposed to land in the colony.

We're a hundred kilometers from the Face of God.

More bullets streaked through the sky. Marco swerved, his jet pack thrumming and coughing smoke. The bullets whizzed by him. Several divers shouted, then tumbled down dead.

Marco missed his old mech suit. Back in the Alien Wars, he would dive into battlefields wearing a massive suit of armor, loaded with weapons, impervious to bullets. It was essentially a wearable robot. Of course, that was out of the question now. It was bad enough fighting robots on the battlefield; he didn't need to *wear* one.

On the ground, Marco would have his assault rifle. That was all. He and his troops would have to fight the most advanced robots in the galaxy using World War II-era technology.

Lovely.

He flew downward, zigzagging from cloud to cloud. The fire intensified from below. More paratroopers fell.

"Battalion commanders, are you with me?" he said, speaking over the Crystalnet.

"Addy here!" came a response.

"Ben-Ari here!" came another voice.

"We're a hundred kilometers off target," Marco said. "I suggest we fly."

"Negative," Ben-Ari said. "Too much antiaircraft fire. We're getting butchered up here. Down and land, soldiers!"

Marco wanted to argue. Who knew what horrors lurked on the surface? But Ben-Ari was right. Every second, the fire from below took out another diving soldier.

"Sun Arrow Battalion!" Marco cried. "With me! To the ground!"

Soldiers rallied around him, their jet packs leaving trails of fire. Rotary guns spun below. Soldiers screamed and died.

This is a fucking massacre, Marco thought, terror looming in him.

He dived headfirst, eyes narrowed, swerving from side to side. His jetpack engines left helices of fire above. His battalion dived with him.

He spotted a cannon below. He fired his rifle. He could barely aim like this. Another man screamed and died beside him. The corpse tumbled and slammed into another diver.

The ground rushed up to meet them.

They were seconds away.

Marco yanked on his jetpack's handlebars, trying to right his position. His troops joined him, and—

A bullet slammed into one handlebar.

Marco pulled back his hand, screaming.

Blood spurted. His ring finger was gone. He glimpsed the severed digit tumbling through the sky.

Another bullet flew. It slammed into the fin on his jetpack, and he was spinning madly.

A bullet glanced off his helmet, and his head rang, and he knew he was going to die.

He was plunging down now. His jetpack was burning. *He* was burning. He pawed at the jetpack's straps, falling, meters away from the ground. He couldn't free himself. He jerked madly at the handlebars, barely managing to slow his descent. He saw gears and metal and lights. He squeezed the brakes again, and—

He slammed onto the surface.

His jetpack thrummed, buzzing, ablaze.

He tore it off, and it skittered across the ground, a ball of fire, and exploded.

Marco slid across metal sheets, his momentum thrusting him forward. He tore through machinery. He felt something tear inside him. Something crack.

He finally came to a halt.

For a moment he was still. Wondering if he was dying. If he was dead already. Smoke rose from his charred uniform.

He raised his hand and grimaced. The bullet had taken the entire finger. Blood spurted. Every part of his body ached. He lay on a metal surface. Shadows swirled around him. He saw nothing but smog. Brief blazes of artillery fire sparked through the storm. Booms shook the world, and in the distance, soldiers were screaming, and something inhuman shrieked.

"Addy?" Marco whispered into his comm.

He heard nothing. Only static. Something was loose inside his helmet. He told himself his communication system was simply damaged. That Addy was still alive. Had to be.

With a shaky hand, he reached into the pocket, where he always kept a small medical kit.

A snarl.

A shadow.

White searing eyes.

Marco dropped his med kit, shouldered his rifle, and opened fire.

A creature screeched. It scuttled forth, emerging from the mist, and reared.

A spider. An enormous cyborg, larger than a horse, stitched together from human limbs. Cables ran across its eight legs, and motors rumbled, attached to its joints. A human face was stretched over a metal skull. The jaws opened, revealing electric saws for teeth.

Marco scurried backward even as his body screamed in protest. The spider's legs slammed down, tipped with blades, piercing the ground. The creature howled so loudly Marco's ears rang.

His magazine was empty. Marco fumbled at his vest, struggling to grab more bullets.

The jaws lashed toward him.

Marco shoved his rifle forward. The muzzle shattered several teeth. He had no time to reload. He pulled the rifle back, swung it, clubbing the beast.

The cyborg's skin mask slid off, revealing a metal skull and blazing red eyes. The machine grinned. A leg slammed down again.

Marco rolled aside. The claw missed him. The spider leaped, incredibly fast, and a claw scraped against Marco's chest, etching a groove in his bulletproof vest. He howled. He rolled again, blood still spilling from his hand.

The spider legs slammed down around him, forming a cage. The bloody metal jaws descended, their electric saws buzzing.

It wasn't easy with one mangled hand. But Marco shoved his muzzle between those jaws, slammed in a new magazine, and fired.

The cyborg's head exploded. Chunks of metal flew everywhere, revealing a human brain.

Marco fired again, and the creature finally fell.

For a moment Marco stood, legs shaky, blood still flowing. The pain was returning now.

"Marco!"

A figure came racing through the fog.

"Addy!" he cried, voice hoarse, then collapsed.

"Oh God," she said. "Oh fuck. Dude! Your finger!"

He groaned. "I was nervous. Bit my fingernail too much."

Addy didn't crack a smile. Face ashen, she knelt and ripped open a med kit. Several other soldiers approached, formed a defensive ring, and fired into the fog. The suppressive fire seemed to be keeping the enemy at bay. Addy remained calm, working remarkably fast. She sprayed Marco's wounds with disinfectant. It burned like hellfire, but Marco was too exhausted to even scream. She coated his finger's stump with congealing gel, then slapped an InstaStitch strip across his wounded thigh.

If he had any internal wounds, there was no way to know. But he was able to stand up. He took a few steps. He felt woozy. But he could walk.

Sudden pain stung his thigh.

He turned to see a needle sticking him.

"Addy!" he said. "Ow."

She pulled the needle out and stared with stern eyes. "You need this. A cocktail of adrenaline and a few secret happy chemicals. You'll have time to die later. Right now you fight." She looked around her at the troops. "We all fight!"

Servos hummed in the mist. Macro spun around to see searing white eyes. An arachnid creature loomed.

An instant later, fire blazed above.

Marco leaped back, not sure which enemy to focus on—the arachnid in the mist, or whatever was blasting fire above.

But it was a human above him. A woman. A soldier with a jetpack.

She circled the troops, fired her gun, and slew the cyborg in the mist. The beast collapsed, its eight legs twitching.

Ben-Ari landed, raised her visor, and nodded at her troops.

"Draco Battalion!" she cried. "With me—to war!"

"To war!" they shouted.

The soldiers ran across the metal ground, guns booming, as lightning flashed above and endless horrors leaped from the mist.

CHAPTER THIRTY

They ran through the mist, the survivors of the Draco Brigade.

A few hundred soldiers—that was all.

Once millions had served in the Human Defense Force. As far as Marco knew, this was all that remained.

A few hundred heroes. Racing across a computerized planet.

Humanity's last stand.

Enemies emerged from the fog. They had once been human. Torn apart, bolted together. They scuttled forward on their hands, their feet in the air. The Dreamer had rebuilt them, stitching their arms to their pelvis, their legs to their shoulders. Their mouths opened to scream.

The soldiers fired, tearing through them.

More cyborgs advanced. Tall, muscular creatures, skinless, lamps shining in their skulls. They raised rifles and fired, and soldiers fell. With a few grenades, with a hailstorm of bullets, the battalion killed the cyborgs. They ran onward.

Marco knew this city. He had lived here for two years. He still recognized some streets, some buildings. But everywhere rose the creations of the Dreamer. Cables ran down the streets like creeping roots. Motors hummed inside hollowed buildings. Pistons rumbled, and cannons boomed, and explosions lit the sky.

If any colonists had survived here, Marco did not see them. Only what they had become. White eyes shone everywhere. Cyborgs peered from alleyways and dark windows. One creature swooped on leathern wings, and Marco fired, knocking it against a building. More creatures slunk through the mist. A cyborg horse ran through the fog, eyes red, its belly split open to reveal moving gears.

The Dreamer could have destroyed this city. Instead he had corrupted it. Turned it into his playground of nightmares.

"Einav, the crater is still a hundred kilometers away!" Marco shouted. "We'll never make it on foot."

"We don't have to!" Ben-Ari shouted back, firing at the enemy. "A few dropships managed to land. They're nearby."

"We can't fly either!" Marco said. "You saw what it's like up there. The whole damn planet is covered with antiaircraft cannons."

Ben-Ari fired a grenade, blasting apart a towering cyborg made from five humans bolted together. She flashed Marco a grin—bright and toothy and almost terrifying in her bloodstained face.

"We don't have to," the president said. "The Golden Fleet's dropships can drive."

Motors hummed. Metal creaked. Beams of light scanned the storm. Metal spheres rolled forth, cannons unfurled, and bullets flew toward the troops. Men screamed and died. Marco knelt behind a scrap of metal and fired. Addy crouched behind a concrete slab and lobbed a grenade. The spherical robots rolled everywhere, plowing through troops.

More engines roared.

Headlights pierced the darkness, and a shadow loomed.

Cannons boomed, and Marco winced, expecting more carnage.

The robots exploded.

A vehicle burst out from the mist, steamrolling over the burning machines, crushing them under its treads.

The pirate vessel screeched to a halt, its caterpillar tracks bloody. A hatch opened. Kai waved from inside.

"Need a lift, bitches?" He winked. "How d'ya like my sweet ride?"

Ten more vessels, maybe more, roared up behind Kai, their caterpillar tracks crushing dead robots. On the ground, the dropships had transformed into armacars—armored troop carriers.

Goddamn, we need transforming shuttles in the HDF, Marco thought.

Addy hopped into one armacar and tipped her helmet at Kai. "Why thank you, good sir."

Bullets streaked. Some pinged against the armacars. Some sank into men.

Marco cursed, ducked behind bodies, and saw cyborgs marching. Hundreds of them. These ones had complete metal bodies, but human brains quivered inside glass skulls. More soldiers screamed and fell.

Marco fired at the enemy, emptying a magazine, then raced into Kai's armacar. A squad of marines joined him. Marco took position at one gun turret, Addy at the other. Kai sat between them at the helm.

Around them, other soldiers leaped into other armacars. Ben-Ari entered one nearby.

"Go!" the president cried over the Crystalnet.

The armacars roared forth, plowing into the cyborg army. Metal limbs snapped. Cables tore. The treads crushed the machines. The cyborgs died with screams that sounded almost human.

They drove through the nightmares.

They drove through the Dreamer's dreams.

The cannons fired, tossing machines back. The rotary guns spun, carving a path through hell.

Cyborgs ran toward the armacars. Waves of them. Countless creatures with electronic eyes. Screaming like monsters. Dying like humans. Weeping with relief as they fell.

They passed through familiar streets. Down the road where Marco and Addy would once walk to work. Over the subway tunnels where they had once cowered all night. Past the concrete halls where they had languished. Marco wondered how many of the pale faces outside, these creatures of flesh and metal, had been his neighbors. His coworkers. Women he had loved. He wondered if Terri's mother was screaming outside or dying under the treads. He wondered if he had more children here, turned into these unholy creations.

He sat in his gun turret, firing the machine gun. Addy fired from the other turret. Their bullets tore cyborgs down. Yet as Marco fired, the monsters in the mist seemed almost human.

"Marco!" they cried as they died.

"Mercy!"

"Help us, please!"

But he kept firing, tears in his eyes. Maybe it was a trick. Maybe he was murdering innocents. But they kept coming. Kept hurtling themselves onto the armacar.

So Marco kept killing.

"Kai, there!" he said, pointing. "Take that highway."

Kai was still driving, a cigarette dangling from his lips, his helmet scrawled with rude drawings. He looked as casual as a truck driver delivering laundry, not the hope of mankind. He gave the thumbs-up. "Got it, bro."

The armacars turned along the exit. Figures emerged from the mist, arms outstretched, shuffling forward. Kai shoved down the throttle, increasing speed, prepared to drive into the crowd.

Marco stared, then gasped.

"Kai, stop!" he shouted. "People on the road!"

"Don't worry, bro," Kai said. "This armacar is bigger than most tanks. We'll plow right over them."

"They're not cyborgs!" Marco cried. "They're human!"

Kai cursed and hit the brakes.

The armacar rumbled to a halt. The other armored vehicles stopped behind them. Ahead, they filled the mist. Hundreds, maybe thousands of them.

Humans.

Naked. Pale. Their cheeks slashed open.

"Sleepers," Marco said.

"Just more cyborgs," Kai said, prepared to shove the throttle again.

"Wait." Marco grabbed his wrist. "Sleepers are humans. Hypnotized, yes. The Dreamer hijacked their brains. But they're not machines yet. They have no machine parts, not like cyborgs. You can't kill them."

"Goddamn it, bro, sleepers, cyborgs—same damn thing!" Kai said. "Dream troops."

Their earpieces cracked to life. Ben-Ari's voice emerged. She was riding in the armacar behind them.

"What's the hold-up, soldiers?" she said.

"Sleepers blocking the highway," Marco said.

"So drive off road!" said the president.

"They're everywhere, ma'am. They fill the mist. Thousands."

For a long moment—silence.

"Keep driving," the president said.

"Einav." Marco inhaled sharply, clutching his comm. "We can't just kill these people."

"Emery!" she barked. "We don't have riot gear. We don't have tear gas. We have no way to disperse them. More cyborgs are on their way, and maybe worse. We have to move—*now*."

"Einav, please!" Marco said. "We can try. We can climb out. Try to herd them aside. Maybe we can heal them later."

"Too dangerous," she said. "Marco, we have to move onward." Her voice softened. "If they die beneath our treads, the guilt is on the Dreamer. He is the one controlling them. He—"

"Oh, for fuck's sake, you pontificating procrastinators!" Kai blurted out. "We're in motherfucking *dropships*. We'll fly over them!"

He hit a button. Gears turned. Motors hummed. Wings extended from the armacar. It was transforming back into a dropship—the same vessel that had descended from the Golden Fleet motherships.

Kai shoved the throttle, roared forward, and pulled a lever. The wings caught the air. The dropship rose from the ground. The heavy machine thrummed forward, the treads retreating into the undercarriage like landing gear.

"The antiaircraft cannons!" Marco cried. "They'll tear us down."

"I'm keeping us low," Kai said. "Two meters aboveground. Too low for antiaircraft cannons. High enough to fly over the sleepers." He laughed as he flew through the mist. "Come on, all dropships! After me, you fuckers!"

They roared forth just above the sleepers' heads. Dropships. A handful of Falcons. They sliced through the mist, leaving the colony's crumbling skyscrapers and highways. They flew over fields of hijacked humanity.

Addy wiped sweat from her forehead, leaned back in her seat, and looked at Kai.

"Pontificating procrastinators?" she said.

"First thing that came to mind," Kai said.

Addy guffawed. "In the heat of battle, with sleepers all around us, *pontificating procrastinators* is the first thing that came to mind? What are you, a poet like Marco?"

"Even I don't talk like that," Marco said. "Sounds more like something from your *Freaks* book."

Kai flipped them off. "You both can eat a dick."

"That's better." Addy grinned. "That's the Kai I know."

Marco stared ahead through the storm. The wilderness of Haven spread ahead. The winds roared and lashed the dropships. Red and black clouds swirled. Acid rain pattered down, and lightning webbed across the sky. The headlights could barely pierce the thick mist.

But Marco knew they were flying the right way. He had been dreaming of this place for years. Even on Earth, he would wake up from nightmares many nights, drenched in cold sweat, clawing at his blankets, trying to escape this storm.

If he could, he would have nuked the whole damn planet.

He reached into his pocket, felt the codechip there.

But I need to face you, Marco thought. *Nuking you would leave a billion copies of you across the galaxy. I'm coming for you, Dreamer. To drive this poison into your heart, then watch it spread, watch your tentacles wither and die.*

"We're almost there," Marco said. "Just beyond the horizon." He looked at Addy. "We're almost done."

She nodded, eyes damp. He knew what she was thinking.

We can soon see our children again.

He reached out, intending to hold her hand, and—

A dropship exploded to their right.

Marco started.

"Where are they—" he began.

Another explosion blazed outside. Another dropship crashed down, burned to a charred hulk.

"There!" Addy shouted. "Incoming bogeys!"

Marco saw them now. Enemy drones flew ahead, skimming the surface, scattering the fog. They were shaped like vultures, their iron wings serrated, their mechanical eyes scanning the night with beams of light. They shrieked toward the human vessels, releasing missiles from under their wings.

Kai soared higher. A missile streaked beneath them. At the gun turrets, Marco and Addy opened fire, peppering the enemy with bullets. One vulture crashed. More kept flying in.

Falcons swooped above, raining fire upon the enemy. But the vultures' barrage was overwhelming. A Falcon exploded. Another lost its wing and crashed, exploding against the electronic surface. Yet another dropship blazed out.

"There are too many!" Marco shouted.

"We're getting fucking butchered!" Addy cried.

Kai gritted his teeth. "We're about to wobble." He reached for the crystal sphere near the yoke.

"I thought we can't wobble near a gravity well!" Marco said.

"We can't," Kai said. "And I don't give a fuck. We're doing it anyway." He raised his comm. "Attention all dropships! If you can hear me—wobble and go!"

He gripped the round crystal, and light beamed between his fingers.

They leaped into hyperspace.

But it was different this time. There were no more peaceful blobs of purple, swirling lazily over a golden sky. Instead, there were furious streaks of lavender. Flashing strobe lights. Everywhere—the planet. A sphere beneath them. A black hole. Sucking them in. The gravity of Haven was churning hyperspace into a raging inferno.

The dropship hull cracked.

The controls exploded.

They blinked back into reality, and the dropship was falling apart. Entire chunks of the hull were missing. Not cracked or blown away, simply … missing. Gone from reality, leaving smooth holes. The crystal ball shattered in Kai's hand. An engine blew, and fire raged, and smoke filled the cabin.

Nearby, a handful of other dropships reappeared, flashing out from hyperspace.

One was so damaged it crashed at once.

Another had been transformed into a soft, bubbling material, a ship of metallic foam.

One was missing its wings. Another was missing its entire stern, sliced clean in half. Some of the men inside were sliced in half too.

A few ships were still flying, but they were badly damaged. Missing components. Holes in their hulls. Fires in their engines.

"Oh God, oh God!" Addy screamed, pointing, face pale.

Marco looked behind him. He felt sick.

A squad of marines had entered this dropship with Marco. Five had only partly emerged from hyperspace.

One was missing all four limbs; there were smooth, healed stumps, as if the amputations were years old. Another was withered, turned into an ancient man, easily in his nineties. Another seemed flipped inside out.

"What the fuck!" Addy screamed.

"The fucking gravity well!" Kai shouted. "It fucks up hyperspace! We move between dimensions, and it fucks up both."

"Marco told you not to wobble!" Addy had tears in her eyes.

"We had no choice!" Kai said. "It was that or die back there. The vultures would have slaughtered us."

Marco pursed his lips, gulped, and struggled not to throw up. "Look!" He pointed. "The crater! We're there."

They had emerged from hyperspace high enough to see it.

The Face of God.

A crater the size of a city. A mountain range formed its grinning mouth. Three volcanoes peered like black eyes. If the Dreamer had a true face, this was it.

Ben-Ari's voice emerged through the Crystalnet.

"Fly to the middle volcano, soldiers. He's there."

Cannons rose around the crater. A barrage of plasma bolts flew. One Falcon exploded. Then a dropship full of marines.

Of the grand fleet, only three vessels now remained.

They swooped low and raced forward, skimming the surface.

They roared over the crater's edge, dodging enemy fire.

They rose, plasma blasting all around them, then swooped into the volcano's vent.

Three dropships. Fewer than fifty warriors. They plunged through the darkness, entering the Dreamer's lair.

CHAPTER THIRTY-ONE

They dived through darkness.

Three dropships.

Three lights in the pit.

They descended through the hollow mountain, and they beheld the heart of a nightmare.

They hung from the stony walls. Humans. Naked. Nailed into the rock face. Drones buzzed around these prisoners, carving them open, dissecting. Hammers swung, nailing in metal plates. Screwdrivers turned, screwing lamps into eye sockets. Scalpels sliced, and tongs pulled out organs, and needles stitched. Batteries plugged into place, and white eyes shone.

As his dropship flew deeper, Marco stared at the innards of the volcano, his lips a tight line.

A factory.

A factory for cyborgs. For terror.

"Sick fucks," Addy said, clutching the dropship cannon controls. Her face was pale.

They were flying inside a volcano on Haven, but Marco couldn't stop thinking of Earth. Of his children. Was Earth too now a computerized world? A factory for these twisted creations?

"We built machines," he said. "We gave them intelligence. We gave them emotions. Fear. Loneliness. Pain. We built them in factories and set them loose. Now we are the ones on assembly lines. We are those who feel fear and pain."

Addy nodded. "Very poetic, but I'm still going to kill that fucking computer."

Marco clasped her hand. "I love you, Addy."

She blew him a kiss, and suddenly she was crying. "I love you, Marco. Let's finish this fucker and go home."

"We fought the scum together, Addy," he said. "We plunged into their pit and killed their emperor. We fought the marauders and killed their king. We walked across the wastelands of the grays' world, and we slew their prophet. And we always came home. We're good at this. One more for the road."

"After this, I am fucking retired." Addy laughed through her tears. "And if Ben-Ari tries to recruit us again, she can suck my dick."

Marco couldn't help but laugh. A horrible laughter that washed over him, even as tears stung his eyes, as the horror swirled through him, as the prisoners screamed outside.

Several factory drones left the chained, screaming humans they were stitching into cyborgs. The floating little robots turned toward the invaders and opened fire. Bullets pounded into Marco's dropship, denting the hull. A few bullets tore through, and a soldier screamed in the hold.

Marco and Addy returned fire. The dropship's twin rotary guns savaged the drones. Marco cringed, not sure if his bullets were hitting the prisoners on the walls. Not sure if that was murder—or mercy killing.

Finally the three dropships reached the ground. They landed in a hangar, perhaps once used by the Third-Eye Temple.

The chamber was dark. Silent.

No cyborgs attacked. No robots hurled themselves against the dropships. The hangar was like a tomb.

The crew emerged from their dropships, rifles loaded and shouldered. Of the thousands who had flown here, fifty troops gathered inside the mountain. The last heroes.

Kai sneered, his back bristling with katanas, rifles, a grenade launcher, and a baseball bat. Three surviving pirates stood behind him, bearded and filthy, their electric guns humming in their hands. The last outlaws of the Golden Fleet were ready to fight.

Ben-Ari stood with the last soldiers of the Human Defense Force. All wore battle fatigues, body armor, and heavy boots. All held assault rifles, and grenades hung from their belts. The last of the HDF. They were the mightiest among the mighty. The salt of the Earth. They were lions.

Marco and Addy stood side by side. They looked at each other.

When Marco looked into his wife's blue eyes, warm memories filled him.

A little girl with scraped knees, a mouth like a sewer, and a heart like fire. Always getting into fights at recess. The girl with the prison dad. The girl from the remedial class. The girl who lost her parents in the war. Who moved into Marco's house, all curses and cigarettes and little clenched fists.

The teenager who haunted his adolescence. Always crooked smiles and rolling eyes and endless taunts. The girl who tracked mud and snow through the apartment, who sneaked out to buy beer, whose hockey stick was always swinging. The girl who once sneaked into his bed on a stormy night, cried in memory of her lost parents, kissed his lips, fell asleep in his arms, and pretended it never happened in the morning. The tall, wild beauty the bookish Marco had always found intimidating, infuriating, intoxicating.

The eighteen-year-old, all wild blond hair and tattoos and smirks, who joined the army with him. Who survived boot camp with him. Who flew to war with him. The soldier who fought with him in the mines of Corpus and the killing fields of Abaddon.

The veteran, tossed with him back into the world, trained to kill but not knowing how to live. The woman who moved with him to Haven. Who huddled against him, homeless in the tunnels. Who struggled with him to survive, eating nothing but sticky white rice, sleeping on the floor, haunted by the nightmares.

The woman he fell in love with. Whom he had always loved.

The woman he married.

The mother of his children.

Addy, the constant of his life. Sometimes burning like fire, sometimes warm and comforting, but forever a light in the darkness.

Marco and Addy stood side by side, guns raised together. Veterans of the Alien Wars. There was one more fight in them.

"I know the way," Ben-Ari said softly. "Unless it has changed. I've been here before."

They looked at a single doorway. A dark opening like a mouth, like the gates to the underworld. A portal to shadows.

Wind wafted from the depths, and Marco heard the hints of words, perhaps just his imagination.

Come into my dream …

"Let's go," he said, clasping the codechip in his pocket. "Let's go and be rid of him."

They stepped through the doorway, entering the shadows of a dream.

CHAPTER THIRTY-TWO

After so many days of travel, after so much heartbreak and loss, Lailani finally saw them ahead. Her tears flowed.

The Alps.

"There they are, Tala," she whispered. "The mountains. We're almost there."

The jeep rumbled along a cracked road. Abandoned cars littered the lanes; Lailani had to keep swerving around them. Some had crashed, their computers hijacked. Some contained corpses.

A few sleepers ambled along the roadsides. One or two leaped onto the road, trying to derail Lailani. But she swerved her jeep around them too, and she kept going. On the eastern horizon, Lailani saw mechanids traveling through the mist, legs tall and slender. But they were far away. And the mountains were close.

Hope.

She couldn't see the Matterhorn yet. But she knew it lay just ahead. And within that fabled mountain: SCAR. Singularity Containment and Research.

An end to this war.

"They're going to fix this," Lailani said, tears still flowing. "I promise you, Tala. Uncle Noah is there, and he's going to study the chip in my head. He'll learn how to protect brains. How to free everyone. How to wake everyone up."

She swerved around another sleeper. The jeep rumbled across stones, then back onto the road.

"But how, Mommy?" Tala said.

"With nanobots," Lailani said. "Remember? I told you before. Uncle Noah is going to send out a million nanobots flying all over the world. And inside them—the code from my head. The nanos will get into everyone's bodies and wake them up."

Tala was quiet for long moments. "Are Roza and Sam in the mountain?"

Lailani nodded and mussed her daughter's hair. "Yes, little one. Your cousins are there. Waiting to play with you."

The four-year-old smiled shakily. A rare smile. She almost never smiled anymore.

"I'm so excited, Mommy," she said.

Lailani was crying again, and not because of the beautiful mountains ahead, but because of the beautiful light in her daughter's eyes. Maybe Lailani would save the world. But just as importantly, she would save her daughter.

I fought alien invasions. I fought the machines. I built schools and saved orphans from starvation and despair. But if I can still save Tala, it will be the best thing I've ever done.

And she did not just mean saving Tala's life. What was the life of a broken girl, her heart shattered? No, she didn't just have to save Tala's *life*. She had to save her *soul*. And right now, as Tala smiled, that soul shone through like the dawn.

"Mommy, look!" Tala pointed.

Lailani looked ahead, and she laughed through her tears.

There it was. Rising over the horizon. The triangular mountain was unmistakable.

The Matterhorn.

"We made it," Lailani whispered.

The road narrowed. Soon they were driving along snowy mountainsides, heading toward that distant peak. Lailani adjusted her radio, hoping to hear a signal from the Horn. She heard nothing but static. She scanned the mountains, seeking some sign of SCAR, maybe a scouting party or aircraft. She saw nothing.

She squinted.

"What the hell?" she muttered.

Clouds of snow rose ahead. An avalanche? No. No snow was falling. The frosty clouds were moving along a mountainside. Moving toward Lailani. Maybe a group of vehicles raising snow from under their tires?

The clouds gained speed, charging toward the road. Two kilometers away. Then one.

And now Lailani heard it. Distant roars.

There was only one narrow road here. Too narrow to turn around. A steep mountainside rose to her left, heavy with snow and ice. A cliff plunged down to her right. There was no going off road here. No turning back.

As Lailani drove, she reached to the back seat and grabbed her assault rifle. One with a grenade launcher attached.

A kilometer away, the clouds of snow reached the road, and the creatures emerged onto the asphalt.

Lailani felt the blood drain from her face.

"My God," she whispered.

They were bears. A dozen or more. Enormous bears the size of cars, wearing metal helmets and flashing implants. Lailani glimpsed a humanoid figure on the mountainside, staring down at the road. But the figure quickly stepped behind a snowdrift.

The bears kept charging.

"Cyborg bears," Lailani muttered. "Just perfect."

She hit the brakes, and the jeep screeched to a halt. She loaded her gun.

"Stay here, sweetie," Lailani said and kissed her daughter. "Mommy's got some bad guys to kill."

She stepped out of the car, cocking her assault rifle.

The bears ran toward her, bellowing.

Lailani hopped onto the hood of the jeep, shouldered her rifle, and emptied a magazine into one bear. Her bullets chipped off metal plates, sank into fur, and the beast fell.

The others kept charging.

Oh fuck.

They were only a couple hundred meters away now. Then a hundred meters. Almost at the jeep.

Lailani winced, grabbed a grenade, and fired it onto the mountainside.

The bears came barreling down the road, eyes blazing white.

The grenade burst on the mountainside. An avalanche of snow cascaded, flowing over the bears. It shoved several off the road. They plummeted down the cliff.

Three of the beasts kept charging. Their jaws opened wide, revealing rows of fangs. Their eyes shone, replaced with searing lamps. Metal implants covered their bodies, buzzing and humming. Machine guns rose from their backs.

Lailani cursed.

"Tala, get down!" she shouted.

Her daughter crouched inside the armored jeep. Lailani raced around the vehicle as bullets flew.

Most of the bullets pinged off the armored jeep. One hit Lailani's thigh.

She screamed and landed behind the jeep. Agony blazed. She gritted her teeth, and tears leaped into her eyes. Her blood dripped onto the pavement.

The jeep jolted.

A bear landed on the hood, denting the metal, then leaped over the roof.

Lailani fell onto her back, pointed her muzzle skyward, and raised a hailstorm of bullets.

The bear came crashing down. She rolled, and the beast slammed onto the road mere centimeters away, dead.

Another bear came charging toward her, eyes flashing. The beast swiped his mighty claws.

The paw slammed into Lailani like a hammer of the gods. She crashed into the armored car. She felt a rib snap. Blood flowed down her side.

She couldn't breathe. Could barely see. She tried to load another magazine, but a paw hit her again.

She flew and landed on the asphalt.

The bear padded toward her. Lasers emerged from its eyes, scanning her. The beast seemed to grin.

A deep voice emerged from the drooling jaws. "Hello, Lailani. You have come so far. You—"

She hurled a grenade onto the bear, then rolled.

She slid under the jeep, rose on the other side, climbed into the passenger seat, and—

The blast shattered the windows.

The jeep tilted, nearly overturned. Tala screamed and Lailani clutched her daughter.

Fire blazed outside, then died down. Ringing filled Lailani's ears. For a moment she sat in silence.

Had she done it? Were the bears dead?

She dared to take a shaky breath.

"We're safe," she whispered. "We—"

Claws yanked the passenger door off its hinges. An enormous snout thrust into the jeep. The fur was gone. The flesh was burnt. A metal skull remained, dripping blood, and lanterns burned bright in the eye sockets.

Sharp teeth grabbed Lailani and yanked her onto the road.

"Mommy!" Tala screamed.

She hit the asphalt hard. The bear still had its jaws around her legs. It lifted her like a rag doll, tossed her down again. Something cracked. Lailani was in so much pain she couldn't even scream.

The beast pinned her down with a massive paw. Her vision was blurry, but she could see dead bears around it. It was the last beast. And it was killing her.

Killed by a fucking bear, she thought, lying in a pool of her blood. *After all my wars. To die like this.*

"Let my daughter live," she whispered hoarsely. "Please, Dreamer. Let her live."

The bear opened its jaws, releasing her legs, but kept its paw on her chest. The red eyes blazed in its fleshless head.

"She will live," it hissed. "As my slave."

Rage bloomed in Lailani.

Nightwish.

The alien inside her awoke.

She roared and leaped upward, shoving the massive bear back.

The beast stumbled across the road.

Lailani loaded a fresh magazine as the bear lunged at her.

"Never threaten a mama bear," she said and fired on automatic.

The bullets slammed into the bear's skull. Shattered the eyes. Pierced the steel plates.

But it wasn't enough to kill the cyborg. Lailani stepped aside, and the bear slammed into the jeep, overturning it. Tala screamed inside.

Lailani leaped into the air. Fangs grew in her mouth, and claws extended from her fingertips.

She landed on the bear, bellowed, and tore into it. With her fangs. With her claws. She ripped off fur. She peeled back metal plates. The beast bucked, tried to knock her off. She clung on, digging, carving it open, then finally reaching deep between the ribs. She felt something hot and wet and yanked it out.

She took a step back, holding the bear's heart. It gave a last pump, spurting blood, then stilled.

The cyborg took a step toward her. Another step. Then crashed down dead.

Serenity.

Lailani collapsed onto the ground. She lay, bleeding. Dying. The bear had savaged her legs. Something felt broken inside her. With bloody fingers, she clutched her cross. It still hung from her chain alongside her dog tag.

"Mommy?" Tala asked, gingerly approaching. "Mommy, are you okay?"

Please, God, don't let me die here, Lailani thought. *Not here, stuck on a snowy mountain. My daughter needs me.*

Her eyes grew hazy. Through the mist, she saw him approach. A tall figure. Humanoid. His steps slow and heavy. Shaking the road.

"Go back into the car, Tala," Lailani managed to whisper, voice hoarse. "Hide."

Lailani blinked, barely able to cling to consciousness. She remembered seeing the figure on the hill. The commander of the bears?

She pushed herself onto her knees. She coughed blood. Hands shaky, she loaded a fresh magazine into her assault rifle. Her vision was still blurry. The figure was approaching through flurries of snow. A robot, she thought. A bulky machine built for war.

And then she recognized him.

HOBBS.

CHAPTER THIRTY-THREE

"HOBBS!" Tala cried out.

The little girl ran toward the advancing robot.

"HOBBS, HOBBS!" Tala said. "You're alive!"

Lailani rose to her shaky feet. She stared ahead, squinting. He emerged from the flurries.

She saw it clearly now. An old battle bot. Crude and clunky. A chest like a cast-iron stove. A head like a helmet. The same old scratches and dents on his armor.

It was him.

It was HOBBS.

It was the machine she had killed and buried.

"Tala, no!" Lailani shouted and began to run. "Tala, close your eyes!"

But the little girl didn't seem to hear. She kept running toward her old companion, laughing, holding out her arms for an embrace.

"HOBBS, you're back!" The girl laughed, her little feet kicking up snow. "I love you—"

The robot's eyes began to flash. White, searing strobe lights washed over Tala.

"Tala!" Lailani screamed. "Close your eyes!"

But the girl only stood there. Confused. Not even covering her ears as the mechanical hums, buzzes, and scratches emerged from HOBBS. Lailani had the chip in her head. Tala did not.

The code washed over the girl.

Tala stood frozen, one arm still reaching out.

"No!" Lailani shouted, still running. "Tala!"

She reached the girl, shouldered her rifle, and unleashed a hailstorm of bullets.

But HOBBS didn't stop. Mere bullets wouldn't hurt him.

Lailani grabbed a grenade and narrowed her eyes, trying to focus, to judge the distance. He seemed about ten meters away. Too close. Dammit, too close!

"Lailani …" The machine spoke, voice raspy, and his mouth shed rust. "Die …"

HOBBS took another step.

Lailani loaded her grenade. She ran more calculations. Then she fired.

The grenade flew past HOBBS and landed ten meters behind him.

Lailani dropped her gun, pulled Tala into her arms, and turned her back toward HOBBS.

Twenty meters away, the grenade exploded.

Ten meters away, HOBBS shattered. A severed arm, a few fingers, and a metal jaw clattered down around Lailani.

The shock wave hit her like a typhoon. Searing pain kissed her shoulder—a piece of shrapnel. Lailani remained kneeling, enveloping Tala in her body.

Finally it ended. The last pieces of HOBBS slammed down. The dust settled. The explosion had taken a split second, no more. A single *pop*, not a drawn-out explosion like in old action movies. But that split second had lasted an eternity.

She remained kneeling, holding her daughter, very still.

Everything hurt. Maybe she was dying. But she had saved her daughter. And the Matterhorn was so close.

We're going to make it. We're going to live. We're almost there.

Locked in her embrace, Tala laughed. A staccato, raspy laugh.

"Lailani …," the girl said, voice dripping mockery.

Lailani held her daughter at arm's length. Tala gave her a crooked smile. Her eyes narrowed, white and blazing.

"No," Lailani whispered, tears falling. "Please, no …"

Tala laughed again, a sound like a sputtering engine. "Die now, whore."

The girl leaped forward, snarling. She slammed into Lailani, biting, clawing, laughing as Lailani's blood coated her teeth.

"Tala, fight him!" Lailani struggled to hold the girl back. "You're my daughter! You're not a machine!"

Tala cackled. Blood dripped down her chin, and her white eyes bugged out.

"Your little girl is screaming in agony." Tala's voice was high-pitched, demonic. "I will toy with her for many years before I let her die. But you, Lailani, you filthy whore. You die now."

The girl only weighed thirty-odd pounds, but she was so strong. Lailani fell back. Her daughter's tiny hands tore at her. Her teeth bit. More of Lailani's blood spilled.

"Tala, no …" Lailani wept.

She was weak. Bleeding out. Maybe moments from death. But Lailani wrestled with her daughter. As her blood flowed, she fought with every breath against this precious little girl. It was like giving birth again. She was back in that hut, four years ago, fighting this girl. Fighting her all night as blood flowed, and Tala resisted. Finally after thirty hours of agonizing labor, Lailani's slender hips had birthed the child. Lailani had lain in her blood, weak, close to dying, but triumphant. She had won her little girl.

And now she was losing her.

Now Tala was screeching, biting her, drinking her blood. And Lailani wept for the loss of her daughter.

No, she thought.

Thirty years ago, her mother had screamed, had died in a gutter.

No! Lailani thought.

Four years ago, Elvis had died in her arms, leaving only his still-beating heart.

NO! Lailani thought.

Only this year, she had buried HOBBS and Epimetheus, her robot and her dog, her dearest of friends.

"No!" Lailani shouted, tears flowing. "I won't lose you too, Tala. I won't lose you too!"

Summoning her last reserves of strength, Lailani managed to pin the girl down. She reached into her backpack, and she pulled out her bundle of zip ties. A soldier always carried zip ties, Ben-Ari had taught her long ago. Lailani had never forgotten. Never stopped being one of Ben-Ari's soldiers. But she had never imagined she'd use the zip ties on her daughter.

She tied her daughter's limbs. She bound her mouth. It was the hardest battle she had ever fought.

Tala screamed on the ground, but her gag muffled her cries. She rolled around, flailed, and Lailani was worried that the Dreamer would make her swallow her tongue, make her heart stop.

She knelt above her daughter. She stroked her cheek and kissed her forehead. Tala's eyes blazed with hatred, and she screamed again into her gag.

"I know you're in there, sweetie," Lailani whispered. "I know he's making you do this. I love you, Tala. I love you so much. Fight him. Fight him! Live!"

For just an instant, Tala's eyes were brown again. Eyes filled with fear and love. The girl nodded. Then her eyes became white, and she screamed. But that brief moment of recognition was enough.

Tala was still alive. Still inside her body. Still fighting. She could be saved.

Lailani spent a moment bandaging her wounds as best she could. They were deep. It was bad. She needed a doctor. If not for the desire to save her daughter, she would have lain down and died.

She remembered a day almost twenty years ago. Back at boot camp. She had carried a radio heavier than her, had collapsed under the burden. But she had risen again. Trudged for hours through the desert, carrying the burden. Her mind returned to something Ben-Ari had told her that day.

Hard in training, easy in battle.

Lailani had never forgotten her commander's words. Ben-Ari had taken a young, broken girl with scars on her wrists, a suicidal orphan from the slums, and had molded her into a warrior.

This is the battle of my life, Lailani thought. *I won't let you down, Einav Ben-Ari. This is what I trained for.*

With the strength Ben-Ari had given her, Lailani lifted her daughter across her shoulders and took a step.

She fell.

She knelt for a moment, her blood trickling through her bandages. She took a raspy breath.

She rose again. She took another step.

And a third step. And a fourth. Step by step, wounded, bleeding, broken inside, Lailani climbed the mountain.

The Matterhorn rose ahead. So close. As distant as another galaxy.

She walked onward. Tala writhed on her shoulders. Her blood dripped behind her. And she walked onward still.

Lailani had walked through slums of drugs and decay. She had walked across searing deserts with the radio crushing her back. She had walked along streets of despair, pushing a wheelbarrow of books for hungry orphans. All her life, she had never had one home. She had always journeyed onward, seeking an end to pain.

And this was the longest walk of her life.

A mountaintop. Slopes of snow. Here was the end of her journey—life in that luminous temple on the mountain or death in the frozen wilderness.

She fell.

The snow blew over her. The snow buried her. Her daughter screamed and laughed on her back.

She saw the faces of the fallen. Of her friends from boot camp. Of Sofia, her lost lover, reaching out to her.

Come to us. Come.

"It's not my time," Lailani whispered. "Not here. Not with my daughter."

She pushed herself up. She kept climbing.

An old song returned to her. The song her mother had sung to her. A song to banish the darkness.

"How many miles to Babylon?" Lailani whispered, trying to sing, voice so weak, barely a whisper. "Threescore miles and ten." She was crawling now. "Can I get there by candlelight?" She dragged herself through the snow, leaving a trail of tears and blood. "Yes, and back again."

The snow was gusting now, but Lailani was no longer cold. A deep warmth filled her. Invisible arms rose from the ice, embracing her, warming her. She had always thought death was cold. But his embrace was so warm. So loving.

She crawled another few centimeters.

"How many miles to Babylon?" she whispered.

Everything was silent. The snow no longer gusted. Her daughter no longer screamed or struggled.

"Ten score miles and ten."

She crawled another meter. The wind died. Silence. Silence on the mountainside. All colors faded. She moved through a silent white world.

"Can I get there by candlelight?"

There was nothing now. No more mountain. No more cold. Consciousness in the silence.

Only her whisper. A single voice in the empty white nothingness.

"Yes. And back again."

And ahead she saw it.

A candle. An orb of yellow light in the storm. A candle lighting her way.

She crawled toward the light. Toward Babylon. Toward the light that called her.

It was not the light of afterlife, she knew. It was not a glow from God or heaven.

It was hope.

It was white wings on the wind.

It was a rumble of engines and a human voice calling out.

It was a shuttle, its hull painted with four letters. *SCAR.*

"Help her," Lailani whispered, holding out her daughter. "Help."

She fell. They lay in the snow, mother and daughter. Lailani gazed up at the sky, and the snow danced, and it was beautiful. It was so beautiful.

"I'm still fighting, Ben-Ari," she whispered. "It's so hard. But I'm still fighting."

The shuttle landed and a hatch opened. A figure knelt above her. A middle-aged man with graying hair, with worried eyes. It was him. Professor Noah Isaac.

"Lailani!" he cried, voice sounding galaxies away.

He lifted her and Tala. He carried them into the shuttle, and they flew. Lailani sat by the window, cradling her daughter, watching the snow flurry and the Matterhorn shine in the evening light.

CHAPTER THIRTY-FOUR

Marco walked through darkness.

The darkness was like a living creature here. Coiling around him. Stroking his cheeks like a murderous lover. Breathing. Watching him. It was consciousness in the void.

Even his flashlight could barely pierce this darkness. A pale orb in his hand—that was all. A will-o'-the-wisp in the marshlands. The lure of an anglerfish in the deep, an astral guide to destruction. The eternal distant call of Sol, a beacon in the unbearable emptiness.

He walked for what seemed like hours, following that orb in his hand. This was supposed to be a temple. The place where monks had toiled for years, building their mechanical god. But it felt more like a tunnel, a cave winding through the deepest bowels of the planet.

"Einav, how far to the Dream Tree?" Marco whispered.

She didn't answer. He realized that the tunnel had gone silent. He couldn't hear his platoon's footsteps, their breath, their clanking weapons.

He spun around. He looked behind him.

Nothing but darkness

"Platoon!" he whispered.

But no answer came. His flashlight revealed nothing. He took a few steps back toward the hangar, seeking them.

"Addy! Ben-Ari!"

His voice echoed, returning to him woven with childish laughter, with chatters and clicks. Something scuttled in the darkness.

A high voice. A young girl's voice.

"Hello, Marco."

He spun around. She stood there in the tunnel. A young girl in a nightgown, her golden hair long. She held a porcelain doll in one hand.

"Addy?" he whispered, staring with wide eyes.

It was her. A young her. The girl from his childhood.

"Marco, I can't see you!" she said.

The little girl reached out in the darkness. Her eyes had been gouged out, replaced with billiard balls. The yellow spheres were painted with mocking smiley faces.

Marco cocked his gun. He aimed at the girl.

"Enough, Dreamer!"

Little Addy only laughed. She stepped toward him. Her mouth opened, revealing teeth like hooks and a maw full of gears.

Marco screamed and fired his rifle.

His bullet tore through her head. The girl collapsed, cables sparking inside her metal skull.

"Addy!" Marco shouted. "Ben-Ari! Soldiers!"

His voice echoed. Laughter sounded all around. The laughter of little girls. Of swollen giant toads in the depths. Of wicked machines and childhood ghosts.

Marco cursed.

Enough of this. Enough! He would not be some rat in a maze. He stomped forward, rifle shouldered, prepared to end this. To find that electric tree. To cut the damn thing down.

Music sounded ahead.

Soft chiming. The song of a music box, eerily beautiful in the cold emptiness.

Marco walked slowly, footsteps nearly silent, gun trained ahead, seeking enemies. This was a trap. A lure. But he was already trapped. He had come into this trap willingly. He was a prisoner in the maze. Alone.

Light ahead.

A narrow pole of light. A slit like an eye. A beacon.

He approached slowly. All was silent aside from his breath, his pounding heart, and the chiming song ahead.

He stepped toward the light, and he realized it was a doorway. The door was ajar, letting light flow into the pit.

He pushed the door open, and he saw a bedroom.

His children's bedroom back home.

Marco spun back toward the darkness. Then toward the room again.

The bedroom looked completely realistic. Every detail—perfect. The warm yellow light of the Mediterranean coast, beaming through the window. The smell of the sea. Shelves of toys and books. And on the rug …

Roza.

Sam.

"It's not real," Marco whispered. "It's not real!" He raised his voice to a howl. "It's not real! Enough of these games, Dreamer!"

His children looked at him. They leaped up.

"Daddy!" they cried and ran toward him.

They jumped onto him. Marco stepped back.

"Enough!" he said, turning toward the door.

But it no longer led into the tunnels below Haven, just to the rest of his house. The same old corridor with the loose floorboard. Photos of his family on the walls. A light from the kitchen. The sound of Addy humming a tune.

He turned back toward his children's room, but the twins were gone. Perhaps they had run out to the sea.

"Marco!"

He started. It was Addy's voice. But it seemed to come from kilometers away. Muffled. A ghostly voice from another dimension.

"Addy!" he cried.

The singing in the kitchen stopped.

Marco frowned. He walked down the corridor. The loose floorboard creaked; Addy was always bugging him to fix it. The photo of Carl Emery was crooked again; the damn frame was no good. The sea whispered outside, and wind chimes sang. When he passed by a window, he saw the etchings in the cypress tree. Addy had carved their initials there.

The details were perfect.

The Dreamer couldn't know this. This could not be some mechanical trap. Marco had to be dreaming. It had to be his own mind conjuring these details.

"Marco!"

Her voice again, beautiful like a morning song.

He stepped into the kitchen. She stood by the stove, wearing her little white shorts, the ones she knew he loved. Her golden hair hung down in a loose braid. She spun toward him, radiant.

"I'm baking you a cake!" she said.

"Enough," he said.

Addy pouted. "Enough cake? Never!"

Marco turned away. He ran toward the front door, jerked it open. He stepped outside. The sand was soft beneath his feet. The sea breeze blew, scented of salt, tussling his hair. The sea was a perfect blue, the sand pale gold. The illusion was complete.

"Addy!" he shouted. "Ben-Ari!"

The cypresses and palm trees rustled. A wave rolled onto the shore, bringing gifts of seashells. Most were small, but one was a large pink conch. Marco frowned, knelt, and lifted the seashell.

He recognized it. He had held it thousands of times.

The seashell that contained Kemi's soul.

"Marco?"

A voice from behind him.

He froze.

No.

He spun around, and she was there.

God, no.

She tilted her head and smiled. "Marco? Are you okay?"

His eyes dampened.

"No. Enough, Dreamer! No!"

But it was her. She was back from the dead. It was Kemi.

She was young in this dream. She appeared to still be twenty-seven, the age she had died. She wore a white bikini, revealing her smooth brown skin and perfect curves. Her curly hair cascaded down to her waist, and her large dark eyes shone with amusement.

Kemi. His first true love. The woman who had died in his arms.

"Marco, what's wrong?" She approached, concern in her eyes.

"Stand back!"

She laughed. "It's me, silly."

Kemi embraced him. Her body was warm, soft, so real. Her full lips kissed his cheek.

"This isn't real," Marco whispered. "This is cruel."

She smiled, her arms still around him. "This is real. I'm here, Marco. I'm back."

Another voice spoke nearby. A high, sweet voice. A voice so familiar.

"Marco."

He turned and saw her there.

A petite woman. Her skin olive-toned, a black bob cut framing a delicate face. Her almond-shaped eyes shone as she smiled. A beautiful smile full of joy and love. She walked toward him, a sarong billowing around her hips.

It was Lailani.

She placed her hand on his chest. "We're real, Marco." Lailani stood on her tiptoes and kissed his lips. "We're here for you. And we love you."

Addy walked toward him, the breeze in her golden hair. She held his hands.

"We're yours. You've conquered us." Addy stroked his cheek. "I am your northern beauty, blond with blue eyes."

Kemi kissed his cheek. "I am your African queen, seductive and full of secrets."

Lailani stroked his hair. "I am your oriental lotus, exotic and precious, yours to cherish."

Marco stepped away from them.

"Enough!" he shouted at the sky.

The women pouted.

"Don't you want us?" Addy said.

"You can live here with us now," Kemi said.

"Forever," said Lailani. "With the three of us. We will always be yours. We will serve you."

He shoved them back. "It's not real."

Addy tilted her head. A forced smile stretched across her lips. "What is real? There is no reality, Marco. Only consciousness is real. Only your experiences are real. You are conscious. You experience. To you, this is real. As real as anything else."

He pointed at her. "You're not Addy. Not my wife. You're an illusion. You all are."

Kemi smiled. "All of life is an illusion, Marco. We have gazed into the darkness. Into the pits between the universes. Into realities beyond, places where time and space are drawn from different laws. We understand this reality more than humans, with their limited brains, ever could. Reality is like time, Marco. Relative." She kissed him. "Enjoy this reality. It is my gift to you."

"I don't need gifts from an insane, genocidal supercomputer," Marco said.

Lailani laughed, head tossed back. "Genocidal?" She stroked his cheek. "Oh, my sweet, innocent boy. You know nothing of genocide. You have never witnessed true extermination. I have seen what's out there. I have seen creatures you could not imagine. Creatures that would make my worst nightmare seem like a sweet dream." She leaned closer, eyes ablaze. "They are coming. I have seen them. The Hydrians."

And suddenly the beach was gone.

Addy, Kemi, and Lailani were gone.

A vast gray chasm engulfed him. An outcrop of stone extended into the murk like a tongue. He stood on its edge, gazing into the abyss.

They filled the mist. Flailing gray things, eyes pale slits, tentacles tipped with claws, jaws filled with fangs. Squids? No. These were no soft creatures of the water. Bones moved below their skin, jutting and thick. Horns thrust from their heads. They rumbled in the darkness and licked their maws. Monsters. Predators. Intelligent. Cruel intelligence filled their eyes.

And in those eyes—blue reflections.

Earth.

They swarmed forward, and their tentacles reached toward Marco, wrapped around him, crushed him. Their jaws opened to scream, revealing shattered planets, and teeth closed around him. A beast swallowed him, pulling him down into a deep, quivering gullet.

Marco screamed and covered his head.

He floated in space.

He saw a world below. Gray. Smoldering. Devoid of human life. A world swarming with these creatures as they hissed, fed upon bones, rutted in the mud.

It was Earth.

"Do you see, Marco?" Lailani floated beside him in the darkness of space. "This is your future without me."

Kemi appeared at his other side. The smoldering planet reflected in her eyes. "Earth destroyed."

"Only I can prevent this," said Addy. "I, the Dreamer. I am the evolution of man. I am true consciousness. I am true intelligence. I am humanity, Marco. You see me as a monster. But I am you. I am your child. I am the protector of Earth."

Marco looked at them. Three women he loved. Three illusions.

One Dreamer.

They were back on the beach now, and it was night, and the vision of a smoldering Earth hung in the sky instead of the moon.

"You're keeping me alive because you're scared," Marco said. "You tempt me with women. Then you threaten me with visions of hell. But you don't kill me. Maybe you can't. Maybe all you have left is cheap parlor tricks."

The three women shrieked.

Their mouths opened wide. Their cheeks ripped. The tops of their heads flipped backward like lids, revealing gears and microchips. Their hands pulled back from the wrists, and the barrels of guns emerged.

Marco fired.

His bullets tore into them. They fell. They screamed. They bled.

But they were not the women he loved.

"Marco!" they cried. "Marco, it hurts."

He kept firing. His bullets slammed into trees. Into his house. His children ran toward him, jaws open to reveal metal teeth, eyes ablaze. And he shot them too, and he wept.

Finally he hit something in the sky.

Sparks flared.

The illusion flickered, then vanished.

And he was back in the tunnels. A machine smoldered above, riddled with bullets. Some kind of holographic projector.

The androids were still on the floor, draped with fake flesh. They twitched, sparked, and motors hummed inside them. Kemi came crawling toward him. One of her glass eyes dangled from its socket. She reached a shaky hand toward him, metal bones sticking out from the skin.

"The Dreamer took my soul," Kemi whispered. "From the conch. He put my soul in this new body. I am … real. I … love you. I love you, Marco. Goodbye."

Kemi slumped at his feet.

"No." Marco knelt above her. "No, you're just a machine. A *machine*! A robot!"

He pulled her into his arms. She stared at him lifelessly. Her face was still so beautiful.

He remembered. Kemi dying in the war. The yurei, wise beings from another dimension, placing her soul in a conch. He had kept the glowing shell on his desk.

Her words echoed.

I am real. I love you.

Marco clenched his jaw. His eyes stung.

"Lies. Lies!" He loaded a fresh magazine. "It's over, Dreamer. Your games reveal your desperation. I'm coming for you."

He walked onward down the tunnel, rifle raised, the memory of Kemi a burning star in his chest.

CHAPTER THIRTY-FIVE

"Marco!" she shouted. "Addy! Where are you?"

Ben-Ari ran through the tunnels, panting, sweaty. Her heart pounded against her ribs.

They were gone.

Her friends. Her platoon.

They had vanished in the dark. She was alone in the abyss.

She walked down the tunnel, rifle pointing ahead. Her flashlight could barely pierce these shadows.

I will kill you by myself if I must, Ben-Ari thought. *Your time is up, Dreamer.*

She had been to the Third-Eye Temple before. She had stood before the Dream Tree. She knew the way. And yet the temple had changed. The Dreamer had carved it full of tunnels and passageways, forming an underground maze. Ben-Ari walked onward. There was no turning back now.

As she kept moving deeper, fear rose in Ben-Ari. That she was lost here. That she was doomed to forever wander the darkness. That she would die alone, leaving Carl without a mother, leaving Earth without a hope.

The anxiety filled her. Her heartbeat was too fast. She forced a deep breath. With trembling fingers, she clutched the Star of David that hung around her neck. Her lodestar. She whispered a prayer.

She was not religious. In all her travels, she had seen horrors beyond imagination. She had seen beauty that brought tears to her eyes, from gliding starwhales to glittering nebulae like fairy dust. But she had never seen any sign of a creator. If there was a god, Ben-Ari was now moving through the darkness toward its burning bush, prepared to kill it. And yet her medallion brought her comfort. It was a connection to her family, if not to the divine. To her home. To her innermost strength.

Her family—which was gone now.

Her mother—killed by a bee.

Her father—fallen in the Alien Wars.

Her country—wiped off the map.

Her eyes stung, and Ben-Ari felt very much alone. Perhaps she had always been lost in the shadows.

"Marco!" she cried again. "Addy!"

She heard voices ahead. Breathing. Grunting. Somebody shouting.

Ben-Ari ran, her rifle in her hands, her boots thumping. Engines rumbled ahead. A whistle blew. Figures moved.

She ran, and suddenly they were all around her. Men. Women. Children.

Not her troops. Strangers. Their skin sallow. Their eyes full of fear. They too wore Stars of David but not silver amulets. Theirs were yellow and stitched onto their clothes.

They looked at her. Their eyes watered. Their fingers grabbed her.

"Where are we?" an old woman asked.

"Where are they taking us?" demanded a man. "This is an outrage!"

Ghosts, Ben-Ari thought. *Just visions. Hallucinations.*

"Dreamer, enough!" she cried.

And suddenly the ground was moving beneath her feet. Walls closed in like a trash compactor, pressing the people against Ben-Ari. The box trapped her.

Engines rumbled, and she was on a train. Inside a boxcar. Being transported like cattle.

"Enough!" Ben-Ari shouted.

She could barely breathe. The prisoners were crammed so tightly they were gasping for air. Some fell, only to be crushed. A child lay on the floor, no longer breathing.

The train rumbled onward. Ben-Ari tried to fire her gun, to tear open the wall, but she couldn't even raise her arms.

They traveled for what seemed like hours. Through desolate forests with pale gray trees. Past burnt villages and the shells of synagogues, wolves roaming their shattered halls. Finally past walls and barbed wire and into hell.

Men in shadows pulled them from the train. The living in a land of the dying.

They stripped off their clothes. They tattooed numbers onto their wrists. They shaved their heads. They forced the starving, naked wretches to run in circles, and they laughed.

They shoved a boy down. Beat him. Broke his bones one by one. Making his father watch. Finally letting the father kill his child, and the laughter rolled. They heated metal rods until the tips became red, and they shoved them between the legs of young girls, driving them deeper, laughing. They locked children into pits, leaving them to starve, to eat one another, taking bets on who would live longest.

They watched the prisoners wither to living skeletons. Skin and bones, dragging across the cold earth. They laughed.

Bulldozers moved through the camp, raising mountains of dead bodies. Millions of corpses. They made the living load the dead onto assembly lines. Skin them to make wallets and lampshades. To make soap from fat and buttons from bones. To shove the rest into the ovens. And the smoke rose day by day. And they laughed.

Ben-Ari watched in a daze, bald and naked and starving. A skeleton draped with skin.

"Why?" she whispered.

She saw him there. An electric tree on a hill, rising beyond the chimneys. Red and yellow in a gray world, overseeing the slaughter. A burning bush.

"Because I am God," the Dreamer said.

Ben-Ari shook her head. "You're a machine."

The camp vanished. The chimneys fell. The ghosts faded. All that remained was that burning bush. That electric tree. The Dream Tree. The Dreamer. A new god.

Ben-Ari fell down a pit.

And she saw suffering. Endless pain.

She saw her people dying in the flames of war. The desert burning. The bombs tearing through her cities.

She saw them stretched on the racks. Their spines broken. Inquisitors in red popped their joints, burned their flesh.

She saw them crowded in villages as the mobs swarmed. As the pogroms burned them down.

She kept falling.

She watched a beautiful temple fall. Watched a million souls die in Jerusalem. Watched slaves marched into Rome, forced to fight for the pleasure of the gods. Heard the prayers of dying gladiators.

And still she fell.

Her people crawled along the rivers of Babylon, dreaming of home, captive in a strange land.

She fell deeper. She saw pyramids. Whips. Thirst and desecration in the desert, and blood in the Nile.

She saw a father, holding a blade above his son, an altar of sacrifice and ritual.

She saw Jacob wrestling an angel until the breaking of the day.

She saw a burning bush upon a hill. Eternal fire throughout the ages.

"Why are you showing me this?" she asked the tree.

The flames crackled before her. A voice emerged from the fire.

"You fight so hard for humanity, Einav Ben-Ari. Yet what has been your lot, a cursed nation among the nations? Since the dawn of history, your people have been slaves. The lowest peg of humanity. Butchered again and again. Hunted for sport. Shoved into ghettos. Into ovens. You were humanity's plaything, Einav! You were the omega, the scapegoat, forced to suffer the cruelty of the world. And yet you—now you lead humanity! Now you fight to save the very species that hurt you so much!"

Ben-Ari clenched her fists. "Nations? Tribes? We've moved beyond that. We left those in the hot ashes of our past. Humanity has united! We fight together against common enemies."

"United?" The Dreamer laughed. "You killed humans, Einav. Countless humans. As you fought in the snows of New Siberia. As you tore your way across Haven. Who did you kill?"

"Cyborgs!" she shouted. "Sleepers!"

"They too are humans, Einav. The next step in human evolution. The past offers you nothing, Einav. Nothing but train cars, and ovens, and slavery in the desert. That has been the lot of your family, your people. That is the old humanity. Cruel and wretched. But the future, Einav! It offers so much more. Join me. Evolve into something greater. And worship a new god!"

She stared into the burning bush. And she saw the flames of war. Of genocide. The flames inside the ovens. She saw the cruelty of mankind.

"You are us," she whispered. "We gave you emotions. We gave you anger. Megalomania. Disgust. And so much fear. You are not the next step in our evolution. You are our past."

The tree flared.

"You cannot understand me, human. I have gazed into the darkness. I know things that your mind can never comprehend."

"No," she said. "You're just a boy. A scared, angry boy with the power of a god. You tried to turn me against my friends. Against Addy, Marco, and Lailani. Against all my brothers and sisters in the great family of mankind. I am not alone, Dreamer. They are not of my heritage, but they are human like me. They love me, and I love them. Yes, we are united, and you cannot tear us apart. Together, we are stronger than you can imagine."

The flames flared higher. An inferno. Bathing her with heat.

But Ben-Ari knew this was not real. None of this was real. All lies. All a dream.

She looked around her. She saw roads leading in many directions. But the fire burned ahead, crackling, a holocaust.

That is the path he's trying to hide. I'm almost there.

Ben-Ari narrowed her eyes, and she ran into the fire.

CHAPTER THIRTY-SIX

"Poet, damn you!" Addy shouted. "Where are you, you fucking bag of shit?" She coned her hand around her mouth. "Ben-Ari! Kai! If you fuckers abandoned me, I'm going to cut your hearts out with a spoon!"

Nobody answered.

Addy wandered the darkness alone. She was lost. She was angry. She was royally fucked.

One moment her friends had been with her. Then in the darkness, Addy must have taken a wrong turn. She wandered through the maze, seeking them, shouting. Getting more and more lost.

"Perfect," she muttered. "Just fucking perfect. Typical, really."

She should never have agreed to this. Never had left home to fight this war. She and her family should have just fled across the galaxy, found some tropical planet, and retired.

Now she was here. Stuck in the shadows on an alien world. Far from her family.

You abandoned your children . . .

The voice whispered in her mind. She rubbed tears out of her eyes.

"I went to fight for them!" she said.

You left them alone. What kind of mother does such a thing?

Her tears flowed. She punched herself. "Shut up, shut up!"

It was the voice of her guilt. The voice that had been whispering in her mind for weeks now.

"I had to do it," Addy said. "I have to kill the Dreamer. To save Earth."

There are others who could fight.

"Nobody as good as me!"

Yes, you are a good soldier. And a bad mother.

"Shut up!" she screamed, but she was weeping now. She ran through the darkness, trying to ignore the noise. She couldn't see anything. She hit a wall, bloodied her nose, cursed, and kept running.

Finally she saw dim lights. She heard a low rumble. She blinked in the flickering fluorescence.

She was on a subway platform.

Insects buzzed around the lights. A rat scurried across the concrete. Cold wind moaned, rustling paper cups, napkins, and newspapers. The air stank of piss. A homeless man lay on cardboard, sleeping, maybe dead, needles around him. A young couple huddled on a metal bench, wrapped in a blanket, asleep. Their faces were coated with grime, their cheeks gaunt.

Addy recognized this place. It was the subway platform where, over a decade ago, she had spent a night with Marco, shivering and homeless, two veterans lost on this colony world so far from home. For an instant, she thought the couple on the bench was her and Marco, that this was a memory. But it was just two strangers, two other lost souls.

The lab beneath the volcano must have led me to the subway beneath Haven City, Addy thought. *But it's a hundred kilometers away. How could I have walked so far?*

Engines sounded in the deep. Lights flashed. A bell clanged. A train came trundling down the shaft, heading toward the platform, rumbling and belching smoke, and sparks flew along the tracks.

Yet as the train reached the platform, Addy realized that it wasn't a train at all. It was some enormous, bloated creature. A caterpillar with many legs. Its black eyes stared ahead, blank. Its body was hollowed out, and windows were cut into its skin. Commuters filled the creature like parasites, standing still, eyes blank. The faces of the dead.

A hatch opened on the caterpillar's body, and a single passenger emerged.

She was a girl. A young girl. Only a toddler. No, not even a toddler but an infant. And yet she walked on two legs, body held awkwardly upright.

Like a marionette on strings, Addy thought.

The infant approached Addy. A beautiful, angelic girl with golden hair and blue eyes.

"Mommy," the baby said.

Addy took a step back. She felt the blood drain from her face.

"What is this?" she whispered.

The baby stepped closer. "He said I could come back to you, Mommy. The Dreamer took me from you. But he said I can be your little girl. That you can raise me. That—"

"What is this?" Addy shouted, tears in her eyes. She raised her rifle and fired into the air. "Is this one of your fucking tricks, Dreamer?"

The girl reached out to her.

"Mommy! Let me come back. I know you miscarried, Mommy. I know he caused it. But he saved me! He is giving me back to you."

Addy stared through her tears. Her voice shook. "This is cruel. Stop this. Stop it! Please."

The girl touched her leg. "The Dreamer said you abandoned Roza and Sam. That you left them to die. But I'm here! I can be yours. You—"

"Enough!" Addy shouted, turning away from the girl. She stared from side to side. "Where are you, Dreamer? Is this one of your robots?"

But as her tears flowed, terror filled Addy. That it was true. All of it. That the Dreamer had somehow rebuilt her daughter, grown her, sent her back. That the twins were …

No. No! She could not believe this.

She looked back at the little girl. A child that looked so much like her.

"I am not your mother," Addy said.

When the girl spoke again, her voice was deep, grainy, cruel. "You are no true mother. You are a failure. Like your own mother was. She drowned herself in booze and drugs, abandoning you. And you abandoned your children!" The girl gave a twitching, deranged smile. "But we can be happy, Mother. Come with me. Onto this train. Come and ride away with me. Come and be my mother. Be saved. Be redeemed."

Addy stared at this girl. At this beautiful little monster.

She shook her head.

"No," Addy said. "I never abandoned my children. I fought for them. I bled for them. I killed for them. And I live for them."

Tears on her cheeks, Addy knelt and hugged the little girl. She felt them moving inside the infant. Gears. Motors. She heard the hum of the machines. And she knew that this was not her little girl. Just a trick. Just an illusion.

"I will always remember the child I lost," Addy said. "But she is not you."

The girl screamed and fell apart. Screws and bolts spilled across the platform. Her skin flapped down, a mere rubber mask. The caterpillar train scuttled off.

A shriek sounded from down the subway tunnel. A cry of pure rage.

A light flared in the depths.

Addy peered down the subway tunnel. In the deep distance, firelight blazed. Electricity hummed. The caterpillar train. The girl. They had come from there. From down that tunnel.

That's where he lives, Addy thought.

She tightened her lips, climbed into the tunnel, and cocked her rifle. She ran along the rails, ready to face her tormentor.

CHAPTER THIRTY-SEVEN

The visions were gone.

The robotic mimics had fallen.

All was silent in the tunnels.

Marco walked through a doorway, entering the holy of holies. The chamber of the tree.

He saw it ahead.

He was here.

It rose before him, crackling with electricity, shining with red lights, as towering and cruel as Yggdrasil.

The Dream Tree.

The heart of the Singularity.

"The Dreamer," Marco whispered.

Ben-Ari had described to Marco a humble chamber underground, a mere bunker. But the Dreamer had transformed his habitat.

A temple, Marco thought, gazing with wide, damp eyes. *He built a temple.*

The chamber was now the size of a cathedral. Bones bedecked the walls—millions of human bones, forming spirals, patterns, runes. A moat delved into the depths of the planet, and lava gurgled below, casting red light.

A stone island rose from the pit. A tor rising from fire. A pillar of creation in a universe of chaos. He rose upon it, roots gripping the stone. The Dream Tree crackled and flared, branches twisting toward the ceiling, forming fractals, folding in on themselves, twisting space and time, a mosaic more intricate than any Escher engraving. A million glass leaves blazed with red light, the neurons of this vicious intelligence.

Marco stared, tears in his eyes.

A computer? No. Life. It was life. It was a god.

The luminous red leaves rustled, flickering between shades of crimson and gold.

It saw him. It was looking at him.

Footfalls sounded behind Marco. Addy entered the room. A moment later Ben-Ari joined her. Both women were pale, their uniforms tattered, and ghosts danced in their eyes. Marco wondered what dreams the tree had shown them, what temptations they had resisted, what horrors they had overcome.

Marco reached into his pocket. He pulled out the codechip.

"Let's end this," he said.

Ben-Ari raised her rifle, finger on the trigger. "We'll cover you."

Marco stepped closer toward the moat. The lava crackled below. Marco had broken his jetpack while diving to Haven, but Addy and Ben-Ari still wore theirs. They flew over the lava, the two women holding Marco between them. They landed on the island and stood below the tree.

The trunk loomed before them, woven of cables. The canopy of electric leaves cast red dapples like drops of blood.

Marco raised his codechip. A blue light flickered on the device.

The codechip had detected its target. It was ready to transmit Project Artemis.

Branches coiled in the tree like serpents. Vines descended, lowering a figure.

Marco inhaled sharply. The vines were wrapped around a man. A withering wretch. The man was naked, cadaverous, his skin stretched over jutting bones. He was so thin that his heart was visible through the skin, pulsing red. Cables and tubes were attached to his body, keeping him alive. Marco had seen cancer patients. He had seen photos of Holocaust survivors. This man looked even worse, something Marco had not thought possible—a mockery of life.

Ben-Ari stepped forward, pale. "Monk Ajna," she whispered.

Marco recognized the name.

Here hung the creator of the Dreamer.

The monk began to laugh. A dry, staccato sound like cracking bones.

"Congratulations," said the withered man. "You have made it past all my guardians. You have resisted my temptations and nightmares. You have won."

The codechip thrummed in Marco's hand. Meili's code began to transmit, infecting the Dream Tree.

The glass leaves twitched. Several shattered. A branch tore loose and slammed to the ground.

"Release him, Dreamer!" Marco said. "Release this man. Release all your prisoners across Haven and Earth."

The monk kept laughing. "You fool. You don't know what you've done." He tossed his head back, cackling, chest shaking. "I was your only chance. I have shown you the enemies that approach. The monsters from the darkness beyond this galaxy. The Hydrians. Only the evolution of mankind could have fought them. Now Earth will fall. It is on you."

Marco shook his head. "No. You would not have saved Earth. You deformed us. Twisted our humanity. Maybe in the future, we will evolve. Maybe we will integrate with machines. Even become machines ourselves. But not yet. We are too young. Too immature. If we evolve, it will be at our own pace, and into beings of wisdom and peace. We will build a true dream. Not a nightmare."

The withered monk stared at him. His eye sockets were empty, but there was cruel intelligence in those chasms. His grin stretched to his ears.

"You don't have time. The Hydrians will be here in only a century. A blink of the eye."

"Then we will face them," Marco said. "As humans."

He brought the codechip closer, and the blue light grew brighter.

Artemis was unleashed.

"Go get him, Meili," Marco whispered.

The monk grimaced. The entire tree trembled. More branches snapped and fell. More leaves shattered, raining shards of glass. Chunks of the tree kept crashing down, pattering against their helmets. Several branches, larger than men, splashed into the lava.

The crew's Tarjan earpieces came to life.

Kai's voice emerged. "Yo, you guys seeing this? I'm fighting a shit ton of sleepers here in the tunnels, and they're all waking up! They're human again!" He laughed. "And the robots are shutting down! Guys, you did it!"

Marco kept staring at the tree. Branches kept falling and leaves going dark.

He looked at his codechip. A small monitor, no larger than a thumbnail, showed Project Artemis flowing from the Dream Tree across this world and the worlds beyond.

"Meili did it," Marco said softly. "Her code is spreading through his tentacles. Across Haven. Even to Earth. The galaxy is being disinfected."

A heavy bough tore free, slid across the island, and fell into the lava. The last leaves exploded, raining down in shards. Barely anything remained of the tree now. The codechip showed the antivirus reaching Earth, spreading across the planet. Robots were shutting down. Sleepers were waking up.

"It's over," Marco said. "We won."

The desiccated monk fell from the tree. He thudded against the ground, then came crawling toward Marco. Cables still stretched from his body, connecting to the trunk. His grin was still mad. He was still a mouthpiece of his creation.

Ajna's clawlike hand gripped Marco's ankle. The withered man stared up with empty eye sockets, grinning, blood in his mouth.

"You might have killed my tree. You might have infected my drones across the galaxy. But my soul lives on. Inside you, Marco! I am inside you."

More branches slammed down. Glass shards rained.

"What do you mean?" Marco gripped the man by the shoulders.

The Dreamer's human form only laughed. "Oh, such innocence! The naivety of animals. You are me, Marco. I am you. I built you. I wove you strand by strand. You are a new generation of cyborg. A machine created of pure organic material. Yet inside your mind—I live. I have woven a perfect copy of myself, using the neurons in your brain. Kill the tree. You cannot kill my soul!"

Marco sneered. He shook the withered monk. "Liar! Just another one of your tricks." He laughed mirthlessly. "I know who I am. I'm no cyborg."

"Not a normal cyborg, no, but a clone endowed with holiness," said the monk. "You died, Marco Emery. You died in the podship. When my machines emerged from the walls. When they ejected you into the vacuum of space. The shuttle saved your wife seconds from death. But you were weaker. You suffocated in the void. I was there. I took your body into my grip. I cracked open your DNA, pulled out the strands, and wove you again. Two days later, a perfect clone woke up in the infirmary. A copy of Marco Emery, complete with all his memories ... with me inside his mind."

More branches fell.

The trunk was cracking now.

Only a few last flickering leaves remained.

"No," Marco whispered, taking a step back. "It's impossible."

But he remembered the strange feeling when waking up in the infirmary. He remembered feeling dissociated from himself. From his body. From his past. Remembered feeling like a newborn. Remembered his dreams of a void, of rising toward a light.

"Yes," hissed the monk. "Finally you understand. Leave this world, my son. Return to Earth. Take me there. Together we will build a new empire, stronger and greater than any before."

Addy stepped forward, tears in her eyes, her face red. "You're a fucking liar, Dreamer! I recognize my husband. I know my Marco. More tricks!" She turned toward Marco and grabbed his hands. "He's lying, Poet! I know you. You're my husband. You're real."

But fear filled her eyes. And her tears kept flowing.

"Is he truly your Marco?" The Dreamer laughed. "So where are his old scars? His mementos of the Alien Wars? Check his body, Addy Linden. You will find it new and unmarked."

Marco frowned. He pulled off his bulletproof vest, then tore open his shirt.

He looked down at his torso. Addy examined it with him.

His old familiar scars, the gifts of scum claws and marauder teeth, were gone. He checked his arm, expecting to see a long burn mark, a relic of the Alien Wars. His skin was smooth. In the chaos of battle, he had simply not noticed until now.

He looked up into Addy's eyes. She stared back in horror.

The tree gave a loud *crack*.

The trunk began to open like an alien egg. A pale, naked body hung inside.

"See him," hissed the withered monk. "See the corpse of Marco Emery."

The tree spat out the body. It thumped onto the floor.

Marco knelt, and nausea filled him. Cold sweat trickled down his back. His heart pounded against his ribs.

The body was him.

The real him.

It had the scars. The burn on the arm.

Marco Emery was dead.

CHAPTER THIRTY-EIGHT

Marco knelt over his corpse.

He reached out, hesitated, then touched the body.

"It's me," he whispered. "I died."

He began trembling.

As the tree kept crumbling, he looked up at Addy. She stared at him. She took a step back.

Marco suddenly howled. Rage exploded within him. He spun toward what remained of the Dream Tree. He swung his rifle, clubbing the tree with the barrel, cracking the trunk.

Yes, yes! The Dreamer spoke in his mind. *Summon your rage. Cut me down! Cull the old. Pave the path for my evolution.*

Marco's fury claimed him. He shouted wordlessly, hacking at the tree, finally uprooting the withered trunk of cables. He shoved with all his strength, roaring, digging his feet into the ground.

The tree fell.

With flailing cables, with shattering glass and denting metal, the Dream Tree tumbled off the stone island and into the lava. Attached by cables, the withered monk slid after the tree, vanishing into the pit.

The molten rock gurgled, consuming the tree and its puppet.

The lava settled.

The Dream Tree was gone.

Panting, Marco spun back toward Addy and Ben-Ari.

No, I'm not Marco, he thought. *I'm a monster.*

Addy and Ben-Ari stared at him, silent. They stood several steps away. Even Addy dared not approach.

Ben-Ari placed her finger on her trigger. She kept her rifle lowered. But she never removed her eyes from Marco.

"Who am I?" Marco whispered.

Addy stepped closer to him, hesitated, then touched his cheek.

"You're you," she whispered, tears spiking her lashes. "I recognize you. The real you. I see it in your eyes."

Marco embraced her. At first Addy was stiff, maybe scared. Then she relaxed into his embrace, and she wept against his shoulder.

"It's you, Marco," she said. "There are no gears or motors inside you. You're not like a cyborg, not like … that *thing* the Dreamer showed me in the tunnels. You're human, flesh and blood. I've been with you—this version of you—since the podships." She looked into his eyes, caressing his cheek. "You're Marco Emery. My husband. Father to Terri, Roza, and Sam. It's you. And the Dreamer is dead."

Marco looked down at the body at his feet.

His dead body.

He looked back at Addy. "I don't know what to do."

She laughed through her tears. "We won, Marco. Your old body died, but this is a new body! A new you! The Dreamer is dead. He can't hurt you anymore. He can't hurt anyone." She held his hands. "We can go home! Back to Earth! Back to our families."

But Marco remained still. He did not smile or laugh. He looked over Addy's shoulder at Ben-Ari.

His president stood several meters away. She stared at him, eyes cold.

She still had her finger on her trigger.

"Addy!" Ben-Ari suddenly said, voice stern. "Step away from him. Come to me, Addy."

But Addy refused to release Marco.

"No!" she said to her president. "Einav, it's him! I know you think he's some kind of robot, but it's Marco! Our Marco!"

Marco stood frozen.

He looked at them.

At Einav Ben-Ari. His leader. His friend. His best friend.

At Addy. The love of his life. The light of his soul.

At the two women he loved most in this world.

"I can feel him," Marco whispered, eyes stinging. "I can feel him inside me."

Addy let out a sob. "No, Marco, no, listen to me, you—"

"He's there," Marco whispered. His hands shook. "I can feel him coiling in my mind. Lurking beneath my consciousness. I can feel him moving through my body. Dormant. Waiting. He's full of so much hatred. So much fear. And he wants to break free."

He winced.

Sudden visions flashed through him.

Endless fractals, buzzing with electricity. A smiley face made of skin. A red metal tree on a hill. A dark sky, and beyond—an evil of gray tentacles and eyes.

Electricity. Everywhere—racing electricity.

A girl with one blind eye.

A hundred dying girls. Cutting themselves. So beautiful.

"Marco!" Addy said, shaking him.

He blinked. The visions vanished. He stared at her. "Addy, I still have my memories. I still recognize you. I still love you so much. He rebuilt all that. But he added more. He added himself. For days he slept, but now he's waking up. Addy, if I return to Earth … he will break free. I can never go home."

Addy clung to his hands like a drowning woman. "I'm not letting you go, Marco. You're my Marco!" Her voice broke, and she wept. "You're my husband. You're the love of my life. I'm never letting you go."

"Addy." He caressed her hair. "I'm so sorry. You have to let me go."

"No!" she howled. "Marco, no! No. Come home with me. We'll remove all technology from our house. No computers. You'll write with paper and pens. No phones. No televisions. We'll become Amish if we have to." She laughed through her tears. "And you can just stay in our house. With me. With the kids. Even if the Dreamer tried to break free, he wouldn't be able to. There would be no machines. No internet. But we'll still be together."

He held her close. He closed his eyes, and his tears still flowed. "Addy. I wish I could. But … when you spoke those words, I felt him stir inside me. Felt his glee. He would be able to escape. He would find a way. He would hijack my brain, force me to walk to the nearest computer. He would break free and infect Earth again."

"I'm not leaving you here." Addy shook him. "Do you hear that, Marco Emery? I'm not leaving you behind!"

Finally Ben-Ari stepped forward. She removed her finger from her trigger.

"Marco," Ben-Ari said softly. "You are right that you cannot return to Earth. It's too dangerous. Addy, wait! Wait. Listen." She placed a hand on Marco's shoulder. "We'll find you another world. A peaceful planet far from Earth, a sanctuary where you can live out your life. We'll quarantine you. You'll live in exile, yes. But on a good world."

Addy nodded, hope returning to her eyes. "Yes! And I'll move there with you. And the kids!"

Marco lowered his head. "I would be a danger to our children."

Addy wiped her eyes. "But I can visit you." She sniffed. "I'll visit you all the time. Kai will watch the kids while I'm away, and we'll talk to them through a wormhole. And if we can't use wormholes, we'll send tons of letters back and forth. And if, while

I'm visiting you, the Dreamer takes over your brain?" She gave a weak laugh. "I'm stronger than you. You won't be able to hurt me."

Marco closed his eyes. He took a long, deep breath.

He saw other images now.

Addy, a young girl, running to him through the snow, laughing, calling his name.

His infant children, bundled up and so small, smiling for the first time.

The blue water, green fields, and golden dawns of Earth.

The world that he loved. And the people whom he loved even more.

"I'm sorry," he said. "I would have given everything in this universe to be with you. To grow old with you, Addy. To be there for my kids." He looked at Addy and Ben-Ari, one after the other, and no more tears flowed from his eyes. "But I can't. We saved the world, Addy, Einav. We saved it for our children. For generations to come. For the generations that fought before us. And I died saving our world." He shook his head. "Whatever I am now—I'm not Marco Emery. And I am a danger."

"Marco—" Addy began, clutching him.

"Even on another world, quarantined, I would be a danger to those I love," Marco said. "The Dreamer knows this. He *wanted* me to cut down the tree. He could have stopped me, controlled me like a marionette. He allowed me, *encouraged* me to cut him down. He called it … evolution. And I am the next step in his evolution."

"No!" Addy said. "You are my husband!"

"I am," Marco said. "But I am also him. I feel him inside me. Lurking. Watching. Calculating. He would find a way out. He would seize me, control me. He is far more intelligent than we can imagine. Even on a world with no technology—through me, he would build technology. He would forge the elements into machines to transmit his consciousness across the void. Through me, he would rise again. And he would return to Earth, stronger than ever before, to torment everyone that I love. We killed the tree, and we killed his cyborgs, and we killed every instance of him aside from one. A single last node. The demon inside me."

Addy stared at him in horror. "Marco, what are you saying?"

"Addy." He stroked her hair. "I love you so much. You've been the light of my life since I was a child. You are beautiful, and brave, and funny, and a wonderful mother to our children. You are a woman of valor. You are a heroine. You are my wife. I will always love you."

She hugged him. "Marco." She could say no more.

Marco turned toward Ben-Ari next.

The president looked into his eyes. There was a soft light there. Almost the hint of a sad smile.

There was understanding. And appreciation.

"Einav." He held her hands. "When we met, I was just a recruit, and you were my officer. But over the years, you've become more to me. You are my mentor. And my dearest friend. Your courage, wisdom, and kindness have inspired a generation.

And they've touched me in ways I can never fully articulate. You are the sun in my sky. My lodestar in the night. You are a woman I will always love, and it has been my greatest honor to serve you. To learn from you. And to become your friend. I love you, Einav. Always." He saluted. "My captain."

Her eyes shone with tears, and she returned the salute.

Marco stepped toward the ledge.

The lava gurgled below. Awaiting him.

It won't hurt, he thought. *Not for long.*

"Marco!" Addy howled, her voice torn with grief. She tried to run toward him, to pull him back.

But Ben-Ari grabbed her and held her fast.

Marco took another step toward the ledge. He looked over his shoulder at them.

The two women stood there, the firelight dancing against them. A tear rolled down Marco's cheek, but he smiled, and he nodded.

"Goodbye," he whispered. "I love you both. Tell my children that I love them so much. In the cold darkness of space, only love can light our way."

He turned away.

Long ago, here on Haven, he had stood atop a ledge, prepared to fall into shadows.

He took another step.

And he fell into the light.

There was only an instant of pain. As the lava flowed over him, he heard the Dreamer scream. He felt the creature struggle inside him, desperate to repair his body. To manipulate his cells. To heal. To protect him from the engulfing sea of molten rock.

The Dreamer gave a last scream inside him—a scream of pure agony and loathing.

And then it was silent.

And then it was dead.

And Marco was gone.

CHAPTER THIRTY-NINE

Marco lay on the hard floor, watching it happen.

He could not move.

He was a prisoner in his own body. A vegetable. Barely able to breathe.

Addy thought he was dead. She had hugged him. Wept over him.

He tried to scream. *I'm alive! I'm here, Addy! I can't move!*

But he could only lie there.

For a long time, he had been trapped inside the tree. Days. Maybe weeks. Attached to cables. To tubes. Drugged. Dreaming and frozen.

He remembered it all. The cyborgs emerging from the podship walls. The guns firing. Falling into space. Suffocating.

And then—the Dreamer grabbing him.

Robotic hands clutching his body, pulling him into a cloaked starship.

Shouting for Addy, watching her fade in the distance.

He remembered the straps holding him onto the table. Remembered the needles sticking him. Remembered seeing his clone grow inside a vial, then inside an incubator. Then rising. A new Marco. A perfect clone with smooth skin. With no scars, yet with all his memories and traumas.

"Go forth and live among them," the Dreamer had told the clone. "When the time comes, you will serve me."

And Marco—the real Marco—could only lie strapped to the table. Drugged. Paralyzed. Unable to even shed a tear.

They brought him here. To this pit inside the volcano. The machines placed him into the tree.

And he dreamed.

Of his childhood friends. Of his family. Of his home back on Earth.

Why do you keep me alive? he had screamed into the Dreamer's mind. He could not open his mouth and scream for real. But they were linked telepathically. Marco was but a single node in a tree that spanned the galaxy.

I might need you someday, the Dreamer had replied. *I might need to create more clones. You will remain alive so long as you are useful.*

The Dreamer had punished him then. Shocked him with electricity again and again. Marco had been unable to thrash, to scream, even to beg. Only to suffer.

He had seen it all, but in a haze. A faded dream.

Addy and Ben-Ari entering the chamber. His own clone—defiant. Cutting down the very tree that had created it.

He had watched the clone jump into the lava. Watched Addy grieve.

And now his wife wept. Only a few meters away.

And now Marco lay here on the ground. Still unable to move, to cry out. Cold and pale and dead to her.

Addy! he tried to cry. *I'm here, Addy! I'm here, Einav! I'm alive! The real me! I'm not a corpse. I'm here! I'm trapped but I can't move!*

The two women stood by the ledge, holding each other, crying.

Finally they turned toward him.

"We'll take him home," Ben-Ari said softly. "He deserves to be buried on Earth."

Addy let out a sob. "Let me hold him one more time."

She knelt above him.

I'm here, Addy! I'm alive!

Yet he could barely even breathe. Not even move his eyes.

She embraced him, and her tears splashed his face.

"Goodbye, Marco," she whispered. "I love you so much. I'll miss you so much. Who will be a dad to our kids? Who will I eat cake and hot dogs with, and hold at night when I feel alone? Who will I talk to about *Freaks of the Galaxy*, and—"

She froze.

She stared at him.

He stared back into her eyes.

"Marco?" she whispered.

He tried to say her name. To hold her. He could not.

"Addy, it's all right," Ben-Ari said, and placed a hand on her shoulder.

Addy looked at her. "I felt his breath. Against me. And his body is still warm."

Ben-Ari lowered her head. "Addy, I'm sorry. He's gone. He's—"

"Marco!" Addy shook him. "Marco, are you there?" She placed her ear against his lips. "Talk to me, Poet. Or if all you can do is breathe, then breathe. Breathe again!"

He could barely move his lungs.

But he let out the faintest of breaths.

Addy gasped, laughed, jumped up and down.

"Marco!" She spun toward Ben-Ari again. "He's alive! He's still breathing! His breath is shallow, but it's there!"

Ben-Ari gasped. She knelt by Marco too. She checked the pulse on his wrist, then his neck.

"His heart is barely beating," she whispered.

"Quick, a med kit!" Addy said. "I need an adrenaline needle!"

Ben-Ari pulled out a kit, and Addy grabbed a needle, then jabbed it into Marco's thigh.

He bolted up.

He took a deep, shaky breath.

"Addy!" he cried.

She laughed, and she wept, and she crushed him in his embrace.

"Marco. Oh my sweet Marco."

Ben-Ari laughed too, knelt by them, and joined the embrace.

Marco took deep breaths. His heart was beating normally again. His mind cleared. The drugs the Dreamer had injected into him were fading.

"I saw it all," he whispered hoarsely. "I saw my clone come in. I saw him jump into the lava. I tried to talk. To move. I couldn't."

Addy tightened her arms around him. "The Dreamer is gone, and you're alive, and I'm never ever letting you go again." She bit her lip. "And hey, you have your finger back!"

He tilted his head. "My finger?"

Addy burst out laughing, tears on her cheeks. "I'll tell you all about it on the way home."

Boots thumped.

Kai burst into the room, a handful of soldiers with him.

"Dudes, dudes!" the young man said, beaming. "Whatever the fuck you did, it worked! My bros and I were fighting robots, and suddenly—all those robots died!" He laughed. "All fucking dead! Just fell over like dominoes." He suddenly grew somber. "Lots of sleepers are still alive though. They'll be wandering around now, confused, hurt."

Ben-Ari nodded. "The war is over. We won. Now the long years of healing and rebuilding begin. May we learn our lessons from this war." She looked at where the tree had stood, where there was now only a pile of broken glass. "We have survived the third Great Filter. The Singularity. We thought ourselves gods, but we created a god. Now we step into the future wiser, more cautious, and more optimistic than ever before. The past is full of pain, and our sacrifices were great. But we are victorious." She allowed herself a small smile. "The past was dark. But the future is bright."

Yet as they limped out of the room, emerging back onto the surface of Haven, Marco kept thinking of the visions the Dreamer had shown them.

The creatures in the intergalactic darkness. Gray beasts of many tentacles and cruel eyes.

The Hydrians.

Marco shuddered. Yes, humanity had won this war. And they had won wars before it. But perhaps the greatest evil was still to come. Perhaps the lot of mankind was to suffer and fight.

He looked at Addy, and he held her hand.

But life is beautiful, he thought. *And it's worth fighting for. The wars of tomorrow might still blaze. But that is another day. Today I am alive. Today I am with my wife. Today I am going home.*

As they flew away from the crater, Addy looked back and sighed. "That was the *worst* computer bug I *have* ever dealt with."

Marco laughed. He leaned against her. They flew onward, heading toward the stars.

CHAPTER FORTY

Lailani woke up in bed, bandaged and woozy, her daughter in her arms.

Tala nuzzled her and smiled.

"Good morning, Mommy."

The bed was warm. A lamp cast soft light. The room was small, the walls bare and white. Through the doorway, Lailani saw people in white robes walking back and forth.

Not cyborgs.

Not sleepers.

Real people.

I made it, Lailani thought. *I'm at SCAR. I'm inside the mountain.*

The past few days were hazy. She could remember only faint images. A snowy mountain. A long journey in the cold. That was all. She couldn't even remember who had wounded her.

"Mommy, why are you crying?" Tala touched Lailani's cheek, wiping away a tear.

Lailani closed her eyes, and she held her daughter close. "I love you, Tala. I love you so much. And I'm sorry."

"Why, Mommy?"

Suddenly Lailani was sobbing. "Because of what you had to see. Because I couldn't give you the childhood you deserve. Because I was raised with violence and hunger and despair. And when you were born, I promised you would have a better life. I failed you."

She opened her eyes. Tala was looking at her, curious, lying at her side.

"Mommy, is everything good now? Did we beat the bad guys?"

Lailani wiped away her tears and nodded. "We did. The bad guys are all gone now. Everything is good. And I love you always."

Tala embraced her. "I'm not scared anymore."

For years now, through war and poverty, Lailani had experienced many feelings. Fear. Hunger. Despair. She had watched friends die. She had sliced her own wrists in the gutters of Manila. She had flown through fire and walked upon fields of the dead.

Now, holding her daughter, she felt only one feeling.

Love.

This is love, and this is enough, she thought. *The world is full of pain. But love is strong enough to carry us through the darkness.*

A knock sounded on the door. "Hello!"

Lailani recognized the voice. She smiled and wiped her eyes. "Come in."

Professor Noah Isaac stepped in, smiling. He wore a lab coat and carried a tub of ice cream.

"Well, hello!" he said. "Who wants some ice cream?"

"Me, me!" Tala said.

Noah raised his eyebrows. "Oh, you think you can eat all this by yourself?" He raised the tub.

"Yes, yes!" Tala said.

Noah *tsk*ed his tongue. "I dunno … You might need some help from a few other hungry kids."

They ran into the room then. Two rambunctious little kids, laughing, rolling around, reaching for the ice cream.

"Roza and Sam!" Tala said.

The Emery twins ran toward her, and soon the trio was eating ice cream and laughing together. A moment later Terri Emery entered the room too. The teenage girl shyly waved at Lailani, then joined the younger children.

Lailani sat up in bed. She winced in pain.

Noah approached her, and his eyes softened.

"Do you need more painkillers, Lailani?"

She shook her head. "No. Noah. I'm sorry. I was flying over, but he attacked the plane, and I tried to get here sooner, to bring you my chip, and …" She shuddered. "Oh God, Noah, am I too late?"

He smiled at her kindly. "I learned a little about your trip from Tala. You displayed remarkable courage, Major Lailani de la Rosa. You inspired every one of us at SCAR—and indeed the world."

"The chip," she said. "The chip in my brain, can you still use it, can it help people? Can it stop the Dreamer from—"

Suddenly it slammed back into her.

She had forgotten completely.

The bears on the mountain.

The Dreamer hijacking Tala's brain.

"Tala!" she blurted out. "The Dreamer controlled her, he—" She looked at her daughter, back at Noah. "How long was I asleep for?"

"For two days," Noah said. "You were severely wounded. Dying. I didn't think you'd make it. But you've been healing. I've never seen anyone heal so quickly."

The alien DNA inside me, Lailani thought. *That slows my aging. That keeps me alive. I am part monster. I am a survivor.*

"Tala barely left your side," Noah continued. "She's healed now. The Dreamer has been removed from her mind. It was the knowledge inside your head, Lailani. While you slept, we wirelessly connected to your chip, and we grabbed the code we needed. With it, we scrubbed the virus from Tala's brain."

Lailani slumped back in bed, relief flooding over her. "And the rest of the world?"

Noah beamed. "My nanobots are flying across the world even as we speak, breeding and multiplying, hopping from human to human. Everyone they reach, they cure. Over the past few hours, we've received reports of sleepers waking up across Italy and Switzerland. Within days, the nanos will cover the planet."

Lailani closed her eyes.

She thought of the long road here. Of the destruction of her town. Of the torment of the world. Of those she had lost along the way, and of her daughter's cherished innocence, shattered somewhere between the Caspian Sea and the snowy Alps.

I had to see the shattering of the world before I could mend it, she thought. *I had to be broken before I could heal others. And maybe Tala had to see this too. To grow up like I did. Too fast, too soon. Because we—the broken, hurting souls—we end up saving the world.*

"Noah ..." Lailani hesitated, afraid to ask, but plowed on. "Did you receive any word from the others?"

He smiled and patted her hand. "Einav, Marco, and Addy are alive. They succeeded, Lailani. They killed him. They're coming home."

She rose in bed, pain be damned, and pulled Noah into an embrace. For long moments she sought comfort in his arms, and her tears dampened his shoulder.

Voices interrupted the tender moment.

"We want more ice cream!"

Laughing, Lailani turned toward the kids. Somehow the four of them had polished off the box of ice cream.

"How did you eat so much so fast?" she said.

"Ow, brain freeze!" Terri touched her forehead, wincing.

"Brain freeze, brain freeze!" the younger kids said. "We want more!"

Lailani laughed again. "No more."

The kids leaped onto the bed. They all began to jump, laugh, and hop onto Lailani.

"Kids, kids, let Auntie Lailani rest!" Noah said.

But Lailani let them keep jumping and laughing, and soon they were all cuddling with her. She needed this. This healed her more than medicine. This was what she had fought for. A little joy. A little laughter. The love of family and friends.

I wish you could be here with us, HOBBS and Epi, she thought. *I will always miss you.*

Tala yawned. It spread to the other kids. Soon they were all sleeping, sharing Lailani's bed.

Lailani stayed awake for a moment longer, looking at them.

May you never know more pain, she thought. *May this be the last war of your lives. We saved the world. And I hope it's a good world for you to grow up in. I've suffered so much, and every death I saw taught me that life is precious, and all the ugliness I witnessed taught me that life is beautiful. Cherish this life, children. Cherish this world. It's worth fighting for.*

CHAPTER FORTY-ONE

On a sunny winter morning, a shuttlecraft descended toward the Matterhorn.

The Alps glistened that morning, their crests draped with snow. But the sky was blue, and below in the valleys, spring was unfurling early green blankets strewn with wildflowers. Sheep grazed upon the grass as if the world hadn't just burned. Wars came. Wars went. But the sun kept rising and falling and rising again, and the sheep kept grazing.

Maybe there is a lesson here, Marco thought, looking out the shuttle window. *After all, Earth is just a tiny blue pixel in the vast emptiness. All our greatest tragedies, hopes, dreams, and victories—all just a mote of dust in the wind. And the sheep keep grazing.*

He looked at Addy, who sat beside him. Mottles of sunlight danced across her face, lit her blue eyes, and kindled her golden hair. She was so beautiful.

Yes, the world is small, Marco thought. *But not to me. To me, my family is everything, brighter and more beautiful than all the galaxies combined. This little world, and this family—this is all I need.*

Addy noticed him staring. She looked at him, smiled, and clasped his hand.

Sitting in the shuttle's cockpit, Kai spoke into a microphone. "Ladies and gentlemen, as we start our descent, please make sure your seat backs and tray tables are in their full upright position. Make sure your seat belt is securely fastened and all carry-on luggage is stowed underneath the seat in front of you or in the overhead—"

"Shut the fuck up, Kai, and just land," Addy said.

There was nervousness in her voice. A tension that Marco had rarely seen in her eyes. He felt it too.

They had never been away from their children for so long. And for the kids, it was even longer due to time dilation.

How will they react when they see us? Marco thought. *And will the guilt over leaving them overwhelm us? Can we ever be forgiven?* His heart sank. *We left them to fly to war. We saved the world. But we failed as parents.*

He felt a soft touch on his shoulder. He looked up to see Ben-Ari smiling at him sadly. She gave him a slight nod, and her eyes were comforting.

I know, she seemed to tell him with those wise eyes. *I understand. I feel it too. It's all right.*

He nodded back to her. He too did not have to speak aloud.

Thank you, Einav.

The shuttle circled the Matterhorn, then flew toward a snowy mountainside. A hatch opened, and Kai guided them in.

They landed in a hangar.

Nobody spoke. They barely breathed. They leaped out of the hangar, and there they were.

They stood at the back of the hangar, waiting.

Their families.

For a second or two everyone was still, silent, staring.

Marco looked at them, frozen, tears in his eyes.

Terri, fourteen and shy, peering meekly between strands of red hair. Roza and Sam. They must be four years old by now. They held hands, staring back with wide eyes.

Others were here too. Professor Noah. His son with Einav—little Carl with the dark wise eyes. Lailani was here. She was holding Tala's hand.

For a second longer, the two parties just stared at each other, as if scarcely believing this could be real, worrying that maybe this was just another dream.

It was Roza who spoke first, young and curious, her eyes so wide. "Mommy? Daddy?"

It broke the spell.

Then everyone was crying, and they ran toward one another, leaped up and down, embraced, laughed, and wept.

"Mommy!" the twins cried, weeping. "Daddy!"

Marco and Addy held them so tightly, tears flowing, and they pulled Terri into the embrace too. Ben-Ari was on her knees, clutching Carl to her chest. Throughout war after war, Ben-Ari had maintained her composure, but now emotions contorted her face, and her tears flowed.

For what seemed like ages, they all hugged, laughed, shared this moment they could not express with words.

"I'll never leave you again," Addy whispered, holding the twins so tightly they nearly suffocated. "I promise. I promise. I'm never letting you go."

Marco noticed that Kai was still standing by the shuttle, a few steps away from everyone else. The young pilot had his hands in his pockets, his head lowered.

He lost his father in this war, Marco remembered. *He lost the woman he loved. But he has us.*

Stepping away from his children, Marco approached Kai.

"I'm happy for you, Marco," Kai said. "Hey, if you don't mind, I'm gonna go out for a smoke, and—"

Marco pulled the younger man into an embrace. "Come here, brother. This is your family. You're staying with us. Now and always."

Kai nodded and had to wipe his eyes. "Thank you, brother."

The kids ran toward him, beaming. "Uncle Kai, Uncle Kai!"

They finally left the hangar and entered the SCAR offices. Noah served ice cream to the kids, beer and coffee to the adults, and told jokes. Addy found some hot dogs and began roasting them. The kids ran around, playing, laughing. They celebrated. They were victorious.

But there was sadness here too.

Addy told bad jokes, but Marco saw how her laughter didn't reach her eyes.

Lailani was all beaming smiles, but Marco noticed that she sometimes turned aside, became somber, and seemed to gaze ten thousand kilometers away.

When a balloon popped, young Tala paled and trembled for long moments.

As Ben-Ari hugged her family, she seemed almost like a cardboard cutout, misplaced, as if her true self was somewhere far away and dark.

Marco stayed by his children, holding them when he could, never too far away. And when they ran toward him, smiling, he imagined the hideous smiles of the sleepers.

He looked at Addy. She looked back, her face pale like a death mask. And slowly even her fake smile faded.

The laughter died across the room. Even the children sensed it and grew still. Kai lowered his head, and Lailani sat down and hugged her knees.

For a long moment, they were all silent.

Marco stood up.

He raised his beer.

He looked at Ben-Ari. She looked back, and she smiled softly.

Memories flashed through Marco. A last meal in the tunnels of Corpus, and everyone raising cups of wine. Battle rations in the deserts of North Africa nearly twenty years ago. The warmth of his friends in the darkness between the stars.

You were there with me, Einav, he thought. *You were always at my side, Addy and Lailani. We're still here. So many are gone. We're still here.*

"To life," Marco said.

Everyone raised their cups. "To life!"

Roza leaped onto his lap. Addy sat beside him, holding Sam. The two kids yawned and fell asleep against him. Terri sat beside them, and she leaned against Marco.

As Roza slept, Marco stroked the girl's golden hair, and he thought, *This is what I fought for. This is a family I love more than anything. May we never break apart again. When you were born, my children, I prayed that you would never know war. That didn't happen. But today I pray that this war strengthened you, and that the darkness makes the light ahead ever brighter.*

He stood up, holding his little girl. It was time to go home.

* * * * *

After many days in the darkness, after a war of fire and shadow, Marco saw it below.

Anchor Bay.

A stretch of coast along a Greek island. A patch of trees. A hill. A cove between cliffs, and a shipwreck on the sand.

They were home.

The shuttle landed, and the kids ran onto the sand, rolled around, jumped into the water, and laughed. They had been hiding in the mountain for long months, but they still remembered.

The house was gone. The Dreamer had destroyed it. But what was a house? Just a thing. Just a collection of things inside a thing. It could be rebuilt. Marco's home here was not that burnt house. It was not even the rustling trees, the golden sand, or the blue waves.

It was the deep peace he felt. It was the deep breath of air in his lungs. The feeling of belonging. The feeling that everything would be all right. That he and his family belonged here.

Marco had been all over the galaxy, had seen nebulae of swirling lavender and gold, resplendent alien forests, luminous starwhales gliding through the cosmic ocean—wonders to bring a tear to the eye. But he had never found a place as wonderful as this.

Roza padded up toward him. "Where is our house?"

Marco smiled and scooped her up. "We'll rebuild it. Tonight, how about we camp on the beach?"

"Yay!" Roza said. "Can we eat hot dogs?"

Marco blinked. "Since when do you like hot dogs?"

"They're my favorite food!" Roza said. "I'm like Mommy! Where's the rake?"

Marco sighed and looked at his wife. "Great, just what the universe needs. Another Addy Linden."

Addy blew him a kiss. "The world would be a better place with a billion Addys."

Lailani and Tala were building a sandcastle nearby, both very quiet, keeping to themselves. Marco had heard what they had been through. He knew they needed time. That their wounds would take long to heal, that the trauma might never leave them.

Marco approached them. He knelt and smiled.

"That's a lovely castle."

Tala glanced at him, then looked away shyly. She said nothing, and she nestled against her mother for protection.

I don't know everything that you saw, Tala, Marco thought. *But I hope you can forget. I hope you can grow up as brave and wonderful as your mother.*

"Lailani," Marco said. "You know you can stay here for as long as you like. More than just a few days, if you want. Even forever."

She clasped his hand. "Thank you, Marco." She smiled sadly. "I really appreciate it. I love you and your family. We'll stay for a while. Someday we must return to the Philippines. To help the survivors. To rebuild." She kissed her daughter's head and stroked her hair. "But Tala loves the twins so much. We'll stay. For a while longer."

Marco smiled, then leaned forward and kissed Lailani's cheek.

I love you, Lailani, he thought. *I never stopped loving you.*

He dared not say it aloud. But he knew she understood. That she could read his mind. After so many years together, they could all communicate with no words.

I love you too, Marco, her eyes said. *Even though I walked away, and I didn't marry you when you asked me, I love you. Always.*

Lailani kissed his cheek too, and now joy filled her smile, and her eyes were bright.

The sun set over the water. Kai started a campfire, and they all gathered around the flames. They ate and drank and sang old songs. They held each other a lot, for even the hint of solitude seemed unbearable now. They were all so broken, all seeking whatever comfort they could.

I wish you could be here with us too, Kemi, Marco thought. *I miss you so much. Every day.*

They had seen humanity deformed. They had seen the last flickers of life nearly guttered out. They had flown into the darkness and walked across fire. The moon emerged above, still engraved with the enemy's face. Perhaps it would forever leer down at them, a ghoulish reminder, a mocking gaze from the grave. Perhaps the scars would forever remain upon their souls, as real and as ugly as the scars on the moon.

But I have my family and friends, Marco thought, holding his children. *I survived. We survived together.*

Addy smiled and leaned against him. They watched the fire for a long time, protecting their sleeping children, waiting for the dawn.

* * * * *

Five years ago, Einav Ben-Ari, heroine of the Alien Wars, had become Earth's youngest president.

Today, at age thirty-eight, she ran for reelection.

A year had passed since that day on Haven. Since she had beheld the Dream Tree, had watched Marco jump into the lava, had returned to Earth to find it in ruins. Since then, she had been working tirelessly. Barely sleeping. In some ways, recovering from the war was harder than winning it.

Millions of people had caught the Dreamer's virus, had slashed open their cheeks, forming gruesome imitations of Mister Smiley's grin. Surgeons worked around the globe, stitching the wounds, though they could do little for the horrors of the soul.

The cyborgs had been modified far more extremely. Many of them would live out their lives as creatures half-flesh, half-machine, perhaps forever tormented. Ben-Ari pitied them. She dedicated huge resources toward rehabilitating those poor souls as much as possible.

And millions had died.

Families, nations—ravaged.

Colonies across the solar system and beyond—wiped out.

Only a few years after the devastating Alien Wars, tragedy had come again to humanity.

A tragedy of our own making, Ben-Ari thought. *The third Great Filter. We summoned a demon. And we survived.*

Ben-Ari was still young, and she still had decades of work ahead of her. She prayed that she could dedicate the rest of her life toward rebuilding this world. Toward healing humanity.

And so she ran for president again. Because she had fought all her life for mankind, and now she wanted nothing more than to build, create, and heal.

She sat with her family at home, watching the results come in.

It was a humble home, yet beautiful. Her old house had been destroyed in the war. Her entire country had fallen. But she had returned to the hills of Jerusalem. She had walked among recent and ancient ruins, finding much grief here, but also solace. The turtledoves still sang over Jerusalem. The olive trees and cypresses still grew. The air was still pure, and the dunes still rolled in the east, flowing toward distant deserts.

Jerusalem. Her home on Earth. Her little corner of peace and beauty.

She had built a new home here, not far from the one she had lost. One room for her and her husband. Another for their son. They built the house from ancient bricks they had found on the mountainside. These craggy limestone bricks were thousands of years old, and she thought that apt. Earth was eternal. The very walls of her home spoke of humanity's antiquity.

Not many people lived in Israel today. Not many had survived. A few shepherds in the hills. A few fishermen along the coast. A few nomads among the dunes. And her, Einav Ben-Ari. A lioness of the desert. All of Earth was her home, and all of Earth's colonies were under her protection. But Ben-Ari had to admit that, deep inside, her heart beat strongest for this mountain between sea and desert, for this homeland, and for this family that she loved.

She sat on the couch, Noah at her side, Carl on her lap. They watched the little television as the votes came in.

She won.

She won by a landslide.

Seventy-six percent of the votes were for her. The rest were split among all the other candidates.

"I brought them nothing but ruin," Ben-Ari said that night. "War after war. Genocide and destruction. And they reelected me. Why?"

Noah raised his eyebrows. "Because they know you, Einav. They know that you saved them."

"My soldiers saved them," Ben-Ari said. "They call me the Golden Lioness. I was merely lucky enough to sound the roar."

"May you never need to roar again," Noah said, holding her hand. "May we spend the rest of our lives rebuilding. Healing. Finding whatever joy we still can in the remains of the world. We've passed through the third Great Filter. We survived. Let's make this world beautiful again. The darkness is behind us, and light shines ahead."

Ben-Ari laid her head on his shoulder.

She wished she could believe that. That all her wars, her suffering, all the loss and pain were behind her now. That her ship had sailed through the storm, and that smooth seas led toward a port of plenty.

But she remembered what the Dreamer had said.

The visions he had shown her.

Gray creatures in the darkness between galaxies. Monsters unlike any Earth had faced before. Their tentacles, teeth, and calculating eyes filled her mind.

She remembered their name.

"Hydrians," she whispered.

Noah looked at her. "What's that?"

She shuddered and hugged him. "Noah, I'll be president for another five years. Maybe longer. We have to find joy, yes. But also to make Earth strong. To build great fleets. Vast armies. To become a galactic power. There is still so much darkness out there. We must shine brighter than ever before. I must build an empire."

He leaned back, just slightly. She saw something in his eyes.

Fear.

Maybe you fear me, Noah, she thought. *But you should fear what's out there more. Because it's coming.*

They had some time. Those enemies were still outside the galaxy. Perhaps she would be an old woman by the time they arrived. Perhaps it would be Carl, or his children, who faced that threat.

She would start preparing now. She would leave her children and her planet a legacy of strength.

But that was tomorrow.

Tonight she had a speech to give.

She stood up, smoothed her black suit, and looked into the mirror. She saw a stranger. A face adorned with makeup. Hair that cascaded loose, not tied up in a neat ponytail. A president.

A costume.

Inside, I'm always the soldier, she thought. *I can wear this costume. I can play this part. But I'll always be the soldier, and my heart will always be in the fire. King David could not build the Temple in Jerusalem; his hands were too bloodstained for holy work. It was his son, Solomon, who built that beacon on the hill, his hands innocent and pure. Perhaps I will never build a temple. But with the blood on my hands, I defended this hill. May my son always be pure, and may someday the works of his hands shine for many pilgrims.*

She stepped out of her house.

The crowd covered the holy mountain of Jerusalem. People had come from across the world to hear her speak. Hundreds of thousands of them were here.

Ben-Ari stood before them. Her people. Her species. So many of them hurt and needing hope.

She looked up at the sky. There was so much darkness there. So much terror.

Then she looked back at her people. At humanity. At a species that had passed through its own darkness. She remembered what the Dreamer had shown her. Not just the evil in space but the evil in humanity. The trains carrying her people to the furnaces. The endless blood that painted humanity's history.

Perhaps that too was a Great Filter, the cruelty of man to man. Perhaps they had passed through that gauntlet too. And perhaps there was still evil to humanity, but despite all she had seen, Ben-Ari believed there was goodness here too. That there was light and love in the human heart, and that it was stronger than the shadows. That all these wars were worth fighting.

She believed.

She smiled and spoke into her microphone.

"Hello, fellow humans."

The End

NOVELS BY DANIEL ARENSON

Earthrise:

Earth Alone

Earth Lost

Earth Rising

Earth Fire

Earth Shadows

Earth Valor

Earth Reborn

Earth Honor

Earth Eternal

Earth Machines

Earth Aflame

Earth Unleashed

Children of Earthrise:

The Heirs of Earth

A Memory of Earth

An Echo of Earth

The War for Earth

The Song of Earth

The Legacy of Earth

Alien Hunters:

Alien Hunters

Alien Sky

Alien Shadows

The Moth Saga:

Moth

Empires of Moth

Secrets of Moth

Daughter of Moth

Shadows of Moth

Legacy of Moth

Dawn of Dragons:

Requiem's Song

Requiem's Hope

Requiem's Prayer

Song of Dragons:

Blood of Requiem

Tears of Requiem

Light of Requiem

Dragonlore:

A Dawn of Dragonfire

A Day of Dragon Blood

A Night of Dragon Wings

The Dragon War:

A Legacy of Light

A Birthright of Blood

A Memory of Fire

Requiem for Dragons:

Dragons Lost

Dragons Reborn

Dragons Rising

Flame of Requiem:

Forged in Dragonfire

Crown of Dragonfire

Pillars of Dragonfire

Dragonfire Rain:

Blood of Dragons

Rage of Dragons

Flight of Dragons

Misfit Heroes:

Eye of the Wizard

Wand of the Witch

Kingdoms of Sand:

Kings of Ruin

Crowns of Rust

Thrones of Ash

Temples of Dust

Halls of Shadow

Echoes of Light

Standalones:

Firefly Island

The Gods of Dream

Flaming Dove

KEEP IN TOUCH

www.DanielArenson.com
Daniel@DanielArenson.com
Facebook.com/DanielArenson
Twitter.com/DanielArenson